BENEATH THE BURIED SEA

Cover art and case design by Robert Kraiza

Title page and header art by Rachael Ward

Editing by Erin Vere at The Word Faery

Proofreading by Erin Larson-Burnett

BENEATH THE BURIED SEA

for ACW—I love you and could not do any of this without you.

& for every chaotic bisexual with a sacred rage burning hot and righteous in your belly. if they won't give you peace, then give them hell.

Content Warnings

Please take a moment to review the list below and ensure my book is safe for you. Though *Beneath the Buried Sea* is a fantasy romance novel, it deals with heavy themes. Take good care of yourself and seek the support of your community when you require it.

- **strong** scenes of parental death
- grief
- suicidal ideation
- gun violence
- brief description of gunshot wound
- brief, historical mention of child death
- sexism and brief violence from a male side character (no SA on the page or implied)
- multiple, detailed, on-the-page scenes of physical intimacy

Pronunciation Guide

NAMES

- **Blodeuwedd**: bluh-DIE-weth
- **Emrys**: EM-riss
- **Danu**: DA-noo
- **Raegan**: American pronunciation is RAY-gen, Irish is REE-gan
- **Bronwyn**: brahn-WIN
- **Coblynau**: cob-learn-eye
- **Caledfwlch**: KAL-led-fulk
- **Defynogg**: DEV-in-non

PLACES

- **Hiraeth**: here-AYETH
- **Sgwd Yr Eira**: skood uhr EAR-ah
- **Carn Goedog**: CARH-n koy-dog

MISC.

- **Cariad**: KARR-ee-ayd (Cormac and Oberon
  would both slightly roll the "r")

NOTE

*I'm American of Welsh descent and have included this guide
for fellow non-native speakers of the Welsh language.
Because there are quite a few unique sounds and letters to
the Welsh language that are very difficult for non-native
speakers to emulate, this guide will certainly not be perfect,
nor will it account for differences in regional dialect.
However, if you're a native Welsh speaker and find something egregiously wrong, please don't hesitate to let me know!*

Book Two
of the
FATEBOUND
DUOLOGY

BENEATH THE BURIED SEA

—— *a novel by* ——
VICTORIA MIER

CHAPTER ONE

Inside the train car, gloom crouched in every corner. The air smelled of dust and steel and blood. Beyond the tracks, endless miles of vast and hopeless desert stretched out, barren and parched—a scene perfectly set for retribution.

Good. Because Raegan Maeve Overhill was finally going to get her revenge.

She set her jaw, gripping the handrail. The train began to move, scuttling beneath her like a scarab. For a heartbeat, she hesitated—if she looked back now, she might catch a glance of the King, trapped beyond the warded barrier that held him fast.

But it would've only broken her, so Raegan swallowed hard and prepared herself to continue forward instead. She'd clawed her way to the Timekeeper's realm through the ritual her father had left behind for her, but she'd been forced to abandon the King to do it. And now she was alone in the mouth of a beast, unable to access the vast majority of her magic. Raegan gritted her teeth, steadying herself as the train rumbled forward. What the fuck had she *done*?

Doom settled onto her shoulders, an unwelcome weight, as panic surged poisonous in her stomach. Her hands shook on the handrail. But going forward was the only way she might know the truth of her father's fate. The dry wind tugged at Raegan's hair, the metal connection beneath her feet writhing as the iron beast crept along the tracks. There was one car to her right—the engine, it seemed. The rest of the dull silver train snaked off in the opposite direction.

Releasing a long, trembling breath, she glanced through the train car's windowed door to her left, finding nothing but rows of empty seats on the other side of the glass. She turned right, pressing her face close to the fogged-up window of the engine's door to peer inside. She tracked a flash of movement: a slip of tweed, the ticking of a clock. Fear and fury slid hot down her throat, igniting something in her belly. Fuck Fate. Fuck the ouroboros. Fuck the Gates and the Prophecy and her destiny.

She was here to find her father. Magic had already waited hundreds of years. It could wait a few more if it meant she might know what had become of him, if she could finally silence that keening howl in her chest that kept her awake at odd hours. Besides, Raegan's father was the only reason she had gotten this far, thanks to his protective wardings and the spellcraft he had tucked away in that little safe deposit box. She owed it to him.

Raegan plunged into the empty carriage at her left. The door swung shut behind her, entombing her in the deathly quiet, sealing away the clang of machinery as the train picked up speed. She paused at the threshold of the car, wary as she scanned the space. Doom pressed in all around her, thick as a wool blanket on a summer's day. She set her jaw and forced herself to focus, to be sharp and sure like a folktale's heroine. Unease curled in her stomach as she noticed that the light refracted strangely inside the train, coming from the wrong places. No sun was visible through the windows. The car smelled of nothing at all. Rows of brown leather seats crouched beneath handsomely appointed black iron luggage racks.

Narrowing her eyes, Raegan searched the luggage racks but found nothing. All the seats were empty, too, though they bore the signs of past passengers: sagging leather and old ticket stubs, stains and scuffs.

The train car bucked suddenly, and Raegan reached desperately for a luggage rack. Her fingers just caught the edge of it and she steadied herself, though her hip banged roughly into a nearby seat. She ignored the damp clamminess that swept over her body, forcing herself forward. But something held her in place with a firm grip on her jacket. Confused and more terrified than she wanted to admit, she twisted at the waist, expecting to find the mocking smile of the Timekeeper, snatching at her like a kitten grabbed by the scruff of its neck.

Instead, the train car's passenger seat was somehow restraining her. The seat's leather looked utterly normal to her eyes, and yet it held her jacket fast, as though armed with a thousand barbs. She pulled again, her heart thudding noisily, blood beginning to pound in her veins. One more desperate yank, and then the leather released her with a sickly tear, leaving a gash in her jacket.

"What the fuck," she whispered, her voice hoarse. She'd almost grabbed the back of a seat instead of the luggage rack above her for balance—and what could've happened then? Fear swept through her, but a tide of fury beat it back. If she was going to die here, so be it. But she'd save her father first, and then she'd take this entire goddamn place down with her.

Continuing along the aisle, Raegan examined the seats more closely, her feet shoulder-width apart, both hands grappling either side of the luggage rack to keep herself steady. The indentations she'd considered normal looked alarming up close—more like bloated bellies of a beast recently sated, or perhaps one filled to the brim with a ferocious hunger. She grit her teeth, wishing with every shred of her being that the King walked this place beside her. It was all civilized on the outside—orderly platforms, polished rod iron, ticking clocks. Beneath the surface, though, lurked something ancient and predatory.

She picked up her pace, headed for the door to the next car, turning it over in her mind. Oberon had said the Timekeeper was likely behind much of mortal folklore about the Devil figure. The god made deals, she suspected. Ten years of all the success you could want, but the rest of your natural life would be spent on this train as the very essence of the place feasted upon everything you were, on any time you had left.

Raegan forced a deep inhale, the exhale coming out as a huff. She'd reached the other end of the car without further incident. A sudden awareness of *something* prickled the back of her neck, and without turning, she fled through the door, across the connection and into the next car. She pulled the door shut behind her, breathing much harder than warranted, her heart running away in her chest. Dread yet again threatened to drown her.

Raegan slid her hand into her pocket, fingers closing around the bundle of meadowsweet from Blodeuwedd. That night at Gossamer felt a thousand miles away as she continued her unsteady trek into the train's belly. She pushed away the thoughts swirling in her head—that she was not equipped for whatever this place held, full of knowledge but no power. Or that, worst of all, she'd perish at the hands of the Timekeeper without even finding her father.

"Steady," she told herself, wishing the word had come from the King's lips instead of her own. But in her gut, she'd known the moment they'd stepped into the station, the brick raw red and gleaming in the low light, that this path was hers alone. Perhaps it always had been. Perhaps everything always led here. Perhaps she was little more than a snake devouring its own tail. She ached tenderly for the King all the same.

Raegan grit her teeth and did her best to shut off her racing thoughts. Only her father mattered right now. Was he on this train, the Timekeeper devouring his years? An answer sang out from deep in her marrow, but it tasted sour in her mouth, so she pushed onward instead. She opened the door at the end of the train car, that prickling awareness on the back of her neck growing more intense, needle-like in its insistency.

Outside on the connection, she paused, gripping the handrail hard. An expressionless landscape flashed by her, something maybe like a desert but rendered in shades of gray. On either side of the train tracks, the earth bore jagged cracks, like the soil here had never known rain.

Raegan pushed through into the next car, expecting more dried-out leather with lumps and bloats. Instead, what awaited her stole the breath from her lungs. Horror gripped her stomach with a cold, iron hand. She blinked once, twice, three times, hoping the image before her would vanish.

It did not. People—*remnants* of people, stray limbs and bleached bones—filled the train. At the front of the car, one passenger was only the barest suggestion of a rib cage beneath the seat's smooth surface. Another was little more than the wet rasping of lungs trapped in scuffed leather. Raegan quelled the nausea climbing up her throat. How could she possibly free her dad from trappings such as these? She curled her hands into fists, fingernails biting into the flesh of her palm.

Forcing herself to continue walking down the aisle even though all she wanted to do was flee back into the King's arms, she examined each passenger for as long as she could bear it. The farther she walked, the more that remained of each person—sometimes a full limb or even a head, hair and glasses and moles still in place. By the end of the car, most seats held at least torsos, many clothed in what she thought might've been fashionable seventy years ago.

To find her father, Raegan would have to keep going, no matter how hard doom beat at her, no matter how much she wished she'd never left Oberon's side. Shame burned her face. What a fucking coward she was, and yet she had thought she was strong enough to face down a god.

With no other choice, Raegan let her rage carry her farther into the train, shouldering through door after door, moving carefully to avoid the hungry grasp of this place. She did not know for how long she walked—maybe a second or a moment or a century—that prey's sense of a nearby hunter growing louder and louder with each step. The sharp, searing inevitability of it all roiled in her stomach. She was going to die here. But first, she was going to tear the Timekeeper limb from limb. Either way, Raegan held little hope of seeing Oberon again. Not in this life.

Her eyes burning with tears, she pushed through into yet another car, biting off the urge to peer over her shoulder or hide beneath one of the seats. The door closed behind her with a sigh, the sounds of the train's rumblings falling away, leaving only the soft breaths of the passengers. She scanned the car, finding more modern clothing and intact people, though all of them looked straight ahead, blind to her presence.

Just as she steeled herself to push through another door,

to bear the horror of the train's twisted and unnatural passengers, she caught sight of auburn curls. So much like hers. So much like her father's. Forgoing her handholds on the luggage racks, Raegan rushed forward, every beat of her heart heavy with poisonous, stupid hope.

"Dad?"

CHAPTER TWO

Her breathing came in ragged gasps, her mind struggling to comprehend what she saw before her. In the back of the train car in that empty, horrible place, sat her father. He wore the same clothes as on the day he'd disappeared: a brown blazer with a hunter green pocket square, cream crewneck sweater, and olive corduroy pants. His hazel eyes gazed straight ahead. In the indirect light, Raegan could see more wrinkles than she remembered lining his face, and the tight auburn curls were shot through with gray.

"Dad?" she repeated, her voice hoarse. Remembering the gash in her leather jacket, she shoved her hands in her pockets to stop herself from touching him. God, after all these years, she just wanted to touch him. She swallowed a sob, shoving tears away from her face. She needed to get closer if she wanted to save him. But the idea of actually doing it tore her in half; she was so happy to see him, and she was so devastated it had to be *here*, caught in a bargain with a cruel god.

Raegan forced herself into a crouch at her father's feet, bracing herself on the floor. His hands had melted halfway into the seat, she saw, and there was little way to determine where the back of his neck ended and brown leather began. He seemed smaller, sunken-in, like the Timekeeper had already taken anything good and only a husk remained.

Black spots danced across Raegan's vision, nausea blooming thick in her stomach. She squeezed her eyes shut, trying to regulate her breathing. When she forced herself to look at her father again, nothing had changed. "Dad?" she repeated, desperation unfolding in her tone this time, tears choking off the word. "Daddy?"

Despair wrapped hands around her throat, and she struggled to fill her lungs with enough oxygen. She'd need an entire *army* to save anyone trapped in this forsaken realm, and yet she'd walked in here alone, thinking she would be enough. Thinking she'd be some grand hero, her name sung by the bards for generations to come. But Raegan was so small. Just a half-mad, not-quite-mortal woman who had more rage than real power.

The train rumbled on, the light remained blank and strange, and the person in the seat before her did not move or react. Perhaps she was simply too late. After all, she'd been meant to undertake this path at thirteen years old—not nearly two decades later. Raegan bit into the side of her cheek, forcing herself to her feet.

The car jolted hard to the right, nearly sending her into her father. At the last possible moment, her leg about to brush the hungry leather of the seat, she caught herself. Her breath rattled in her chest as she wrapped her fingers tightly around the iron luggage racks above her head.

Once she'd somewhat slowed the galloping pace of her heart, Raegan turned to look at her father again. He was practically a corpse—grayish skin, unseeing eyes, a sick, garish imitation of the person she had loved so much. A sob tore at her throat, and she squeezed her eyes shut. All this time, he'd been *here*. Right here, at the end of the spellcraft he'd left for her. And she'd just let him waste away in this horrific realm of death and sun-blistered metal. Raegan didn't know if she could save him—if she could do anything other than curl up on the floor and sob for everything she'd lost, all the ways she'd failed.

In the deluge of her despair, she ached fiercely for the King. She clung to those last few days finally returned to his side, visiting Fey clubs and researching in the archives, traversing pocket realms and hidden doors—

She opened her eyes, her mind seizing on the memory of the way he opened a porticus:

that brief touch somewhere in the air, like an acknowledgment and invocation at once. With a shaking exhale, she summoned up all the broken remnants of her power, hoping beyond hope that it would be enough. Her hand trembled as she reached out, careful not to touch her father's unnaturally hued skin. She clenched her jaw hard, tried to remember exactly who she was, and on an exhale, she brought her fingers a hair's breadth from her father's forehead.

Replicating the King's posture—the fore and middle fingers straightened, the thumb activated, the ring and pinky fingers bent downward—she sent everything she was into that single forward dip. Somewhere from within that vast and blank plane came a screech of metal on metal. The train car rattled and bucked, but Raegan held her ground, the muscles in her arms screaming, her heels dug into the floor.

And then her father opened his eyes. She reeled back, her knees almost giving out beneath her. For the first time in almost twenty decades, Raegan was looking her dad in the eyes. She was staring at one of the people she loved most in the world, returned from the grave by some strange twist of

Fate, a flick of the snake's tail. A shriek or maybe a sob gathered in the pit of her stomach, all those years of grief and ache building like a hurricane.

"Raegan?" came a rasp from the lips of what had once been her father. She stared at him, dumbfounded, her mouth moving to speak, but no sound came out. Her throat caught on a thousand unsaid words, her body feeling like it may give out at any moment.

"Raegan?" he asked again, straining toward her, trapped by his own skin and whatever bargain he'd made. "Is that really you?"

She clenched her jaw and shoved down her feelings as best she possibly could, sealing shut the floodgates that penned all her ferocious, tender emotions inside her chest. If she didn't, she'd drown. "Is it really *you*, Dad?" Raegan asked, eyes searching his.

"Yes." He coughed, as if he had to clear dust from his lungs. Beneath the years of disuse, his voice was just as it had always been—mid-toned, soft around the edges, his accent lightened by years in the States. The sound of it made her want to weep for a century.

Then his eyes suddenly sharpened. "Oh, Raegan. You should never have come here."

Ice slid into her veins, and she shifted away. "You're the reason I'm here," she protested. "You *led* me here."

"How?" her father rasped, his eyes wild, straining against the places where his body was stitched to the leather of the train seat. "I never would've . . . I . . ." The words died in Cormac's throat, and his face slackened, whatever she'd woken in him fading.

"Dad," Raegan said, loud as she dared. "Dad, I need to know what's going on."

His eyes tracked slowly to meet hers, and then his brow furrowed, as if he was struggling to place his own daughter.

"Where are we, Rae-Rae?" he asked in reply, trying to pull himself out of the seat again, only to be held fast.

Hopelessness crashed onto Raegan's shores, and bile flooded her stomach. Every inch of her body was too hot, clammy with sweat, prickly with fear. Her mind raced, but no answers materialized, as if all her cleverness had evaporated in this dry, dead realm.

"Dad, I really need your help," she said, her voice breaking. She clasped her hands in front of her, hoping it would be enough to stop herself from reaching out to touch Cormac. All these years, she'd yearned to pull the pocket square from his jacket once more, to bury her face in the wool of his sweaters, rich with the scent of books and oakmoss and cedar. Here he was, *right* in front of her for the first time in decades, and yet more out of her reach than ever before. Bottomless sorrow threatened to swallow her whole.

Cormac was listless again, and the train car had taken on a deadly, eerie silence—the forest when a predator stalks, all the little soft things gone into burrows and shadowed places to avoid claw and fang. Raegan grit her teeth. A cold current of rage swelled within her.

"I . . . I left the book and . . . the box," her father said suddenly in a choked voice, his eyes squeezed shut with the effort, "only . . . so y-you . . . would understand. Understand w-why . . . why I h-had to go. The letter, Raegan. If you . . . if you read the letter, why are you here?"

His gaze lifted to meet hers, and suddenly, she saw her father again—a shadow of the man she knew, yes, but still Cormac.

"What letter?" Raegan asked, though as the words left her mouth, she remembered the empty envelope affixed to the book she'd used to summon the kelpie.

"I m-made . . . the deal," Cormac rasped, "to keep you *out* of all this."

She opened her mouth to tell him that she was hopelessly entangled in it, had been for a thousand years, long before Fate had made him her father. Her head throbbed. She felt small and insignificant, a speck of dust to the primordial forces that used her and her dad like chess pieces.

Then, at the other end of the train car, the door swung open. Raegan snapped to attention, all her fear and misery forgotten as a man in a three-piece tweed suit appeared from the gloom. He was of average height, his eyes shadowed by the brim of an old-fashioned hat. If not for his choice in clothing, he was someone Raegan would've barely noticed on the street.

And of course, if not for the way power emanated from him, pulsing like a million heartbeats, a thousand stolen lifetimes. Her gut twisted, doom raking its claws across her chest.

"Finally," the Timekeeper said, his voice the low, vibrating timbre of a grandfather clock. "The Deathless One comes to meet her fate."

CHAPTER THREE

Fury flushed hot against her skin, and beneath its warmth, a cool tide of rage lapped onto her shores. She rose to her feet. "Fate," Raegan spat, "can go fuck Herself."

The Timekeeper laughed, the sound buzzing in the air around her. "Your father is too weak to give you the answers you desire. Shall I offer them instead?" He slunk closer, all his movements so utterly wrong, lacking a single shred of humanity. "If you are to rot here for all eternity, I want you to know *everything*. I want it to haunt you, all the things you could not stop, all the machinations you were too blind to see."

Raegan clenched her jaw, eyeing the average-looking man in the suit. She slid her hand into her pocket on some strange, half-remembered instinct, her fingers searching for the bundle of meadowsweet Blodeuwedd had given her at Gossamer. Horror gripped her spine when she found the lush, soft plant was little more than dust.

"Your father wanted you to shirk your birthright to the Protectorate," the Timekeeper continued when she said nothing, his eyes twin black holes beneath the brim of his hat. "He made a deal. Twelve years and a day with you and your mother, wardings to keep you unseen."

Raegan swallowed. So this, too, had been all her fault. Had she ever done anything but cause pain?

"And then he'd follow the working to wherever it led," the god said, clearly enjoying the way each word tore deeper and deeper into her. "He tried to warn you against following him and completing the spellcraft in full. A letter and a book and a key. And how easy it is to pluck a letter out of existence. Perhaps if he loved you more, he would have tried harder."

The world lurched. It wasn't the train this time, just Raegan, her knees threatening to buckle. "That spellcraft takes two," she said, the words barely audible, her rage drowning beneath the dust storm of despair. "So it was—"

"Oh yes, it was *you* I wanted," the Timekeeper said, prowling another step forward. None of his movements were right, almost like a large, powerful predator had stuffed itself into a suit and stood up on its hind legs. "Fate's little undying dog. All those years. All that *power*. And Fate was willing to trade you for just a little more magic to flow through my Gates."

Raegan stood up straight as an arrow, feeling like the god had driven a dagger right into her heart. *No.* That would mean—

"Enough for Her Seers and Her Oracles and whatever else She holds so dear," the Timekeeper continued. "So She paved the way to ensure you would play your part and the King would not stop you."

Nausea exploded in Raegan's gut, and it took everything in her not to double over and vomit. The entire Prophecy had been a lie. Fate had crafted it all to put a particularly difficult pawn where She wanted it. No one was at fault— not the Keeper nor Cordelia nor the Oracle. If Fate Herself spun a Prophecy, who in the universe would have the power to see it was false?

"What did you do to the King?" Raegan asked because apparently the Timekeeper liked to talk and that might buy her a few moments. And maybe help her stop thinking about her father, a sickening heap of gray skin and crumbling bones in her peripheral vision.

In response to her question, the god waved a gloved hand in the air lazily, as if shooing away a fly. "Nothing," the Timekeeper replied, taking another slow step down the aisle toward her. "You're Gods-touched and just mortal enough to get into my realm. But your Unseelie king? He's Goddess-blessed, which is another thing entirely, and not welcome here." He smiled then, all teeth, no warmth. "I can make this easy, soft, gentle. You can even sit next to your father. I know how much you've missed him."

Raegan's anger took her two furious, lightning-quick steps forward before the river of ice deep within slowed her pace. She steadied herself, fists clenched at her sides. The Timekeeper was assessing her every second; he had to know her Seal had been removed. But what he couldn't know was how much of her power she had gotten back. Raegan would not give him anything to use against her. With all her might, she tried to dip her hand into that cold current and summon what she had back in the cafe with Maelona.

"Dad," Raegan said, though she didn't—couldn't—take her eyes off the Timekeeper, "I love you and I'll see you again. I promise." It was all she could get out. Because she couldn't save him. She had known that the moment she'd seen him sutured to that train car by the bargain he'd kept. All for her. He'd done it all for her.

And now, for nothing at all.

The Timekeeper smirked, taking another step forward, drawing parallel with the seat Cormac occupied. "Enough.

Have a seat." His spindly fingers, hidden beneath the dark brown leather of his gloves, suddenly clasped her father's shoulder. "He does not have much time left, after all. I've nearly had my fill."

Fear ate at Raegan. Not for herself, but for her father. She didn't know how to get both of them out of this alive. Her heart pounded hard in her chest, anxiety sparking like a flare. The river did not answer her call, unable to reach into this world of death and slow, agonizing decay.

"Sit," the Timekeeper said, more forceful now. "Or I'll take everything he has left."

Raegan's heart froze in her chest. Her mind failed her; she could see the validity of the Timekeeper's threat, the way the ancient thing in a three-piece suit had devoured so many of Cormac's years. That old darkness sang a hymn inside her chest. She'd found her father. Perhaps her quest was complete. Oblivion had always called to her so sweetly, and there was no use denying it—she was, after all, very tired.

"*Cariad*," Cormac wheezed, shattering death's thrall. "I'm sorry. I love you. Run. *Live.*"

And still her body did nothing, a deer in the headlights. She'd either spend the rest of eternity hating herself for not saving her father, or she'd die utterly in vain at the hands of a primordial power she detested. It was no choice at all.

As if sensing her thoughts, the Timekeeper laughed. His attention sliced at her skin, a shard of broken glass. "Time's up."

The hand resting on Cormac's shoulder flexed, the fingers spider-like, and then Raegan watched as her father disintegrated. It happened so quickly that for a fleeting moment, she thought—foolishly, hopefully—that it was only a cruel illusion. She stared, helpless and useless, as her father simply fell apart as if he were only made of fresh, powdery snow. Dust particles drifted through the train car like funeral ash.

Raegan choked back the horror that reared in her chest. She'd come so far just for her father to die before her eyes. And he *had*, she knew—the fierce warmth beneath her breastbone that had insisted for all these years he was still alive blinked out, a dead star in a cold, uncaring universe. She looked at the Timekeeper to find his gaze already on her. She screamed.

And then he pounced, moving like the hands of a clock spinning with no care for the rules of its making. In a heart-beat, or less than one, or maybe in an interval so quick it could not be measured at all, he loomed over her. Beneath the brim of his hat, his eyes were bottomless pits—devourers of light, the harvester come reaping.

She clawed at him, eager for revenge, not caring if she didn't live to celebrate it, but the primordial monster slipped out of her hands like smoke. With another snarl, Raegan lunged for him, and the Timekeeper let out a cruel bark of laughter, tripping her. She barely caught her balance, stumbling back a few steps. He was playing with her—had been doing so from the second she walked into this place, and probably long before that, too. If she was going to die, Raegan refused to give him any further satis-faction.

She held her ground as he prowled closer, hot tears of rage spilling down her cheeks. Her fingers closed around the meadowsweet dust in her pocket. With no time to think, she yanked her hand free, held her palm flat before her lips, and blew the dust into the Timekeeper's face.

She expected only a momentary distraction, but instead, the thing in the tweed suit howled, reeling back from her. The train bucked and bristled, screws rattling and metal scraping. The luggage racks shook, one detaching from the wall, landing on the leather seat beneath with a heavy, crushing thud.

Run. Live, her father had pleaded before he turned to dust before her eyes. Raegan saw no other choice. The promise of revenge burned hot and bright as she turned and took off down the aisle. At the end of the train car, the door flapped madly on its hinges. She caught the handle, throwing herself through the doorway. Outside on the connection, the train seemed to be moving faster, gearing up for another strike. Desperate, she looked to either side, finding only gray, cracked earth. But she could not stay here. She could not share her father's fate, even though part of her wished for it, yearned for oblivion.

Raegan grit her teeth and wrapped her arms around herself. Then she took a running step toward the edge of the connection platform and threw herself into the air. Dusty ground rushed at her, but she cared little whether it crushed all her bones and split her skin open. As long as it was not those empty, world-devouring eyes of the Timekeeper that took her. That was all that mattered. Perhaps in whatever life came next, she would get to see Oberon again. If that were true, then death could come as quickly as it wanted— as long as it ferried her back to the King.

A hard impact to her left arm, then a sickly roll: gray earth, blank sky, gray earth, blank sky, over and over again. Dirt filled her mouth, and she smelled blood—hers, this time, she thought. And then Raegan realized she could only see the expressionless sky. She was still breathing. Her left ribs stung, and the right knee of her pants was torn open, exposing skinned flesh. She raised two shaking hands, finding both heels of her palms bloody and raw. Touching a few fingers to her face, she discovered a gash across one eyebrow.

But Raegan was alive. With a shuddering groan, she

pulled herself up to a kneeling position. The fabric of her pants scraped against her skinned knee, and she cried out, trying to bite off the sound at the last moment. Hot, stinging tears rolled down her face.

She wrapped her arms around herself, tucking her chin to her chest. She needed to move, to find a way out. Otherwise everything had been for nothing and she would never see Oberon again or drink cocktails at Gossamer or sit by the fire with Baba Yaga or tell her mom she was sorry.

But despair closed in all the same, a tidal wave of dim gray, and she began to weep. Her father was *gone*, just like that, after so many years of searching. Sobs gripped her shoulders and crushed her ribs. Her throat ached and her lungs cried out for air, but she couldn't stop. The tears were as relentless as that river inside her, swollen with stormwaters. She fed the dry, cracked earth her sorrow, unable to move or think or do anything but cry out for everything that she had lost, and all that she thought she still might lose at the hands of a hungry god and foolish men.

Raegan managed a deep breath, though her lungs hitched and tears still stung the tender flesh of her face. She sat back on her heels, raising her head to look around. The realm had not changed. The tracks lay to her left, the steel spine of a monster fading into the gray horizon. The train was nowhere in sight, though she had little doubt the Timekeeper would come to collect her when he had recovered and she had exhausted herself attempting to find a way out.

Hopelessness crooked a wing over her shoulder, and Raegan hung her head. But then, before her, just a few inches past her skinned knees, she noticed a shimmering pool. It was small—only about two feet in diameter and so shallow she could see the scarred earth beneath. Her tears, she realized. She shoved the despair aside. How many times had she read that the tears of a phoenix held magical properties? And was she not a phoenix of some sort—constantly rising from her own grave?

Tentatively, Raegan reached out a hand and skimmed the top of the pool. The water was cool, nothing like the feverish tears she had shed. Planting her palms on either side of it, she peered over the edge. There, she found her own face reflected back—auburn curls hanging down like a curtain on either side, the hazel eyes and freckles and cheekbones, the soft, square shape of her features she'd detested so much as a teen.

She gazed into her own eyes, breathing ragged. In a rush, she remembered the King holding her gaze outside the Oracle's Temple, his body so close, the heat and intensity and darkness of him surrounding her.

"What are you going to do, Lady of the Rivers?" he'd asked.

Raegan looked at her own reflection, settling her shoulders into a firm line.

"I'm going to a kill a fucking god."

CHAPTER FOUR

The words tasted like a promise on her tongue, all hellfire and retribution. She pulled herself to her feet, stumbling on unsteady limbs. With her Seal peeled back, she remembered enough of the way of things to know that she'd have to walk through this door without a single shred of disbelief. Certainty had always been the key, strung on a silk ribbon of wild-eyed hope.

Raegan brushed her hands off on her thighs and immediately regretted it, having forgotten the torn-up skin on her palms. She winced, clenching her teeth to fight the wave of pain. But then something else stole her attention entirely: the rumble of a train in the distance, of time devouring its own tail.

She turned to look over her shoulder and saw the train approaching, shaking its mechanical hide like a bull about to charge. A dust storm gathered in its wake, the sand writhing like locusts. Upon a set of steps at the front of the railcar stood the Timekeeper. His tweed coat flapped ferociously in the wind, though his hat stayed firmly in place, casting his devouring eyes in that ever-present shadow. He did not look like Death or even the Devil—he looked, Raegan thought, like something much worse, something mortals had not even dared to name.

She inhaled, dust and blood and steel thick in her nose. This moment would be an extraordinarily bad time to be wrong. But fuck it. Ignoring the searing pain in her side, Raegan raised both hands to the Timekeeper, displaying two proud middle fingers.

"I'm the rising tide," she shouted, her throat raw and aching, the wind tearing the words from her mouth. "When we meet again, you and everything you've built will drown in my flood." Then she turned back to the pool of tears, brought her palms together above her head, and swan dove into the shimmering surface.

Cool currents greeted her, singing old riversongs, a language she'd learned some thousand years ago when the earth still spoke freely. Relief bloomed so suddenly in her chest that Raegan let out a gasping cry, accidentally inhaling water into her lungs. But she found none of the discomfort or sting this body remembered from weekends down the shore. So she swam on, trusting the dark blue of the dazzling currents to guide her home.

Home was not a place; she had lived too long, seen the borders change a hundred times, watched the soil be cut into by men who knew nothing of honor or stewardship. No —home was *him*. The ocean eyes, the dark waves of raven hair, the low and quiet intensity, the powerful hands and unwavering relentlessness. So she swam toward that shadowy harbor, the place where she knew he waited. Where he always waited for her.

An hour or a year or maybe a millennium passed, and then all at once, Raegan broke the surface. She gasped, pulling air into her lungs on instinct. Her leather jacket and boots were suddenly far too heavy to keep her body buoyant, and she flailed for a handhold. Her fingertips found only slick, cool stone. Fear shot through her as she surfaced again, panic beginning to choke the air in her throat. Had the Timekeeper somehow turned the Rivers against her?

She reached up, desperate, fingers sliding uselessly against the smooth surface. But then a hand grabbed her wrist—a touch she'd know anywhere. Raegan sobbed in relief as she was lifted from the water by the King of the Unseelie Fey. Despite her waterlogged clothing and all her sorrow, he pulled her ashore as if she weighed nothing. He wrapped strong arms around her, and she collapsed into the darkness of him, black pepper and woodsmoke and damp rain.

Shifting back from his kneeling position to sit on his heels, the King clutched her to his chest like he may never let her go again. "Raegan," he murmured in the same tone someone prays for one last time, hoping it might finally work.

"He's gone," she sputtered, her words choked by tears. "My father's gone."

He did not pry as she dissolved into sobs. He only held her close until her shivering slowed, until his black wools and dark eyes and expansive sweep of coiled muscle felt more real to her than any blank plane stitched together by a steel railroad.

And then, gently, he pulled back to examine her, his fingertips trembling as he brought them to her jaw. "Your wounds need tending, but you are back, and you are safe, " he said, his voice breaking like a storm upon the shore. "Raegan, I . . . I do not—I do not know what I would do if . . ."

For the first time since she'd lost him in that horrible place, the King's oceanic gaze met hers. She saw a thousand things within the storm of gray, but most of all, she saw that shared oath of unconditional love. The bloom she'd discovered in herself at Gossamer unfolded, petals seeking the dark, dangerous heat of him that she preferred to any sun.

So Raegan gripped the front of his shirt with both hands and pulled his mouth to hers—never mind the split skin and wind-worn lips. Oberon met her eagerly, his hands sliding around her waist, crushing their hips together. Despite her exhaustion, his touch reminded her body it was alive after all. That living was revenge in itself.

He broke the kiss gently, long fingers brushing wet hair away from her face. She opened her mouth to speak and then closed it again, the memory of her father's frail body disintegrating into dust choking out the words she'd wanted to say. So she put her head to the King's chest and cried some more instead.

"I promise," he murmured, holding her tightly to him, his powerful grip near-crushing, "you will have your vengeance. My love for you knows no bounds. Neither does the violence I will gladly wreak on your behalf."

Raegan nodded, her hands shaky as she sat up straight, brushing the tears off her cheeks. How many times would she have to grieve the same person? Was there no end to this ouroboros? There were so many different kinds of death. But here was the last, she supposed—the final door through which she could not go questing beyond. For the first time in her entire life, Raegan's father was actually, truly, irreversibly gone.

A cold chill spread across her body suddenly as her mind ground to a halt, as if her survival instincts refused to allow her to contend with such a thought in her current state. In the King's arms, Raegan trembled—with sorrow, with rage, with exhaustion, with things she did not even know how to describe.

"Can you walk?" Oberon asked, straightening. When she tried to move her lips and speak, she found she could not answer. She thought he might pull her up anyway, dragging her along behind him like he had so many times before. Instead, the King stayed put on the cold tile floor beside her. The only move he made was to gently shift her fully into his lap.

"I do not know what awaits us beyond this chamber," Oberon warned her as he tucked the top of her head under his chin, not seeming to mind that her hair was cold and soaked. His words registered slowly; Raegan's mind felt like a blank, white room—not dissimilar to the one currently surrounding them. Oh gods—had she even escaped the Timekeeper at all? Was her mind tumbling through some homecoming fantasy while her body stitched itself to the leather seat of that forsaken train?

"Oberon," she ground out. "What happened to you? After, I mean."

"I waited for you. As I always do," the King explained, gesturing to the space around them; his hands still shook like a storm-ravaged willow. With a start, she realized it was the same room where they'd opened the door to the Timekeeper's realm at the Oracle's Temple, bare but grand with its high ceilings and golden light and expansive creamy marble floors. "I have not left this room in a number of days. Perhaps a week."

She looked up at him as sharply as her frozen muscles would allow. "Why?" Raegan asked, her throat raw, heart pounding as she tried to convince herself the King and the marble and the Temple were real.

"If I left," he continued, his gaze skipping away from hers, the long, dark lashes dipping down, "you would have had no chance of coming back at all. Once the chamber is unsealed, the protection warding burns away any spellwork completed here." The King's voice—that dark, melodic, eternally steady voice—shattered into silence. A moment stretched long and lonely before his eyes met hers again. "And then nothing would connect this room to the In-Between any longer." A muscle in his jaw leapt, broad chest rising in a quick, sharp inhale.

"Fuck," she whispered, digging her knuckles into her eyes. So much unimaginable power, and the King had been reduced to nothing but breathless waiting and razor-edged hope. She fought to find the right words, her body drooping like a wilted flower from the effort. With a low, pained breath, she decided to say nothing, turning to bury her face in his chest again. The dark heat of him loosened the cold stiffness of her joints, the icy sludge that seemed to grip her thoughts easing.

"I tried," Oberon whispered, hands cradling the back of her head. His voice hitched, tone growing thick and heavy. "Raegan, I need you to know I tried so hard to reach you."

"I know," she replied into the fabric of his shirt. "The Timekeeper *wanted* me there. Fate fucked us over. She made a deal for more magic to flow through the Gates. I was Her fattened calf for Kronos, and I went fucking willingly. Imagine how he could gorge himself on all my endless time. I don't even want to know how long She's been planning this."

Oberon's body went still against hers. She waited to feel that rare tide of rage spill through him, bloodthirsty and wild. But he only let out a long sigh. No words left his mouth. For a long moment, there was nothing but the sound of their breathing echoing against the marble. They stayed like that, a tangle of trembling limbs and damp clothing, until Raegan spoke again.

"It feels like everything is even worse now," she said in a raw, forlorn whisper. "We've tried so hard. We've done so much. And somehow we've only lost more."

Oberon did not deny it. "Can you try to stand?" he

asked again instead. "Let me care for you. Let me make something better than it was."

Raegan nodded, the corners of her mouth lifting even as tears spilled down her face. Oberon helped her to her feet, bracketing her body against his larger, sturdier one. She tried to take a step toward the door and found she had absolutely nothing left. Her legs shook, ankles and knees screaming in protest, every muscle liquified. Before she could even voice her distress, the King swept Raegan off the floor and into his arms. Her vision pitched, black spots swarming on the edges, until the darkness consumed her entirely.

~

*S*he opened her eyes to a familiar place: that autumnal meadow, the mountains rising into gray skies, the river snaking low in the grass. Woodsmoke slunk into her senses. Heavy wool draped over her shoulders. Instinctively, she turned to her left. There he was—always, relentlessly, endlessly. Tall and powerful, inhumanly beautiful in the overcast light. He wore his past self well—every inch the mysterious, dangerously charming knight he'd been a thousand years ago.

He turned to face her. That oceanic gaze did not belong to Mordred, she knew; it was the Unseelie king staring back at her. "What is this?" he asked, his younger voice—less husky around the edges, more melodic, the accent thicker—a mismatch for the weight of those eyes.

"I don't know," Raegan—and she was Raegan, not some echo of Nyneve—murmured, looking around. The dreamscape was the same as it always was—except both of them seemed to have autonomy. As if the ouroboros could be broken, as if they could do more than retrace the same

28

patterns in river mud over and over again until it broke them.

Her senses prickled. She turned away from the knight, back toward the rushing waters in the distance, her heart pounding like a wild thing against her ribs.

Just a few paces from her stood something tall and terrifying.

Someone. A woman, perhaps, but only because Raegan lacked more expansive language. Blue tattoos marked cool, pale skin—woad, Raegan recalled. Intricate plaits of raven hair fell around angular shoulders, which were cloaked in a cape of feathers that shifted from black to cobalt in the light. The mouth was thin and serious, the eyes large and bottomless.

"Phantom Queen," Raegan breathed at the same time the faerie king beside her murmured, "Morrigan."

"There is not much time," the goddess said in the voice of a thousand crows cawing into a thunder-swept sky. "You must listen closely."

Raegan's marrow hummed. She nodded because what else was she to do in the presence of the ancient goddess of war and sovereignty she had once trusted with her life? With his life. Because she had, after all, been involved in his creation—alongside Nyx, the Morrigan had torn a wound in the midnight sky and crafted the King from the obsidian jewel it bled.

"You opened a door through the In-Between," the Morrigan said, those ink-black eyes falling on Raegan. "And now, finally, we might have our revenge."

The goddess raised her long arms and then shot forward in a terrifying movement of black braids and crow feathers. She stopped a hair's breadth from them both, fingertips pressed to their foreheads. The moment the Morrigan's divine body touched hers, Raegan's vision went black—the black of congealed blood on a battlefield, the black of war banners, the black of the things that fester when too long denied.

And then, all at once, she saw.

A set of ancient stone steps leading into water.

A sword the color of ocean water during a storm.

The mortal king who had once wielded such a blade.

The blood of the Fair Folk he had spilled with it.

An isle shrouded in mist.

A snake shedding its skin.

The feeling of something winged taking flight in her chest—hope, if she dared.

"Find Avalon. Seek Excalibur." The Morrigan's voice boomed in her head, heavy as death, magnetic as destiny. "All doors that were once open to the deathless witch remain so. If the faerie king can return the faerie blade to its original state, so too might he return the world to what it once was. Together, my children, you could liberate us all."

CHAPTER FIVE

Scent came back first: perfumed waters heavy with spring thunderstorms, chilly vanilla, a soft sprig of lilac, and beneath it all, something rich, herbal, and slightly medicinal. She breathed in deeply, clearing stagnant air from her lungs. Smooth, silky fabric pressed against her skin, a gentle cocoon from which she might emerge more glorious than she had entered. She opened her eyes—slow, steady—to warm, golden light floating down from somewhere high above her. The space held a downy silence, but just beyond it, she could detect running water and the gentle tinkling of silver bells in the distance.

The Temple of the Oracle, Raegan knew—a familiar place, as familiar as the heavy weight of grief that swept into her body like a homecoming. Her father was dead and she'd watched it happen, unable to save him from the Timekeeper. Nausea shot through her, and she doubled forward, gagging. "No, no, no, *no*," she stammered through a torrent of unshed tears, squeezing her eyes shut, doing anything she could to banish the memory of the worst thing she'd ever witnessed.

Her hands reflexively curled into fists. Raegan hissed as

the torn flesh on her palms smarted. She yanked her hands from beneath the blankets to find the heel of each hand wrapped in a thin, spidery gauze—far more organic-looking than any medical gauze she'd ever seen.

And her right hand, it seemed, was not empty. Tucked along the indentation in her palm that some people called a fate line was a crow feather. In the golden light of the Temple, it shimmered like an oil spill. All at once, Raegan remembered the dream—or perhaps the vision—in that meadow she knew so well, the goddess she hadn't seen for a thousand years speaking directly to her.

Speaking of a way they might know revenge. Of an ancient blade and a hidden place and the true nature of things.

Raegan sighed, looking away from the crow feather and all its responsibility. To combat the anxiety swarming her mind, she began to catalog everything in the room. To her right, a side table with a pitcher of water and glasses. Beyond it, dark blue velvet draped from the ceilings in soft swathes. The bed frame was made of twisted willow branches, the sheets and blankets varying shades of porcelain white and rich cream. To her left, a tasseled silk loop caught the wall of heavy velvet in a swoop, exposing a sliver of the hallway. Along the outer edge of the room, a fawn-colored tufted leather chair sat empty, two teacups stacked beside its leg. Raegan forced a long inhale and equal exhale.

Every atom in her body dragged her eyes back to the crow feather waiting in her open palm. She stroked its silky black surface. She wondered if she was strong enough. It would be easier, kinder, to let the grief swallow her whole—to forget about gods and magic and destiny. To mourn. Her father was finally, truly gone. And yet that did not stop the Morrigan from crawling through the tiny door she'd opened and throwing another crucible at her feet.

Shadows stirred beyond the swoop of velvet at the threshold of her room. Raegan glanced up from the feather and met the King's oceanic gaze.

"Hey," she said weakly.

"You are awake," he replied, stepping into the room and pulling the plush blue fabric curtain closed behind him. His expression was wary, guarded, holding hers as if the rest of the world did not exist.

Raegan looked away, swallowing hard and wondering if she should even tell Oberon about what she'd seen. She did not doubt that it was real—and that was exactly the problem. But as her gaze skipped down, she caught sight of the King's powerful hands.

Tucked between long, elegant fingers was a crow feather, gleaming wildly in the diffuse light of the Temple.

"You too?" she asked, holding up her feather.

Oberon nodded, measured and grim. "It would be madness."

"To follow the Morrigan's quest?" Raegan asked, meeting his eyes again.

The King sighed, raking a hand through his hair. "Quite frankly, I do not care much about goddesses and quests. I care about *you*. How are you feeling?"

Raegan moved to sit upright. "I'm okay. Well, no, that's not true. I just watched my father die, felt pretty sure I was going to die, too, and then when I was trying to sleep that off, a fucking goddess showed up in my dreams and told me I have more shit to do."

A sardonic smile ghosted Oberon's lips as he sat down on the edge of her bed. He reached out and gently—far more gently than he should even have been capable of—took her hand into his. As always, the dark spell of the faerie king rolled over her like a heatwave, lighting a spark low in her belly despite all the horrors she'd so recently suffered.

"You look well, all things considered," Oberon said, eyes meeting hers. "You have only slept for about a day. After your ordeal, more rest would be wise."

Raegan was only half-listening. In her head, she was replaying the Timekeeper killing her father over and over, one of the people she loved most in the world dissolving into dust because he'd had the misfortune of caring about her.

"I can't lose anyone else," she said, looking up at the King, tears hemming her words.

For a long moment, he was silent. "I wish I could tell you that you will not."

She raised her free hand—the one that still clutched the crow feather—and pushed her tears away with the back of her palm. "That *was* real, wasn't it?" she asked, hollow, knowing she didn't need to specify.

The King sighed, his fingertips moving in a slow serpentine over her skin. "Yes."

"And Excalibur was a faerie blade?"

"There have always been rumors that Myrddin perverted a Feyrish weapon for the king of men," he replied. "It would not surprise me, no, though I cannot say for certain."

"Even if it isn't," Raegan mused, digging through the recesses of her mind, "Excalibur siphons the power of gods and Fair Folk, right? That's why it's so legendary. The first weapon that could not only stand against magical beings, using their own power against them. So maybe it *could* actually harm the Timekeeper."

Oberon nodded, his mouth in a grim line. But they'd have to actually find Avalon first. Raegan dropped the feather into her blanketed lap, raising her hand to massage her temples. The soft hush of running water and tinkling bells in the background lulled her, the halfway light tempting her with more sleep that would delay all she faced.

"And Avalon . . ." she mumbled instead, the hopelessness of it all threatening to crush her. "Apparently even the goddamn Morrigan doesn't know where its door lies."

"I would think not. Danu's safe refuge for Her first generation has not been located by anyone in living memory," he replied, something not unlike grief slipping into his words. "That door has been closed for nearly three thousand years. She sealed it behind Her."

Raegan let out a long breath. The Morrigan's vision had been a call-to-arms screamed from the top of a windswept hill, not a murmured sweet-nothing from a honeyed tongue. She might be a fool for it, but Raegan believed she could follow black feathers and the cry of a crow better than she had ever chased windsongs and the soft rustle of white wings.

"The old gods have not been able to reach into this world for centuries," she said, choosing her words slowly as she raised her eyes to Oberon's. "And even though it was all bullshit, the false Prophecy that Fate set up for us created the situation that allowed me to tear open a door—no matter how small—between the realms."

The King said nothing. He only watched her, his eyes restless as the sea, the candlelight-like illumination of the Temple turning the strands of silver in his hair golden. Shadows draped across his angular face. His powerful body was utterly still, more statue than living thing. He looked like destiny. He looked like defiance embodied.

"You want to seek Avalon," he said, his tone tinted with reverence like stained glass. "You want to quest for Excalibur. After everything, you wish to follow the words of a goddess."

She held his gaze, her jaw clenched. She did. She

wanted this to be over, once and for all. No more resurrections. No more hopelessness. No more of this. Rage kindled deep within Raegan. All her endless sorrow and grief wove itself into the fabric of her never-ending anger, creating something sharp and shining, chainmail-like.

"My love," the King breathed, closer to her now, the intensity of him like a wildfire, "I know not where you find the resilience to follow another Thread that may well give out from beneath our feet."

Raegan bared her teeth at him in something that was not quite a smile. "Spite's as good a reason as any. Besides, you said I would have my vengeance. Could there possibly be a better revenge than destroying everything the Timekeeper holds dear with the single swipe of a long-lost faerie blade?"

At that, the King smiled back, all nightmare, all predator. "I told you I would follow you to the ends of the Earth." A promise for her, a threat for their enemies.

"Oberon," she said, her tone sharp, "I think we should do this. The Morrigan has never led us astray."

A long moment passed where he said nothing, though he reached up to cup her face in one large, warm hand. "You need to mourn."

She ground her teeth, the truth of his words swelling up in her like stagnant lake water thick with algae. "We all mourn in different ways," she replied, arching an eyebrow.

"And I suppose you have usually mourned by seeking revenge," the King observed wryly. Then his expression went still, serious. "It is possible. We would need a few weeks to prepare, and we should move in secret. Only our most trusted comrades can know of this vision, this hope. But Andronica could hold the wards once more, Kamau could lead the Court's defenses, and the kelpies would no doubt aid our quest." He paused, cocking his head to one side, examining her. "What do *you* want, truly?"

Raegan let out a long breath, looking down at the creamy fabric that stretched across her lap, at the gauze covering her body, at the bruises developing on her forearms. It was going to take a hell of a lot more than that to keep her down. If she destroyed the Timekeeper, she'd avenge her father—and she'd make his sacrifice worthwhile. What had Cormac wanted more than for people to be free to choose their own paths? Magic could do that.

"I want to find Avalon," she finally replied, meeting his gaze again. She shifted her weight on the bed, moving toward him. "But first, I want you to distract me. Is that fucked up?"

The King's expression didn't change as he leaned in, his fingers sliding between hers. He brought his mouth to the underside of her forearm, trailing soft kisses down her flesh. A thick drumming started up in her core.

"Is this the sort of distraction you were hoping for?" he asked, gaze meeting hers.

"It's nice," Raegan teased. "But maybe something a little more . . . full-bodied?"

Without saying a word, the King gently folded the blankets back, down to her legs. Then he gathered her up in his arms. "As always," he said, his lips moving against the shell of her ear, "your wish is my command."

Tucking her close against his chest, Oberon strode to the opposite wall and parted the shimmering fabric, revealing a square room tiled in a deep, opalescent blue. A stone basin crouched on what appeared to be a giant slab of moonstone, an antiqued silver mirror hanging above it. To the left, roughly cut stone stairs led down into a large bath. The waters sparkled metallic in the light, as if a current danced beneath. The entire space carried the scent of spring thunderstorms and a cool whisper of lilac.

Along the wall, a bench had been carved out of the stone and then covered in soft blue mosaics. There, the King set Raegan down. The tiles were cool through the thin fabric of her long dressing gown. He settled beside her.

"May I see your bandages first?" he asked, gesturing to her palms.

"Fine," Raegan replied, sighing dramatically as she extended her hands to him. Tenderly, Oberon peeled the spiderweb-like gauzing away. She braced herself for bruised, torn skin, but when he finished unwrapping the bandages, there was little more beneath than some pink scrapes.

"Good," he murmured, pulling his hands away from hers. "How do they feel?"

"Okay," Raegan said, realizing it for the first time as she examined the tender pink flesh. Then her eyes slid to Oberon's, her heart beating faster. Nervousness fluttered in her stomach like she was a tween again, experiencing her first crush. "Still hurts a little. A kiss might help."

Amusement slid across his angular features like a mirage, the corners of his sculpted lips lifting. Gaze on hers, the King bowed to bring his mouth to both of her scraped palms in turn. Heat slid through her belly.

"And your knee?" he asked, eyes dropping down to her legs.

Raegan obliged without a second thought, pulling up the hem of the gown. Oberon gently maneuvered her legs to lie across his lap. The knee she'd torn after jumping from the train was bandaged in a similar fabric, and Oberon unwound it with the same care. Much like her hands, the skin was pinkish and scraped, still a little sore, but far more healed than it should have been after one day.

"Hurts a bit more than my hands," Raegan said, not able to stop herself from smiling.

The King returned the expression, and gods, to see playfulness on his face was such a balm for everything. He lowered himself over her legs, brushing her knee with his lips. She bit back the soft sound of pleasure, watching as Oberon trailed his mouth along her thigh, both of his hands sliding up her legs. Then his powerful grip was on her waist and he sat upright with an elegant contraction of predatory muscles.

"Do you think you can stand?" he asked, eyes on hers like no one else existed.

"Don't flatter yourself," Raegan replied, pushing to her feet, though he caught her halfway, bracketing her smaller frame against his. Heat sparked deep in her belly as their bodies met, her soft curves pressed against his hard musculature.

She permitted a brief detour to wash her face and brush her teeth at the sink, noting that it was very much her own reflection looking back at her in the antiqued silver mirror. More or less, she wagered. She'd been a lot of people, after all.

At the edge of the stone bath, the King pulled her dressing gown up and over her head, and all thoughts of the past melted away like swollen stormwaters. Beneath the garment, Raegan wore nothing save for another spiderweb gauze pad on her side. With a touch so gentle no one else in the world would believe he was capable of it, Oberon peeled the bandaging away. Beneath, her skin was bruised and scraped, but nothing like she'd imagined—no horrific sights of bones breaking through skin or flesh torn away entirely.

She opened her mouth to make the request, but Oberon was already sinking to one knee, his mouth brushing the sensitive, bruised skin where the gauze had been. Her entire body woke up all at once, a thunderstorm rolling across the horizon, and she gasped his name into the steamy air. The tender place at the apex of her thighs throbbed.

He stood then, like she'd commanded it, cupping either side of her face in his hands. The intensity of the King's gaze threatened to consume her. Good. She'd like to be devoured—by him, and only him. The thought alone sent a spike of desire, lightning-hot, into her chest.

Then his mouth was on hers, the dark, throbbing intensity of whatever they shared washing over her. Oberon wrapped powerful fingers around her waist, mindful of the bruised rib, his hands sliding down to the generous curves of her ass. Raegan deepened the kiss, something desperate rising within her, every inch of her body aching for his touch.

"I thought I lost you," Oberon murmured against her mouth, his voice low and husky. As he spoke, one of his large, warm hands slipped to her belly, and then lower, finding precisely where she wanted to be touched. Raegan let out a soft moan at the wave of pleasure, arching into him. His other hand moved to cup her breast, teasing until her moan deepened into something full-throated and breathy. Her breath quickened as her heart began to race.

"I thought I had grown accustomed to that pain," the King continued, increasing the pressure of his touch. "I have not. I *will* not. I will destroy anyone who seeks to steal you away from me."

Pleasure uncoiled within her and she gasped, half-strangled by desire. She clung to him, as if the harder she gripped, the more she might prove he would never lose her again. Or maybe she just wanted him to remember this—to remember the heat of her body, her heavy breasts pressed into him, the way she said his name. She left him with little more than memories; they may as well be good ones. With that end in mind, Raegan began to unbutton his shirt with shaking hands. A few moments later, she'd gotten what she wanted—nothing between his skin and hers, only fervent kisses and the sound of her name in his mouth. Desire pounded between her legs, her breath coming in quick gasps.

He coaxed pleasure from her body as if he spoke the same language as her flesh. A powerful sensation mounting in her depths, Raegan rolled her hips harder into his hand, desperate for more. At that exact moment, Oberon pulled his touch away from where she wanted it, sweeping her into his arms instead.

"Fuck you," she panted, limp in his grasp, her chest blushed pink and heaving.

"That is the intention," he replied in a low voice that sent her core curling in on itself.

Raegan met his gaze and rolled her eyes as Oberon carried her into the bath. There, he gently set her on a ledge cut into the stone wall. Hot, silky waters stretched over her, rippling around her collarbones. A soft exhale slipped from her mouth. She closed her eyes and tilted her head back, leaning the base of her skull against the lip of the stone.

"I don't remember asking for a bath," she murmured when a few moments had passed without the King's hands on her—too many to bear, though it embarrassed her to admit it.

"I will have you know I am capable of accomplishing more than one task at once,"

Oberon said, the weighted warmth of his palms roving to her shoulders, his hands soap-slick, perfumed with honey and oatmeal.

Raegan laughed, and some of the tension and fear slipped away with it. The sound melted in her throat as the

King massaged soap into her shoulders, his mouth meeting the sensitive skin just below her ear. His hands traveled lower, powerful fingers working out the tension in her back. But tension flared hot and hungry elsewhere, a torrent of desire building with each breath. Raegan pulled him closer, and in response, Oberon let his hands slip from her collarbones and then to her breasts. His mouth met hers again to capture the resulting moan.

Cupping the heavy flesh, he teased her where she was most sensitive. Need seared through Raegan's body as his touch traveled lower, across her belly and then her lower back, working in more soap as he went. By the time she was feeling thoroughly clean in perhaps the dirtiest way possible, her muscles had finally softened, but the thick, beating need at her core had only wound tighter.

Oberon began to rinse the soap from her skin, one hand slipping to the damp heat between her legs. Her thighs slid open for him, a thousand years' worth of desire relentless and throbbing. Pleasure pounded her from every angle, the material world melting away, leaving only the curvature of his muscled, scarred body and the softly swaying curls of steam.

"I thought I had lost you," he repeated, deep and breathy, as both of his powerful hands gripped her by the waist, lifting Raegan to the lip of the bath. "And it is only a half-life without you, my witch." The temperature of the air was a welcome relief, her hair plastered to her neck, her face red. Before she could say anything, Oberon slid between her thighs, sinking to his knees.

The Unseelie king kneeling before her usually only meant one thing.

"Permit me to memorize your taste," Oberon asked, right on cue, his gaze sliding to hers.

"What have you done," she murmured, her breathing hard and fast, "to deserve that?"

His mouth moved into something dangerous and feral, and it sent a thrill through her. "I have spilled blood," the King murmured, his lips meeting the inside of her thigh. "Killed legions. Defeated a hundred armies in your name. Toppled kings. Destroyed worlds. All for you. Always you. *Only* you."

His breath moved across her skin with each word, mapping her generous thighs with hot, open-mouthed kisses, his long fingers hooked behind her knees. Her blood pounded.

"I think," she panted, digging her nails into his shoulders, "that will do."

Dark and dangerous amusement simmered like a heatwave across his face, and then his mouth met the yearning heat of her core. Raegan fought to savor the moment, to do everything in her power to never forget, but Oberon knew her body too well and had worked her into a frenzy. She crested the wave of her release a few minutes later, body melting into his as she cried out his name.

He held her against him, one hand splayed across her lower back. Raegan closed her eyes and pressed the side of her face into his chest, her heart still fluttering behind her ribs. They stayed like that, the ancient king of shadows bowed over the witch who refused to die, and for a long moment, even destiny and Fate and ancient goddesses did not dare to disturb their peace.

But their peace never seemed to last.

CHAPTER SIX

L ittle was visible through the rough hood they'd forced over her head. She closed her eyes, focusing on her other senses instead. Through the fabric, she smelled sunburnt dust and sweat—her own or that of the Protectorate dragging her, she did not know. For a third time, she fought to plant her bare heels into the hard-packed earth, but her body responded with little more than a pathetic jerk. Still, the Protectorate man to her left halted abruptly, taking a handful of her hair and yanking hard.

"It's no use, love," he laughed in her ear, the sour warmth of his breath making her flinch away.

They dragged her forward again, her feet catching on the ground, a stray rock scraping her skin. She hardly even felt the pain. Panic was too thick in her throat now, the hood suffocating, her anxious inhales dampening the fabric. Whatever they'd done during those long, endless hours deep within their stronghold, she had no magic. Her body did not obey her commands. Desperate, she fought to do something as simple as flexing a few fingers. Nothing.

She opened her mouth to scream because at the very least she'd make this as unpleasant as possible, but no sound came out. A few tears, however, did manage to tumble down her face. Her heart still pounded, and a heavy weight still crouched on her chest. Hunger still sat sticky in her stomach and her head still hurt. So she'd feel every last unpleasant thing but have no control. Rage boiled in her, and for a long, skittering moment, she thought she could feel the edges of the Protectorate spellwork.

A harsh pain in her ankles and knees broke her concentration.

"Oh, apologies," the Protectorate on the right mocked. "Stairs."

The pair dragged her to her feet, and she scrambled for dignity, but to no avail. She could see little more than faint outlines through the hood, and the depth or number of the stairs beneath her were a mystery. She tried to put her shoulders back and tilt her chin up as she struggled, but her muscles didn't even seem to hear the instruction.

Then the stairs stopped and the air changed. Woodgrain beneath her bare feet, a dry breeze tickling her arms. She strained to listen—murmurs of a crowd, pennants snapping in the wind, the thump of boots. Peaceful, almost, if not for the sense she was perched at the top of a hill about to give way beneath her.

And it did—the Protectorate men forced her to her knees, the wood biting into her skin. A hard push at her upper back doubled her over, and then a gloved hand grabbed her hair again, positioning her head so the side of her neck rested on cold stone.

Oh. Well, she should've expected that.

The hood came off in a violent flourish, sending stark sunlight streaming into her eyes for the first time in . . . days? Weeks? Her vision was sideways, the platform stretching out before her, banners embroidered with the Protectorate's dragon rampart flying proud and cruel. She strained but could not see beyond the platform, though the sudden jeering told her there was, of course, a crowd.

She squeezed her eyes shut and fumbled for the spellwork that held her fast, trying to find the weave in her Threads. She could feel it, the way it strung her like a puppet, but she could not reach it—vast miles seemed to separate her magic from theirs.

A commotion caught her attention. At the other end of the platform, a group of at least ten Protectorate were climbing the stairs, looking for all the world as though they were trying to drag a wild animal along with them. Her mouth went dry.

She knew immediately what—who—was at the center of that tangle of chainmail and dusty cloth, surrounded by straining magic and anxious shouts. The rest unfolded like terrible poetry: a large, masked man stepped forward into her vision, his wicked ax glinting in the high sun. At the same moment, the Protectorate group at the other end of the platform split, revealing the High King of the Unseelie Fey.

Despite the magicked chains that wrapped around almost his entire body, despite the deep cut over one black, swollen eye, he lurched forward and screamed. She'd heard that sound before, once—in the crumbling walls of an old stone building, her body laid out on a rough slab of wood, the life bleeding out of her.

A figure stepped between her and the King: a mountain of a man, his chainmail well-used, his familiar weathered face pulled into a victorious sneer. She summoned every ounce of her rage, her defiance, fighting to dip her hand into that cold, dark current.

"S-see," she sputtered, every movement of her tongue a monumental effort, "you soon."

"No," Bedwyr replied, tucking his hands behind his back, strolling forward on the platform, allowing her to look *at the King again. Just once more.* "Not this time, I don't think."

Then the sharp glint of sun on steel raised high, followed by nothing at all.

~

Darkness. The manic scream of a banshee. And then someone saying her name, just audible beneath the grating shouts. Raegan's throat hurt, which probably meant that she was not dead and also that she might be the one screaming.

She opened her eyes, panting, but only more darkness greeted her, a few rough outlines visible in the dim light. Panicking, Raegan raised her hands to her face, clawing to remove the hood from her head. But there was nothing there; her nails only scraped skin.

A large, deft hand caught her fingers, gentle but firm. "Raegan," murmured a voice that sounded like dusk over the lake and heather on the hills. "*Cariad*, you are safe."

Golden light fluttered in from no direction in particular, illuminating the foot of the willow branch bed, blue velvet walls, creamy marble floors, and the familiar face of the King leaning over her. As they made eye contact, he released her hands.

"Fuck," she muttered, dropping her head into her palms, pulling her knees to her chest, bedsheets snagging at her ankles. A shiver wracked her body, the slick sweat on her skin turning cool. "It was the same dream again."

Ever since she'd made it back from the Timekeeper's realm—nearly three weeks ago—Raegan had been haunted by this particular dream. Three weeks of careful planning, intensive training, and relocating Fair Folk to safer places, every bit of it made that much more difficult by the sleep stolen from her each night. As if she needed anything else on top of the horrendous, bone-deep grief that she'd barely had the time to feel, let alone process.

"May I touch you?" Oberon asked, his broad, powerful frame a comforting shadow in her peripheral vision.

"Please," Raegan pleaded, biting down on the tears climbing her throat.

Oberon pulled her into his arms, tucking her head beneath his chin. She buried her face in his chest, woodsmoke and black pepper and damp stone washing over her. Wrapping her arms around his waist, Raegan clutched the fabric of his shirt with all her might.

"Your dream will not repeat itself in the waking world," he murmured, one hand stroking her hair.

"You can't promise that," she whimpered into his chest, misery climbing her throat. "What if I doom us all *again*?" The memories pressed in all around Raegan, thick and suffocating. "Why do you still trust me, believe in me?"

The King lowered himself to be eye-level with her, cupping her damp face in his hands. "Perhaps I am an old fool," he murmured, his long fingers brushing away her tears, "but I do not believe a love as enormous, as magnetic, as unending as ours, could be a path to destruction."

Raegan saw in his dark gaze how much he believed the words tumbling from his mouth, but doubt still sat like tar at the bottom of her stomach. It was too easy to remember the way he'd treated her less than a month ago when they'd first found each other. How he had framed their love not as enormous or magnetic, but as poison that had torn his world apart.

"My liege, are you— Oh," a voice boomed from the doorway. "Apologies."

Raegan raised her head, dragging the back of one hand across her eyes to wipe away the tears. Through blurred vision, she saw Kamau, one of the King's most trusted knights, standing in the doorway, concern etched across their features.

"The Rivers are clear," Oberon said in a low, soft voice, stepping back to look at her.

Raegan forced a shuddering exhale, fighting to pull herself out of the dream and into the present moment. "It's time to go, then," she muttered.

"Yes," he replied, brushing away a fresh tear with the pad of his thumb.

Raegan threw back the sheets and scrambled to her feet, pushing down the thick swell of fear and horror clamoring in her marrow. She reminded herself that they'd been desperately waiting for this moment, holding on to the Philadelphia Temple by the skin of their teeth through an increasingly brutal onslaught by the Protectorate.

She would not destroy this sacred, shimmering chance because of a bad dream. A memory from another life, she knew, but it was so much easier to imagine it as only a nightmare—then she could tell herself it was not a portent, not some horrible omen. That dreaming repeatedly of how she'd destroyed their chance at liberation last time as the Seelie Queen was not some kind of very bad sign.

"Is Rainer ready?" Raegan asked, shedding her sweat-dampened t-shirt with little concern for Kamau being nearby. She scrambled into the clothes she'd had neatly folded on the nightstand since they'd decided to follow this path.

"Yes," the King replied, moving aside to give her room to pull on a bra and then a pair of jeans. Thanks to the light seeping from the hallway, she noticed that he was dressed already—an ink-black suit with a charcoal waistcoat and midnight leather boots, all sharp angles and deadly shadows. His appearance settled her; if she had to walk into the mouth of a beast, at least it would be at his side.

"Is Andronica in position?" the King asked, breaking her thoughts, his question directed at Kamau.

She didn't hear an answer as she pulled her gray wool sweater over her head, so Raegan assumed everything was ready. Anxiety twisted her gut. Only a handful of people knew about the vision from the Morrigan: the Keeper, Andronica, Kamau, and Rainer. This last, mad hope was too precious, too delicate—so they'd opted to pursue it in secret.

Raegan leaned against the bed to pull her boots on, turning to glance at Kamau. The towering knight looked capable and sure, no hint of doubt in their large, expressive brown eyes. Raegan set her jaw and straightened, grabbing her leather jacket—the tear inflicted by the Timekeeper's train since mended—from the willowy bed post. The King handed her a familiar luggage tag, and she slipped it into her pocket.

Then they moved for the doorway. Kamau held up a hand, glancing back out into the hallway, and then gestured them forward. The three of them fell into stride abreast, Raegan bookended by the much taller statues of the King and Kamau.

"Let us run through it one more time," the knight said in a hushed voice, their fingers rubbing the pommel of the dagger at their waist—something they usually did when they were nervous, Raegan had noticed. "Rainer will take you as far as possible in the Rivers. The Protectorate will almost certainly intercept you at some point. The kelpies can only hold them back so long."

Raegan grit her teeth, lengthening her stride to keep up, trying to stay mindful of ensuring her footsteps were quiet. The plush blue carpet that ran down the marble hallway helped, and the two Fey beings on either side of her moved like silent shadows despite their size.

"You'll be forced to surface," Kamau continued, holding out a hand, their head whipping to one of the curtained archways. Raegan slammed to a halt, trying her best to not even breathe. The Unseelie Court had been reduced, yet again, to refugees, thanks to the ongoing Protectorate assault. The city crawled with operatives, and apparently, the United States's paramilitary force that governed magical affairs had given the Protectorate much more leeway than they usually did on American soil. Most of the Court was hidden away in the remaining pocket realms, trying to weather the storm—a task only made harder by the way residual magic bled from this half of the world faster and faster every day.

Kamau gestured for them to move forward again. At her left, the King let out a long, low sigh, raking his hand through his hair. "I hate misleading our people," he muttered.

Kamau's dark brown gaze shot to the King, their heavy brow furrowing. "We have discussed this," the knight said, remembering halfway through the sentence to lower their voice. "It would cause panic. And we still do not know the identity of the turncoat in Blodeuwedd's faction. We cannot take the chance of the Protectorate knowing your intentions."

The King nodded, his jaw clenched. Up ahead, something clattered—metal on marble, Raegan thought as she froze. The three of them held their breath. Her blood thundered in her ears. But then nothing—only the silence of the witching hours.

"When you surface," Kamau continued, moving forward again, "you'll only have the River Wye's protection.

Maybe the hawthorn trees, if you can find them. It will be a hard road to Hiraeth."

Raegan's vision tunneled, nothing but blue velvet and marble floor and golden light. Her hands shook at her sides. She didn't know if she was strong enough for this. The Protectorate were at the height of their power on the Isles, both in magic and bureaucracy—they were part of the government in the United Kingdom and enjoyed all the freedoms that came with it. The Americans didn't let them use time magic or most modern weapons—some centuries-old squabble Raegan didn't care to learn about. But where she and the King were headed, the Protectorate had anything and *everything* they wanted at their fingertips.

"And you absolutely must be clear of any Protectorate interference when you cross Hiraeth's walls," Kamau said, the muscle in their sharp jaw working. "It is a risk to allow Hiraeth to host you while you search for Avalon."

More nervousness roiled in Raegan's gut. Her palms were damp. How long was this goddamn fucking hallway? It felt like walking to the gallows.

"The last Fey city on the Isles," the King murmured, the gravity of the situation clear in his tone.

"The Protectorate have hunted it for so long," Kamau replied, something not unlike fear coming across their features. "We cannot hand it to them on a silver platter."

The King reached behind Raegan to grip his knight's shoulder. "I know you have loved ones in the city, Kamau. I would die before I exposed Hiraeth."

The tall, broad knight nodded, biting down on their bottom lip. "I know," they murmured. "Truly, I do. I just . . ."

"This is fucking terrifying," Raegan supplied, wiping her hands off on her jeans. "It's, like, endless risks for a *vision*."

"The Keeper was convinced the vision was true, direct from the Morrigan," Kamau reminded her, their expression softening. "And Octavia, too. I spoke with her before she evacuated with the other Seers. The Keeper and the Oracle herself, both utterly convinced, Raegan. That is not nothing."

She looked away from the knight. The Keeper and the Oracle had *also* been convinced of the false Prophecy. Setting her jaw, Raegan stopped herself from saying just that to Kamau, instead staring at the path ahead. The Fey viewed an Unrequited Prophecy and a vision from a goddess as two very different things, but she—admittedly—did not. At least they moved in the opposite direction of the Vaults—it was almost like a declaration they would do this their way. She reached for Oberon's hand as the corridor's terminus came into view: a large door stained in woad, so dark blue it was almost black. Carved rivers of abalone shell snaked through it, glimmering in the golden light of the Temple. Its doorknob was shaped like the long, powerful body of a kelpie, rendered in patina-blackened silver.

Beside the door, the Keeper and Andronica stood like silent guardians. Doubt rushed into Raegan's chest. What if they were wrong? *Again?* The stakes felt higher than ever. The King could not hold the protective wards around the pocket realms from where they were headed—across an ocean, on a quest strung upon a few words from the thin, sly lips of a goddess who had been locked on the other side of the Gates for a thousand years.

Raegan steadied herself, attempting to clear her mind of the doubts clustered there, thicket-dark. The King squeezed her hand, sending a memory skittering out of her recesses—another time, another place, but still facing a door, the weight of too many hopes perched on their shoulders with clawed talons.

"My liege and my lady," the Keeper said, the sound of his voice pulling Raegan back to the present. "Everything is prepared."

"Thank you, Anakletos," Oberon replied, reaching to embrace the Keeper. The smaller besuited man returned the King's gesture, gripping for a moment or two like he may not let go at all. Raegan knew the feeling.

To her surprise, the Keeper released the King and immediately swept Raegan into a tight hug. "I feel it in my marrow this time," the ancient thing murmured close to her ear, his words sounding for all the world like prophecy.

Raegan pulled back to look into the Keeper's eyes, where she thought she might have caught a glance of the galaxies turning. He nodded once and then stepped clear of the door, out of her vision. Kamau pulled Raegan and the King into a tight embrace, long, heavily muscled arms easily encircling both of them at once. The knight murmured an old Fey blessing and then stepped aside. Andronica moved forward, reaching for the King first.

The two of them exchanged low, fervent promises in the Old Tongue. Oberon bowed his head, bringing his brow to meet Andronica's—an Unseelie expression of deep mutual admiration and trust, Raegan remembered suddenly. Andronica would once again bear the weight of the wards in the King's absence.

Raegan gathered herself up to offer some kind of parting word to the deadly swordswoman who understandably hated her guts. Before she could say anything, Andronica grabbed her by the shoulders and pulled her into an embrace.

"Don't fuck it up this time, yeah?" Andronica said in a tone that was almost friendly and definitely playful. She pulled away, still gripping Raegan by the shoulders, near-black gaze searching hers. "It's different. *You're* different. I know we only had a few weeks to train together, but I hope it pays off."

Raegan's heart soared; she hated how much she craved the approval of this gorgeous, talented, dangerous Fey version of Lucy Liu. "I'll do my best," she replied, not able to contain a grin. To her delight, Andronica grinned back, as sharp and bright as the edge of a blade. Raegan tried to savor the moment, a dewdrop in a drought, but then she saw the Keeper approach the door, his ornately carved ring of keys flashing in the low light.

The moment her eyes fell on the keys, every door in the Temple sang out to Raegan all at once, a chorus of silver bells. She rooted herself to the spot, fighting the tide—though she didn't have to for long, because then the way of the kelpies swung open before her, and the pull of it was so strong that she didn't hesitate.

Raegan swept into the room with the King at her side, the dark and constant shadow looming beside her frantic, chaotic flame. Inside, the room was blank—creamy marble floors, walls tiled in pearl. It was similar to the ritual room they'd used to complete her father's working, but much smaller, the ceiling a more reasonable height. She did her best not to think about that.

At the chamber's center, Raegan noticed gentle movement—the sway of a large puddle. She took a step closer, the King keeping pace. The door closed behind them, and even though she'd known it was coming, the feeling of being cut off from the world made her stomach flip. Raegan gripped Oberon's hand harder as they approached the dark waters lapping at shores of marble.

There was no summoning this time—no drops of blood or shared whiskey, no precise words or wardings drawn in chalk. Instead, the puddle rippled twice, like a giant walked somewhere in the distance, and then the surface of the water broke into a thousand droplets.

From the shadowy depths rose a massive head and thick, curved neck, a seaweed mane hanging in heavy waves. Backwards hooves rang out on the marble floors, and Raegan's mouth went dry as she yet again took in the kelpie known as Rainer.

"I understand that I am a very impressive sight," the kelpie intoned, lowering his head to look at both of them in turn. "But we must go. *Now*. The Rivers will only remain clear for so long before the Protectorate finds a way to dam them up again."

"Then let us be on our way. The Unseelie Court delights in partnering with the kelpies once again," the King replied as he helped Raegan onto the creature's back. He mounted behind her, sliding one arm around her waist.

Rainer began to move immediately, hooves ringing out against the marble. Raegan took a fistful of slippery, dark green mane into her hands. She reminded herself to breathe.

"I have you," the King murmured in her ear. "I will not lose you again."

Raegan gritted her teeth and nodded, fighting the fear that gnawed at her stomach. Rainer came to a halt a few paces from the puddle, his entire body pointed toward it like an arrow.

"To long-overdue revenge. Let there be blood," the kelpie announced, his voice a thousand rushing rivers. Before Raegan could prepare herself, Rainer gathered himself up and without another word, launched into the surface of the water.

CHAPTER SEVEN

Raegan didn't know if they'd been traveling the half-lit, watery realm on Rainer's back for seconds or days. Time slipped out of her grasp entirely, a snake slithering away through dew-damp grass. It didn't help that even though her eyes told her that they were deep underwater, her breath came easily and her body remained dry as bone.

We shall surface soon. Rainer's voice boomed in Raegan's head so suddenly that she jumped, causing Oberon to tighten his grip around her waist. *Prepare.*

For the hundredth time, Raegan tried to summon a memory of their destination: Hiraeth. The final stronghold of the Fey in the Isles, a city hidden by mist and magic and a wall of hawthorn trees. She'd been there before, she knew, but the magic that concealed it seemed to have stolen her ability to remember it as well. Hiraeth operated on very old, very powerful workings—the kind that could have only been crafted on this half of the world before the Gates existed. She was eager to be within its walls again, though she wished it were for much different reasons.

But for now, only the dim blue-green of the Rivers

surrounded her, kelp forests looking more like thick black thunderclouds in the distance. Rainer's hooves did not travel across a sandy floor or river-worn pebble underfoot; instead, he moved through the water like a fish, his back legs transformed into a massive tail covered in glimmering scales. Raegan took a quick look down, not comforted by the vast darkness lying in wait beneath them.

They'd encountered no one else traveling the same section of the Rivers. Beyond the occasional shadow of a horse-like body or watchful, shimmering eyes at the edge of a kelp thicket, it was only the three of them. Or at least, it seemed that way until Rainer spoke.

The Protectorate is near, the kelpie boomed in her mind, a warning. *They cannot enter the Rivers, but they can dam the waterways and attack from the surface. I believe we are about to encounter both.*

As if on cue, Raegan watched a shining silver spear pierce the space just to her right, moving far faster than anything metal should in water this deep. Rainer launched forward, veering toward the open mouth of a kelp forest. The King pulled her back against his chest, his sword—an impossible thing woven from pure shadow—appearing in his free hand.

We may need to take a path through the deep places, Rainer warned, sending a delicate whisper of dread skittering up Raegan's spine. Such places were not for mortals; they were not even for something like the King, not without invitation. Things older and far more terrifying than Rainer lurked in the low places, sunk deep and sleeping in the river silt, kelp woven over them like a thatched roof. It would not do well to wake what slept in the Rivers.

At her back, Raegan felt Oberon tense in response to Rainer's words, and she watched his hand wrap tighter around his sword's pommel. She grit her teeth, panic fluttering like a moth somewhere in her throat. White-knuckling Rainer's slippery seaweed mane, Raegan tried to focus on staying with the kelpie's quickened movement. She wished she could talk to Oberon in this place, but the only voice she'd hear until they surfaced was Rainer's. It was the way of things, she knew.

Another spear sliced through the murky depths, alarmingly close to Rainer's right shoulder. In response, the kelpie banked left hard and would have unseated Raegan if not for the King's arm around her waist.

They are trying to kettle us, Rainer said, surprising Raegan with his choice of vocabulary. She might've laughed if she weren't deeply afraid for her life, a delicate thing in this game they played. *Fools. I am far older than such tactics.*

Raegan peered ahead through the dim watery light, catching sight of what she instantly knew was one of the dams Rainer spoke of, looking for all the world like a wall of chainmail. Dull, lifeless metal stretched across the path ahead, kelp forests looming on either side. Even from a distance, Raegan felt the way the Rivers could not flow through the Protectorate's dam. The water seemed to rear away from the chainmail entirely, fronds of kelp wilting when the current pulled them too close to the unnatural thing.

A chorus of spears sang through the water just behind them, the King batting most of them away with a slice of his sword. Beneath her, Raegan felt Rainer gather himself, powerful muscles bunching in anticipation of his next move. Head thrown high, he surged forward, as if he intended to run straight into the wall of metal. Oberon ducked lower to the kelpie's neck, sheltering Raegan with his body. She flattened herself against the seaweed mane, heart hammering in her chest.

At the last possible moment, Rainer swung himself to

the side, an impossibly elegant pirouette. But the tight turn slowed his pace, and for a second, it felt to Raegan as though they hung dead in the water. Dread danced in her gut, and she looked up, responding to a prickling sensation at the back of her neck.

From above, a net of thick, rusted metal descended on them, diving through the depths at an unnatural speed. Terror slunk low through Raegan's chest—after everything, here she was, about to be captured like a prize, dragged back to a hunting lodge, throat slit.

But she was not prey. Not anymore. No—she was more predator than the Protectorate could even begin to imagine. She was the Lady of the Rivers, and this was *her* domain. Raegan straightened, squaring her shoulders, gaze locked on the descending net. Then she swung one hand above her head, palm-up, fingers claw-like and ravenous. With all her might, she called to water, reaching for that cold, dark current that ran through the very center of her being.

Something serpentine and sharp exploded into existence between Rainer and the Protectorate's net, razor-toothed and keen. A dragon, maybe, Raegan thought, its body slim as a torpedo, its mouth a gaping maw of destruction. To her eyes, it seemed to be made entirely of water and river silt, a darker shade than the space around it, pieces of kelp layered on its body like scales or armor. The water dragon tore into the net with its barely corporeal teeth, a shriek emitting from its empty belly. Without hesitation, it turned and dove for the chainmail wall.

When the dragon's jaws met the chainmail, the metal exploded. Instead of shrapnel, a thick wave of dust plumed from the impact before floating down into the depths of the Rivers below. Rainer righted his course and surged toward the now-open path, the dark shadow of the kelp forests on either side forgotten in favor of the way illuminated by crystalline blue light.

Raegan might've raised a triumphant fist or even let out a soundless battle cry if not for the darkness creeping in from the corners of her vision. She swayed in the King's arms, trying to shake off the intense dizziness that spun her world around. But the shadows slipped in closer and her stomach flipped, and then everything went black.

～

Raegan blinked her eyes open, expecting the diffuse golden illumination and blue velvet of the Oracle's Temple. Instead, she found the deep oil spill of night. Dead leaves rattled on branches, and everything smelled of damp vegetation and cold mud. She narrowed her eyes, trying to make out the form before her by the light of the moon. With a start, she realized it was Rainer, curled on his side like a regular horse in a farmer's field somewhere in the mundane world. His neck was upright, his head alert, ears swiveling.

"We are safe," the kelpie said, toad-like eyes finding hers easily even in the gloom.

"Right," Raegan replied in a hoarse croak, wondering why her back hurt so much until she realized she was wrapped in a thick woolen blanket and propped up against the base of a hawthorn tree. Its jagged bark bit through her leather jacket.

"We have surfaced," Rainer added, his words almost obscured by the wind humming through the bare trees surrounding them.

"Yeah, I see that," she grumbled in response, rolling her neck. "Figured there wasn't a forest in the middle of the Rivers."

In the wan moonlight, she saw Rainer cock his head. "Well, actually—"

"You are awake," came another voice, deep and low, as the King melted out of the shadows. He moved to crouch by Raegan's side. "How are you feeling?"

"I'm fine," she said, though her heart panged at the urgency in his movements. She wondered what it was to love something so fragile. "Just frustrated that every time I use magic, I lose consciousness."

Oberon glanced at her with one of those knowing, sideways looks. "Perhaps," he began with a wry smile, "you might consider starting smaller than creating a monster from water when you reach for your magic."

"I know," she said, shivering as a cold late autumn wind cut through her. "It's hard to reach past the Protectorate magic. I always have to go farther than I think, and then I end up going . . . *too* deep."

Baba Yaga's removal of Raegan's Seal had restored the potential for her to reliably reach her older powers, but it did not erase this body's birthright. As such, whenever Raegan did any sort of working, she had to evade the Protectorate magic. It was like the ocean, she had thought a few times—right beneath the surface was that mortal, god-granted power. She had to dive deeper to find the Lady of the Rivers or Titania or the Witch of the Wood. And when she found that low place, thick with black currents and heavy with the ages, it was far too easy to drown.

"That, too, will fade with time," the King replied, leaning his shoulder into hers. The contact, even through multiple layers of clothing and quite chaste in nature, sent warmth sweeping through her body.

"Now that our lady has awoken," Rainer said from across the small clearing, his tone dry, "might I suggest we save our discussions for when we are within Hiraeth's walls, not in some unwarded Welsh forest where our enemy may appear at any time?"

Raegan's heart leapt into her throat. "You said we were safe," she hissed at the kelpie, who got to his feet far more elegantly than she'd ever seen a regular horse manage.

Rainer tossed his head, eerily similar to a teenager's eyeroll. "Yes. Relatively speaking. But we could be saf*er*."

The King stood, extending a hand down to her. Raegan unwound the wool blanket from her body and hauled herself to her feet with Oberon's help. Leaves and damp soil clung to the fabric, the smell of late October heavy in her nose. The King reached for it, and when his fingers brushed it, the woolen textile disappeared from sight.

Rainer eyed him. "The Protectorate's reactivity to magic is much more sensitive here, my liege, as you'll surely recall."

The King slid one arm through Raegan's and gestured to the hawthorn trees with his free hand. "They agreed to harbor us as Raegan recovered. We will lose such protection when we return to the riverbeds, but for now, the hawthorns keep watch."

Rainer acquiesced with an elegant nod as Oberon helped Raegan mount. She settled onto the kelpie's broad back, comforted by the feeling of the King behind her—like a bonfire on a cold winter night. All the world hung still for a moment, and she felt Rainer take a deep breath. Then the kelpie plunged through the trees as if neither he nor his passengers were made of anything of all but shadow and night air. The exhaustion clinging to Raegan faded away— she sat astride an ancient kelpie with the Unseelie king, and she'd used that old, sleeping thing she'd always known was within her to turn back the Protectorate. The embarrassment she'd felt at needing to rest faded, too—her body was, after all, only mortal.

When Rainer broke the treeline, Raegan saw that dawn clung to the horizon, casting the world in hues of golden gray. The River Wye awaited them up ahead, a wide silver python cutting through the damp browns and muted oranges of late autumn. It was quiet—no birds had begun their morning revelry yet, and the only sound was the soft splash of Rainer's hooves. For a moment, Raegan found herself lost in it—the thick, heavy crest of the kelpie's neck, the faint remains of moonlight sketching a path on the water. It looked like an illustration in a children's book, the rightful princess returning to her realm upon the back of her trusted steed.

If it were a children's book, though, the enemies and the dangers would be surmountable. But the hush with which Rainer moved, not even offering a snarky quip when she dug into his sides too sharply with her knees, indicated their safety balanced on a knife's edge. She felt it, too, with her Seal removed—the river offering all the protection it could, the path wavering as the moon slipped behind the sky.

The sun began to rise in earnest, flipping the power balance back in the favor of their enemies. Thickets of trees huddled on the river's banks, and Raegan had to stop herself from inspecting every shadow for a flash of chainmail. She cast her gaze ahead instead. The large, lichen-covered stones dotting the river were damp with dew, each drop catching the light like a tiny crystal. It should've been a quiet, beautiful, early morning in the Wye Valley. But instead, the hair on the back of Raegan's neck stood on end. The air was wrong—still and dead. Everything around her seemed three shades too light, like the vibrancy had been leached out of the landscape. Behind her, the King tensed, and she watched as shadow-spun armor burst into existence, quickly covering the arm he held around her waist.

"We are very close," Rainer finally said in a low voice. "But so, I fear, is the Protectorate."

Raegan glanced over her shoulder at Oberon to find him scanning the horizon, his head thrown back like he scented his prey's blood on the wind. With a deep breath, she reached out to the river, fighting to do what he'd tried to teach her during their weeks recovering at the Oracle's Temple—imagine a wall between the Protectorate magic of this body and the older, stranger things that had clung to her soul for millennia.

Then words shattered the air and Rainer jerked to a halt.

"I have to say I'm surprised," bellowed a voice that Raegan knew well and liked much less. From behind the wide, dappled trunk of a sycamore tree on the opposite bank stepped an all-too-familiar mountain of a man. Bedwyr. "I never thought you'd dare to walk these lands again. I'm glad you proved me wrong, though—now you get to see how far we've come and how far *you* have fallen."

Raegan did not know if the once-knight of Arthur was addressing her or the King or perhaps even both. All she knew was that behind her, the air exploded with that teeth-rattling magic, and when she called for the river, it did not answer.

CHAPTER EIGHT

Her heart pounding, tongue sour and acrid in her own mouth, Raegan whipped her head around, looking for the source of the attack. But instead of Protectorate operatives, she found herself staring at an eerily beautiful orb of slinking, transparent shadows that now surrounded them. Beyond the veil of gloom, she could just make out a group of figures, predictably dressed in drab suits. Their magic assault landed on the surface of the shadowy shield with a half-hearted boom and then dissipated.

Raegan twisted to face forward again, delighted to discover a willow tree on the opposite bank had wrapped thin, snaking branches around Bedwyr. He hacked at them with his sword, but another of the tree's limbs shot out and plucked the sword from him, promptly chucking it into the river. Beneath her, the kelpie pranced in place, sleek muscles contracting, as if eager to commit his own violence.

"Do not waste energy on anything but keeping him at bay," the King said to Rainer, gesturing to Bedwyr. "The Timekeeper does not allow death to touch him."

No, Kronos certainly did not—the only reason Raegan

hadn't killed the fucking monster herself for what he'd done. She blanched, nausea rising in her throat at the memory: of being carried like a carcass over the man's shoulders, brought to the crumbling manor where she'd found moments of peace and refuge with the knight she had known then as Mordred. Laid out on a damp, rotting table like a prize or a feast, a trap for her beloved. Her hands curled around Rainer's mane in white-knuckled fists.

But for all her power, she'd been human then. Mortal. She was not any longer—not entirely. Raegan let that thought sink deep into her, into the bones of this vessel and then through her legs to the kelpie and finally into the earth beneath her—the soil that had known her for a thousand years. She felt something stir, dark and deadly.

At that exact moment, the King grabbed her waist with both hands and spoke a single, sharp word. Rainer charged forward, moving down the river like a jousting destrier. She had little choice but to hold on for her life, his long stride and powerful gait dangerously close to unseating her. Up on the banks, more Protectorate were gathering, though they met a hearty resistance from the willows and ash trees.

A blow of attack magic whistled right past Rainer's ears, slipping around him as if the Protectorate's magic could not touch him at all. But the kelpie threw his head back and screamed anyway. The sound was a low and awful thing of ancient folklore and hungry riverbanks.

It stirred something in Raegan, and she almost got her hands around it before she noticed with a jolt that Oberon was trembling. The muscles of his arms were nearly convulsing. She raised one hand to his forearm, laying her palm flat.

"Are you doing *all* of this?" she asked, raising her voice to be heard above the din. "The trees, the shield?"

"Yes," Oberon grunted in her ear, his voice pained, unwinding his sword arm from her waist. "Hold on."

Raegan barely got both hands back into the kelpie's mane before Rainer leapt straight into a gallop, somehow moving even faster than before, the river spraying as his massive hooves struck its surface. Guilt and shame reddened Raegan's face. Oberon was aware she still couldn't defend herself and saw no choice but to fight on the defensive and the offensive at the same time.

"More ahead," Rainer said over the thunderous roar of his gallop.

Raegan felt the King draw a quick inhale against her back, and then his shadow-blade appeared in his hand. Rainer galloped through a section of the river where the willow trees grew together closely, their branches hanging low. On the other side, the banks opened up to little more than tall grasses and woodland flowers.

The river was lined with Protectorate. For a long, terrible moment, Raegan's world moved in quarter-time, showing her every single drawn bow in horrifying detail, too many iron-tipped arrows winking in the sunlight. Between the tightly regimented formation, she could see foot soldiers waiting behind the archers, armed with swords and guns and spears and rifles. And then she realized, no, it was *not* adrenaline slowing the world down for her. It was something so much worse.

Rainer's earth-eating strides had nearly halted, too—like they were doing little more than crawling through mud when just moments ago, they had been gliding across the surface of the water. The protective shield of shadows surrounding them blinked out. She had a terrible feeling that the Protectorate forces would move in real time, which was confirmed less than a second later when arrows and bullets drew down upon them, quick and numerous as raindrops. Raegan's heart leapt into her throat as she ducked instinctively, gripping hard with her knees in a way she knew Rainer would scold her for later. If they lived long enough for such things.

Oberon had no choice but to release her waist, throwing his free arm out in a sweeping motion. Darkness rippled above them, like someone had cut a bolt of the night sky and fashioned it into a cloak. The majority of the arrows and bullets pinged off it harmlessly, falling to the ground, but she saw a red slash open on Rainer's shoulder.

All of the warnings when they'd formulated this plan came roaring back to her—that the Protectorate was much stronger here on the Isles, that pursuing this alone meant that it would be three of them against all the Timekeeper's horrors—of which there were many; Kronos and his armies knew much of the old Fair Folk magic still slept in the ancient cairns and beneath grassy hills, and they defended it as fiercely as water in a drought.

But Raegan had thought the waters would answer her. She did not think she would sit helplessly on a kelpie while bullets and arrows and magical attacks rained down on her.

Rainer's voice split her concentration, but she couldn't make out his words over the vast thundering of her own blood. She threaded her fingers tighter into the kelpie's dark mane and, despite the danger, squeezed her eyes shut. The King's arm slid back around her waist, for which she was grateful, and a second later, she felt the contraction of his muscles as he cut someone down with his sword. He moved, she thought, faster than Rainer, but his speed was clearly reduced by the Protectorate's time spell.

Raegan bit down on her lip until she tasted blood—a thick rush of warmth, like the river's summer storm surges. Her eyes still closed, she leaned over Rainer's side, hoping the King would keep her astride, letting her fingertips sweep the surface of the water. With all her might, she forced her Protectorate magic into a box—small and dull, a container no one would bother to open. She had not asked for this birthright, and neither had her father nor her aunt nor anyone at all in her line, she wagered, for many hundreds of years.

No more. No more of this. No more of Maelona's endless exhaustion, of her father's wild-eyed and shattered hopes. No more early graves for blood-conscripted soldiers who maybe, like Cormac, had yearned for a different world despite their inheritance.

Her fingers slick with river water, Raegan sat up straight on the back of the kelpie. She remembered that arrows and bullets rained down upon her, iron swords not far behind, and that she rode astride a water-horse whose kind had haunted folklore for a millennium. Her truer, older birthright had always been the water. The river. Life and death given in tides, ebbing and flowing with moon and storm and season. And then delicately, softly, she reached into that cool, dark place inside her, where currents rushed unseen beneath pearly gray waters.

For a heartbreaking moment, Raegan felt nothing except a sureness that she would fail everyone she had ever loved. She grit her teeth, told the river to go fuck itself, and then plunged her hand into the black water deep within her.

Something *roared*.

Raegan opened her eyes. The water ahead of her rumbled and roiled like a witch's cauldron. Any of the Protectorate soldiers who had made their way down and into the river began to scream, rushing back up the banks, breaking their formation. Some tripped and fell, and Raegan watched with a pleasure she did not even try to deny herself as they were boiled alive. Blistered, bubbling corpses began to dot the surface, and the Protectorate forces closest to the water scrambled to step back and close ranks.

Raegan almost couldn't believe it—the river had answered. Her eyes brimmed with tears that blurred her vision, which would not do on a battlefield, so she raised one hand to wipe them away. Despite the clamor and the chaos, she felt Oberon pull her closer to him, his palm opening on the curve of her hips.

"You are terrifying," he murmured, his lips brushing the delicate shell of her ear. "I find myself jealous of those who are ravaged by your power."

Suddenly, for the first time in her life, Raegan understood the true meaning of bloodlust. She leaned back into him, sliding her fingers through his, and then she steadied herself. The river, she remembered, would give her everything. She need only ask.

What she wanted was for every single Protectorate to die here, on these banks, by her hands, and for whatever haunted these waters to feast upon their bodies. Let this section of the River Wye serve as a monument to magic's return, to defiance of the Timekeeper's reign. Let any Protectorate who survived tell their children to stay away from these banks, lest the old ghosts of war and horror awake in their graves, open-mouthed and bleating like a slain lamb.

Both the King and Rainer seemed to have shaken some of the time spell, or perhaps it had been weakened by Raegan's onslaught. Rainer's pace quickened, though he did not attempt to return to that full-out gallop; instead, his movements were agile and sharp, veering around attacks like a warhorse, snatching at flesh with his teeth as he passed.

Raegan trained her eyes on the formations along the banks. They had broken, she could see, and some Protectorate were still stumbling in the mud at the shore, clutching burned and boiled limbs.

She leaned low over Rainer's thick, arched neck, her muscles somehow no longer in need of constant willpower to keep her astride. With a deep breath, she threw out one hand, letting her fingertips graze the top of the waters again. This time, she heard riversong the moment she touched the surface—ringing in her ears as loudly as if someone were right beside her, singing ballads of teeth and silt and bones picked clean by currents.

"Feast," Raegan murmured, the word coming out long and lilting, like it was a song all on its own. And perhaps it was, because the moment she spoke, the river ahead of them reared up like a snake, every ounce of water leaving the bed entirely. Rainer veered around the neck of the riverbeast, his hooves thudding on wet mud instead of the water's surface. The creature she had summoned, Raegan saw, was not impacted by the time spell in the slightest.

With awe, she watched the river do her bidding. The creature was similar in shape to the water-dragon she'd summoned deep in the Rivers, but so much larger and realer. Currents and vegetation shimmered like scales, and when the beast opened its mouth, sharp stones studded the cavern-like maw. Someone screamed, just once, and then the river was upon the entirety of the Protectorate on the left bank.

Throwing his head back, Rainer let out a battle cry that hummed in Raegan's bones as he leapt onto the opposite bank, effortlessly navigating the damp, thick grasses and hidden rocks. Higher up the bank, a red stag appeared, so glorious in the early morning light that it made Raegan's breath catch. For a moment, she wondered what had called the stag to this place—but then it caught sight of the nearest Protectorate, took three running steps, and impaled the man on its antlers. A laugh bubbled in her throat, raw and drenched in violence.

Raegan stretched her arms wide to either side, only her legs gripping Rainer's flanks, her hair flowing behind her like a bloodstained banner. She turned to the left, focusing her energy on the riverbeast that decimated the Protectorate's forces. When she saw only a few remained, she beckoned the beast to her. It reared back and screamed before snaking across the wet black riverbed, its jaws open for more.

The sound of grown men imbued with an unnatural and unearned power screaming at the top of their lungs would live in Raegan's bones forever, she thought, and she would store it carefully. Wrap it in wax paper, bind it with blessed twine, and take it out only to feast in the most hungry and lonesome of times. It was a sacred sound, and it was worship—just as good as any prayer or offering.

The Protectorate had gone against the natural order, the Timekeeper had taken more than he needed while others went hungry, and the woods and the fields and the waters had been razed and polluted and bled dry.

And now they would pay for what they had done.

CHAPTER NINE

Her river monster tore through the Protectorate's ranks. Anyone who managed to miss the creature's riverstone teeth met the King's blade or Rainer's hooves. In a few minutes, it was all over, leaving Raegan breathing hard and shaking. Light-headed and nauseous, she slid off Rainer, moving to stand at the kelpie's shoulder. She watched the King roam the battlefield, chewing her bottom lip raw in the process.

In the old times, the Morrigan would've appeared with her crows. If neither side of the battle had her favor, she'd feast on the hearts of brave warriors while her crows devoured whatever flesh they could find. But if one army had the Morrigan's allegiance, then the goddess would roam the battlefield with one of her many daggers and dispatch any of the enemy that remained.

With the Gates still standing and the door Raegan had torn long since sealed back up, there was no goddess of war, death, and magic to do this work. Instead, the King took it on, examining each prone body for signs of life and sliding the point of his sword through every heart he could find. Unable to continue watching, she turned away from Rainer and made her way to the banks to give thanks to the river instead. It was necessary, yes, but in truth—she could not handle the task Oberon had silently taken up. Fighting in the heat of battle was one thing, but ensuring there were no survivors, ending the lives of those who could not fight back —it turned her stomach. She supposed it was a mercy for some, and she understood the strategic advantage of leaving no one alive. It probably made her a coward that she saw the reasoning but couldn't carry it out herself.

When the river had been properly sated—a long, tumbling prayer Raegan hadn't remembered until now, a lock of her hair, and seven drops of her blood—she felt the King appear at her side. Raegan straightened, dusting the dirt off the front of her jeans. The birdsong had returned a few minutes prior, and the wind danced coyly through the dry leaves. She examined Oberon in the bright morning light. His shadow armor had dissipated. Barely a hair was out of place, his elegantly cut suit unmarred, as if he had wandered in from afternoon tea, not a battle.

Oberon sheathed his sword without saying a word. Then he closed his eyes. Raegan took a step toward him, surprised to find that upon closer inspection, he looked harrowed. An exhausted shadow clung to every sharp angle of his face, sunken and sallow instead of feral.

Movement rustled a few paces down the river, and the King turned, all predator again, his eyes gleaming hungry in the sunshine. A low groan came from behind a willow tree's curtain of limbs. Oberon moved like a panther, nothing but shadow and grace and violence. Before Raegan could fully process the scene before her, the King was dragging some-thing—*someone*—by the scruff of their neck from beneath the willow.

"P-p-please," a voice—young, shrill—sputtered. Raegan moved to meet the King as he stalked out into the open, pulling the person behind him like they weighed nothing at all.

Raegan stood facing the King, peering down into the grass. In Oberon's deadly grasp was a mortal who looked barely out of their teenage years. The sight of their sandy brown curls sent discomfort skittering through her stomach. Hazel eyes peered up at her, wide with horror and brimming with tears. Without a word, the King released his fingers from the back of their armor, sending them slamming into the earth. They let out a long, low hiss, squeezing their eyes shut.

"Oberon," Raegan murmured, reaching out to brush his arm as he went to draw his sword. He looked down at her, the angle casting a hood of shadow over his eyes. He said nothing, but he didn't have to—her lover was not present. Only the Unseelie king, the faerie rebel who had survived a thousand years of warfare and near-extinction, stood before her now. He had no mercy left, and part of Raegan didn't blame him.

"They're just a kid," she said softly, looking up at him.

Without a word, the King gestured to their chainmail and gray suit, the gun holstered at their waist, the empty scabbard—probably missing a shortsword, Raegan identified reflexively.

"I know how much some of us don't want this," she implored, reaching for his hand. The King allowed her to touch him, but he didn't curl his long fingers around hers in his usual reflexive motion. "We aren't given a choice, Oberon."

The young Protectorate hacked a horrible-sounding cough, and as Raegan looked down, she saw blood bubbling from their mouth. They laid their head back down in the grass, eyes staring up at the sky, roving about like maybe it might be the last thing they ever saw.

"And my people are?" the King wanted to know, his voice low and slinking. "Perhaps you noticed during your time with my Court that there are very few Fey children. Has the removal of your Seal reminded you why that is?"

Raegan flinched. The cruelty of his tone felt unnecessary; she hated the Protectorate, too. For gods' sake, they'd executed her once. In that life, Fate had either played Her most fucked up trick, or She'd simply made a mistake, and Raegan had lived as the High Seelie Queen. She knew the way the Protectorate would seek out Fey children and slaughter them. She'd held limp and gray faerie babies to her chest and wept. She fucking *knew*.

"They're a kid," she repeated, her voice louder now.

"They are dressed and armed for battle," the King roared in response, his lip curled, his eyes all black, none of that fathomless gray sea she thought she might like to drown in. "If they are indeed a child, that transgression is on the Protectorate for sending their little ones into the fray."

"I–I'm t-twenty," the soldier piped up unexpectedly, their teeth beginning to chatter. Shock, Raegan realized.

"Did you want to fight today?" Raegan asked, placing her palm flat against the King's chest. She knew it was as good as hoping a single strand of silk ribbon might hold back a charging panther. To her surprise, the soldier laughed.

"Do I l-look like I'm having f-fun?" they wanted to know. Their voice was clearer now, the accent Irish. "Besides, d-don't think you'd b-believe anything I s-say."

Before the King could stop her, Raegan stooped low, settled her hand on top of those uncomfortably familiar curls, and spoke softly to the river. The waters had fed today; there had been much death. Allow a little life, she pleaded. Her fingers warmed, and something effervescent and sparkling bubbled in her chest, golden as an August sunset. She felt the warmth leave her fingertips and rush into the young Protectorate. They gasped, clutching their hands to their chest as their pallor changed from gray to pale sand. Freckles suddenly stood out on their cheekbones, and they blinked, breathing raggedly.

The King let out a long sigh.

"Did you—did you just . . . ?" the soldier asked, their voice trailing off. They groaned, moving stiffly to sit up. Surprisingly, they made no attempt to flee, though Raegan hadn't intended to heal them completely—just stave off immediate death. The soldier took a deep breath and then looked up at Raegan and the King. Their eyes widened as they took Raegan in, but when their gaze fell on Oberon, pure horror shattered their little heart-shaped face.

"May Kronos save me," the soldier whispered reflexively, trying to use their arms to propel them backwards, but the King caught them by their scruff again. At the mention of the Timekeeper, Oberon flinched and then looked at Raegan, as if to prove a point.

"I still say 'Jesus Christ,'" she said before the King could speak, one eyebrow arched at him. "Or 'for God's sake.' I don't actually *believe* in it."

The soldier was struggling hard against the King's grasp, completely ineffectively, like a fish on land, the hook already in its mouth. Raegan walked around their captive, kneeling down to face them.

"What's your name?" she wanted to know.

The King let out a long string of curses in High Feyrish, a beyond-ancient language that even most Fair Folk didn't know anymore.

"Reilly," the mortal replied, their eyes never leaving the King's broad figure. " T-thank you for healing me. For . . . for w-whatever it's worth, no, I didn't much fancy fighting t-today. Or any day, really." Oberon's grip did not slacken. Raegan chewed her lip, examining the soldier. "Makes n-no bloody sense, but, you know—thanks," Reilly added, hasty and nervous.

Wordlessly, the King lifted the soldier from the ground by their collar. Their feet dangled, and their breath came out in panicked gasps as Oberon raised them to eye level. He held them aloft, saying nothing, and Reilly visibly panicked more and more with each passing second they were forced to spend staring down the nightmare they'd been raised to fear beyond all else since birth.

"It was the Lady of the Rivers who spared you today," the King said in such a low, cruel tone that goosebumps prickled Raegan's flesh. "Not I. Not the Unseelie king."

Reilly nodded furiously, like they were in full agreement, though Raegan knew the King could have spouted nonsense and the young soldier would have readily complied.

"Go," the King commanded, barely letting Reilly's feet graze the earth before he released them. The soldier scrambled for their footing and then stood there, their eyes wide, breathing shallow and quick, completely frozen in place.

"Go," the King repeated in a roar, one powerful hand moving for the pommel of his sword. At that, Reilly bolted like a deer, taking off along the narrow riverside path, almost invisible beneath the willows. Raegan watched them go, grinding her jaw.

"*That*," the King snarled, suddenly so close that his breath stirred Raegan's hair, "will almost assuredly be a problem later."

She turned back sharply to face the King, away from the direction Reilly had run, her stomach boiling, poisonous words on her tongue. But as she did, she saw that Rainer had joined them.

"There appear to be no reinforcements coming for now," the kelpie said, sticking to the shallows, moving like

79

the shadow of a large fish beneath the waters. "May we depart?"

Raegan bit down on her tongue, unsure if Rainer hadn't seen any of what had just transpired or just simply chose to not comment. No, she was sure he hadn't seen anything. When had the kelpie *ever* managed to refrain from commenting?

"Yes," the King agreed, offering his arm to Raegan despite their argument. Unsure, she took it, and he helped her onto Rainer's back. The kelpie moved into a lofty trot, the gash on his shoulder appearing to bother him only a little. Raegan thought she'd have energy to heal it when they found a safe place to rest, though she felt a pang of guilt for helping Reilly first.

Silence sat heavy as they followed the river. None of them spoke, though that storm still brewed between Raegan and the King.

A mile or more had passed when the waters twisted into a copse of ash and alder trees, the branches thatched together to create a roof of gloom. Rainer slowed at the copse's mouth. The King tensed behind her, and Raegan cast her eyes into the dimness, desperately awaiting her vision to adjust from the bright sun of the unsheltered banks.

"I hope you enjoy it, for now," came a voice—a voice Raegan knew so well, had hated before she even remembered who she really was—from up ahead.

Rainer let out a snarling, carnivorous sound and plunged forward. On the right bank, his back against the trunk of a tree, lay Bedwyr. One hand was pressed to his side, and even in the low light, Raegan could see the blood pooling between his fingers. Triumph surged through her before she remembered he could not stay dead—he could bleed and he could die, but the Timekeeper always brought his favorite pet back.

Rainer approached, his footfall heavy and threatening, moving like a cat about to pounce. Bedwyr watched them, heavy-lidded, his breathing uneven. Raegan shuddered with revulsion

as she realized Bedwyr might be one of the only other people to ever exist who knew intimately what she went through. Rage flared to life in her chest; how *dare* Fate and the Timekeeper link her to her once-murderer like this?

"How long will you last this time?" Bedwyr asked, his gaze meeting Raegan's. "A year? Maybe two? Time never seems to be kind to the Unseelie king's little whore."

Raegan rolled her eyes at the predictability of men, but behind her, Oberon stiffened. She felt his hand clench tighter around her waist, and some twisted kind of heat pooled between her legs.

"May I?" the King murmured in her ear.

Raegan froze, bloodthirsty desire racing up her throat, open-mouthed and wanting. But why would he *want* to after their disagreement? Why would he still seek to exercise the sharp, violent edges of his devotion—wasn't she too hard to love?

"Be my guest," she managed to reply breathlessly. With her consent, the King slid down from behind her and stalked toward Bedwyr. As much as she wanted to watch the King's movements—imbued with an impossible predatory grace that set her entire body on fire—Raegan found her eyes falling onto Arthur's fallen knight. The myths remembered Lancelot and Arthur being so close, but the fabled king had always favored Bedwyr more, particularly toward the end. Arthur had valued Bedwyr's penchant for cruelty—and put it to good use.

Which made it even more satisfying to see that Bedwyr

was afraid. She didn't bother holding back her laugh. Didn't she know that feeling so well? Neither of them could melt into the quiet, dark embrace of death, but they could both *die*. Death was soft and lovely. But dying? Raegan found that it usually fucking hurt.

The King lifted Bedwyr from the ground by his throat, pulling his sword from its scabbard with his other hand. He moved languidly, like all of this was a ballroom dance and not a cold-blooded murder. Bedwyr scrambled, reaching for his own sword, but the King batted his hand away, pinning the knight against the trunk of the tree. Then he buried his sword in Bedwyr's existing gut wound, twisting it in slowly. The knight screamed, the sound reverberating through the trees and deep into Raegan's bones.

The limbs of the alder Bedwyr had just been impaled against began to reach for him, sliding through his legs, driving slowly into his flesh.

"It doesn't make a difference," the knight wheezed, trying hard to sound triumphant and failing. "I'll come back."

"When you do," the King said, his voice regal and horrible all at once, fingers still tight around Bedwyr's neck, "stay *far* away from her."

And then the King tilted his head, bared his teeth, and tore out Bedwyr's throat.

Chapter Ten

The King let Bedwyr's lifeless body drop to the ground like spoiled fruit at late harvest. Then he turned, sheathed his sword, and met Raegan's eyes. A pulse flared hot and hungry deep in her bones, every part of her igniting, flint-sparked. Blood streaked dark across his full, sculpted lips, a harsh shadow on his ivory skin. Sparing the young Protectorate soldier had deeply angered the King, and yet here he was, looking at her like he'd devour the entire world if only she'd ask. With a deep breath, Raegan tried desperately to center herself, digging half-moons into her palms. She did not even want to think about what the kelpie she sat astride might be able to sense.

But as the King approached, the dark, raw power emanating from him overpowered Raegan entirely. He stopped, standing silent beside her, gaze tipped up toward hers as one powerful hand slid onto her thigh. She thought of nothing—not the kelpie, not their exposed position, not magic nor Fate nor the Protectorate. Nothing at all but *him* as she reached out with both hands, seized the King by the front of his shirt, and brought her mouth to his.

He met her with a palpable hunger, his palms slipping

to the curve of her waist. Raegan tangled her fingers in the obsidian waves of his hair, Bedwyr's blood—like iron and ash—mixing with the taste of the King, all woodsmoke and folklore and the endless reach of night. She could've stayed there forever, but Oberon broke away gently, though his hands still roamed her body.

"We must keep moving," he murmured, long fingers brushing back curls that had escaped her braid.

"Thank you," Raegan replied, holding his gaze, wondering why she had ever tried to love anyone else.

"Always," Oberon replied, fingertips brushing her lips—now bruised with Bedwyr's blood, too, she imagined—before steadying himself and swinging onto Rainer's back.

The three were silent as they traveled down the River Wye. Raegan dabbed at her mouth with the sleeve of her sweater, perversely pleased to find the gray fabric darkened with blood. The thrill lasted only a few moments—then her adrenaline crashed entirely, and Raegan realized exactly how exhausted she was. Every muscle in her body ached, particularly her legs, and sleep pawed at her. The temptation to doze off to the gentle sway of Rainer's movements, tucked into Oberon's muscular arms, was thick and sweet as honey. But she knew that for all her exhaustion, the King must be feeling it tenfold. With a sigh, she sat upright in his arms, not wanting to ask him to give anything more than he already had.

The banks ahead seemed clear of Protectorate, and at some point, Rainer broke the silence by relaying that the kelpies thought the soldiers had withdrawn to regroup. That should buy enough time to get to Hiraeth. Raegan ran her fingers through Rainer's thick, wavy mane, hoping beyond hope that they could actually find the door to Avalon. That they could actually turn back the faerie blade. Actually save magic.

Early morning slipped away, the sun rising higher, as Rainer ferried his cargo along the river. Raegan watched, fascinated, as the kelpie slipped by hikers and kayakers and fishermen, all completely unaware of their presence. She'd just thought she had a grasp on the magic Rainer was using to render them undetectable when the kelpie spoke.

"Nearly there," he said. "We should be able to cross quickly. The Protectorate is licking their wounds, at least for now."

She straightened, peering around the tight bend of the river. All she saw was a vast meadow nestled in the curve of the river, nearly obscured by the slant of the trees and roll of the hills. She narrowed her eyes, fighting to engage her second sight—something that had once been as easy as breathing in previous lives, but since the Seal's removal in this body, took intense concentration.

For a moment, the kelpie beneath her and the solid mass of the King behind her faded away, and she almost had it—a slide of another lens across her vision, like a lizard's inner eyelid. The meadow disappeared. Or rather, it was no longer empty. An image flickered to life instead: rain-damp stone and smoke-wreathed chimneys and narrow, twisting pathways. Something in her heart panged, familiarity wrapping around her like an old, worn-in blanket.

But then it was gone, only an empty meadow staring back at her. Frustration simmered in Raegan's body, but then she realized that this time, she hadn't failed. Instead, her sight had been fiercely and definitively rejected.

"What exactly *is* this place again?" she asked Oberon, not stopping the awe from creeping into her tone. As far as she knew, they were still deep in the Welsh countryside, but the village—or small city, perhaps—she'd glimpsed for a heartbeat looked more like photos she'd seen of Edinburgh.

"A hold-out," the King replied. Rainer began to work his

way into the shallows as the sun dipped behind a thick coil of incoming rainclouds, casting the picturesque surroundings into grayscale. "An exception to the Protectorate rule of the Isles. A last defiance, if you will."

"And do you trust it?" Raegan wanted to know.

"I do not trust anything," Oberon replied, an amused laugh leaving his lips when Raegan reacted with an overly dramatic sigh at his predictable answer. "But I trust the people of Hiraeth, and in particular, I trust our host more than most. He has done this work for many centuries, never ceding an inch to the Protectorate."

Raegan nodded, anticipation fluttering beneath her breastbone. Another glance through the worn spot in the tapestry, another foray into the world-behind-the-world.

"We won't put them in danger?" she asked, though her heart ached to even ask the question; now that she knew it existed, the idea of not getting to visit a secret Fey city filled her with sadness. But she didn't want to sow more destruction, either, like they had for the Unseelie Court back in Philadelphia.

"We will," Oberon replied, his tone soft and hung heavy with all the weight of a throne. "But it is a necessary danger, and more importantly, one that the people have accepted. Their wards are strong and have stood for many years."

Raegan nodded, feeling a bit better, though anxiety still churned in her stomach. A column of wind blew hard across the river, bringing a spray of rain with it. She examined the meadow, eager to be tucked away behind stone walls, no longer out in the open. Through the raindrops, she spied hawthorn trees dotted around the space and smiled. If she thought it was only open land, she wouldn't have given the hawthorns a second thought—but knowing what she did, it was hard not to see a circle of trees sacred to the Fey. It was hard not to see a faerie ring.

The river barely reached Rainer's ankles now, and he carried them up a marshy bank, coming to a halt a few strides from the water's edge. Behind her, the King dismounted, and though the movement itself was full of his usual grace, the landing was unsteady. Concern and a small trickle of fear shot through Raegan. He needed rest as much as she did. She scrambled down from the kelpie's back on her own, not wanting to further tax him, and earned herself a grumble from Rainer about preferring that her flailing elbows stayed away from his ribs.

"Thank you, Rainer," the King murmured, reaching out one hand to rest it on the kelpie's thick, heavy mane. In response, Rainer said nothing but turned to nuzzle the King's shoulder in an alarmingly equine-like manner given the rest of his personality and tendencies.

"Into battle we shall always go as brothers," the kelpie said eventually, his tone low and sonorous. Oberon nodded, leaning forward to rest his forehead against Rainer's. Raegan settled for reaching out to stroke the kelpie's neck.

"Thanks for not drowning me," she said, preparing herself to follow Oberon as he straightened. Then she noticed the wound on Rainer's shoulder from their clash with the Protectorate. "Oh. Here. I think I can do this again."

Raegan spoke to the water, wondering if it might grant one last boon. The goddess of this river, Gwy, had been slain by the Protectorate during the Uprising, so nothing divine could answer her call. Only the water—the water blackened with blood, the primal and ancient wells of life and silt and death.

When she opened her eyes, the gash on Rainer's shoulder was certainly still visible, but it had gone shiny and pink, a wound at least one week healed.

"I am in your debt, Lady of the Rivers," the kelpie told

her, bowing his head. "Now go. Beyond the wards with you both. I doubt such a small act of healing would alert the Protectorate in their current state, but we must move with the utmost caution."

Raegan nodded and took one more look at the kelpie—right now, every single time felt like it could be the last—and then turned toward the meadow. The rain bore down, bringing with it the smell of woodsmoke and beeswax and damp oilskins. Raegan shivered.

Beside her, the King offered his arm, and together they climbed up the slope from the river. Raegan felt a soft pull at her very essence, like the waters bid her to stay, to forget the world above and sleep in the muck, where she would be hidden and safe. But Raegan did not want to be safe and she did not want to sleep. She wanted to fight.

"You should know," Oberon said, glancing over at her, his profile regal, "many years ago, there was a Temple here and, of course, an Oracle. After the Uprising, the Protectorate destroyed the Temple and killed its Oracle."

Disgust simmered in Raegan's gut. An Oracle's Temple was one of the most sacred places on earth, and there were so, *so* few. To destroy one felt profane, even for the Protectorate.

"But our people took what they could back, and the Temple became something else—a teahouse for the city's citizens and a waystation for its visitors. Our host," the King continued, soft grass underfoot now, something shimmering in the air around them, "was once the Temple's Keeper."

CHAPTER ELEVEN

A door opened in the rain. Despite all she'd seen, Raegan struggled to process it for a long moment —a rectangle cut out of the meadow, drenched in blues and greens, the silhouette of a man standing within it, backlit by the dancing orange glow of a hearth.

"Come inside," said the shadowed man in a clear, strong voice, each letter enunciated. "And welcome to Hiraeth."

The King laced his fingers through Raegan's and pulled her across the threshold. Behind them, the roar of the wind through the meadow abruptly cut off, leaving her ears ringing in the silence. But different sounds quickly trickled into her ears—low murmurs and the clink of porcelain and the crackle of a fire.

The man who had invited them in stepped back, the light from a nearby lantern illuminating his features. He was tall and distinguished in a casual sort of way, just as easily thirty as fifty or three hundred. His sharp jaw and deeply-set monolid eyes revealed wisdom but defied exact age. Round metal glasses perched on his nose, and his hair was black-brown, shot through in some places with shimmering silver, a handsome contrast against his warm, rich skin. His expression was kind but guarded, and his dark eyes held a sharpened sort of intelligence that Raegan liked immediately. Unlike the other Keeper she was familiar with, this man dressed in worn jeans, brown leather boots, a faded chore jacket, and a gray sweater.

Raegan's eyes swept around the narrow room surrounding them—a vestibule, maybe, considering its small footprint and high, vaulted ceilings. Behind the man were beautiful double doors, all glinting leaded glass and carved dark wood; she couldn't make out anything on the other side.

"Merry meet, Emrys," the King greeted, regal as always.

The Keeper inclined his head with a slight smile, his gaze dipping toward Raegan, something that might have been distrust crossing his expression for a moment. "It has been some time, my liege," he replied after a moment's pause. "Please, follow me."

The King moved forward, his hand still in Raegan's, and she went with him. Together, they passed through the grand, heavy doors, which led into a stone-walled antechamber. An iron chandelier hung from the highest point of the vaulted ceiling, the flickering candles upon it casting uneven shadows around the room. At the far end stood another set of large double doors, and through the glass, Raegan thought she saw movement. She strained her ears and caught more of the sounds she'd heard earlier— conversing voices and clinking porcelain. The teahouse, she figured.

"We appreciate your hospitality despite the dangers," the King said, coming to a stop when Emrys did, atop a beautiful if threadbare rug. Raegan looked to either side and found a hallway leading off in both directions, cloaked in shadow. It was the kind of room where assailants might slip from the darkness, knives gripped in steady hands, but Raegan found she felt no apprehension.

"It is our honor," Emrys replied with a bow of his head. "As I discussed with the kelpies, I think it is best that no one knows you are here. Every year, the people of Hiraeth have renewed their centuries-old agreement to harbor the Unseelie Court when and if necessary, so understand that you are not imposing on innocent townspeople unaware of the risks. But that does mean you'll be a bit cooped up."

"It is for the best," Oberon replied with that easy authority of his. Raegan, realizing that Emrys was looking to her for her agreement as well, nodded.

"Then please, follow me," Emrys said, turning to the hallway on the left. "You'll be staying with me in the old Temple."

The passage was much shorter than she would've expected before entering the shadow-cloaked space—or perhaps it was only brief and painless because Hiraeth had permitted them within her sanctum. There was a soft pop as she passed over the threshold, and then she found herself standing in a large room. At the far end, a fire crackled in a massive stone hearth, engraved with figures and creatures Raegan couldn't make out. To her left, the rain lashed a large bay window that offered a view of a narrow stone street and roving tendrils of mist. Nestled beneath the bay window was a heavy wood table with high-backed chairs.

She moved deeper into the space, Oberon at her side, and noticed two faded tapestries hanging on either side of the fireplace. One depicted a maiden peering into a large, shallow dish of water; the other showed a tall, elegant figure standing before a small fire, arms raised skyward.

Oracles, Raegan realized. Remnants, she imagined, of the Temple that once stood here. The only parts of that place its Keeper could still watch over, kept beside the hearth in a place of honor. Her heart panged. Such was the story of magic—endless losses, a thousand funerals, the few survivors holding tight to the tiny fragments of what once was.

"Have a seat, please," Emrys instructed, gesturing to the table. He shrugged out of his chore jacket and hung it on a much-used iron hook set into the wall. He was more muscular than the Keeper Raegan knew, and a voice at the back of her head whispered that he was likely quite comfortable with sword and bow.

"If what I hear from the kelpies is true, you must be exhausted," Emrys called before ducking through a dark archway on the far side of the bay window, disappearing into another room.

Oberon pulled a chair out for her and then settled into one beside it, his elbow resting on the table's dark, shining surface. "I would never encourage you to be completely without suspicion," he murmured, eyes meeting hers, "but we are safe. We can rest. Emrys has kept the path longer than most."

Raegan nodded, sagging back into the chair. Despite the heat of the fire, she didn't remove her leather jacket yet.

A door creaked open, and Emrys appeared from a shadowed hallway, carrying a black metal tray with swooping, scalloped edges. Upon it was a plate piled high with tea cakes, two large pots of tea, a selection of jams and creams, and three teacups with saucers. The teaware was beautiful —a shining sterling silver pot in the shape of an elegant gourd, a stylized vine curling off the lid. The teacups were pitch black, gilded with silver around their wide mouths.

"Thank you," Raegan said, reaching for a cup the second the tray hit the table. The three of them prepared their tea in silence. After a few large, perfectly brewed gulps that burned her mouth—she did not mind—Raegan reached for a tea cake. They were perfect: a little sweet with hints of cinnamon, dotted with dried currants.

"Do you have any injuries that need attending to?" Emrys asked after a few minutes of companionable silence. "Any other immediate needs?"

"Only rest for now," the King replied, folding his hands on the table. "Raegan will likely require a larger meal, yes?" He turned to look at her to confirm, and for a moment, she clearly saw the deep exhaustion on his angular face.

"Yes," she said, meeting Emrys's gaze. "Still very much human in that regard."

"I expected as much," the once-Keeper replied. "Should be ready in a few hours, if that's alright."

Raegan nodded, adding a few more biscuits to her plate, this time sampling some of the different jams and jellies.

"I encourage you to rest today," Emrys said, pouring more tea into his cup. "If you have cause to walk the streets of Hiraeth, please use one of the glamoured cloaks by the door. The glamour workings are linked, so wearers of the cloaks are visible to each other, but no one else. Try your best not to speak to anyone. Hiraeth's people will question new faces. Remember, we keep this city safe because those of us who become citizens agree to never again leave its walls."

The jelly's flavors of earl gray and strawberry bursting delightfully on her tongue seemed much at odds with Emrys's grave words. But Raegan nodded, casting another look out the large bay window to her left.

Across the winding stone street, tall stone rowhomes rose into the mist. Most of the first floors seemed to be occupied by shops—she could make out an apothecary and a stationery store. The path was lit by elegant lamps, dark metal stalks curling from the street, delicate pools of honey-colored light hanging like lily of the valley buds. Her heart ached to explore this place.

"We thank you and Hiraeth's people for providing us a home as we search for Avalon," the King said, his tone mild, long fingers tracing the silver-rimmed mouth of his teacup.

"We should speak of Avalon after you've rested," Emrys replied, expression softening. "No offense, but the two of you look like hell."

Oberon and Raegan laughed in unison, the amusement genuine but the sound itself ragged, torn around the edges.

"There are many places Modron could have buried her door," the King mused. "I look forward to hearing your theories. The Unseelie Court is lucky to have a mind as vast and nimble as yours to call upon."

At that, Emrys beamed, his kind but serious face looking far more human for a few moments. Raegan smiled into her tea; the way so many Fair Folk blossomed under Oberon's praise delighted her, and probably, if she was being honest, helped assuage any concerns she felt over possibly choosing the wrong side.

Looking up from her teacup, she examined Emrys's features. He *was* Fey, she was fairly sure, though he lacked the feral angles and his ears were only slightly pointed. Perhaps, like her, he was something altogether more complicated, though Raegan did not have the mental energy to tackle that at present.

"Will you actually be safe?" she asked suddenly, looking into Emrys's dark brown eyes, scrutinizing what she found there. Thoughts of the Philadelphia Temple laden with makeshift bedchambers and displaced Fey who didn't know if they'd ever see their homes again filled her mind. "Will your wards hold? I don't want to fuck up your life, too."

Emrys evaluated her, and then his mouth twisted into something arch but not unkind. "Hiraeth's wards have held for more than three hundred years, and nearly a thousand before the attack on the Temple. And alas, even if they do not, my Lady, it is our choice to make the sacrifice."

Raegan held his gaze and said nothing for a long moment. Then she sighed, shrugged and settled for, "Thank you, Emrys." She took another sip of tea, hoping the weight of so many peoples' hopes and faith would not crush her.

Once the remaining tea cakes had been polished off—mostly by Raegan, with some support from Emrys—Oberon got to his feet, grimacing when he shifted weight onto his left side. "Emrys," he began, "would you be so kind as to show us to our room?"

"Of course," the distinguished man replied, pushing his chair back. "Follow me, please."

Emrys led them through a passage that branched off from the far end of the room, near the fireplace, and then up a set of grand stone stairs. The stairwell was adorned with portraits, each painting featuring a silver nameplate affixed to the heavy, ornate black frames. A plush rug of deep plum florals softened the landing where Emrys paused for a moment before continuing down a wide hallway lit by Art Nouveau-style lamps.

He opened the third door on the right. Raegan kept close on Oberon's heels, curiosity overpowering her tiredness for a few moments. The room that greeted her was breathtaking. Clad in gray stone and dark wood, the space included an ornately carved fireplace, a four-poster bed with a tapestry-like quilt on it, and a heavy armoire. The far wall was mostly taken up by gabled windows. One deep windowsill was lined with round velvet pillows in moody jewel tones. Raegan eyed the little nook with delight; it was so easy to imagine herself tucked away there with a book, looking down on the twisting, rainy streets of Hiraeth. But then she remembered her path held little room for pleasure and turned away regretfully.

Emrys showed them the narrow door that led to the bathroom. The dark wood continued there, too, accenting the high ceilings with carved crown moldings. The wallpaper depicted a meadow scene not unlike the ones visible in the valley beyond the city's walls. A clawfoot tub, pedestal sink, and separate glass-surround shower—the only modern-looking thing in the room—were arranged beautifully in the space. Another large bay window of leaded glass invited in the delicious sound of the rain's pitter-patter.

"I have some work to attend to," Emrys said, looking between Raegan and the King. "But help yourself to anything in the old Temple. Take care if you step beyond its walls. You'll know you've neared one of the city's edges when you come across the hawthorn trees. Our wards are strong, and the city moves constantly, shrouded in old workings—which is why you'll find it's always raining in Hiraeth. And that reminds me—I'll need to add your blood to the wards. They are . . . hungrier than most."

At that, Emrys pulled a glass vial from his pocket, along with a sharp sewing needle. Oberon and Raegan pricked their fingers without protest, squeezing a few drops into the vial. At the bottom, Raegan noticed a curl of paper, as well as some dried herbs. Rosemary, maybe, and angelica. In any other situation, she'd pause, refusing to give her blood until all her questions were answered. But as difficult as she normally found it to trust people, she felt no apprehension at following Oberon's lead. She had trusted him—and often *only* him—for more than a thousand years. Besides, truth be told, she just didn't have the energy.

Raegan barely had the bandwidth to run a bath and climb into it, which was exactly what she did after Emrys departed. Once the bath had filled, dosed with some of the lavender-scented salts kept in a lovely glass jar beside the tub, she gleefully shed her blood-and-river-mud-streaked clothes and slipped beneath the hot, silky waters. In moments, she was half asleep, and she barely even registered when Oberon entered the bathroom and stepped into the shower. By the time she felt a bit more like a living, breathing person, he'd long since departed and her bathwater had gone cold.

Raegan climbed out, supposing that not everyone spelled their bathtub to stay hot like the King had for the guest rooms in his archives. She toweled off, rubbing condensation from the mirror above the sink with the flat of her forearm. It felt like a hundred years since she'd been in the archives, though in reality, Raegan knew it hadn't been more than a few weeks. She splashed some water on her face, brushed her teeth, and pulled on one of the soft flannel robes that hung on the back of the door.

Then she walked out into the main room, finding Oberon on the bed with his eyes closed, though she very much doubted he was asleep. Just in case, Raegan tip-toed to where she'd left her clothes, digging into her leather jacket pocket for the luggage tag—the spelled object the King had given her back at her apartment in Philadelphia that condensed all her belongings to a slim piece of leather. She found the tag and placed it on the gabled windowsill, waiting for the spell to unfurl and reveal her travel bags.

As she did, Raegan caught a flash of movement outside the window. A Fey toddler and their parent walked down the street, the child stopping at every puddle and jumping into it as hard as they could, splashing rainwater everywhere. A strangled noise escaped Raegan's throat as panic surged in her chest.

"What if the Protectorate find Hiraeth because of us?" she asked, her voice raw.

"We will do what we can to ensure they will not," Oberon reassured her.

Raegan spun, hands clenched into fists. He hadn't moved from the bed, but his eyes were open.

"But they're so much more powerful here," she said, thinking back to the time magic they'd worked at the river, at how taxed Oberon was.

She'd *known* this—it had been discussed in all their planning. The American government had its own shadowy paranormal organization, but they hardly considered the Protectorate their brothers-in-arms. The Protectorate, in their eyes, were superstitious and obsessed with the Fair Folk. Operatives were under strict rules of no gunfire and absolutely no larger workings like time magic while on American soil. Raegan suspected the United States just didn't like to be outgunned; *their* organization certainly didn't have a thousand-year-old pact with a god. But the Protectorate still followed the Americans' rules. Leave it to two imperialist empires to begrudgingly respect each other, if no one else.

"They are indeed more powerful here," Oberon agreed, sounding a bit ragged.

He did not offer any other words of comfort as Raegan grabbed a pair of sweatpants and a t-shirt from her bag. She took one last look at the narrow, winding streets below, which were busier now that the rain had lightened up. When the guilt felt like it might swallow her whole, she gave up with a sigh and walked over to the bed. She'd been planning to get dressed and go make another pot of tea, but the sight of him derailed her thoughts.

She'd never quite seen him like this—barely able to keep his eyes open, but also unable to sleep. His brow was heavy, his jaw clenched, the vast tides of his breathing interrupted by sharp hitches. Hesitating, Raegan stood on the other side of the bed, biting down on her lip.

"Can I do anything?" she asked, the words coming out hoarse, scraping her throat as she spoke. Shame spun a web around her lungs. She could've done more at the river, she knew. Been stronger. Fought harder. Gotten her shit together. And then Oberon wouldn't be suffering like this, laid out like a corpse.

"No, but thank you for offering," he replied, barely more than an exhalation.

Raegan told herself it was just the gray light of Hiraeth's rain that made him look so sallow, so wan. She swallowed hard and gritted her teeth. Her hands went clammy, her insides twisting tight as a hangman's noose. How close, Raegan wondered, her eyes pricking with hot, burning tears, had she come to losing him again this morning?

Trying to shove the thought away, she settled onto the quilt. "Is it okay if I lie down, too?" she asked in a whisper.

At that, Oberon opened his eyes. "Of course," he replied, his gaze sweeping over her, a frown twisting his full mouth. "I will be alright, *cariad*. I am in a great deal of pain, but it will improve with rest."

"Okay," she replied, pushing away a stray tear before he could see. Gods—he was only in so much pain because of her, and here he was, comforting her all the same. Raegan curled onto her side, keeping her back to Oberon so he wouldn't notice her distress. With a long inhale, she tried to stifle her emotion, to drown her shame. Tracing the quilt's pattern with her fingertips, she rooted herself in the vast, defiant warmth of the faerie king beside her. The pitter-patter of the raindrops striking the windows on the other side of the room lulled her into drowsiness.

It might've been peaceful, but then Raegan made the mistake of closing her eyes. In an instant, Oberon and the four-poster bed and the rain and Hiraeth were gone. Instead, that platform creaking beneath her bare feet, the feral cry of her lover, the rough hood over her head, the inescapable doom.

With a stifled gasp, she opened her eyes, fingers fisting the quilt. Raegan fought to reason with herself. Spiraling would not help. But her thoughts spun out anyway—all her past failures, every moment of this morning's battle played on an endless loop. She wiped her clammy palms on her thighs and then pulled her knees to her chest. What if Reilly *did* become a problem later, just as the King said? She'd have no one to blame but herself. It wouldn't be the first time she made a decision that felt so right in the moment and only brought ruin in the end. The dream of Titania's execution stalked the edges of her waking hours, baring its teeth.

Anxiety and shame and self-doubt pounded in her blood. She turned to look at Oberon—*really* look at him, cataloging the scars and the fierce angles and the full mouth and the dark, silken waves of hair. Fuck—she loved him. Absolutely and completely, madly and irrevocably. Raegan bit down on her lip, choking back tears. In all the fairy tales she'd spent her childhood reading, love was a pure thing. Divine, even.

But in the dim, rain-shook light of the teahouse's room, she worried that *her* love amounted to nothing but destruction and demise.

CHAPTER TWELVE

Raegan awoke to the violet-hued light of late dusk seeping in from the window. She didn't even remember falling asleep, and for a moment, panic enveloped her at the sight of an unfamiliar room. But then she remembered—*Hiraeth*.

She turned to check on Oberon, a knot releasing from somewhere beneath her ribs when she saw he was actually sleeping. A bit of tension had eased out of his brow. For a few moments, Raegan basked in it all—the murmurs of the city outside, the safety of the teahouse, the opportunity to rest. But then all the usual ghosts and bad dreams returned to her conscience, and she knew more sleep was out of the question. Even if she managed to fall asleep again with her heart racing like this, she knew where she'd end up: back in that hellish nightmare of her past mistakes.

So she stood, careful not to disturb Oberon, and dressed, pulling on boots and grabbing an oversized sweater from her bag to ward off the evening chill, and then slipped out of the room. She found the kitchen easily enough, returning to the first floor by retracing her steps. As Emrys promised, dinner was indeed in the oven, and the smell of it made Raegan's mouth water. She tasted rich spices, savory broth, and delicious vegetables in the air. Her stomach rumbled. The old-fashioned lemon-shaped timer on the counter indicated there was still a little time to go before the meal was ready, so she wandered through the archway into the main room.

The fire in the hearth had gone out, and the space was colder for it. She walked over, determined to stoke the flame, when the front door opened. Raegan's body tensed, and that dark current deep inside her flexed—but it was only Emrys.

He nodded at her as he pulled the door shut. "I thought you'd still be resting," he told her, unlacing his muddy boots.

"I probably should be," Raegan replied mildly, crouching to position a log in the hearth's hungry mouth. Doubt and shame still gnawed at her, so she looked for a distraction. "Hey, I was wondering. Why do your wards need blood?"

In her years of journalism, she'd found a shocking amount of people would answer not-so-pleasant questions if she asked them in a pleasant enough voice, like it hardly mattered to her, anyways. This technique did not work on Emrys.

She glanced up from the heart to find him already looking at her, eyes glittering in the low-lit gloom. Raegan watched as he considered her, the sensation not unlike staring into one of those endless trick mirrors. She wasn't easy to read, never had been—but all at once, Raegan was overcome with the thought of what it might be like for Emrys to try to get a handle on her. What was it like, she wondered, to look at someone who was not only the person standing before you, but also a thousand others, all beating about like birds caught in a too-small cage?

"When the Temple fell after the Uprising," Emrys said,

examining Raegan as she lit a match and held it to the kindling, "my Oracle was murdered and only a handful of my Seers survived."

His use of possessive language was not precisely that—not as if these people had belonged to him but as if they had been his responsibility. Emrys said it the same way someone might say "my child" or "my sister." He paused, moving into the room, his jaw clenched.

"I held on to a scrap of the Temple's realm," he continued, gesturing to the space around them. "We built something out of the ruins our enemies left us with. A place where they could not find us. A place that moved with the rain and the mist. A place that might be a home for our kind."

The fire took, and Raegan leaned low, infusing it with a long whoosh of her own breath, which the flames gobbled up. Then she stood, considering Emrys in the dancing shadow and light of the fire. He stood at the back of the armchair now, hands gripping the rich fabric.

"To create Hiraeth, I set new wards," he continued, meeting her gaze, unwavering. "Ones with more teeth. It's an old working—very old—and like many of the old things, it requires blood. But I had to be sure my Oracle had not died for nothing. I had to be sure nothing like that attack could ever happen again. So I dug deep into the earth here, just at the center of what remained of the realm, and I buried seven Protectorate soldiers alive."

Raegan found she could not read Emrys as well as she could most people, and she respected him for it. That said, she didn't see any remorse in his face as he retold the tale of his actions, but to her judgment, there was no glee, either.

"And once wards have a taste of blood . . ." she replied, her voice trailing off, one eyebrow arched expectantly.

"They begin to require it," Emrys confirmed, standing

up straight and folding his arms. "I bleed myself for them, and any visitors must make offerings, as you have."

"And the annual tithe?" Raegan asked, Seal-less and knowing the way of things.

Emrys smiled, dead-eyed, all teeth and no warmth. "You are a witch, my Lady. I imagine you know."

Raegan did—the wards would almost certainly require seven more Protectorate lives every year, and if Emrys strengthened or added to the working, the wards would want even more. It explained their power, the way Hiraeth existed in ancestral lands plagued by the Protectorate and remained hidden. It also explained why Oberon felt confident the Protectorate could not cross the wards. Not only would it be an incredibly hard spell to undermine but the wards already knew the taste of their blood and apparently rather enjoyed the flavor. She briefly wondered how he'd convinced his own working to let her within the city's walls.

But if Emrys wanted surprise or horror from Raegan, he would not get it. Yes, Protectorate blood ran in her veins, but it felt more like a technicality than an immutable element of her existence. Besides, she found it difficult to imagine herself in Emrys's shoes and not doing the same as he had.

"Well," Raegan said, dusting her hands off, "I might actually feel safe enough to sleep through the night here, then."

Emrys smiled again, fox-like and genuine this time, and she smiled back. She liked this Keeper and opened her mouth to say so, but a shrill sound from the kitchen cut her off.

"Ahh," Emrys said, firelight catching the silver in his hair as he moved across the room. "That'll be the ramen."

"Need any help?" Raegan asked, which was how she found herself pulling chipped porcelain bowls from the teahouse's cabinets and setting the table. She ducked back into the kitchen for glasses, only to find the King had arisen and was filling a large pitcher with water from the farm-house-style tap. She took in the sight, amused—three ancient, deadly creatures preparing themselves a little meal that, in appearance at least, would not be unwelcome in a Beatrix Potter scene.

Either the ramen and its accompaniments were perfect, or Raegan was very, very hungry. Perhaps a bit of both. She greedily filled her bowl of broth with Emrys's perfectly cooked noodles, brisket, soft-boiled eggs, bok choy, scallions, and miso paste. With the knowledge of the wards, the setting sun behind the mist, and the fire burning merrily in the hearth, she nearly summoned a shred of peace.

"What are your initial thoughts on our path, Emrys?" Oberon asked, an untouched bowl of broth, noodles, and vegetables before him. Raegan could tell he was still in pain by his careful, deliberate movements and the ever-present crease between his ink-dark eyebrows.

"I have a list," Emrys replied after a long swig from his ale. "Only a few places seem possible when human folklore and Fey texts are cross-referenced. Though, I admit, there are many tales of Modron and Danu, and there is much oral tradition among the Welsh that I may not be accounting for."

"Especially as Modron and Danu are viewed as sepa-rate entities by the mortals," the King mused, his gaze a thousand miles away.

Raegan paused in thought, turning over the Irish and Welsh goddesses in her head, the result of two similar but separate cultures interacting with the same expansive, ancient being—the All-Mother, the Creatrix of the Fair Folk, the Maker of the Gods-Touched.

"We knew Her long before anyone called her Modron

or Danu," Emrys said, pausing to consume another spoonful of ramen. "The Druids also came to know Her true history by way of their relationship with the Seelie Court, but of course the Romans destroyed their libraries. So yes, this will be difficult. I think beginning the search at Tintagel, the Sgwd Yr Eira waterfall, and Carn Doedog is the best course, considering you saw water and a mound of earth in the vision from the Morrigan."

Raegan considered, scooping up a piece of egg, the fragrant scent of seasonings and vegetal musk curling into her senses. "None of those places are connected with Danu or Modron. But I guess neither goddess has many associated sites. Which is . . . peculiar, now that I'm thinking about it."

"Or a very intentional obfuscation," the King replied drily, giving her a side-glance that would have been mischievous if not for the pain she could clearly read in his features. The events of this morning had taken too much from him. "Those three are an excellent start, Emrys. Thank you."

Raegan decided that, after she'd slept more, she'd ask Emrys for access to his library—she had no doubt in her mind that there *was* a library somewhere in this ancient and magical place—and do a bit of her own digging. Two heads were better than one, and if she was honest, Raegan wasn't capable of entrusting this task to someone she barely knew.

The thrum of the quest and the hunt sang in her, a sharp thrill rolling through her body, as if her tendons were all harp strings to be plucked. Her father had taught her this folklore for a reason, intentionally filled her head with stories hastily costumed in Christian robes, the thick haze of the past waiting just beneath.

Oh. Her father. All at once, the thrill swept out of her and she abandoned her spoon with a clang. It was strange how easily she forgot he was dead, gone, lost to her forever despite all she'd suffered to find him. Such a thing should plague the forefront of her mind, destroying any ease or pleasure that rose up inside her. And yet Raegan found she could almost tuck the loss away like a handkerchief. Perhaps because she'd been practicing it for so many years, Cormac good as dead all the while.

And there was her mother, too, undoubtedly losing her mind, the lie of an in-patient stay worn thin nearly a month later. And Henry and Saanvi, who might have taken it upon themselves to hunt for her the way they usually hunted down a source or a lead. Regular, everyday people who—against their better judgment, surely—cared for Raegan, who would be hurt by her choices.

"What's going to happen to mortals when the Gates are opened?" Raegan asked, the words coming out of her before she quite realized what she was saying.

Across the table, Emrys went entirely still. She felt the heavy weight of Oberon's eyes land on her. She lifted her own gaze, somehow finding Emrys's the easiest to meet first. She had to remind herself she did not know this Keeper, and unlike the Temple in Philadelphia, had not known him in another life, either. And yet—she felt so incredibly sure that if the King hadn't been right across the table, Emrys might have shrugged and said, "Who cares?"

Raegan swallowed hard. Why had she never bothered to ask this before? She let out a long breath, flexing her hands. Because she hadn't wanted to know. She'd wanted only magic and questing and to see behind the curtain. She'd leapt without looking because she thought her father would be beyond the door. He had been. Just not for very long.

"I suppose we have not yet had time to discuss this matter," Oberon said, annoyingly diplomatic.

"Yeah, well, it's kind of important, isn't it?" Raegan snapped, though of course she was mad at herself, not him.

Who in their right mind would ask a faerie king to put mortals first, to consider their needs above that of his people's?

"It is," Oberon replied, turning in his chair to face her, even though she could see the movement pained him. "It is important to me. And also complicated."

Emrys, still silent, stood, collecting his dishes and then reaching for Raegan's nearly empty bowl. She watched him, daring the Keeper to say something she could sink her teeth into, but he only gathered up his napkin and departed for the kitchen. So she turned on Oberon instead.

"Go ahead," Raegan snapped. "I know you want to say it."

The King narrowed his eyes, tilting his head as he examined her. "What do you think I wish to say?"

She threw her hands up in the air, her face reddening. "Why didn't I ask this question before? Why in all our weeks of planning at the Temple did I never once bring up the fate of mortals if we accomplished our task?"

Oberon's mouth parted slightly as he watched her, saying nothing for too long. In the firelight-soaked silence, all Raegan could see was the raw-red brick and sepia-colored sunset and her father's fading red curls, trapped forever on that train, beyond her reach.

"No," Oberon replied, leaning forward onto his knees, his clasped hands close enough to Raegan's thighs that she could feel the heat of them. "I wish to know exactly what happened to you in the Timekeeper's realm. You refuse to speak of it, and *cariad*, I am sorry, but the time has come to do so, lest it fester within you."

"Fuck you," Raegan laughed, hoarse and battered, though traitorous tears gathered in her eyes. "Don't turn this around on me, Oberon. Answer my question."

He watched her with such gentleness in the silken gray

velvet of his gaze that Raegan wanted to punch him. It was so much easier to be angry, to point fingers and make accusations, especially when Oberon had such an infuriating, unerring ability to be correct, *particularly* when it came to her.

When she held his eyes, refusing to look away, her jaw working, the King sighed and leaned back. "Revolutions are bloody, Raegan," he said in a way that made it sound like he did not enjoy spilling blood when she knew very well that he did. "There is little way around it."

Silence slipped its arms around the remnants of the Temple within the city now called Hiraeth. Raegan let it string itself tight and uncomfortable, all of her attention on the faerie king. He relented, but only because he chose to do so, she knew.

"The world will profoundly shift," Oberon continued, staring out the bay window into the city, dressed in dusky silks and the honeyed cloaks of streetlamps. "Many people —your mother's included, the *Cymry*—speak to gods that can no longer hear them, acting out rituals that are meaningless without a free flow of magic. In my years, I have seen only those who seek conquest and oppression align with the Timekeeper and the Protectorate. If magic is freed and the gods walk the earth once more, power might yet be returned to its rightful places."

Raegan leaned toward him, crowding the King in against the wall and the window. The next question was already falling from her tongue before she even realized she was speaking. "Have you ever helped humans?" she demanded, her fingernails digging into the table as she refused to dive into her own freed memories for the answer. She needed to hear it from *him*. "You've been on this side of the Gates for a while. You've seen a lot of atrocities. But have you actually done anything?"

Her anger surged out, no longer roiling in her stomach but excised like a demon, filling the room with its flame and fury. And she allowed it, knowing that she couldn't hurt him—not like this, at least. Not as badly as she'd hurt herself if she let all this anger and shame and guilt turn inward—and oh, how the tide strained for her harbors.

"You know well that I have spilled my own blood for human rebellions and dispatched monsters before they could make it to the pages of your history books," the King said, reaching for his glass of water, unbothered. "But there is only so much I feel my people should interfere. I will not strip mortals of their agency or their ability to shape their world. No matter their transgressions."

"How noble of you," Raegan sneered, caught between bursting into tears and screaming curses until her throat bled. "I suppose once the Gates open, you'll just sit around the fire with us and we'll all hold hands and imagine a new world together. If you're so generous with us puny mortals, why didn't that happen the first time, before everything went to shit?"

She watched Oberon's jaw clench and reveled in it; how many beings could say they alone could make the Unseelie king lose control? The fire crackled in the background, and Raegan felt her own anger smolder and spit.

"I tried," he said, sounding miserable and weary instead of sharp and cunning like she wanted. "When the Time-keeper made his offer, many of the mortals on the Isles had already forsaken the old gods and turned against the Fair Folk. Christianity promised eternal life, and the Gates offered prosperity and safety until they met their god. The Timekeeper did not require worship—not in a way they understood. So they made the deal without understanding the depth of the cost."

With her Seal peeled back, Raegan remembered most

of this history as he said it. The Fair Folk—the Unseelie Court in particular—*had* tried to warn mortals of what aligning with the Timekeeper would bring. But men could not bear to see a great, powerful, immortal race walk among them when their own eternal life was more hazy promise than certain inevitability.

In their eyes, the Fey had everything and refused to share, whereas the Timekeeper offered everything he had and didn't even care if they worshiped another god. But only because the Timekeeper did not want churches or idols or prayers; he hungered for much, much more.

"I know our history," Raegan spat, even though she'd asked the question. "What will happen to mortals? Will you allow the kelpies to lure us into puddles and murder us? Will your court return to kidnapping our children and hunting our loved ones through the woods for fun?"

Oberon's body language changed abruptly. She watched him push aside all his pain as he turned on her, finally giving her what she wanted—the hated and feared Unseelie king who haunted human folklore.

"Your people murder each other for no reason," he snarled, his voice low and impossibly cold. "You war over gods that cannot hear you, or worse yet, ones you invented entirely. Murder and assault and enslavement were not enough for you—no, you had to colonize and pillage, to oppress those who are different from you, and now you have the audacity to pretend none of it ever happened. Your history is soaked in blood, yet you act as though you are morally superior to the Fey. Spare me this nonsense."

Raegan shot out of her chair, its legs screeching against the stone floor. Her entire body aflame and red with rage, she slammed her fist onto the table, leaning into Oberon's space in a way she knew he loathed. "And does that make it alright to murder us and pile your feast tables with our carcasses?"

Part of her was surprised when the King stood to meet her immediately, rising from his chair like a rogue wave in a quiet sea, tall and fathomless and unspeakably deadly. "Mortals routinely consume intelligent, sentient creatures," he replied, his eyes level with hers, and all of a sudden, she felt like the one pinned in the corner. "What issue could you *possibly* take with my people doing the same?"

CHAPTER THIRTEEN

Horror slipped down Raegan's throat, sour and sharp, turning the heated flush of her anger razor-edged. How *dare* he?

"You're a monster," she snarled in return, knowing it was the thing he feared most, though at this moment, she might've believed it. She waited for the hurt to ease his features, for the feeling of triumph when she won against such a mighty opponent. But the feral angles of the King's face did not soften. He made no attempt to walk his words back or apologize. He did not reach for her. He simply held her gaze, everything about him predatory and ancient. So Raegan, out of any other options, the hungry anger inside her coiling traitorous with a desire to hurt him, did the only thing she could.

She left him behind.

She darted for the entryway, where she barely remembered to snatch a glamoured cloak from the pegs before throwing herself through the front door. Raegan tumbled out onto the winding cobblestone streets of the hidden Fey city, tugging the cloak's hood over her head. She abruptly chose a direction and took off, hating herself all the while—

for her weakness and her inability to control her anger, her need to express poison because she wasn't immune to her own bite. For being exactly what her ex-girlfriend had said she was: hard to love.

No one looked her way as she plunged through the rain-damp streets. The gray stones ramped upward, the tall, narrow buildings jutting into the sky like broken teeth. Raegan barely stopped to consider her surroundings; she just continued to run, following the path lit by the honey-hued glow of the streetlights, dodging pedestrians as she went.

Then the angle of the rain-slick cobbles steepened sharply, slowing her pace to a walk. By the time she reached the summit, Raegan was breathless—and then, her remaining breath stole away for another reason entirely. From this vantage point, all of Hiraeth spilled out before her: a thousand pathways spiraling in on each other, a world of rain and mist and stone, a quilt of gray stone and damp green parkland. It was *much* larger than it should be—much larger than the riverside meadow it had appeared to occupy. At the edges of the city, the crown of clouds met the hawthorn trees. From inside Hiraeth, they were towering and unreal, curling in a half-dome around the city, like a hand cupped around a butterfly.

She liked the idea of having something else to focus on, so Raegan pulled her cloak tighter against the wet, dark evening and began to make her way down the hill. Walking helped. It always had. Her dad had taught her that at an early age, taking her for a loop around the neighborhood or down to the corner store, or even on the bus to Pennypack Park when a particularly difficult problem arose. What was difficult at eleven years old, of course, paled in comparison to the things she faced now.

But still, Raegan continued through this neighborhood

of Hiraeth, pleased to find she didn't even need to bother keeping her head down. She realized upon peering into a shop window and not encountering any reflection of hers at all that Emrys's cloaks were glamoured for full undetectability. The realization pulled her shoulders down her back a few inches, something at the base of her neck loosening. She felt so visible, so central, in this war. It was nice to be no one, nothing, just a stir of the wind.

And at this precise moment, she was just a person hovering outside the raindrop-painted window of a bakery, admiring the pastries on display beneath soft, twinkling lights. Each creation was decadent, sugar-spun, perfectly delicate. Like the happy ending of a fairytale. At that thought, Raegan felt her heart pang for a reason she refused to investigate. Instead, she sighed and continued walking.

Hiraeth passed gently by in soft blurs of dove gray and storm blue and rain-drenched black. It was the thoughts devouring her from the inside-out that felt dagger-sharp and dangerous.

Raegan slipped around a group of shorter, stockier Fey leaving a pub, their expressions a-glitter with faerie wine. She'd really thought that with her Seal removed, she might make better choices—be a better person. Scoffing, she kicked at a pile of wet leaves that had drifted onto the cobblestones from an ancient sycamore in someone's neat front yard. Here she was, still playing the same stupid song. How had her therapist phrased it? That she'd figure out how to provoke people so they would treat her the way she thought she deserved. And then everything was easier with her darkest suspicions proven correct. Raegan could walk away, firm in her belief that she brought out the worst in people. Firm in her belief she was better off alone. And it would be better if Oberon remembered why he had grown to resent her sooner than later—before she couldn't live without him. Didn't her failures haunt him as much as they did her? And yet he still trusted her, still followed her into the dark.

Up ahead, the cobblestone walkway came to a T, a dark and rambling garden devouring the path she'd been following, the hawthorn walls rising up starkly behind it. To the left, the cobbles widened, leading to taller buildings, broad avenues, busier foot traffic, brighter streetlamps—a commercial corridor, it seemed. To the right, the way turned narrow and winding, bending sharply and then disappearing behind a block of elegant townhomes; she had the sense it wound back up the hill she'd just come down. Raegan wavered, examining the options, the cold, rainy night air making her feel alive and almost fragile in a way she welcomed. It served as a reminder that her next grave could always be her last.

Fuck.

And she'd called him a *monster*. Jaw clenched, she held very still, never mind the nearby pedestrians blind to her presence. "What is wrong with me?" Raegan whispered. "I love him more than I even understand."

Suddenly, the grand charcoal sweeps and Art Nouveau arches and golden lamplight and low murmur of other living creatures became far too much to bear. She needed to be alone, *now*. Raegan barreled forward to the gates of the shadowed garden. The towering metal had been bewitched into the shapes of hawthorn leaves, tiny glittering stones emulating dewdrops. A small silver plaque, green with patina, was set into the low stone wall, indicating it was a public garden—no surprise, given the general Fey sensibilities about how the world should operate. At this hour, night having thrown its velvet skirts over the city, the garden should probably be closed, but the gates opened at Raegan's touch and she slipped inside.

Beyond the ornate metalwork, the garden was damp and hushed. Despite the late autumn season outside Hiraeth's walls, deep purple hellebore clustered around the path, fiddlehead ferns curling just behind, shading the dark shadows a lush green. The graceful furl of the ferns reminded Raegan of Oberon's hands. She ground her teeth and kept moving.

The twisting path was clearly charmed against mud. Despite the mist still pouring down from the skies, the dirt was firmly packed and dry, lined by twinkling willow-o-wisp lights. Amusement stirred inside Raegan; as a child, she never would've thought that willow-o-wisps would be safe to follow. No matter how much she'd wanted it, she had never dared to *actually* think she might not belong to the world she'd been born into but a stranger, wilder place entirely.

Ash and alder and willow grew denser and tighter for a few moments, barely more than looming shadows despite the blueish-green light lining the path. But as Raegan continued, the garden opened up again, the tree line creeping farther and farther back. In its place, strange ferns in a shimmering shade of pitch, wine-dark tulips, black roses, and deep purple flowers she didn't recognize grew instead, creating an impossibly lovely—and poisonous, she suspected—carpet of midnight foliage.

And in the distance were the hawthorns, looking for all the world like something created by a witch in a fairytale to trap a sweet princess. Gnarled, reaching limbs twisted and climbed into the evening sky. The hawthorn wall was much closer now; this must be a very old garden, Raegan realized, to back directly up against the wards. All of the newer sections of the city typically had a boulevard for travel and security between any structures and the wall itself. But even by the faint willow-o-wisps studding the edge of the path like phantom jewels, she could see the garden's dark, tumbling flora stretched all the way to the hawthorns.

Something else caught Raegan's eye—a wooden arch, old and sagging, barely standing. If not for the lush vines wrapped around the entire structure, she suspected it might not stand at all. There was something familiar about it, so she walked closer—though familiarity with strange things was beginning to feel normal these days. Gravel crunched under her feet as she approached.

All at once, she understood—the structure was just like the portico from the overgrown community garden back in Philadelphia. The King had still been able to use it for traveling within the city, but *that* was why she'd felt such profound sadness, why the sight of it had stirred her memories. This gate had once connected entire realms, spanning oceans and deadly wards and planes of existence, a relic from the days before the Protectorate's attack on the Temple that had been Hiraeth's epicenter once.

Now it stood ancient and forgotten, a reminder of why the last Fey city had cut itself off from the rest of the world. Raegan let out a long, shuddering breath, raising a reverent hand to brush her fingers against the portico's structure.

Before she could, the hawthorn wards at the end of the path *shivered*. The hair on the back of her neck stood on end. "Okay," she said, taking her hand away from the portico. "Sorry."

But the prickling across her skin did not ease; if anything, it intensified, as if her nearly touching the dead gate hadn't mattered in the first place. No, some voice inside Raegan told her that there was some other disturbance that had caused the wards to react and that she only felt it because whatever had triggered the hawthorns was close. *Very* close.

Instinct took over, and Raegan ducked behind the wide

trunk of an ash tree, letting the shadow and mist obscure her form. Her blood pounded. She desperately peered through the gloom, searching the open space beyond the portico where the path curled up at the hawthorns' feet. Emrys and Oberon had both been so confident nothing could cross the wards. If they were wrong, this entire city—this entire way of *life* the Fey had carved out from the world that had been stolen from them—was at risk because of her. And if anything happened, Raegan didn't think she could survive the guilt.

Seconds trickled by. There was only the soft murmur of the misty rain and a few distant lashes of wet branches. Maybe she was just being paranoid. But then her senses prickled again, and this time, Raegan found her eyes falling on a specific place at the end of the path. A few of the hawthorn branches didn't look quite right. Discomfort perched on her shoulders, sharp and taloned, as she realized there was a strange shape on the wall. And then everything got worse.

In the depths of a tiny, half-forgotten public garden, right at the edges of Hiraeth's wards, crouched a woman in dark clothing. The willow-o-wisps turned the long locs falling over her shoulders to a shadowed blue-black. Raegan watched, her breath dead in her chest. The intruder's hands were moving, and Raegan was terrified to realize they did so with spellwork. One section of the hawthorn roots shimmered like wet blood, a symbol appearing. Raegan narrowed her eyes, craning her neck, desperately wanting as much information as possible before she made a decision. The swoop and the shape of the symbol felt familiar, but she had only faint faerie lights to see by. Before she could inspect further, the woman straightened.

Raegan stood stock-still as the woman looked left and then right. Her heart hammered in her throat; she was sure the trespasser had sighted her, even though she knew it was impossible thanks to the glamoured cloak. But then the woman glanced around and took a tentative step closer to the path, away from the wards, which still hummed like slightly offended bees. As blue-green illumination drenched the trespasser, Raegan noticed two things: the stranger was beautiful, and she was also not really there.

It was the best way to describe what she was seeing: the woman was faintly translucent, a gentle glow tracing the outline of her form. Raegan's mind moved sluggishly. God, she was too tired for this shit. She examined the stranger for a moment longer, noting her strong profile and tall, curvy frame, the perfect obsidian skin and high cheekbones. Beautiful but mortal. The woman moved forward again, looking like a deer on high alert, terrified to make even the tiniest of sounds. Silence bled into the woods, the rain and the wind ceasing all at once, like they'd taken note of an unwelcome guest. The stranger froze, afraid to shatter the quiet.

But Raegan was not, so she stepped from the shadow of the trees onto the path and pushed back the glamoured hood, moving directly into the woman's line of vision. "Shadewalker," she boomed in a voice that was once the Witch of the Wood's. "You don't fucking belong here."

CHAPTER FOURTEEN

Hiraeth moved constantly across the Isles, so Raegan had no way of knowing how close they were to any river beyond the city's walls—and yet, she heard a current *roar* somewhere. Good. Anyone capable of shadewalking in a realm leached of magic by the Timekeeper was a formidable creature—so let them make no mistake that Raegan had buried legions beneath silt and tide.

"You know what I am," the trespasser said, her eyes wide, brows furrowed, her chest rising and falling quickly. Her voice was rich, inflected with hints of London and the Caribbean.

"Yeah," Raegan replied, moving toward the woman, who took a backwards step. "Not. Fucking. Invited."

Holding her ground, Raegan called to the water in the core of all things, not knowing if attempting to work such dangerous, difficult magic would be the death of her. But a *shadewalker*? It shouldn't even be possible with the Gates standing—not to mention that the Protectorate had hunted those born with the gift into extinction. Or so she'd thought.

The seconds stretched too long, and Raegan realized a

few things all at once: the woman was young, maybe mid-twenties at most, rooted to the ground, absolutely terrified, and most disconcertingly of all, had Protectorate blood and magic running through her veins.

"How are you even here? And *why*?" Raegan demanded, taking another step forward, this one more aggressive, which sent the stranger tumbling back two, three steps. She could see in the woman's body that every instinct was pleading with her to flee, to never look back and forget whatever madness had possessed her to follow this path.

And yet the stranger remained, her jaw set, hands curled into fists. "Where . . . where exactly *is* here?"

Raegan blinked. Behind the intruder, the hawthorns curled the tips of their limbs, as if awaiting a command. "What?" she demanded, the word coming out a hoarse shriek that was not exactly intimidating.

The stranger released a long, hitched breath, and Raegan realized exactly how much the unwelcome mortal was trying to rein in her panic. "I don't . . . I don't think I meant to come here," the Protectorate explained weakly, retreating another step. Her back bumped into the hawthorn's outstretched limbs and she jumped, scrambling forward again. "I was just looking for . . . okay, well, I *was* looking for you."

Raegan stared, pushing away a swell of horror. The Protectorate had a terrifyingly useful asset—someone who could stow their body safely away and then wander the land, looking for signatures of magic that only they could see. Wards, pocket realms, protective workings, curses, bindings, blessings—all exposed by a shadewalker's sight. Such a power could allow the Protectorate to track the Fair Folk far too easily, as was terribly clear by this woman's presence inside Hiraeth's wards. A place she should never have been able to locate, let alone enter.

"Looks like you found me," Raegan replied flatly, desperately trying to summon her quickness, her cleverness. Maybe the Protectorate stranger didn't realize she was inside Hiraeth? She pleaded for that to be true and for the ability to ensure the woman did not find out. Gods, only a few hours in Hiraeth's walls and she'd already fucked everything up. "Strange thing for the Protectorate-oathed to be looking for me without being a lot more . . . murder-y."

Good. This was going great. Raegan absolutely sounded terrifying and confident. Silence clung to the garden's branches, thick as a woolen blanket on the first day of winter.

"Yeah, but the thing is," the woman began, her eyes darting away, though her voice grew stronger, "you spared Reilly. And I need to know why."

Raegan's mind wheeled, but the calculations were too slow, too thick with the emotional turmoil of her and Oberon's argument. She'd come here for peace and quiet, for fuck's sake. "So you want me to believe you risked performing outlawed magic and being killed by the Unseelie Court just to . . . ask a fucking *question?*"

A large raindrop plopped down from an outstretched tree limb to land directly on the top of Raegan's head. She gritted her teeth. She could've just not been a bitch for once in her life, and then she'd be tucked in Oberon's arms, probably in front of a fire, maybe with another helping of Emrys's ramen.

A few steps down the path, the stranger wavered, though her body relaxed a little. She swept her long tendrils off one shoulder with a shaking hand. "Yes. Because it doesn't make any sense. When Reilly made it back alive from the fight, rambling some nonsense about being spared by the Lady of the Rivers, the generals took it pretty bloody seriously. They're being kept under surveillance that does not feel friendly, and they're my best friend, and I need to know what happened so I can help them. No one will let me speak with them, so I came to find the only other witness. I didn't track you, by the way. I *couldn't*, actually. I just looked for old wards, starting at the river where everything happened, and then spiraling out." The shadewalker paused, a little out of breath. "If it's not obvious, I'm pretty desperate."

Raegan blinked. The woman's thought process was absolutely fucking insane. Shadewalking involved the practitioner entering a deep trance that left their physical body vulnerable as their shade walked free. How had this woman found anyone trustworthy enough to attend her body while she walked? And why had she been willing to wander through ancient wards on a goddamn hunch?

With a huff, Raegan realized she had done things just as stupid before, and probably would again. So she went for a different angle. "What do you think the Protectorate will do to Reilly?" Raegan asked, tilting her head, scrutinizing the stranger. Fuck, she wished she had better eyesight. She needed to watch every muscle in the woman's face, every twitch of the fingers.

As it turned out, the woman was not that subtle. She let out a harsh, arch laugh, looking at Raegan like *she* was the insane one. "Didn't think I'd need to explain the horrors of the Protectorate to you, of all people," she replied.

Raegan raised a brow. "You don't," she said, sly, taking a slow step toward the trespasser, the gravelly earth crunching under her boots. "It's just a rare opinion for those within their ranks to hold." She waited, eyes sharp, knowing everything about the woman's answer would be extraordinarily telling; she had set it up that way.

"That doesn't matter right now," the woman pleaded, bringing her hands together at her chest, her emotions and reactions all over the place—usually, though not always, a sign of genuine despair. "Why did you do it? Did Reilly make a deal?"

The woman said the last three words in a low, hoarse whisper, as if even speaking them might invite the Unseelie king into her very soul.

"No," Raegan replied, resisting the urge to roll her eyes. "They were just . . . really young. And there's not exactly a choice in the Protectorate, is there? Moment of weakness, I guess. Clearly a mistake, since you're here now."

That stumped the woman. Her brow knitted together tightly, and then her mouth fell open for a second before she found the right words. "You expect me to believe that?"

Raegan threw her hands out in frustration, startling the stranger into another backward step, but all she did was embed herself between hawthorn branches. The limbs reacted, one sliding across her shoulders as if to hold her in place. "You came to find *me*, and when you crossed wards you had no business crossing, I didn't immediately kill you. But you're going to accuse *me* of lying?" Raegan demanded, incredulous.

The woman grit her teeth, slapping away the hawthorn branches; they couldn't hold something incorporeal, anyway. "I—I've heard rumors," the stranger stuttered, her hands moving in frenzied gestures. "I mean, more than rumors. A lot from your aunt, actually."

Raegan forced herself not to freeze at the mention of Maleona, to not give away any impression she cared about the fate of her father's sister. She only stared at the trespasser, trying to emulate that cold, dead look she'd seen Oberon use more than once.

"Look," the woman continued, straightening her shoulders, making direct eye contact with Raegan for the first time, "if you spared Reilly and the generals don't want any of us to know, that's . . . suspicious. Particularly considering all of the other things I'm already pretty sure are true."

Raegan clenched her jaw. This woman could be valuable. This woman could possibly take her to her aunt, or at least give her information about where she might be. This woman was also mortal, Protectorate-oathed, and capable of passing through Hiraeth's wards, even if only incorporeally.

"What things," Raegan asked, her tone delicate but sharp-edged, "are you pretty sure are true?"

The woman looked hard at Raegan then, dark eyes flashing with a familiar kind of rage. "That the Protectorate either needs to fundamentally change," she replied, voice firm, "or it needs to be dug up by the roots and burnt alive."

CHAPTER FIFTEEN

Raegan said nothing, focused on crushing the hope taking flight in her chest, butterfly-winged and shimmering. After everything that she and the Fair Folk and anyone who fought for magic had suffered, she could not find it in herself to believe that Fate would simply hand her this boon. Unless, of course, it was not Fate at all who had brought this about but the stranger's own defiant free will coursing hot and heady through her veins.

"What's your name?" Raegan asked, exhausted and brimming with energy all at once. The mist clung to her hair, pulling a shiver from her body.

The woman looked at her like she was out of her mind. "You're not going to tell me how convenient it is that I've shown up like this or how you'd rather kill every single human with Protectorate blood than trust a single one of us, or something like that?"

Raegan waved a hand tiredly in the air, suddenly feeling quite old. "Sure, I mean, I might get to that. But for now—your name, please?"

The stranger faltered, her full lips pressed into a firm

line. The willow-o-wisps pulsed, making her appear opalescent.

"I'm not Fey," Raegan reminded the woman. "I can't do anything with it. It's just—I'm assuming you know mine, so it only feels fair."

"I *do* know yours, Raegan Maeve Overhill," the trespasser replied, considering. She opened her mouth, closed it, and then finally spoke. "Alanna. I'm Alanna."

"Nice to meet you, Alanna," Raegan replied, sidestepping to lean against the defunct portico's side because her body was about ready to give out entirely. The sagging wood structure held her weight. "Though usually I prefer people to stay on their side of the wards."

"I know," Alanna replied, genuine, holding her hands up. "I'm sorry. I didn't see another way. I needed to shield myself from the Protectorate, too."

Raegan had figured as much, and she nodded, but then another implication slipped into her mind. She considered it, breathing in the scent of decaying leaves and rain-damp soil. "They don't know what you are, do they?"

Alanna let out a snort that startled some birds in the undergrowth. The sound of their wings flapping filled the air, and then the garden returned to its nighttime hum. "Of course they don't. If they did, I would be dead."

Raegan rested the back of her head against the portico, crossing her arms. "Nah, they'd find a use for you. They're pragmatic. It would be unpleasant, but you'd be alive. Is anyone attending your body, by the way?"

Alanna looked at her incredulously. "Why would I tell *you* that?"

"So no," Raegan said, hiding her smile, drawing shapes in the gravel path with the toe of her boot. "I can't help you with your friend. What they told you is exactly what happened. The Protectorate won't like that story getting around, so I'm not sure what they'll do to Reilly."

Alanna's countenance darkened, eyes narrowed at Raegan. For the first time, the woman stepped closer, her hands balled into fists at her side, despite the fact she could enact no violence in her current form. "So *that's* why you did it. Now I understand."

Raegan stood up straight, pushing off the portico, surprised by how much Alanna's accusation stung. "No," she replied, raising her voice. She swallowed, trying to settle the anger digging its claws into her. "No, that's not why. I barely have four brain cells to rub together right now, and I had even less this morning after everything that happened."

She was surprised when it seemed like Alanna believed her. The younger woman studied her hard, looking for any cracks, but relented when Raegan just gazed back at her. Alanna let out a long breath, cradling her forehead in her hands.

"You said you think the Protectorate needs to change," Raegan said tentatively, keeping her hands at her sides, where Alanna could see them. Her words hung in the cold November air, surrounded by the orchestra of a soft breeze stirring damp, rain-heavy leaves in the ancient botanical garden.

Alanna stared at her, expression guarded and distrusting. "Yeah. I did. I'm trying to do my best to change it, but that won't matter if *you* murder us all first."

"No one wants to murder all of you," Raegan said automatically before wincing and leaning back against the portico. "Okay, yeah, some Fey do. But only because they feel they have no other recourse."

"I know," Alanna said softly, to Raegan's absolute bewilderment.

She was off her game, so tired that her bones felt heavy

—she was in no place to navigate a conversation like this and come out on top. But not everything comes wrapped in a bow, so Raegan took a deep breath and tried her best. "You do?" she asked, matching Alanna's tone.

"Yeah," Alanna replied, glancing at Raegan for a heartbeat before her gaze drifted away. "I mean, I've seen enough Fair Folk. I'm a researcher, but it requires field work. If they wanted all humans dead, despite everything—despite the Gates and the Timekeeper's boon and the fading residual magic—I think . . . I think we would probably all be dead."

Raegan didn't know what to say to that, so she just nodded, grim. This woman had to be part of some Protectorate trick. Just like she'd said herself—if they knew one of their oathed could shadewalk, they'd find a way to use it.

So why was her gut saying otherwise? Why did that rage in Alanna's eyes feel like a twin flame to her own? She would have grown up with this woman—with Reilly, too—and been like an older sister to them both, if things had been just a little different. If her father hadn't run. That was all that would've needed to change—no complex web of choices and paths. Just one hinge. If her father had stayed, she'd probably know Alanna and Reilly as well as she knew herself.

"Part of why I came here," Alanna said, looking self-conscious, refusing to meet Raegan's eyes, "is because I wanted to see you. I needed to know if you were the monster in the briefings or if you're . . . just a person like anyone else."

Raegan chewed on her lower lip and watched a pale green hellebore petal tumble across the path. "What have you decided?"

"Not sure yet," Alanna replied after a moment's pause.

"Then maybe we have more to talk about, you and I," Raegan hazarded, looking up and holding Alanna's dark brown eyes. If she pulled this off—and if Alanna didn't fuck her over, which was very possible—it could change everything. To have not only a deeply embedded source in the Protectorate but also a shadewalker in a world that thought they were dead and gone? The possibilities hummed in her chest, electric-hot and pulsing with a thousand opportunities.

Alanna hesitated, but she'd stayed for this long, so Raegan knew she probably had her already. "Maybe," the woman replied, but there were more words hanging on her tongue.

"Do you feel safe like this?" Raegan asked, gesturing to Alanna's shade and then the wards. "If you do, just come back and we can talk more. Alanna, I think we might want the same things. Or at least, enough of the same things to warrant further conversation."

"I would be executed as a traitor just for coming here tonight," Alanna replied, her shimmering, incorporeal body still clearly stiff, wracked with tension.

"Well, then you might as well get your money's worth," Raegan said with a smirk.

To her surprise, Alanna smiled, that dangerous flame back in her eyes. "*If* I come back," she replied, moving toward the sigil that marked where she crossed the wards, "it will be in two days' time at sunset."

"Okay, we're making this really dramatic," Raegan replied, knowing the power of humor. "Should I wear a red feather in my hat so you know it's me?"

Alanna held back a laugh, standing within a pace of the wards. "I need to go. If you think of a way to help Reilly, please tell me when we talk again."

"I thought it was *if* you come back," Raegan replied, repeating the woman's words with a playful smile.

"If I come back," Alanna agreed, actually smiling now,

her beautiful, young face so different without all the gravity the world had placed upon it. And then, without another word, she slipped through the wards and disappeared.

Raegan stared at the last place Alanna had stood until the interwoven wall of hawthorn trunks and branches nearly burned an afterimage into her retina. She didn't even know if Hiraeth would be in the same place in two days. If Alanna would ever be able to find her again at all. If she'd just come back with a Protectorate army instead of that glorious rage. Raegan heaved a sigh. Was this delicate, slim chance worth endangering all of Hiraeth? She didn't know.

And worse—would a Protectorate shadewalker crossing the hawthorns for the first time in hundreds of years because of *her* just remind the King why he'd avoided Raegan for all those centuries? The thought choked the air out of her lungs. The last time they'd tried to open the Gates, the last time she'd ruined everything, he had abandoned her to empty half-lives where the memory of him was little more than a distant, blurry dream. Where she'd ached and ached and ached, all alone.

Heaving a sigh, Raegan pulled the glamoured hood back up, turned on her heel and walked down the path through the botanical garden, out the gates, and back up the hill. It was no short walk to return to the old Temple, and now her shoulders sagged even heavier with calculations for the future. But she needed to feel Oberon's arms around her, even if it might not last.

With that thought, she gathered herself up and increased her pace through Hiraeth's winding streets, her heart pulling her back to him the way it always did. Thoughts of all the potential futures spilling out before her should've filled Raegan's mind, and maybe as she walked, she would've untangled them. But it was the King who took up space in her head. The dark-haired, gray-eyed being of impossible power and shocking beauty that she just couldn't stop hurting. Between her repeated deaths and her nearly endless mistakes, she was always clawing at his open wounds. Maybe he always *had* been better off without her. But she was too selfish for that, it seemed.

Raegan crested the top of the hill, the majority of the city behind her now. Her breath was quick, a damp sheen coating her lower back despite the cold evening air. She pushed her tired body into a jog, recognizing the bakery she'd passed on her way out. Finally, she saw the old Temple up ahead, the wide bay window of leaded glass, arched black door, and ornate metal lanterns awaiting her. As she approached, Raegan paused, something not quite right about the slant of the door and the light emanating from the window.

A few moments later—her heart skittering through her chest all the while—she realized the discrepancy came from a tall, broad figure lounging in the shadow of the Temple's stone walls. Raegan would recognize his form anywhere; she'd know him blind and only by touch; she could find him in a strange city a thousand years from now after she'd forgotten her own name.

The Unseelie king waited for her in the darkness, wearing one of Emrys's glamoured cloaks. Good—so they were only visible to each other. Everything else melted away and she ran to him. Her boots thudded on the cobble-stones as she threw herself into his arms. He pulled her close without saying a word, the dark heat of him rendering her as senseless and ready to surrender as always. The King rested his chin on the top of her head, wrapping his larger body around hers.

"I'm sorry," Raegan murmured at the same time Oberon spoke. She pulled back and looked up at him, forced to crane her neck back to meet his eyes. "What did you say?"

"I said that I apologize," he told her, amusement glittering in his gaze. "It seems we have both arrived at the same place."

Raegan bit down on her lip to keep the tears she felt brewing behind her eyes at bay. "Can we go inside? It's cold out here."

"Of course," Oberon replied but not before pulling a wool blanket from the windowsill and draping it over her shoulders. He must've brought it out with him, she realized, while he awaited her return.

Silently, they crossed the threshold. She peeled off her damp glamoured cloak and hung it up to dry. Then they made their way upstairs. As she passed, Raegan noticed the dining table had been cleared and wiped down and the fire in the hearth was cold and quiet. Oberon led the way up the grand stairs, the antique structure sighing under his weight in a way she was quite familiar with herself. The second-floor hallway flickered orange in the dark of the night, all the dark metal sconces along the wall aflame. The effect was both cozy and haunting at once.

They slipped through the doorway to their room together. Raegan was relieved to find the ornately carved fireplace was already crackling away with a bright flame. She wrapped the blanket tighter around her shoulders, breathing in the room's scent of old wood and fresh lavender. It looked larger at night, all the shadows carved out and deepened.

She settled on the edge of the bed, watching Oberon as he came to sit beside her. Raegan let out a long breath, leaning over to rest her cheek on his shoulder. She clutched the moment like a pearl between her teeth. Just a little longer before she brought up Alanna and the garden. Just another moment before he hated her again.

"I apologize for what I said," he murmured, long fingertips stroking her back. "It was unnecessary and cruel, a pattern I find myself falling into all too often."

"I'm sorry, too," Raegan said, meaning it. "You only said what you did because I pushed you. I'm always pushing you. Well, anyone, really."

"Anyone who gets too close," Oberon replied softly, his fingertips still making sweeping, gentle strokes down her frame. She shivered at his touch.

"Yeah," Raegan admitted. "I'm sorry I called you a monster."

At that, the King straightened, moving to cradle Raegan's face in his large hands. For a long moment, he said nothing, only holding her gaze. Then, finally, he spoke. "Do not call me that again. Not, at least, until I am about to cross that line. Until I step into that place from which none can return."

"You won't," Raegan said, her brow furrowing with the intensity of her belief, voice firm.

But the King only sighed. "I cannot promise that," he replied, his thumb stroking her cheek. "And you cannot promise to be the only thing holding me back from that ledge."

"But I want to," Raegan said, reaching up to grip both of his wrists with her hands.

"There are many things we want," Oberon said, "that we cannot—or should not—have, my love."

He exhaled and then brought his forehead to hers, hands still against her skin. She closed her eyes, tears gathering on her lashes. The scent of woodsmoke and black pepper settled around her, the familiarity of it reaching deep into the recesses of her memory. Raegan let the scenes roll over her, the current of a cold, thunderstorm-swollen stream in spring.

They pulled apart, only slightly, so he could wrap an

arm around her waist. She settled her head onto his chest, tired and spent and knowing at the same time that the battle had only just begun. With a hard swallow, she tried to find the right words.

"I love you," Raegan said with all her might, reaching to slide her fingers into his. "I love you more than I understand. More than I thought I'd ever be capable of loving anyone. It scares me sometimes."

He turned to look at her so fiercely that she lifted her head from his chest, their eyes meeting. She hated the way her words brought no joy to his expression. Instead, Oberon looked haunted. He was, she supposed. She had been his ghost for more years than she'd ever been his lover, and she brought more horror to his doorstep than happiness.

"Not everything is a responsibility for you to take on," Raegan murmured, reaching up to trace the sharp angle of his jaw. He leaned into her touch. "Don't wear my love like a mantle." *"Even though it weighs as heavily as one, and I'm about to remind you why,"* she did not say.

Oberon took in a deep, jagged breath, closing his eyes. Then he gathered her body against his and kissed her— slowly, deeply, as if they had all the time they could ever want. Raegan drowned herself in his dark tide, a sailor to the siren, moth to flame. His mouth on hers, the feeling of his strong, long-fingered hands roaming her curves—all of it should have torn down her defenses, sent the truth of what had just happened spilling from her lips. But with her father dead and her mortal life forsaken, what else did she even have but Oberon and this quest? So selfishly—as always—she clung to the moment for a little longer.

"Feeling better, I suppose?" Raegan teased, tracing his jawline with her fingers.

"Somewhat," the King said against her collarbone, his voice a low rumble like thunder in the distance. "My pain has eased a little with rest. My desire for you, however, has only grown all the more intense."

He pulled her sweater over her head, bringing his mouth to her neck as he pressed her into the quilt. Raegan let out a soft whisper of a moan, reaching for the hem of his shirt, praying that the deft sweep of his lean, muscular body would pull her from the darkness of her own mind. And it almost did—desire erupted in her at the sight of his moonlight skin, so much power coiled just beneath. Raegan ran her hands down the King's back, wrapping her legs around his hips, her boots long since kicked off somewhere at the edge of the bed.

"I'm sorry I'm such a bitch all the time," she said, the words tumbling out of her, a hundred feelings shouting for dominance inside her chest. Guilt swarmed her like locusts.

Oberon paused, coming up on his elbows, a wave of raven-black hair tumbling across his forehead. Then he examined her, his mouth moving into a frown. "Do not be sorry," he finally said, sitting back on his knees, her thighs still wrapped around him, as he reached to undo the zipper of her jeans. "I have always liked that about you."

He wasn't lying, she didn't think; in this position, the evidence of his arousal was hard and straining against the apex of her legs. Raegan studied him, lifting her hips so he could pull her jeans from her body.

"For what it's worth," she replied, breathless now with want as he slid his hands up the bare skin of her legs, "I've always liked that you can be . . . monstrous."

The corner of Oberon's sculpted mouth lifted, but even though he didn't meet her gaze, she could tell the humor didn't reach his eyes. "A pair of angry, broken things," he murmured, lowering himself back over her in a sharp, controlled movement. The heat and weight of him pulled a low, strangled sound of unbridled want from Raegan's mouth. The King reached forward, cradling the back of her head in his hands as he swept her into another all-consuming kiss.

She wanted to let go. Wanted the dark rush of him to consume her, to be devoured by the terrifying faerie king that everyone else had attempted to kill or tame and only she had tried to understand instead. Raegan gasped, the sound half-choked by desire, as Oberon undid the clasp of her bra in an easy, practiced movement.

"Oberon," she murmured, resting an open palm on his bare chest. With just that light touch and the sound of his name, the King pulled away from her immediately, sitting back to meet her eyes. Concern cut into the languid expression on his angular features.

"How can you love what you know you're going to lose?" she asked, her voice raw, damp desire for him still throbbing between her legs even though her heart felt like it might shatter.

The King's expression hardened for a moment, a faraway gleam in his ocean eyes. But then he seemed to shake it off, parting his lips and taking a long inhale before speaking.

"Like this."

Chapter Sixteen

The next morning, Raegan still hadn't managed to tell Oberon about Alanna. She'd tried, but then they'd fought bitterly about something else entirely, and now here she was at the ass crack of dawn, climbing mist-damp stairs to the mouth of an ancient waterfall looking for a door to Avalon. She felt far too exposed scrambling up the side of the falls, her form clearly outlined by the wide, pearly skies. Down below, the woods surrounding Sgwd Yr Eira were deep and dark, perfectly capable of obscuring gray suits and flashing chainmail. Maybe Oberon was right—maybe she *should've* stayed behind.

Her anger from earlier rekindled in her chest, so Raegan took a deep breath and climbed higher, keeping her attention on the uneven ground and loose soil. At least Hiraeth had its many perks—centuries of Fey history meant its armory was enough to impress even Oberon. They'd left through the city's gate that morning thoroughly decked out in amulets, cloaks, chainmail, and leather armor bespelled to keep the Protectorate's gaze well away. And then they'd taken a merry, exhausting jaunt around the countryside to see if anyone was following them, but all had been quiet.

Raegan paused, inhaling to prepare for hauling herself up across an absurdly large boulder in the path. The King was only a little ways ahead of her, but it felt like miles stretched between them. She'd awoken this morning and desperately wanted to talk about Alanna—but gods, how the fuck *could* she? Not even one full day within its walls, and she'd endangered all of Hiraeth. Kamau's family. Emrys. The last Fey city, found by a Protectorate shadewalker because Raegan had spared Reilly.

Besides—Oberon hadn't told her that he was planning on searching the possible Avalon sites without her. Raegan had only found out when she'd rolled over, discovered that the bed was empty and peered through the darkness to find him fully dressed, about to slip out the door. And when she'd pushed him on where exactly the fuck he was going, he'd all but snarled at her that the task would be easier without her in tow. She ground her teeth, searching for a foothold in the rockface. Only a few things made Oberon as upset as he'd been when she hadn't agreed with his plan. One of the top contenders was the prospect of watching her die again.

"Should probably do a better job helping me up this fucking waterfall, then," Raegan muttered, pulling herself up onto the boulder with a groan. After a few seconds of panting, she continued up the path, frustrated at a million things, including the limitations of her body.

She was city-fit, not witch-on-a-quest fit, and her muscles definitely knew the difference. As if on cue, Raegan underestimated the height of the next step and clipped her toes on the edge, losing her balance.

A large hand caught her by the upper arm, steadying her.

"Thanks," Raegan said as she rebalanced herself, peering up through the mist at the King.

"I did not realize you were struggling," he replied, pulling her closer. "I would not have gone ahead." Oberon slipped his arm around her waist, palm open on her hip, and bracketed her body against his taller, harder one.

Despite everything, hunger uncoiled in honeyed spools deep in her stomach. The pull, as always, was so much stronger than the push. "On second thought, it *is* kind of hotter when you're mean to me," she deadpanned.

He glanced down at her, amusement tugging at the corners of his mouth, and helped her up an enormous, rough-hewn stone that served as the next step. "I am happy to make adjustments for your pleasure," Oberon murmured, turning to face her, his fingers digging into the soft flesh of her hips in a way that sent desire snaking up from her core. "Though perhaps not here, climbing the side of the falls."

"Reasonable, I guess," Raegan smiled, sticking close to the King as they made the final ascent. The sky was still opalescent above them, the sun only just now beginning to think about peering over the horizon. The falls were quiet— no tourists or hikers and hopefully no Protectorate. Only the thunder of the water met her ears, the scents of lichen, damp stone, and rushing currents filling her nose. It might've been beautiful and peaceful if they were there for any other reason. If the fate of magic and the Fair Folk did not hang in the balance, all their will and energy bent toward the scant words of an ancient goddess.

Raegan stepped out onto the rocky shelf behind the falls, the King at her side. She'd been to this sacred place before in other lives, but awe still fluttered in her chest. To her left was a jagged wall of earth, all dark rock and mossy plants, above her a wide arc of thundering falls, and to her right, the water pitched toward the ground, spraying mist into the air as it hit the pool below. The ledge was wide enough for two or three people to walk abreast. She and the King did just that, falling silent as they searched. They'd chosen the falls—and the other sites they'd search next—based on residual magic. Though it was a resource quickly fading from this half of the world, Sgwd Yr Eira still hummed with a memory of its old power.

"We don't even know what exactly we're looking for," Raegan sighed impatiently a few minutes later, mostly to herself. Maybe if she found Avalon's door first, it would forgive the transgression of Alanna. Or at least soften the blow. She ran her fingertips along the slippery stone, searching for a seam or an inscription or anything that might tell her there was something more here, a door that had known her once and might open for her again. "The Morrigan's vision left a lot to be desired."

"I do not think we will find what we seek in this place," Oberon replied. His tone was so definitive and flat that Raegan glanced over at him. In the mist-shrouded gloom, he looked every bit the vengeful Unseelie king, dressed in black clothing and dark leather armor, a sword sheathed at his side. He tipped his head back as if to scent the air like a wolf. "There is old magic here, yes. But not, I fear, the kind we seek."

Raegan hated to agree, but she did. The waterfall was, on its surface, thick with wonder, looking every inch the place a door to Avalon might exist. It'd been Emrys's top candidate, in fact. But there was no sensation of unfurling, of something long-forgotten turning over in its grave to rise again. No matter how much she yearned for it.

Raegan placed two open hands against the fall's rocky spine, trying with all her might to remember. Another thing she'd thought would be different once the Seal was gone. Her memories were there, yes, but accessing them was another thing entirely. It got easier every day, bit by bit, but Raegan had never been a particularly patient person. She wanted all of herself, and she wanted it *now*. Was she not entitled to her own past?

The whisper of the falls suddenly gathered itself up into a symphony, and Raegan's heart lurched, hoping the place would sing to her of doors and salvation. But it was just the wind playing the water like a harp, so she closed her eyes again and focused on the times she'd been to Sgwd Yr Eira before. Snippets of full moon rituals a thousand years in the past came and went, lovely and magical, white blooms floating on the surface and candles lining the pool, but nothing she could use on this quest.

Another memory surfaced, and with a sharp, unwelcome pang, Raegan remembered there used to be nymphs here. She pushed the scene away before she was forced to see the stones stained with blood a second time. Was there any place in this landscape, she wondered, that the Protectorate had not irrevocably altered with their hungry violence?

A hand alighted on her shoulder, jarring Raegan for a moment before she recognized the heavy, weighted warmth of the King's touch. Already deep in her own mind, she lost control of the memory stream and found herself standing in a similar place on the waterfall's ledge. It had been summer then, the air thick with humidity, the forest below like a sea of emeralds. Under the spray of the falls, the air was blessedly cool, smelling of August rain and autumn's promised return.

He'd been there, too—much younger, that beautiful fairytale knight she'd once called Mordred. In her mind's eye, she pressed her back to the stone, beckoning him closer, the waterfall feeling so much like a gauzy curtain fluttering around a four-poster bed. He'd looked at her with those ocean eyes, dark with desire, before stalking over with the predatory grace he'd possessed even then.

If these lands were marred by the bloody touch of the Protectorate, she reasoned, what legacy had she and Mordred left behind? Did the all-consuming, revolutionary kind of love that usually only young people were stupid enough to fall into make any difference?

"Sorry," Raegan mumbled, pulling away from the stone. "I was trying to see what I could remember about this place."

"I recall a few things," the King replied in a low, husky voice, his hands sliding around her waist.

Raegan laughed. "I was thinking about that, too." She turned to face him, pressing her back into the stone just like she had all those years ago. Gods, she'd give anything to be young again. A chance to do it all over.

Oberon slid a long, powerful leg between her own, bringing his mouth to hers. A lightning strike of need electrified her entire body. Raegan ran her hands down his muscular chest and then fumbled at his waistband. Common sense fled her; the keen sense of danger she'd felt so viscerally since they'd stepped beyond Hiraeth's wards earlier that morning evaporated. Even the heavy sweep of guilt faded. There was only the tumble of water, the soft whisper of the mist, and the undeniable pull of the magnificent, impossible thing before her.

The years and her lives overlapped like a double exposure. It could've been Mordred or the King whose strong hands roamed beneath her garments, whose kiss grew so intense and desperate that she wanted to drown in it. A name escaped her mouth, voice thick with unmet desire. All she wanted was to feel his capable fingers at the apex of her legs, the hard length of him buried deep inside her, the rock wall biting into her exposed skin.

"Raegan," the King murmured against her lips, catching her wrists in his hands. "As much as it will pain me to wait another moment, my plans for you are best enacted within the safety of good wards. After all, you *do* get quite loud."

Raegan rolled her eyes and laughed, coming back to herself. It felt good to laugh. She straightened, pushing off the wall. "If you think about it," she countered, looking up at him, "it's *your* fault I'm loud."

"It is an honor to accept that blame," Oberon told her, a smile dancing across his full lips. Then he sobered, a familiar weight coming back to his brow.

That shared, shadowed heaviness returned to Raegan's chest too, and she sighed. "There's nothing here. Part of me wants to search harder. Due diligence, I guess. But I think I would feel something. And you definitely would."

She considered the King, otherworldly in the misty gloom, looking every bit the last of the Tuatha de Danann. Not Danu's direct prodigy, no, but crafted by divine hands in a similar ritual, infused with the blood of fallen warriors and the bite of sacred swords. Two Fey had not tumbled together beneath sheets and born him. Usually the doors sang to her, but she supposed this one would call to him—the last of his kind, locked out of the paradise that was his due.

"There are other places," Oberon said, reaching out to take her hand. "Imagine how long Emrys's list must be now that we have given him an entire morning alone in his library."

Raegan nodded, sliding her fingers into his as they walked along the slippery ledge back to the stairs at the side of the waterfall. "I didn't think it would be *that* easy—that the first place we tried would be the one."

"It would be nice, though, would it not?" Oberon asked,

looking over at her. "For something to be easy for once." The words left his mouth laden with wistfulness.

"Yeah," Raegan agreed, pausing at the top of the stairs, trying to prepare her body for the climb back down. "Easy would be nice."

"I may be able," the King told her, stooping low and sliding his arms around her, "to make *one* thing easier, at least." With that, he swept her off the ground and into his embrace.

"Oberon," she sputtered with concern, "I'm fine to walk. Aren't you still in pain?"

"Yes," he replied without hesitation, his tone even. "The pain never leaves me. You, however, do. So allow me to hold you, and trust me to care for my own body."

Raegan tilted her chin up, holding his gaze. She swallowed down a wave of jagged guilt and settled for nodding before pressing the side of her face to his chest, desperate to hear his heartbeat. She took a deep inhale. Maybe she could memorize his scent of black pepper and woodsmoke and damp stone. Maybe even if he cast her out again, she could at least remember what she had lost this time.

She opened her eyes when Oberon reached the bottom and then slid out of his grasp. "Thanks," Raegan said, her heart fluttering.

The King offered her a rare jewel in return—a smile that actually reached his eyes. Her stomach somersaulted. She ached to kiss him again, but then his lips parted, worry creasing his brow.

"My love," Oberon said, reaching for her in a gentle, graceful movement, cupping her face in his large hand. "I worry there are things you are not telling me. You have yet to speak of the Timekeeper's realm, and I feel your secrets have only grown heavier since."

Raegan's instinct was to lean into his touch and tell the

faerie king everything. Who wouldn't do the same, faced with his beautiful ferocity and long-fingered hands? He would follow her to the ends of the Earth—he'd said it himself. But Raegan clamped her jaw before the words could tumble out and spill the truth of her father and the conversation with Alanna. If it all came out like this, Oberon would finally see that she was too hard to love.

"I'm not ready," she replied, the lie sour on her tongue, but her defenses snapped down like a bear trap, and even she didn't know how to pry them apart. "I'll let you know when I am."

Oberon held still, saying nothing for a moment longer. Her heart raced, anxiety flooding her veins. "I fear we are not in a position to wait until we are less tender," he murmured, brushing the pad of his thumb across her lips. "I have known you too long. You are keeping something from me. I am concerned."

It didn't matter that the King spoke his feelings with the utmost care or that he was absolutely, unnervingly correct. Raegan's heartrate spiked all the same, her anger flashing as hot as if he'd come for her jugular. "I'm not a member of your Court," she snapped, stepping back, away from his touch. "You can't just command me to do what you want."

The King's hand floated back down to his side, the elegant swoop of a prized bird. For a split second, he looked at her in a way that made Raegan question Baba Yaga's sureness he would never harm her. "Raegan," Oberon said, his tone edged with warning, "that was *not* a command. Not even close."

She crossed her arms, planting her feet wide. "You don't get to decide when I talk about really fucked-up shit that happened to *me*. It didn't happen to you."

The King closed his eyes and raked a hand through his hair, which always made him look more human to her. "But it did," he said, meeting her gaze again. "It very much happened to me, too. I waited and hoped for an entire week in empty chambers. Regardless, there is something else, I think, that you are harboring. Do recall we are not regular people. I am not asking as your lover."

"Oh, so you think you're asking as my king?" Raegan snarled, her fingers winding into fists, the blood pounding in her throat, the anger so much more palatable than the bone-deep shame.

He reeled back so hard that for a second, she thought she'd slapped him without realizing she'd raised a hand at all. "No," Oberon said, his expression an open wound. "No. I am asking as your accomplice. Your co-revolutionary. Make no mistake—this is a war. You cannot leave me in the dark in war. Not again."

Guilt crowded Raegan's lungs, his words validating all her fears. Her old defense mechanisms flared, anger roaring up in a dark wave. "It's not like that," she protested, furious that hot tears were pricking the back of her eyes.

Oberon let out a long breath, holding her gaze all the while. "I cannot know how it is if you do not *tell* me."

Raegan paused, feeling miserable and alone. Some horrible part of her *wanted* him to throw his power around like he used to in their youth, when his first language was manipulation and threats and violence, all thinly veiled by effortless seduction. She knew how to handle that—how to not be afraid of him, how to bare her teeth in return. She knew how to fuck him into submission, and she knew damn well how skilled he was at doing the same in return.

She did *not* know how to handle what he was doing now—so open, so gentle. It made her nervous, like a panther delicately eating berries from her hand when she knew it craved blood and flesh instead.

"Is that why you brought up some nice old memories

and carried me down?" Raegan snapped, making an accusatory gesture toward the stone steps behind her. "Did you think I'd swoon and give you whatever you wanted?"

Now he just stared at her, his eyebrows drawn together, bewilderment moving into his expression. For a long, stretched moment, he said nothing at all. Raegan squirmed but held fast.

"We should depart," Oberon eventually replied, moving toward the waterfall's rock-ringed pool to summon the kelpies. "May we discuss this further later?"

She opened her mouth to tell him no and to fuck off while he was at it, but something stole his attention, expression gone cold. Instinctively, Raegan turned on her heel, following his sightline. On the other side of the pool, about a hundred paces into the forest, movement caught her eye. The world dropped out from under her. Shapes of drab gray snuck through the undergrowth. The smell of metal and gunpowder that suddenly filled her nose could only mean one thing.

Despite all their precautions, the Protectorate had found them.

Chapter Seventeen

R aegan froze. Her eyes shot to the King. His head was cocked like a predator's, gaze taking in the enemy on the opposite shore. He *wanted* to fight —she could see it in the flex of his long fingers, his muscles spring-loaded. He wanted to tear limb from limb, to find another throat to sink his teeth into. Raegan swallowed back nausea. How many children would he rip through without a second thought? The Protectorate leadership was as cruel and cunning as the Fey they hated; it wouldn't surprise her if this entire squad was filled with round-faced young adults, their curly hair just like Cormac's.

"No," she said, barking out the word, darting forward to grab the King by his wrist. "No. Let's just leave. Save it for a fight that matters."

He watched her, and for a second, Raegan thought she saw suspicion in his expression, which chilled her to the bone. Oberon's hundreds-of-years-long reign had produced very few traitors, but she remembered what he'd done to the fools who'd dared to cross him. She had no desire to be on the receiving end.

"The kelpies will not reach us in time," the King told her, tone flat, "and there are no porticos left in this land."

"Just get us to the woods behind them," Raegan suggested, her eyes darting to the approaching Protectorate, who admittedly *did* seem very excited to use their guns. "We can lose them and follow the river upstream to call the kelpies. Doing magic now won't matter. They've already found us."

The King did not agree or acquiesce; instead, he reached out and clamped a hand around Raegan's arm. The world spun, the beautiful setting of the falls and the woods turning into a sickening blur that rattled her eyeballs in her skull. When the movement finally stopped, she leaned over and retched onto the damp brown leaves beneath her feet. The King gave her all of two seconds before he tightened his grip on her arm and began to haul her deeper into the woods, away from the river.

"How did they find us?" Oberon muttered under his breath, moving at a pace meant for his legs, not hers. "We used the Rivers and employed no active magic."

Raegan said nothing, her mouth dry, her mind racing. Emrys had triple-checked them for any kind of tracking spells when they'd arrived. They'd been within Hiraeth's wards the entire time, until she and Oberon had left that morning. So how could—

Alanna. Raegan gritted her teeth, trying to keep her footsteps on the forest floor as quiet as possible. She knew a decent amount about shadewalkers, but they were rare and often reclusive or, at the very least, not forthcoming about their abilities. There could certainly be things she didn't know. And that symbol Alanna had conjured on the wards —it hadn't felt like anything much to Raegan at the time. More like a breadcrumb to get back home, a chalked arrow on a tree trunk. But now the events of the night prior returned to her mind as quickly as she tripped through the woods, and her stomach stewed.

"This is why I wanted you to stay with Emrys," the King said in a low whisper, pulling her into his arms as he moved behind a large, rain-slick rock. He pressed his back against it, holding Raegan to his chest, and then lifted his chin, gaze undoubtedly roving the forest.

"You don't know me at all if you think I'm going to sit around while you hunt for Avalon," Raegan replied, whispering despite the anger she felt—and trying to ignore the curl of arousal she felt with her body pressed against his hard, lean form.

"I do not think you will *enjoy* it," the King spat back at her, looking around the side of the rock. The woods had fallen silent, as if all the smaller creatures recognized what hunted within their domain. "I only think it is right."

"Were you even there yesterday morning?" Raegan hissed, trying to keep her balance as he shot around the side of the rock with her body still held against his, a deft movement of shadow and strength. "I made a goddamn river monster eat a bunch of people. I can handle myself."

He said nothing and began to stalk away from the rock, gripping her by the forearm as if she were an obstinate child. Her shoulder pulled painfully, and she broke into a jog to keep up with him. They continued in silence, moving away from the Protectorate and toward the river that fed the waterfalls. It was barely more than a small stream here, but Raegan knew not much water was required to call forth a kelpie—not even for the old-fashioned mortal way, like she had done when all this began. The King's request for a kelpie was so honed and subtle that even the Protectorate were unlikely to notice it.

"I don't think they're following us," Raegan whispered,

just wanting to break the silence, constantly torn between her anger and her yearning.

"No, I think not," Oberon agreed, but he still moved quick and low, a panther hunting. "Your idea was quite sound—the magic I worked would only confuse them, appearing so close to their formation when we were nowhere to be found."

He was trying to mollify her, Raegan knew. She stepped around a large fern, the fronds brushing her leg, leaving her pants striped with dew. He would've thought of the same option in a heartbeat; in fact, he probably had before she'd even said it. But Oberon hadn't wanted to run. He wanted to fight, to maim, to kill.

"Just trying to stop you from murdering people," Raegan muttered, the words harsher than she had really meant.

The King did not even slow down. "Interesting, as you seem to have few qualms about your own actions yesterday."

"I didn't like it," Raegan snapped, yanking her arm from his grasp. "You *like* it."

The King looked at her sideways, his eyes shadowed in the gloom of the November wood. His full lips moved into something cruel. "Yes, you do. Pretending otherwise is a fool's game, and you are no fool."

She opened her mouth to respond, but she was so angry that she didn't think she could say anything without screaming. They seemed to have slipped past the Protectorate, but she wasn't particularly interested in testing that assumption out. So she said nothing, fixing her gaze on the ground ahead of her, anger and frustration boiling in her stomach.

Neither one of them said anything as they moved through the forest, Oberon occasionally pulling her behind a large tree or hulking boulder to double back or check that they had no followers. The silence was not helping. Raegan wanted to have it out—to yell and curse, to make any kind of noise that drowned out her guilt and shame. The King, on the other hand, seemed to relax into the quiet.

Beneath the boughs of a hemlock grove, he finally paused, crouching near the water's edge. Raegan slid as deep as she could into the darkness of the hemlocks, waiting for the kelpies to arrive. When Oberon rose from the stream, he turned back, eyes meeting hers. For some reason, the compassion she saw lingering in those gray depths made her furious, and she didn't know why. Self-loathing sank its fangs into her.

"Nyneve," the King murmured as he approached, saying her first name like she was a goddess and he was only a humble supplicant. She straightened, eagerly awaiting the apology—because when he apologized, she got to pretend she'd done nothing wrong. "You cannot make me love you and then stop me from protecting you."

Raegan's mouth hung open, processing the words he'd said too slowly. "Don't pretend you could love a caged thing," she spat, recovering herself. He turned away from her, his shoulders sagging.

Behind the King, a kelpie's muzzle broke the surface of the stream. Raegan pushed past him, wanting to be back at Hiraeth so she could safely get away from him. As she stepped out from the hemlock grove, she spotted movement on the other side of the stream. But she was already out in the open, and it happened so fast. They'd successfully escaped a close call, she thought, about to return to the old Temple. She'd been about to swing a leg over a kelpie and disappear into the Rivers, hadn't she?

But then there was a man in a pinstripe suit, leather oxfords shining in the light of the now-risen sun, and in his hands there was a gun. He fired, quick as could be, and

Raegan called to the water beneath her—and it began to answer, jaws flexing wider. It didn't matter, though, because the King burst from the hemlock grove like an apex predator, sending the bullet curving back toward the man who had fired it with a simple wave of his hand.

He turned to Raegan, his face a mask of anger and bone-deep fear, and she knew it was only because he loved her so much that he didn't see the other Protectorate man emerging from the shadow of the opposite bank with a shotgun—or something like it, even crueler in design—in his hands. And when he fired, the King wrapped his body around Raegan's and plunged into the stream below. It should've only been a foot or so deep, but the Rivers opened for them.

The shock of the cold water knocked all of the air out of Raegan's lungs, and it took her a few terrifying seconds to remember she'd always been able to breathe in the Rivers. A kelpie—not Rainer—burst out of the dancing river grass to her left, swinging its scaled tail to bank hard. Raegan scrambled onto its back, turning to look for the King. He climbed onto the kelpie behind her, looking no worse for wear until she dragged her eyes down his body, her heart pounding in her throat all the while. Her stomach dropped at the sight of his chest. She urged the kelpie faster.

He'd watched her die, over and over again. That was how it worked, how it had *always* worked, and maybe that was because Fate knew as well as Raegan did that she wasn't strong enough to be the one left behind.

CHAPTER EIGHTEEN

The kelpie didn't hesitate. It broke through the surface of the River Wye and pounded onto the shore, its long, dark legs propelling it up the banks and onto a windswept, forlorn hill. Raegan gripped its slick seaweed mane tighter as she saw a circle of hawthorn trees come into view. And then, a door cut out of the gray morning, the smell of autumn rain and damp cobblestones suddenly thick in her nose.

The kelpie shot through the door, clattering into a small courtyard Raegan hadn't seen before. It was Hiraeth, though—the old Temple's striking stone facade rose into the deep gray-blue sky, the courtyard abutting what she thought might be the kitchen. Having barely broken its pace through the city's wards, the kelpie came to a skidding, clattering stop right by a slim, arched door. It flew open, and Emrys stepped from the gloom, expression tight and drawn. Raegan watched the ex-Keeper register the sight of the King's chest. His ever-present composure promptly shattered. Something about it made her leap into action.

"Shotgun blast," Raegan shouted despite Emrys only

being a few feet away, sliding down from the kelpie. "Definitely iron. Left chest and shoulder." She thanked the fickle vaults of her memory for allowing her to reflexively identify the King's wounds.

The kelpie sank to its knees, allowing Oberon to dismount more easily. He did so unaided, though his jaw was clenched hard and he wasn't moving his left arm.

"How bad?" Emrys asked as he yanked the door all the way open before beginning to roll up his sleeves.

"Not sure yet," Raegan replied, wrapping an arm around Oberon's waist to support his injured side. She thanked the kelpie and shooed it back to the river; the younger ones didn't fancy being on dry land for very long.

"I am fine," Oberon said, though he leaned into her. Not very much, of course—he had more than a foot and at least a hundred pounds of pure, heavy muscle on her. But the fact he leaned into her at all indicated he was probably not fine.

"I have modern medical training and equipment," Emrys told Raegan, coming to the King's free side.

"I can walk quite well," Oberon said, testy now. "They shot my shoulder, not my legs."

"Shut up and let us take care of you," Raegan snapped, trying to match her strides to his.

"She's right," Emrys said from the King's other side as they passed through the door. Emrys kicked it closed behind him. "Not comfortable, I know, but the kitchen table is probably the best place for now."

Raegan nodded and turned on her heel to help the King maneuver toward the large, roughly hewn table. He managed to pull himself up onto it without her or Emrys's help, bringing his right hand to the front of his leather armor. His fingers shook.

"I got it," Raegan said, moving forward to begin unbuckling the breastplate. "Emrys, can you get hot water, rags, and your equipment?"

"Already on it," Emrys called, his voice coming from deep inside the old Temple.

"I will be fine," Oberon told her, catching her gaze, dark hair falling across his forehead, which was covered in a thin sheen of sweat.

"It's my fucking fault," Raegan muttered, trying to get the buckles undone as quickly as possible without yanking on his injuries. She cursed her lack of muscle memory; in other lives, she'd been able to help him remove his armor in a few seconds flat.

"I did not see them," Oberon sighed, trying to sit up straighter, supporting his weight on the flattened palm of his right hand. "So my fault, then. Though I find little use in this exercise. Such things are to be expected. It is war, after all."

"How did they find us, Oberon?" Raegan asked, stooping over to unbuckle the larger straps at the bottom of his breastplate, hoping beyond hope that there was another explanation than Alanna.

"I intend to find out," he told her, closing his eyes. For a long moment, his breathing was so shallow that Raegan's heart nearly exploded, but he opened his eyes as Emrys burst back into the room. The ex-Keeper's arms were filled with a massive first aid kit, a large bowl of hot water, and a stack of clean towels.

Raegan finally finished undoing the armor's closures and slowly pulled the shredded leather off Oberon's body. It had certainly taken some of the brunt of the blast, but his left chest and shoulder were still a mess of gore, muscle fibers visible beneath torn skin, blood glistening in the low light. She was going to wrap him in fucking Kevlar from here on out. Leaning closer, Raegan caught a sickening glimpse of bone, white-gray and shining. She expected a surge of nausea, but it did not come; she'd been a healer in too many lives, she supposed.

Emrys produced scissors and cut Oberon's shirt down the middle, working with Raegan to peel it away from his skin. "Heart and major arteries look okay," he said, examining the King closely. "This is still bad, though."

Moving automatically, Raegan dipped one of the towels into the steaming bowl of water and began to clear away the blood around the King's grisly wounds. Her hands shook. She'd done this. She'd allowed the Protectorate to track them, and she'd distracted him with her stupid anger and her self-loathing. Bile churned in her stomach, and she nearly choked.

But even now, she couldn't make the confession about Alanna come to her lips. A golden opportunity to infiltrate the Protectorate would be ruined, she told herself, even though she knew that deep down, the real reason she couldn't was her own weakness. Because every moment, she wanted to sink to her knees and scream in grief about her father. If she had to contend with the tender sorrow she still bore about the choices she'd made in that life as Titania? If Oberon and Emrys looked at her like she was the cause of all the pain in their world? No. She just *couldn't*, particularly not until she knew for sure that Oberon would be okay.

Suddenly the King reached for her, enclosing her fingers in his right hand. She looked up at him, wordless and spiraling.

"I will be fine," he repeated, looking hard into her eyes, "and I will not allow you to blame yourself."

"What happened?" Emrys asked, pulling a pair of unpleasant-looking tweezers from his medical kit. He began to pluck scattered pieces of iron and leather fibers from the back of Oberon's shoulder. Raegan watched as the King didn't even flinch.

"Th-they came out of nowhere," she stammered. "We thought we had lost them and stopped to call for the kelpies. There were two of them, maybe more. Obviously one had a fucking shotgun."

Emrys grimaced. "I want to look you both over again for tracking spells. There's no reason they should've been able to find you so easily, especially in a remote place."

"Perhaps," Oberon said, his voice breathier than usual, his words slowed, "they know we are looking for Avalon."

Raegan paused, holding a bloodied towel in mid-air, the implications boiling in her gut. Her skin was clammy and hot, but the inside of her chest felt cold, like icicles had slid into her capillaries. Emrys, too, paused, looking at the King with alarm.

"Emrys," the King said, his voice low and dangerous, a predator slinking through the night. "You are one of the only people who know we seek Avalon. Have you betrayed me?"

The destroyed Temple's Keeper straightened like an arrow. "No, Oberon. My liege. You know I want the same things as you."

"I know," Oberon said, twisting to look at Emrys, though it clearly pained him. Somehow, despite being naked to the waist and covered in blood, the King very much still looked like the most dangerous creature in the room. Raegan didn't move, her throat burning, her heart pumping far too quickly.

"If either a threat or an offer was made to you by our enemies, you would tell me, yes?" the King wanted to know. "I will protect what is yours as fiercely as I protect what is mine." His gaze slid to Raegan, something feral and hungry simmering in those gray depths. "The bullet was meant for *her*, Emrys."

The Keeper froze, tweezers still in his hand, and swallowed hard, his Adam's apple bobbing in his throat. With shaking fingers, he set the tweezers down and moved to stand in front of the King. "Oberon," Emrys implored. "Beyond my loyalty to the Unseelie Court and the old ways and my personal desire for revenge, I also am not particularly interested in you torturing me for three hundred years."

Glancing at him with a heavy-lidded expression, the King's mouth curved into something cruel and dangerous but amused all the same. "Understand I do not doubt you," Oberon murmured, his eyes locked with Emrys's. "But something is awry."

Without another word, the King's eternal, oceanic gaze swung to Raegan. "In a thousand years, you have never betrayed me, not truly," he said, his breathing heavy, his words sending a spike of fear and hurt and anxiety right into her chest. "Like Emrys, I do not doubt you. Yet I must ask: has your current vessel's Protectorate blood led you astray?"

In that moment, Raegan would've sworn he was a stranger, that they'd never met before, that he'd never torn out someone's throat for her, let alone loved and fucked and fought side-by-side for a millennium. He looked at her with that cold, dead expression he usually reserved for his enemies.

"No," she said hoarsely, for some reason clutching the bloodstained rag to her chest. "Mordred, *no*. Of course not."

With that, the King seemed to shrink, his shoulders collapsing again, that cruel darkness leaving the sharp angles of his face. "Good," he murmured, his spine curving. "I am sorry I had to ask you both."

Emrys shrugged, clearly less affected by this questioning than Raegan, and returned to plucking bits of iron from the King's shoulder. "You had no choice. Let us patch you up, and then we can try to figure out how this happened."

Her hands shaking, Raegan returned to wiping blood from Oberon's skin. He was alive—talking, breathing. He was going to be fine. And yet, with the weight of her mistakes pressing down on her shoulders, Raegan felt like she was going to lose him all the same.

~

By that evening, Emrys was no closer to figuring out how the Protectorate had found them, and the secret of Alanna rattled around in Raegan's chest. She stared at the plumes of steam curling up from the two cups of black tea she'd prepared. Her heaved sigh sent ripples dancing across the dark waters. She'd planned to tell Oberon first, because she desperately needed his help to explain it all to Emrys. If he didn't hate her afterwards, of course, which felt like a very real possibility.

Steeling herself, Raegan picked up the tea tray and turned toward the stairs. She knew she had to tell him, and she hated herself for not saying anything to Emrys. They'd spent hours checking the spellwork on Hiraeth's wards together after Oberon's wounds were tended to and they'd gotten him settled upstairs to rest. If the Keeper had clocked how hard her heart had been beating when they'd neared the square leading to the botanical gardens, he'd said nothing. Though perhaps he just planned on going directly to Oberon with the news that the King's lover had, yet again, become his doom.

Beginning to climb the wide, grand stairs, Raegan did her best to banish the thoughts from her mind. Over-thinking wasn't going to help. She'd spent too long sitting by the fire, wondering if she was just afraid of punishment or if she hated herself or if she feared nothing quite as much as letting him down. Maybe all three. She didn't know. There was so fucking much she didn't know.

Raegan paused at the partially closed door, taking another long, deep breath. Maybe he'd be asleep. Maybe she could put this off a little longer, refine her words, smooth it over in her own mind.

"Raegan?" the King's voice slipped around the door, as low and dark and melodic as it always was, and despite everything, the sound of it still felt like home. So Raegan walked into the room, her steps slow, her heart thumping louder and louder.

"Hey," she said, her voice shaky, "I brought you some tea. And I wanted to check on you." She set the tea tray down on the windowsill and then turned to face him. Oberon was sitting up in bed, his hands folded over a book that sat in his lap. That Feyrish web-like bandage she'd found on her own body at the Oracle's Temple in Philadelphia wound around his chest and shoulder. Blood seeped through in more places than she would've liked despite the yarrow she'd packed into the dressing. But his color was better and no sheen of sweat glimmered on his brow.

"You and Emrys are quite a formidable pair when it comes to healing," Oberon said, his gaze meeting hers.

She flushed with pride, which the guilt and shame immediately consumed. "I'm glad I had enough in me to at least close up the smaller wounds," she said, stirring sugar into a teacup. Her hands shook, and the spoon clanked loud and sharp against the china. "Emrys got me a Fey anatomy book from his library. I've been studying it to try to close up

164

your larger injuries, but I'm worried about getting all the tendons right."

Healing a superficial tear was one thing, something Raegan could do even this soon after her Seal's removal. But muscle fibers and tendons were another thing entirely, too easy to make worse, particularly on Fey creatures, whom she was now remembering were actually built quite a bit differently on the inside than humans.

"They will heal in due time on their own, but it is appreciated," the King replied, watching her every move and making no attempt at hiding it. "My body, despite its pain, still mends quickly."

Raegan nodded, her lips pressed together as she brought him a cup of tea—strongly steeped Assam with just a touch of sugar. She offered it to him, handle-first, the heat searing through to her palms. He took the teacup, fingers brushing hers. As always, her body keened unnaturally for him.

"I need to tell you something," Raegan blurted out, dragging both hands through her hair. Nausea tumbled slick and bloated through her stomach. "But you have to understand. It's not like before. I wasn't planning to do anything on my own, I was just collecting information until I had enough to tell you."

She bit her tongue, cutting herself off from saying more. The King just watched her, his gaze a fathomless pit. No words stirred on his beautiful mouth, the same one that had touched every inch of her a thousand times before. She swallowed hard, beginning to pace at his bedside. The pale green rug of Art Nouveau-stylized leaves that ran alongside the bed was the perfect length of her footsteps, to-and-fro.

Raegan shook her hands at the wrists, trying to rid herself of the nervous energy. She paused at the end of the rug, her back to Oberon, taking in the brilliant late afternoon sunshine that snuck through Hiraeth's clouds for a moment, gilding all the carved woods and jewel tones of the room with honey.

And then Raegan turned, her heart pounding painfully against her breastbone, her ribs like a cage containing a wild, traitorous beast. She met his gaze again and opened her mouth. "I think I may have allowed the Protectorate to track us. I think this is all my fault."

CHAPTER NINETEEN

The King said nothing, though she saw his long fingers tighten around the teacup. A bird swept by the window, casting a shadow across his face for a moment. Raegan swallowed again, her throat aching, waiting for him to say something.

But he wouldn't, she knew. She hadn't given him enough information to respond to; instead, he would pin her under his terrifying gaze and wait until the words came tumbling out. Only once he felt he understood would he speak.

"Last night, when I went out, a shadewalker came through the hawthorns," Raegan said, wringing her hands in front of her before she forced herself to stop, stuffing her fingers into her pockets instead. "She's Protectorate."

And then Raegan told him the rest—how Alanna had said she might come back the following night, how she was not interested in what the Protectorate wanted but she was afraid of the Fair Folk, too. How Raegan didn't think they could trust her, but they could certainly use her. How she felt so much guilt, so much shame, so much grief, and it was going to break her. Had maybe *already* broken her.

Her heart thrust itself harder and harder against her bones with every word, and she could hear her own voice becoming higher, the sentences quickening. Her chest hurt. She shoved hot tears away, pushing her rage down. She had to stop using anger as a defense. She could not scream at the High King of the Unseelie Court until he went away. He was not afraid of her, and she could not cut him deeply enough for it to matter.

"Raegan," Oberon said after what felt like an eternity, setting his teacup down on the nightstand. "I have never heard of a shadewalker able to work tracking spells away from their body. Regardless, if someone intends harm, the hawthorns have their own defenses. Lastly . . . I need to corroborate this with Emrys, but I believe the place you are describing is the Garden of Doors."

He said those last few words with such meaning, such weight, but Raegan couldn't recall the place name. Besides, she was mostly focused on the utter relief she felt flushing her body, cool spring water after a long drought. With shaking hands, she pushed a few stray curls away from her face.

"And the Garden . . ." she said, looking at him quizzically.

"Hiraeth is sentient," the King replied. "The Garden of Doors is one of the city's oldest locations, the grit around which Hiraeth was formed. It is an ancient place, and it only appears when it wishes to. There is no precise location it can be found. Its gates open to few. I would hazard that the city *wanted* you to speak with this Protectorate woman."

Raegan's head swam, the meaning of those words undoing her entirely. She closed her eyes, silent tears streaming down her face. What felt like her first deep breath in days filled her lungs.

"But," Oberon continued, a sharp edge coming into his

tone that sent her heart hammering away again, "I want to know why you did not tell me what occurred. I want to know why you did not allow me to carry the grief and the guilt with you."

"Because . . . you hate the Protectorate," she said, taking a few steps toward him before she thought better of it, lulled by his words. "And I get it. I do, too. But in this life, I'm tied to them. And I know from my own family how much a lot of them want no part of it. I've told you everything my dad did to get me away. Why couldn't Alanna be the same?"

The King looked at her, his expression a dagger of frustrated bewilderment. "She very well *could* be, but that does not explain why you withheld this from me. If you did not know the Garden's true nature, then you were risking all of Hiraeth's people. *Why*, Raegan?"

Shame wrapped around her body, squeezing the fresh air from her lungs. He saw her too clearly, and now there was nothing left but the bare, aching truth. "I . . . I've fucked everything up so much. More than once. Alanna finding Hiraeth was my fault—because I asked you to spare Reilly," she managed, panic and pain clutching at her chest with clawed hands. "I didn't want you to know until I had a handle on the situation, until I was in control. Because I won't be able to bear it if you go back to hating me. Because maybe you *should*."

Silence settled over the room, downy as fresh snow. Raegan squeezed her eyes shut, unable to look at him, to study the expression on his angular face like a palm reader divining the future's bitter truths.

"I have never," the King said, a petal-soft murmur, "hated you. *Could* never. I admit I have tried."

She opened her eyes, reaching forward to grip the bed's footboard, her knuckles white and strained. "Then why did you forsake me for centuries?" Raegan demanded, the hurt of it hollowing out her bones. Shame crept in to fill the empty spaces. "Why is the first time we've been together again since the Gates closed?"

The King examined her, one powerful hand dug deep into the quilt, his injured arm pressed flat against his torso like a broken wing. "It was not," he said hoarsely, "because I hated you."

Anger took her in one great swell and she slammed an open palm down on the bed frame. "If you love me so much," she hissed, "how could you abandon me for hundreds of years? Maybe I'm not that important to you. And that's why I was so terrified to tell you about Alanna. Because it's just another one of my long fucking litany of mistakes, and you don't handle those very well, do you?"

A muscle in his jaw feathered and he shifted his weight. She paced the side of the bed again, secretly—and shame-fully—glad that he was injured. No, not exactly—of course she wished it had never happened. But if it had to happen, she was grateful it was now. Raegan did not know if she could've had this conversation facing down a fully dressed, well-rested Oberon, not when the angles of his face got so raw and feral that he seemed more animal than human.

"I thought," he said, meeting her gaze again with all the gravitational pull of some grand, alien moon, "I was keeping you safe. I thought that was the sacrifice I had to make. Without me, you might live. Without you, my court might endure."

Raegan threw her head back and let out a choked, sardonic laugh, though tears burned her eyes. "What a martyr you are," she spat. "I've never left your side. Being with you has condemned me to early deaths, to pain, to suffering. Have I ever abandoned you?"

"No," the King admitted, holding her gaze, his face gone expressionless.

"Then how do I know, particularly after last night, that you won't be so quick to leave mortals behind, too?" she demanded, prowling closer, a perverse joy racing through her that she'd turned the tables. The guilt quieted to a low hum, though the shame still burrowed deeper beneath her skin. "If they make a few mistakes, or if it just gets too inconvenient. Like I did."

"Is that truly what you think, Raegan?" Oberon demanded, his voice shaking with anger and hurt. She looked away, unable to reconcile that her words had brought such an expression to his face—unfettered sorrow, deep as a wound.

"All I know is how far you're willing to go, how you'll never stop, and right now it feels like the existence of humans is on the line," Raegan replied, tears choking her words, the tides of her rage and guilt and shame and sorrow all mixing together to form the brackish water filling her lungs. "And maybe that's a price you're willing to pay."

He looked away from her, his jaw flexing, the lamplight pulling out the threads of silver in his hair. "Rarely are situations so black and white."

"But what if it is?" Raegan demanded, coming to the end of the bed again, gripping the footboard. "You would accept that price, wouldn't you?"

"Complete annihilation of mortals in exchange for the return of magic, continued prosperity and health of my people, and reclamation of my throne?" the King asked, giving her his full attention—normally such an electrifying, sensual thing, but it fell over her instead like the cold slink of heavy fog, treacherous with monsters she could not see. "I tend to make my decisions with more information and nuance. But let us say the situation is so lacking in real-life detail. Yes, Raegan. In that scenario, I might have to accept."

She stared at him, looking for any echo of that complex,

yes, but also playful, languid, and fiercely good-hearted knight she'd known so many lifetimes ago. He hadn't smiled enough to reveal the dimples she knew were there in hundreds of years. Mordred's eyes had looked almost blue sometimes, but the King's were undeniably a deep, endless gray.

"Are you happy?" he demanded, his upper lip curling, wolf-like. "Are you pleased to have found a way to make me into the monster you for some reason wish to see?"

White-hot anger flared, igniting Raegan's entire body. "You just said you would annihilate mortals in exchange for what you want!"

To her horror, the King laughed. The sound of it was all windswept moor and lonely wood, the shadowed and terrible places where a powerful goddess had once birthed Her children into this world. "Nyneve," he said with a sigh, leaning back against the pillows she'd propped up for him earlier. "You cannot force me into a corner and then be upset to find me there."

Raegan dragged her hands down her face, unsure—not for the first time—if her anger contorted the world around her or if the faerie king had simply just bent her to his will again. Why had Fate crumpled her into this, all distrust and rage and a throat aching with screams she had to exert every ounce of her effort to hold back?

"Nyneve," Oberon repeated, softer. "Come here."

Raegan hesitated, but her body bucked against her like it was its own being, her bones begging to be near him. So she compromised, taking slow, measured steps toward the King's bedside. Her breath hitched the entire time. When she stood beside him, Oberon reached out for her hand, and she gave in. He brought her fingers to his mouth, those perfectly sculpted lips brushing her skin in a way that made her quiver.

"We are not really talking about what will happen to mortals, are we?" he asked, his voice a low murmur that made her bones hum. His gaze searched hers as he looked up at her, the angle sending lamplight cascading into his eyes, pulling out shades of deep ocean blue. "We are talking about *us*. About how I left you."

A sob tore itself free of Raegan's darkest hiding places. "Because maybe I'm just too hard to love," she managed to get out, her chest hitching, tears pouring down her face. "I fuck up too much and all I do is hurt you."

Oberon cupped her jaw in his hand, raw grief in his expression. "Loving you, *cariad*, is the easiest thing I have ever done," he murmured, fingertips soft as ghosts as he tucked an errant curl behind her ear. "Do not ever say you are too hard to love. There have been some, I am sure, too weak to hold the wild, unrestrained wonder of your love in their hands. I am not one of them."

"Then why," she gasped, her knees buckling, "did you leave?"

"Because I was afraid," the Unseelie king told her, his eyes near-black in the lamplight. "Because I was afraid I could not save you. Because I thought losing you was a fit punishment for my own failures. Because I thought you deserved to be free of me."

Raegan let her body go, sliding down into a crumple onto the side of the bed. His touch never left her skin and she was grateful for the heat of him, a north star in the darkness of her own heart. "I'm sorry," she said, her voice scraping at the sides of her throat. "I'm so sorry. I just—I couldn't lose you like that. Not again. Not after my dad."

"I am so sorry, Raegan," the King whispered, pausing to swallow hard, his eyes bright with tears. "I am sorry I abandoned you. I am sorry I made that choice for both of us. And most of all, I am sorry I created this situation—that you felt so sure telling me what occurred would leave you with nothing."

She nodded, leaning into his touch. She felt wrung-out, like she'd swallowed broken glass, but there was a weight off her shoulders. A relief so intense she thought she might be able to sleep for a hundred years.

"I love you," the King said, sliding his hand down into her lap and weaving his fingers into hers.

"I love you, too," she responded immediately, the words tasting as rich as late summer and black currant juice. With her free hand, Raegan pushed away the last of her tears.

"Would you like to speak of the future for mortals?" Oberon inquired. She looked up, taking in the soft coziness of the room, the curls of steam still curling off the teacup on the bedside table. For a long moment, Raegan wanted nothing more than to burrow deep between the heavy, embroidered quilt and never resurface. She chewed on her lower lip, deep in thought.

"Actually," she finally said, raising her eyes to his, "yeah. That would help. I need ... I need to realize we can just discuss things. Like regular people."

Oberon released a hearty laugh that warmed Raegan to her very core. "Yes," he said, the corners of his eyes creasing with a smile, "I believe we can. Please understand, Raegan. I know that mortals are under the Timekeeper's thumb as much as the Fair Folk. I yearn for liberation, and all liberation is connected at the root. We must do this together—you and I, mortals and Fey—or not at all."

Of course he understood. Of course the dark, powerful king she'd fought beside for a thousand years had always been worthy of her loyalty. She nodded and gripped his hand tighter. "I'm sorry, Oberon."

"I know," he replied, letting go of her hand to cradle the side of her face. "I am, too."

"Would it hurt if I kissed you?" she asked, leaning over, the need for physical assurance all-encompassing.

"Not if you are very careful," he said, his lips moving into something delightfully wicked before she brought her mouth to his. Her body came alive, the taste of him heavy on her tongue—folklore and smoke and revenge. She had to physically restrain herself from spreading her legs over his hips, hunger drumming beneath her breastbone. Despite his injury, Oberon met her eagerly, sliding his hand around the back of her head.

"Perhaps," Raegan murmured against his mouth, "I could make further apologies for how fucking stupid I am sometimes."

She felt his fingers tighten around her curls, mouth trailing to her jaw. "How do you propose to make these amends?" the King wanted to know, his breath quickening. "You may have noticed a shotgun ripped through me earlier today. I would like to make amends of my own, but the hole in my chest may prevent me."

Raegan sat back, laughing, tracing the waves of his dark hair, then his sharp cheekbones, with her fingertips. "I was thinking," she said, trailing her hand down the right side of his body until she found where he was hard and hot and wanting, "you wouldn't have to do very much. You can make your apologies later, when you have use of both of your talented hands. What do you think?"

His gaze slid to hers, his face a mask of desire. "I suppose I could permit it," Oberon said, his lips curving with that dark, slinking humor she loved so much.

"Thank you for your generosity, my king," Raegan replied, moving the quilt aside gently, her eyes on his bandaged chest and shoulder. She motioned for him to swing his legs over the side of the bed, and he did, albeit with a grunt of pain. "I've been a healer in enough lives to know this is probably a bad idea."

"That," the King replied, watching her with hungry eyes as she shimmied his waistband down, "is precisely the appeal."

She grinned, pushing her hair back and sliding down to her knees between his muscular thighs. Then she brought her tongue to his exposed length. When he let out a low sigh of pleasure, Raegan wrapped her hand around his thick base and took him into her mouth. The sound of her name toppling from his lips sent heat sliding through her core. She glanced up, arousal further igniting at the sight of him—his head tipped back, the elegant expanse of his neck and angular collarbones etched out by the fading light.

Raegan couldn't recall the last time she'd done this in her current life, and she certainly never remembered enjoying it in this body. But with *him*—everything was so different, the way she hungered for him, the way he seemed to seek little but her pleasure whenever they fucked. Oberon reached for her with his right hand, saying her name like a prayer, fingers slipping around the back of her neck. He met her gaze and held it, setting a wildfire blazing between her legs.

She took him deeper, and he moaned, tipping his head back again. "Good girl," he told her in a low, raw murmur, his fingertips digging into the base of her skull. Desire exploded inside her, and for a moment, Raegan was little more than burning need.

She pulled back a heartbeat later, pressing hot-mouthed kisses along his thighs and hard length, her jaw needing a break. "Don't say that," she panted against his skin, "or I'm going to have no choice but to fuck you, and then your wounds will open back up."

Oberon laughed, the sound of it rough and undone, his

fingers massaging the back of her head. His eyes slid to hers, and he was about to say something, but then she took him back into her mouth, and all that fell from his lips was a long, breathy groan.

Some time later, after he came apart for her, he needed help returning to his propped-up position in the bed. Naturally, Raegan pounced. "The faerie king got fucked senseless by a human woman," she said with a playful smirk, adjusting one of the pillows behind his torso.

"Not the first time," Oberon answered, his eyes closed, his words drowsy. "And I pray it is not the last."

CHAPTER TWENTY

A very long soak in the clawfoot tub did Raegan more good than she thought possible. The afternoon had grown unseasonably warm, the rain slowing to a mist, so she'd opened the windows opposite the tub and watched the late autumn breeze stir the tendrils of steam rising from the water. She'd grown blissfully sleepy, the intricate greens and golds and tawny shadows of the meadow scene depicted on the room's wallpaper offering a lush, peaceful backdrop. There'd even been a selection of bath salts—the Fey did not fuck around when it came to toiletries—and Raegan had dropped in a few good handfuls of the arnica-infused soak. After the hard climb at the waterfall this morning, her muscles needed it.

When she emerged from the bathroom, the bedchamber was silent. The King was asleep, she hoped—his eyes were closed, the book he'd been reading set on the nightstand. The space smelled faintly of yarrow and blood, but no sickness or rot. Good, all things considered.

Quietly, she dressed in comfortable clothes, grateful that she'd packed so thoroughly back at her apartment. Raegan gently pulled her damp hair through the the neckline of her sweater, scrunching the ends in a practiced motion as her thoughts drifted. It felt like another life. So much had happened since then—in particular, the Time-keeper and her father. She grit her jaw and sighed, moving to the foot of the bed—an ebony-toned swoop of wood, engraved with an ornate triskelion.

Her heart swelled as she took Oberon in; slumber did little to ease his expression. Tension still creased his brow, tight as a bowstring. She studied that nearly imperceptible hitch beneath his eyes that meant he was in a great deal of pain. As she watched, his full lips moved into a grimace. When, she wondered, would he be free?

And then, all at once, the King was awake—no half-aware expression or drowsy in-between, just asleep and then not. "Is everything alright?" he asked.

"Yeah," Raegan said, but her voice came out hoarse and unconvincing. "I was just glad to see you sleeping."

She moved around the end of the bed and came to the empty side—her side; if only she'd known all these years that her preference for the right side of the bed was because he always slept on the left. Then Raegan pulled herself onto the mattress, curling on her side to face the King.

"Is now an okay time . . . to tell you?" she asked, her voice coming out quiet and small enough to ride away on the swirls of mist beyond the windows. "To tell you about what happened? It's okay if it isn't."

The King tried to turn to look at her but stopped with a grunt when his injured muscles protested, so she sat up instead, tucking her legs beneath her and meeting his gaze. "Yes," he told her. "Whenever you are ready, so am I."

His voice was ragged, face a bit gray around the edges. She chewed on the inside of her lip. She didn't want to be unfair, to burden him with more. But she felt vulnerable right now—and more so, comfortable in that vulnerability. And she didn't trust herself to find this place again.

"Emrys has painkillers," Raegan found herself saying instead of, *"I traveled into a god's realm just to watch my dad die in front of my eyes."*

"I know," the King replied, his gaze unwavering.

"Right," she said, the vast river of her memories parting, allowing her to see beneath the rushing currents. "You don't trust yourself to stop."

"No," he said, his eyes sliding away. "I do not. Not with the pain my body brings me every day, grave injuries or not."

Raegan dragged her fingertips across the duvet. The air in the room suddenly felt oppressive, the golden lamplight congealed.

"Raegan," the King murmured, moving instinctively to touch her before remembering the sling and the gashes beneath the bandages. "Please. Go on, if you are ready."

She gathered herself up, holding all of the horrors and losses and unyielding pain in her arms, and opened her mouth to show him everything, to catalog her wounds and sharp, aching places. But then instead of words, a hitched sob came out of her mouth, tears tumbling down her face. She tried to stop herself, to banish this ridiculousness and just get on with it, but the sorrow clawed up her throat with defiant talons. Raegan folded in on herself, all the world a blur, a smear of gore where something she loved had once grown tall.

Whether she realized what she was doing or not, she ended up with her head in Oberon's lap, his uninjured hand stroking her hair. The sobs that wracked her body were not the tormented wails of fresh grief or even the frustrated cries of depression; instead, this sorrow was silent in its passing, a rush of mute tears, a fountain of hopelessness.

At some point, Raegan's lips moved and words came out. "Fate used my dad to get me to the Timekeeper. Can you imagine? Reducing someone vibrant, so full of love and life, to bait on a hook. What if all our suffering is for *nothing*? What if everything my dad sacrificed changes nothing in the end?"

She hadn't wanted to admit that, not even to herself, and dark spots skittered across her vision as she said the words. The world closed in around her like a vice. The King said nothing, still stroking her hair, waiting for her to speak again.

"I'm not scared of death," Raegan murmured into the soft, still air. "Just of leaving you, and what you might become after I've made you love me, only to lose me again."

His powerful hand slowed its gentle movements, and Raegan swallowed hard, biting back a fresh rush of tears.

"That is for me to manage," the King said eventually, his words laced with steel. "You have enough worries. I need not add to your burdens."

"Would it be easier," Raegan began, the ache in her chest nearly crowding out her voice, "if I *do* just make you hate me?" Hours ago, there was nothing she feared more, but now she saw the clarity that hatred might offer. It would hurt, of course. But so did everything else.

A pause, heavy as a millstone, the air weighted with the kind of silence that a Fatesong might've filled if there were any fairness or justice left in the world.

"No," he said, the single word so impossibly gentle in its defiance.

"It's easy to love someone enough to be with them," she replied. Raegan pushed herself up shakily to meet the King's gaze again. His gray eyes were misted with the fog of unshed tears, and his face was pinched, knuckles white. "But Oberon—do I love you enough to do the very thing that would hurt the most: destroy what we have? So you aren't forced to carry around an entire mausoleum of all the things we could've been?"

His jaw clenched, and then he closed his eyes, tears spilling from between long, dark lashes. He opened his mouth only to press his lips back together; all the while, Raegan just waited.

She thought she had finally found what could ease her yearning—the truth of her father, the world behind the world, the glory of magic and all that came with it. But now she feared there was part of her that would always, *always* yearn unreasonably for him and for nothing else. And that meant that part of her would always ache. It didn't matter how many times she returned to the soil. It didn't matter if Fate rewove her Threads completely and made her anew. That ache for him would remain lodged in her chest until the world caved in.

"Do you not realize," the King murmured, breaking the silence, his words as fragile as dew upon a spiderweb, "that I love you enough to lose you a thousand times over and still seek you like a moth to flame?"

Raegan let out a shuddering breath, tears obscuring her vision. Her throat constricted. "I think I'm the moth in this allegory," she said with a damp chuckle, shoving away the wetness on her cheeks with the back of her palms.

"No," Oberon said, reaching to take her hand in his, long fingers slipping between hers. "I am the Unseelie king, the Nameless One, the Render of Worlds, and yet I am little more than ash in your flame."

Raegan's breath caught. She gripped his hand between both of her palms. No words came to her tongue, nor her mind—logic and language fled her entirely, leaving only that bone-deep sense of longing she'd felt for a millennium. And then she raised her eyes to his and saw the truth of what the Unseelie king had spoken in his gaze.

"I love you," the Witch told the King, the words spoken solemnly, like they had the power to dispel prophecies and war.

"And I love you," the King replied in an exhale, as if what he felt for her stole the very air from his lungs.

For a moment, there inside the walls of a hidden city, wrapped in the heavy cloak of mist, she swore the ache buried deep within her ceased its keening. It would return, she knew. But for now . . . for now, there was only the calluses on his powerful hands and the autumnal scent of him and the terrifying vastness of how deeply she cared for someone she could never truly have.

~

When Emrys offered to show Raegan the old Temple's library, she'd been grateful for a distraction. Burying herself in researching any scrap of Avalon left behind was far more appealing than wondering exactly how much longer she had to live in this body, this life.

And for the first hour, she'd genuinely enjoyed the work. The ruined Temple's library was very different from the King's archives—more like a sunken greenhouse than any library she'd ever seen. The entire space sat just below the soil, casting everything in permanent shades of twilight. An enormous Victorian-era solarium glass roof stretched overhead, the towering oak bookcases climbing to the rainy skies above like hungry stalks. Globes and lush plants and orreries and objects she couldn't identify guarded the tops of the shelves.

Beneath her stockinged feet, the gray stone floors were cold, but a fire crackled merrily in the reading area. Antique fainting couches lounged in front of the hearth, covered in moss-green velvet. The parchment-colored rugs were embroidered with scientific-style renderings of local flora. Like every Fey space she had ever entered, it was gorgeous and magical and definitely, fantastically absurd. What charms, she wondered, did it take to stop the sunlight—no matter how diluted by rain—from bleaching all the books on the top shelves? And how were the plants watered without sending damp and rot down to the tomes beneath them?

"You know," Raegan said, leaning against the end of a bookcase, a large potted angel's trumpet brushing her hair, "before I had my Seal removed, I would've asked you a thousand questions trying to figure out how the fuck this place works."

Emrys looked over at her, a faint smile ghosting his lips. He pushed his delicate wire-rimmed glasses up his nose. "Do you not ask now because you can figure it out on your own or because you do not wish to spoil the wonder?"

Raegan paused, running her fingers down the gilded spines of a matching collection on the history of unicorns. "Both, I suppose."

Emrys said nothing, appraising her. For a moment, it looked like he was about to say something in response, but then he seemed to change his mind. "That concludes my tour," he announced. "But I'll be in the dwarvish history section if you need anything."

Her eyebrow rose, but before she could open her mouth to ask, Emrys waved a slim hand in the air. "It's a hunch. If Danu commissioned some kind of a door to Avalon, it's possible they worked on it."

Memory settled onto Raegan's shoulders, and all curiosity fled her. Dwarves were all but gone from the modern world, having retreated far into the earth after the Fall—a common name for the Fair Folk's devastating loss at the battle of Camlann. The dwarves had little desire to see how man would carve into the hills, or to witness the endless war the Fey would wage to take back what was theirs. A tiny part of Raegan couldn't blame them.

"Thanks," she said, pushing thoughts of the dwarvish people from her mind. "And thanks for letting me into your library."

"Oh, it's not mine," Emrys replied as he began to walk away from her, his tone uncharacteristically light. "It was the last Oracle's."

Before she could inquire further, the ex-Keeper was gone, disappearing around a bend of stone floors and shadowy shelves. She stared at the end of the row where he had just been, but there was only the creeping vine climbing the opposite wall and the tiny, ornate fountain that splashed beneath it.

Reorienting herself to the task at hand, Raegan glanced down at her notebook, scanning her list of the sections Emrys had mentioned that she wanted to explore. For half an hour, she did just that, amassing a pile of books on what looked suspiciously like an overly-long potting table, but with banker's lamps and inkwells instead of trowels and shears.

"One more thing to check," she muttered to herself, taking a long sip of lukewarm tea from the mug she'd brought into the library with her. And then she was off, weaving through the shelves, though this time she was seeking a section Emrys had only mentioned, not shown her. She didn't think the Temple's library was that big, but Fey spaces were always larger than they seemed, and in a few minutes, she had gotten a bit turned around.

This part of the library was quite different from the rest.

The shelves were empty, moss growing in the crevices, the surface of the wood pockmarked with decay. No fountains burbled, and the solarium roof overhead was covered in muck, like all Hiraeth's rain hadn't managed to reach it for at least ten years. Raegan almost turned back. Even the floor beneath her feet grew uneven and rough, sections upended like a large creature had burrowed just below the stones.

But something nameless pulled her forward, and before she could stop herself, she heeded the call. Raegan grit her jaw and hoped it was not Fate's Threads stringing her along yet again. She turned down a narrow hallway, which abruptly dumped her into a stone-walled chamber with a rounded ceiling. Unlit beeswax candles crouched in the corners, looking a bit too much like melted flesh. In the middle of the room, an enormous cabinet stood alone. It was a gorgeous piece of craftsmanship despite the dust coating it —even in the low light, Raegan could make out the shimmer of mother-of-pearl inlaid in its veneer. Jade curls of fiddle-head ferns guarded either side of the double glass doors. A key sat defenseless in the lock, a long tassel of much-worn silk hanging from its loop.

Curious as always, Raegan stepped closer, ignoring the way the walls seemed to press in from all sides. She was treading on a grave of sorts, she knew—but such boundaries did not apply to her. She belonged neither to the land of the living nor the underworld. Only Fate and the Unseelie king could lay any meaningful claim to her.

When her eyes finally adjusted to the gloom and she could make out shapes behind the dusty glass, Raegan regretted her curiosity. Inside the cabinet were Prophecies. Her throat closed off, and grief thundered onto her shores like a hurricane. And yet, she reached her hand up to the key and turned it, springing open the door. Old air, heavy with what could have been, rushed to meet her nose, smelling of ancient paper and melted beeswax and long-dried blood. She told herself not to look, but Raegan was very bad at following anyone's commands, even her own.

A dragonfly the size of her thumb, a pheasant in an enormous glass dome, a stunningly beautiful pegasus, and a falcon with its claws outstretched—all made of paper, all impossibly detailed and so delicate. She shouldn't be moved by them, she thought, not anymore. But longing lurched inside her anyway, and Raegan pressed her forehead to the glass door she'd left closed, like a child left outside in the cold.

It was not for her. It never had been, not really—Fate had chosen her for the sole purpose of offering a fattened calf to the Timekeeper in exchange for Her own desires. Raegan had not been picked for her wit nor her daring nor her unerring ability to read people. She'd been chosen because Fate had already cursed her, and there was little Fate liked more than something She could use more than once.

With a long, wavering sigh, Raegan moved to close the door, but something deeper in the cabinet caught her eye. No. Surely she was mistaken. In the gloom of the catacomb-like room, the weak light slipping in from the hallway providing the only illumination, perched a luna moth inside a slender glass dome.

Her hand reached out of its own accord, but she snatched it back. Surely there were hundreds—if not thousands—of Prophecies in the shape of a luna moth, like hers had been back at the Temple in Philadelphia. Surely it meant nothing at all. This Temple was dead, anyhow—there was probably a very practical reason why a few scant Prophecies lingered in its belly, and why one of them had taken the same shape as the Prophecy that had opened Raegan's life.

She hated that she ached for it, that there was little more she wanted than to place her fingers upon the glass and see the luna moth spring to life. For it to all have been for something, some grand design. For Fate to still be on her side, somehow. An ache bloomed enormous and undeniable in her bones. Biting the inside of her cheek, Raegan followed her yearning, unable to hold it back any longer. Her fingertips brushed the luna moth's glass dome. Time hung still, and then, somehow, against all reason, the glass burst like a bubble. No shattered pieces, no sharp edges to draw blood, just there and then gone.

She drew back, her heart throwing itself against her ribs. The glass cages of the other winged paper things in the cabinet thinned, barely more than a translucent film, and then they too faded from existence, a bubble bursting. With equal parts horror and awe, Raegan watched as the creatures moved for each other, just as hungry and desperate as when she reached for the King. The dragonfly and the luna moth curled around each other in time for the pheasant to devour them both in its paper mouth.

The Prophecies, Raegan realized, were cannibalizing each other, creating a single creature crafted from impossibly thin paper. Her throat closed off. Fuck, all she had to do was just not touch anything, to curb that traitorous hunger for Fate that seemed to live in her marrow.

The winged thing—hooves of a pegasus, wings of a dragonfly decorated with the moons of a luna moth, its head a falcon's—grew in size, moving toward the door of the cabinet. Anger pounded in Raegan's body, and she slammed the door shut. She'd had enough of Fate, enough of these parchment creatures flitting about and ripping her life apart.

"Shit," she muttered beneath her breath, watching words appear like a bloodstain on the dragonfly wings: *all become one, so may the once and futur—*

"Emrys," Raegan shouted, desperate to not ruin everything again, to not risk all of Hiraeth again, to not create another monstrous wound of Threads and Fate-kissed paper. She shoved the silk-tassel key in the lock and turned it. And just like that, the creature stilled, words no longer appearing, the Prophecies no longer devouring each other. She let out a long breath, her hands clammy.

When the frantic energy of the catacomb died down, when all felt dead and still, she turned and marched back down the hallway, through the damp, ruined half of the library, until she found the main aisle. Her head down, jaw grinding, Raegan strode for the hall that connected the library to the main section of the Temple. She wanted to throw herself through the front door and back into the winding, rain-damp streets of Hiraeth, where no one would see her and no one knew her name. Where guilt did not gild her shoulders like chainmail, where her mistakes were not lined up like daggers on a belt.

Instead, she nearly slammed into Emrys, who rushed out from around a corner, his eyes wild, the faded chore jacket he always wore sitting askew on his narrow shoulders. Raegan swerved to avoid him, almost losing her balance. Her heart began to thud in her chest. Had Emrys found Avalon? Had the King's injury taken a bad turn? Was the Protectorate upon them like hounds on a fox?

"Raegan," Emrys panted. "An outsider found the edge of our wards."

Her heart climbed into her throat, mind racing.

"She claims," he continued, "that she's your aunt."

CHAPTER TWENTY-ONE

Raegan blinked. "*What?*"

Emrys huffed, gesturing toward the mouth of the library. "Maelona Overhill. That's who she says she is. She found the hawthorns. I have no idea how."

Raegan swallowed, her mouth painfully dry all of a sudden. She hadn't told Emrys yet about Alanna; she'd wanted Oberon to help her with the conversation during dinner, seeing as she hardly knew the ex-Keeper. "Can you take me to her?" she wanted to know.

Emrys stared at her incredulously. "Why? She stinks of Protectorate."

"If it's actually Maelona," Raegan said, slipping past him and beginning to jog down the long passage to the main rooms, "she's not on their side."

"Well, is she on *ours?*" Emrys demanded, keeping pace with her.

"Only one way to find out," was all Raegan said, shouldering through the heavy door to the old Temple. She yanked on a random pair of Wellies from a rack by the front door; this was probably not the kind of situation to walk into without shoes.

"Raegan, how did she find us?" Emrys demanded, blocking her from leaving the small entryway. Though taller, he probably didn't have much of a weight advantage on her, and the magic she'd seen him do was all protective and divinatory. She could probably get past him.

But he was not her enemy, and besides—anyone given the honor of being a Temple's Keeper was formidable, even if they hid it well. "Because a shadewalker found me the other night," she said, her fingertips digging into her temples. "She came through the hawthorns. Into the Garden of Doors. It was a whole thing. I was going to tell you."

"A shadewalker?" Emrys asked, his voice low but eerily calm. He removed his hand from the wall, all his attention falling onto Raegan. "The Garden of Doors opened to you?"

Having known Oberon for more than a thousand years, she never liked when people got quieter when they were angry. It usually meant they had mastered their tempers, wielded their rage like a scalpel—which annoyed Raegan, whose anger was more like a battering ram.

"Yes," she hissed between her teeth, beginning to seriously consider shoving past him to get to her aunt. "And it also opened to the shadewalker, who happens to be Protectorate. Through no fault of her own, I may add. She found us when she searched shade-clad in the general area of our confrontation on the river. Hiraeth's wards are ancient and incredibly powerful. To her, they lit up like faerie lights, if you'll pardon the pun."

Emrys pulled himself up, suddenly much taller than Raegan realized. "And you did not inform me of this immediately?"

"No," she said, tilting her chin to meet his gaze. "And I'm sorry. But right now—"

"Right now, you and I are going to deal with the Protectorate woman gnawing at the hawthorns," Emrys replied, cutting her off, his tone flat and deadly. "And then, we are going to speak about this shadewalker and your questionable decisions."

Raegan ground her teeth together and swallowed her initial reaction, not allowing a sneer to work its way onto her face. "Fine." She buried any thought of mentioning the Prophecy beast deep in the library; besides, she'd sent it back to sleep, hadn't she?

Emrys nodded and then turned, pushing open the heavy wooden double doors to the hallway. It was the same one she and Oberon had entered through originally—long and dark, shadows curled in the corners, the stone floors beneath cold and gray. The ex-Keeper broke into a jog, moving for the vestibule. Her heart clenched, and she quickened her pace to keep up with Emrys. She hadn't allowed herself to imagine Maelona might still be alive. Hope could be a poison. With a huff, she broke into a run, her thighs screaming.

"Emrys, wait," Raegan panted, partially because she really didn't want to fucking run but also because she wasn't sure what he knew of the situation with Maelona. "Let me tell you Maelona's deal."

She watched as he reluctantly slowed his stride, moving from a jog to a quick walk. It was still an exertion for her much shorter legs to keep up with. Why the hell were all these people so tall? Though she'd hardly caught her breath, Raegan told Emrys about Maelona—about how she'd never known her aunt existed, she'd just shown up after Raegan summoned the kelpie and shattered Cormac's protective working. How her aunt had wanted to get her out, how she was hardly some fanatic aligned with the Protectorate's goals, and how Raegan hadn't seen her since that day in the cafè.

"So the shadewalker, who is also considering moving against the organization she was born into, got her here?" Emrys asked, rubbing his forehead furiously.

"I assume, but you know what they say about assumptions," Raegan replied, tripping on the rug that stretched the length of the hallway and cursing profusely. "The shadewalker—Alanna—mentioned Maelona. So I was already aware they knew each other."

Emrys said nothing else, though he looked less than pleased, and Raegan had a very strong feeling his anger was a long, drawn-out thing—that if she somehow managed to survive everything, he'd hold a grudge over this.

Raegan tried to force deep breaths into her lungs, ignoring Emrys for the moment and instead preparing herself for seeing Maelona. Her mind calculated the reasons and motives her aunt might be here, and she fought to formulate responses to them all. She couldn't let that soft, aching space in her chest dictate how she handled Maelona's appearance. No longer could she be a woman pulled headlong down a velveted hallway by a Seer. There were no Fatewinds in her sails. She charted her own course in these deadly waters.

But then they finally spilled into the large vestibule, the tearoom's doors on one side, the massive, ornate, and undoubtedly ancient gates to Hiraeth on the other. She hadn't seen them on her way in, not like this—the gates stretched at least twenty feet tall, forged from some kind of long-forgotten metalworking technique. Living hawthorns intertwined with snaking vines of age-blackened silver, creating an impenetrable and foreboding wall—but strikingly beautiful in an alien, inhuman kind of way.

With one hard look in her direction, Emrys reached

toward the gates. Instead of opening them in a dramatic whoosh, he instead wrapped his fingers around a small metal latch Raegan hadn't noticed. He pulled, and a section of the hawthorns slid away, revealing a door-within-a-door, a clandestine peek into what awaited on the other side of Hiraeth's gates.

Raegan rushed forward, bumping her shoulder into Emrys as she scrambled for a look. And there, standing in what was probably an empty meadow or a windswept moor or some other forgotten place, was Maelona.

Gone was the silver-threaded goddess who looked like she might bring a war ax down on anyone who dared consume another Overhill. In her place was a perilously thin creature propped up against a tree trunk just on the opposite side of the wards.

For a moment, she allowed herself to hope it was just the sunlight dappling her skin, but as Raegan looked closer, she saw that both of Maelona's eyes were blackened—one nearly swollen shut—and a jagged, infected-looking cut ran across her forehead. If Raegan wasn't mistaken—which she rarely was about these sorts of things—Maelona was wearing the same outfit as the last time they'd seen each other, though everything was now covered in grime and blood.

"She can't see or hear us," Emrys told Raegan in a short, even tone.

"Raegan," Maelona rasped suddenly despite the ex-Keeper's words, her eyes hunting but, of course, finding nothing. "Raegan, if you're here, please. If you don't let me in, they will find me. Alanna got me out. Alanna brought me . . ." Maelona's body pitched, one knee buckling, and she skidded down the side of the tree, peeling bark off as she went.

If it was a performance, it was a hell of a job, and better

than Raegan thought straight-shooter Maelona would be able to muster. If it *was* Maelona.

"Is it her?" Raegan demanded of Emrys. "Can you tell from across the wards?"

He glanced down at her, his jaw working. Then he pulled his delicate silver glasses from the pocket of his chore jacket and slid them onto his face, like he was about to inspect a particularly lovely flower, not decide if one of Raegan's last living relatives was within their grasp to save.

"I see no glamours," he intoned, clinical, tapping the rim of his lenses. "She is in true medical distress."

Raegan's heart panged, and she turned back to Maelona. Her aunt had slid all the way down to her knees, and her head lolled. Raegan exhaled and then attempted to summon her second sight. For a moment, a lens slid over the world, sending everything into strange hues and shadows. She grit her teeth and began to examine Maelona, but then the sight slipped out of her grasp.

"Fuck," Raegan snarled, curling her fists and trying again. Sometimes she regretted the Seal's removal, only because now she remembered far too intimately how she'd once worked magic as easily as breathing.

The sight did not come. But instead, instinct rose within her, a wine-dark wave of pure intuition, and she knew without a doubt that the broken form of the woman before her was Maelona Overhill.

"Open the wards," Raegan said. "Let her in."

"Are you out of your mind?" Emrys demanded, wheeling on her. "I am not bringing a Protectorate-oathed mortal within my wards. I'm not even sure if Hiraeth itself would permit such a thing. Your *friend* from the other night only fared so well because she was shade-clad."

And because the ancient, fabled Garden of Doors let Alanna in and had taken Raegan right to her. Ice-cold rage surged in her veins, and she turned to face Emrys, though it pained her to take her eyes off Maelona. "You might recall," she said, lifting her chin, meeting his eyes, "that I am the Queen of the Hill, the Witch of the Woods, and if Fate hadn't been too terrified to allow it, I would have been your High Lady. So open. The. Fucking. Wards."

Somewhere in the back of her mind, Raegan didn't understand why she was suddenly eye-level with the ex-Keeper, who stood at least a head taller than her. But then she watched his gaze widen behind his glasses, and she realized that her feet had left the ground entirely. What a compelling image, her journalist's sense chimed. An ordinary woman, her eyes still puffy with the tears she'd shed, dressed in an oversized wool sweater and loose jeans stuffed into the top of Wellies three sizes too big, levitating above the ground like some kind of vengeful specter.

"If you invite doom into the last Fey city on the Isles, I will hold you accountable," Emrys told her, his tone steady, though she could see all his teeth.

"If you haven't noticed," she snarled in response, "I wear my guilt like chainmail and wield my transgressions like a weapon. So be it, Emrys. If I'm wrong, add it to my fucking armory."

Something like respect might've flitted across the ex-Keeper's angular features, but then his expression smoothed and he inclined his head. "So be it," he echoed.

CHAPTER TWENTY-TWO

I n the end, Emrys and Raegan had to drag Maelona through the gates. Her aunt was barely conscious, flitting in and out, though at some point she seemed to recognize Raegan and relaxed a little. As they pulled her into the vestibule—gently on Raegan's part, not so gently on the ex-Keeper's—the gates closed behind them with a soft sigh.

In that small, square room with impossibly high ceilings and bare stone walls, the entire world seemed to inhale. The space grew restrictive and tight, like all the oxygen had been squeezed out of the air. Raegan tensed, tightening her grip on Maelona. What if Hiraeth wouldn't grant her entrance? Offering a relatively safe meeting place for a shade-clad Protectorate woman to discuss treason was one thing. Permitting a sworn enemy into the city's inner sanctum was another entirely.

Emrys shot Raegan a sharp look over Maelona's lolled head as if to say, *"I told you so."* Raegan narrowed her eyes at him, trying to look calm, but her hands had long since gone clammy, her heart fluttering like a tiny, trapped bird in her chest. Behind them, the hawthorn branches slithered and tightened.

"Hey," Raegan spat, looking up as if she might find some avatar of Hiraeth floating in the darkness above their heads. "You sorta like me, right? I'm useful to you? Well, I'm only alive because of this woman. So let me help her. Also, see how fucked up she is? The Protectorate did that to her because she's a traitor."

At that, the suffocating air seemed to loosen, the room suddenly feeling a few feet larger. Ahead, the heavy wooden doors into Hiraeth became visible; Raegan hadn't realized until now that they'd disappeared from view. She exhaled, black spots swarming her vision.

"Thanks," she said, unsure where to direct her gratitude, before gathering Maelona up and beginning to walk forward. Emrys grumbled something under his breath but did his part, slinging her aunt's limp arm over his shoulder.

"Even if Hiraeth has allowed her in so far," Emrys said as they trudged down the long hallway, "when we give her blood to the hawthorns, I don't know how they'll react."

"We'll cross that bridge when we get there," Raegan grunted, her muscles despairing at the amount of physical activity she'd done today. She needed to ask Oberon to train her. Memories unhelpfully peppered her mind—mages who had met their end on the battlefield because they'd relied too heavily on their magic.

When the door into the ruined Temple finally appeared, Raegan let out a sigh of relief. So far, so good. She hadn't ever thought she'd yearn for the approval and acceptance of an ancient, primordial city, but a lot of weird shit had happened lately.

"Table again, I guess," Emrys said as they shouldered through the door. "Just to check her over for tracking spells."

"And serious injuries," Raegan snapped, trying to be

gentle as she lifted Maelona onto the large table. Her aunt looked like skin and bones, but there was a heft to her, a memory of muscle and defiance.

She examined Maelona's right side for life-threatening injuries and found none, though she saw her aunt's thumb had been broken and reset incorrectly a number of times. She winced. Maelona's ankle was swollen too, a more recent sprain, probably in her flight from the Protectorate's dungeons to Hiraeth's hawthorn door.

Working soundlessly, Raegan switched sides with Emrys and repeated her search, finding a bruised collarbone and a pinky dangling by a few strands of muscle. She swallowed hard and fought to find her extensive knowledge of human anatomy, locked away somewhere in her own mind. To Raegan's surprise and delight, she located it and put it to quick work—reattaching Maelona's pinky, resetting the thumb, completely erasing the black eyes and gash on her face.

"No tracking spells," Emrys confirmed, sounding slightly disappointed. "Let's get her settled. Then you and I are having a long conversation."

"Sure," Raegan said, mostly because her head was swimming and she felt woozy. *Too much too fast*, a voice inside her head chided. She gritted her teeth and blinked rapidly a few times.

"You alright?" Emrys asked, arching a brow at her.

"Fine," she replied, fighting the urge to sneer just for good measure. Clenching her jaw so hard that her teeth ached, Raegan leaned forward to get one of Maelona's arms across her shoulders. Just as she did, the woman stirred, her eyelids fluttering. Then Maelona slapped away Raegan's hands and pulled herself to sit up halfway, a show of sheer will.

Her aunt was surprisingly calm as she took in Raegan

and Emrys. "Oh, good," Maelona mumbled. "Got to you before the Protectorate got to me. So, bit of bad news. They know you're looking for Avalon."

Raegan startled a step back, her blood suddenly running cold and thick through her veins while a thousand pins pricked red-hot across her skin. The world tilted dangerously, and her tongue suddenly felt too big for her mouth.

Even Emrys didn't manage to form any useful questions before Maelona slumped back down onto the table. Raegan's mind plodded along sluggishly, offering her nothing at all as Emrys shook her aunt's shoulder, trying to reawaken her. Only when his jostling began to verge on violence did Raegan snap out of whatever trance she'd fallen into, reaching across to shove Emrys's hands away.

"Can we get her somewhere more comfortable?" Raegan asked, the words coming out slow and slurred.

Emrys considered her, an eyebrow arching again, though nothing else changed about his expression. He turned and waved a lazy hand at the two armchairs by the cold hearth. In the space of an instant, a daybed stretched across the space instead, a flame roaring to life in the fireplace.

"Do not ask me to put her upstairs within easy reach of our injured king," he warned as he scooped Maelona up on his own this time.

Raegan blanched, partially due to the nausea, partially due to the accusation lingering in his voice. "Why the fuck do you think I'd want that?"

"Just want to be clear," Emrys replied nonchalantly, arranging Maelona on the daybed. Raegan dragged herself over to remove her aunt's boots and tuck her into the wool blankets Emrys produced.

"Now we wait," the ex-Keeper said, crossing his arms, staring down at Maelona with a frown.

"Thanks for your help," Raegan said, only a little begrudgingly. Emrys just grunted in reply. The dizziness had faded, but she was suddenly very, very tired, barely able to keep her eyes open. So she told Emrys she wanted to quickly check on Oberon before they had their little chat, warned him to be nice to Maelona in the meantime, and then made for the stairway. It was unfairly far to walk, all rich fig carpeting and sconces flickering sleepily. She made herself keep going, all the way to the room she and Oberon shared.

"Maelona's here," Raegan announced to the King, who was awake, his nose in a book. She kicked off the borrowed Wellies somewhere near the door and caught only a few seconds of Oberon's startled expression before she collapsed onto the bed. Sleep wrapped itself around her like a cocoon and did not let go.

~

Raegan awoke to shouting. Not her own this time, to which she felt a bizarre kind of relief. She swallowed, her mouth dry, and then pushed herself to sit up. Oberon was gone. A quilt had been thrown over her legs, but she still wore the jeans and sweater she'd put on earlier. Silence blanketed the Temple for a long moment, and then a muffled, raised voice met her ears.

Not Oberon, she assumed, groaning as she swung her legs over the side of the bed. Her head felt like it had been stuffed with cotton. She should probably do more of the magical exercises the King had suggested to her a few weeks ago. Maybe she'd build up some endurance and stop passing the fuck out constantly.

"She has ruined us before!" someone—oh, Emrys, of course—shouted, closer now, on the landing, maybe. "My liege, I am begging you to see reason. Two Protectorate operatives now know Hiraeth's location. This is madness."

Silence again. Raegan moved to stand, but the world spun. "Okay," she mumbled, sitting back down on the edge of the bed. The hallway outside creaked under someone's weight.

"Emrys," came Oberon's voice, the sound of a dagger burying itself in flesh. "Stop shouting."

It sounded like Emrys offered a strangled kind of huff in response. She didn't even have time to strategize further before the King ducked into the room, a storm brewing on his expression. Emrys followed behind, face red. For a moment, Raegan saw the depths of terror in his eyes—that he might lose everything he'd ever built, let down everyone he'd ever loved. She sighed, pushing down the anger she felt at his distrust.

"Emrys," Raegan began, her head clearing a little. "I'm sorry. This is fucked up. I have caused you so much stress and worry when you've graciously opened your home to us. I need you to know that I may not always make the best choices—I can admit that—but I *always* have the end goal in mind. For magic to return. For our people to be free."

Emrys looked taken aback for a moment before he slid that mask of composure back on. His gaze flicked to Oberon, who cocked a brow and inclined his head for a reason Raegan didn't understand.

"You don't remember Hiraeth," the ex-Keeper said, fiddling with a button on his chore coat, "because I took your memory of it. You've been here before. With Oberon. You were Titania, the Seelie Queen. You know what happened. We don't need to dig up the past. It is hard for me to not be suspicious of your actions."

Raegan picked a piece of lint from the thigh of her jeans, her hands shaking. How *dare* he? How dare he steal her memories? Why did all of these men think they could reach into her skull and take whatever the fuck they wanted?

And when she raised her chin to say exactly that, her gaze met the King's—the placid waves of an ocean under cloudy skies, the tide pulling at that soft, secret place deep inside her chest. She let that blind, seething anger of hers go, a silk ribbon caught in the seaside winds.

"Let's not dig up the past," Raegan agreed, laying her hands flat on the duvet beside her legs. "Because I'm kinda touchy about my memories, and it really upsets me that you took them. But I understand you just want to protect Hiraeth. That's what I want, too. Emrys, imagine what a shadewalker would add to our power, one who is still oathed to the Protectorate. And Maelona's extensive knowledge. It could change *everything*."

She paused, the words dying in her throat as she snuck a glance at Emrys. His expression had softened slightly, his jaw no longer working back and forth.

"But I'm so scared I'm wrong," Raegan whispered before she even realized she was speaking. "*Again.*"

Emrys inhaled sharply. Beside him, the King was silent, though all his attention was on Raegan. She noticed offhandedly that his color looked better than earlier. It was sort of horrifying that he could take a close-range shotgun blast and be walking around this soon, but it was also kind of hot.

"I'm scared, too," Emrys finally said, his deep brown eyes warmer now, like the soil's first thaw in spring. "Terrified, actually. But you are not wrong. This could change everything. However, we must do it *together*, you understand? You cannot fix a thousand years of history on your own. No one can. Please stop trying."

Something like ease settled into the place between

Raegan's shoulder blades. It was tenuous, strung delicately above a chasm, but it was there all the same. She took a deep breath and nodded. "It's different this time," she said, hoping her words were true. "Even the Keeper in Philadelphia said so."

"Perhaps," Emrys said, narrowing his eyes and adjusting the bridge of his glasses, "it is because *we* are all different this time."

The hope of that statement surged in her chest—that finally the resistance had gathered the strength it needed, been transmuted by the past, and shed every skin it no longer needed. Maybe they could do it this time. Particularly with Alanna's—

"Wait," Raegan said, sitting up straight, a feverish chill crawling across her skin. "What time is it?"

"Almost sunset," Oberon said with a start, realizing the same thing she just had. "You need to go."

Raegan slid off the bed, happy to find her legs were shaky but working. She scrambled for the boots she'd kicked off and shoved her feet inside them. "No," she said, looking up at the two impossibly powerful creatures with what was probably a manic grin. "*We* need to go."

Oberon parted his lips to say something, but then he just smiled instead. It reached his eyes, and the sight of that sent warmth tumbling through Raegan's chest.

"I'm sorry, go where?" Emrys asked, folding his glasses back into the pocket of his chore jacket and looking anxiously between the two of them.

"The shadewalker is meant to return," the King replied, moving toward the door behind Raegan. "If the Garden opens for her. For us."

"The Protectorate shadewalker is coming *back*?" Emrys asked, a hint of despair in his tone, but as Raegan slipped out the door and began to run down the hallway, she heard his footsteps following.

"We have more to discuss," Raegan replied, hitting the landing and grabbing the banister to keep her balance as she thudded down the stairs. "Revolution, namely."

"Are you comfortable with this, Emrys?" Oberon wanted to know, his voice coming from higher up the stairs.

"Comfortable?" Emrys demanded, his voice a half-octave higher than usual. "Gods, no. But perhaps . . . perhaps that is good. Perhaps I have gotten too comfortable with the idea that only Hiraeth could survive. That liberation was only a dream."

Raegan hit the stone floor at the bottom of the stairs and pushed her exhausted body through the great room, coming to a halt when she saw Maelona's prone form on the daybed. Her aunt had been tucked into a wool blanket and a quilt, her head propped on a velvet pillow. She was sound asleep, her deep inhales visible even beneath all the layers.

"She will be fine," Oberon murmured, touching Raegan's shoulder. "She made her choices and her sacrifices. Now it is our work to ensure it was worth it."

Raegan turned to look up at him, her throat closing off with emotion. His words echoed the concern she'd had about her father—that everything he'd done had been for nothing. And here was the Unseelie king himself, doing whatever he could to ensure another Overhill would not succumb to such a fate.

She nodded, slipped her fingers through his, and moved for the front door of the Temple. Emrys was already there, slipping one of the glamoured cloaks over his shoulders.

"Oberon should really stay here," the ex-Keeper said in a tone that indicated he did not expect his king to follow the suggestion in the slightest.

"I should," Oberon agreed, but he only unlaced his

fingers from Raegan's to reach for a cloak. She smiled to herself at his response, pulling the fabric over her own shoulders. Then the three of them stepped out into the streets of Hiraeth.

At this hour, the cobblestone pathways were thick with Fair Folk, the city gowned in gossamer-thin mist. There were more small children in Hiraeth than Raegan could ever have dared to believe—proof that their people would not fall so easily to the desires of power-hungry gods and misled men. She paused on the Temple's steps, watching the crowds as they slipped by, though she had no need to search the faces in that way she always did. Her heart panged in a good way.

And then, across the cobblestones, she saw something that she took a long, skittering moment to comprehend, all her assumptions about the Fey of Hiraeth and what the future would look like with the Gates destroyed feeling so incredibly stupid and short-sighted.

"Mortals are accepted in Hiraeth?" Raegan demanded, her throat aching, spinning to face Emrys. She didn't hold the once-Keeper's gaze for long, her heart longing to look back across the street and take in the mortal florist setting out buckets of blood-red peonies.

"Of course," Emrys replied, genuine surprise in his tone. "Humanity has never been our enemy. Many mortals are just as endangered by the Protectorate as the Fey. Magic unites the people of Hiraeth, not race or blood."

Her breath caught in her throat, and she felt Oberon slip his free hand—the other still in a sling—around hers. "I did not realize you were unaware," he murmured, his fingers stroking the underside of her wrist in a way that made Raegan's mind go blank and white and hungry. "I should have, though, knowing Emrys had taken your memories.

Hiraeth is a sanctuary to those who need it. Who believe magic is not to be locked away by a ruling class."

"Right," Raegan said, clearing her throat, blinking away the tears that were gathering on her lashes. She didn't know why she hadn't bothered to open her eyes and *look* before—surely she had passed mortals on her walk last night. But gods, her rage had blinded her completely, hadn't it? The words of the Oracle came floating back to her—that anger is a useful tool when we control it but not when it controls us.

"So," Raegan continued, that seed of hope buried deep inside her chest growing large, "it took me a while to find the Garden the other night. We might be in for a walk."

"I think you should lead the way," Emrys said, pulling his cloak over his head. "It opened for you before. If Hiraeth wants you to continue speaking with Alanna, it'll lead you to her."

Raegan nodded, looking left and then right. Last time, she'd taken the left turn, winding down the hill into the commercial section of the city. But tonight, when she turned the other direction, she caught an improbable thing —the flutter of a moth's wings in the lamplight up ahead. Pale green, unless she was only imagining it, twin moons on the delicate curve. She inhaled sharply. Maybe she was Icarus, doomed to plummet just when she thought she'd reached the warmth of the sun for the first time in a thousand years.

Or maybe not. Maybe the story ended differently this time.

"This way," Raegan said, stepping out into the mist, hoping the doors would open for her just once more.

CHAPTER TWENTY-THREE

"My gods," Emrys murmured, his words floating on the still, heavy mist. Before the three of them stood the Garden of Doors, willow-o-wisps flickering blue and green and silver through the intricate, stylized gates. "No one has seen the Garden in at least a hundred years."

"Well, here it is," Raegan said with a shrug, swinging one side of the metal gates open. She stepped into the garden, which was just as awash in dewy aubergine petal and rain-damp bark as the other night. The King stayed close to her side, his cloak arranged to disguise his arm, which was still very much bandaged to his chest. In the faerie lights, the sharp angles of his face were all the more apparent, all the more inhuman. Raegan marveled at his fierce beauty, and then at the even fiercer love she felt for him.

"You said she was near the hawthorns last time, yes?" Emrys asked, walking through the gates and onto the path. His gaze was wide, a sort of child-like wonder overtaking his expression that made Raegan feel like things might just be okay in the end.

"Yeah," she agreed, striding deeper into the garden. Up ahead, she saw the path narrow, the thicket of old-growth trees creating a canopy ahead. A vicious wind whipped through the trees, tearing at her clothing. "I still think it's best you hold back. Don't want to terrify her."

Neither the King nor Emrys agreed, but they didn't *disagree* either, which seemed more important to Raegan considering their respective personalities. She moved reverently down the path, her strides constantly alternating between quick and slow—a rush of need to see if Alanna had returned, a deep dread that only horrors awaited them.

But when she arrived at the dead portico, the garden was quiet. The hawthorns were in the shape they ought to be, no strange shadows draping them, no sashay of Alanna's generous hips or elegant drip of her braids down her back.

"Sunset, she said?" the King asked, his voice low.

"Yeah," Raegan replied, scanning what she could see of the sky, though it was hard to gauge time beneath Hiraeth's crown of mist and rain.

"A few minutes still to go," Emrys said, his voice distant. Raegan turned to find the ex-Keeper turning in a slow circle, looking at the garden with unabashed wonder. At least she could give him that, Raegan supposed, if everything ended up going to hell. She pushed her hood back, letting the glamour fall away, and watched as Emrys did the same.

She moved to face the hawthorn wall again, running her eyes across the impossible structure. It was something straight out of a fairytale—her mind almost failed to process the enormity and sweep of it, a tangle of thick, ancient limbs that held the city in the palm of its hand.

At that moment, the air changed, the wind ceasing. Petrichor and damp leaves crushed underfoot filled Raegan's nose, the smoke and warmth of the city streets left far behind. Though groomed and orderly, this garden was a wild place, she realized. It wore politeness on its face, but its heart was all belladonna flower and hemlock root. Raegan smiled.

Then the hawthorns shimmered, just as they had before. Three ancient things held their breath in a place that was not a place, in a time outside of time. The future felt hinged on this moment, Raegan realized, like all of their Threads might change the weave for the better if they could just make this work. If they could prove themselves worthy. If the Fey put aside centuries-old resentment and bad blood, if the mortals of the Protectorate had finally had enough of aiding their own oppression.

The dead portico at Raegan's side shivered, and then a woman, looking for all the world like she'd been dipped in mercury or draped in silver silk, came through an opening in the hawthorn branches. Raegan held her breath. Emrys stood on the other side of the portico, and the King wisely faded into the shadows of the trees, hidden by his hood's glamour.

"Alanna," Raegan called, her voice trembling only a little.

"Raegan," Alanna called back, taking a few paces forward before she sighted Emrys. Then she froze, her young face stricken with fear.

"This is Emrys," Raegan said immediately, though she studied Alanna closely. "He's a friend. He wants what we do."

"I thought we'd meet alone," Alanna said cautiously, though she held her ground. Her long braids were bound in an elegant bun this time. Her clothing wasn't exactly visible beneath the shine of her shade, but it struck Raegan as being more casual than before.

"I'm sorry," Raegan said, meaning it. "I can't keep trying

to do things all on my own. Hopefully you'll figure that out, too, before you're a thousand goddamn years old."

Alanna smiled, relaxing slightly. "Did Maelona make it to you?"

"Yes," Emrys replied, his tone light. "Thank you. It means a great deal to Raegan."

Alanna inclined her head and took the smallest step forward. "They were going to execute her as a traitor. I have friends in the holding blocks. It should look like an accident —a mistake with the shift change, a lucky opportunity."

"Have you endangered yourself by getting her out?" Raegan wanted to know. Her fingers wound into fists of their own accord. No more of this, the Protectorate devouring whatever it wanted for the sake of enriching itself.

"Probably," Alanna said with a sly smile, one shoulder meeting her ear. "Hard to stage a coup without risking yourself, isn't it? But beyond her being your family, she's useful to our cause. She's lived a lot longer than most field operatives. She knows things."

"Like that the Protectorate is aware we're looking for Avalon," Raegan suggested, shifting her weight. The following silence was so heavy she could hear the gravel crunch beneath her slight movement.

"Not for sure," Alanna replied, her gaze flicking to Emrys. "We have Prophecies, too. Which has always seemed hypocritical to me, but that's the Protectorate for you. It's a firmly held belief that if the King and the Deathless Witch return to these lands, it will be to seek Avalon."

"Does the Protectorate have any ideas about where Avalon may be?" Emrys asked, pulling his glasses out from beneath his cloak.

Alanna narrowed her eyes. "So you *are* looking for Avalon, then?" she asked, a grin taking over her face. The expression was pure oxygen in the depths of blank, dead space. "Why?"

Raegan and Emrys exchanged a glance. Silence hung like the gallows in the dark garden, heavy and accusing. "What if we said it was because the Fey are done with this realm and wish to seek safer lands?" Emrys asked.

Alanna looked from one being to the other. A breeze sent pale pink petals tumbling across the path, shaking rain from the tree branches high above the small group gathered in a garden at the end of the world. Raegan held her breath.

"That would be more palatable, I suppose," Alanna finally said, shrewd and sharp. "But I wouldn't believe it."

Raegan bit the inside of her cheek. They'd strategized as they looked for the garden—of course they had—but all three of them knew so little about what Alanna really wanted.

So then, fuck it, Raegan decided. "What do you want out of this, Alanna?" she asked, stepping toward the younger woman. The willow-o-wisps gleamed brighter for a moment, as if the garden approved.

Alanna, to Raegan's surprise, stepped forward to meet her. They stood only a few feet apart now. Alanna was much taller than Raegan, a queenly tilt to her chin. "Revenge," she whispered, her voice hoarse and raw. "They took me from my mother, you know. She'd gotten me out, away from my father—he has the Protectorate lineage. And when they found me, they made her forget me. They didn't kill her, because she's good leverage. They always know where she is. Keeps me in line."

Raegan's throat constricted. Beside her, even Emrys inhaled sharply. That was the Protectorate, though—cruelty had *always* been the point. A strange urge rose in her to take Alanna's hands in her own. But she couldn't, because the woman was shade-clad, oathed to the enemy, and not yet in possession of Raegan's trust.

"So many of us do not have a choice," Alanna hissed, her eyes shining with tears in the willow-o-wisp light, even in her incorporeal form. "There needs to be some protection for mortals in a world with Fair Folk in it—of course there does. But *this*? The Protectorate hasn't protected anything but their own interests in hundreds of years. They are conspiring with a god who only brought misery to this world, and they don't care who suffers."

Raegan clung to Alanna's words, the way she spat them out like poisoned seeds. She could help free so many families of the shackles the Overhills had worn since the Battle of Camlann. She ground her teeth together, flexing her fingers. *If* Alanna was telling the truth. But she'd freed Maelona, sent her to Raegan. She hadn't come for them with an army. Maelona was disposable, though, Raegan realized, and the Protectorate might make that calculated move. It was a smart one, admittedly.

"I think I can speak for Raegan and myself both when I say we *want* to believe you," Emrys said, his voice soft and more blanketed in understanding than Raegan had ever heard. "It's just . . . It's hard."

"You think my first option was aligning with the bloody Fair Folk?" Alanna demanded, crossing her arms, looking over Raegan's shoulder to address the ex-Keeper. "I'm not enjoying this either."

Raegan inhaled, shaky and unsteady. This was so different from pursuing her father—it wasn't just about her anymore. Now an entire world was nestled in her hands like a delicate, speckled egg. One wrong move, one stumble, and it would shatter.

"Risk something, Alanna," she suggested, meeting the woman's large brown eyes, which were rimmed lightly in kohl. "Something tangible, something we agree on. Not a random bone to a dog you're thinking about killing anyway."

Anger flitted across Alanna's face, and she drew away from Raegan. "Have I not risked enough?" she wanted to know, her voice a harsh rasp of disbelief.

Maybe Raegan finally *was* growing as a person, because her own rage did not ignite with the spark of Alanna's. Instead, sadness flooded her chest, the tides leaving salt clinging to her ribs. "You have," she replied, surprised to find tears pricking the backs of her eyes. "My gods, you have. And yet I have to ask you for more."

Alanna shook her head, taking two steps backwards toward the opening in the hawthorns. "What could you possibly even ask of me?" she demanded, but she hadn't left yet.

"Speak with us in your body," Raegan suggested, knowing it was an enormous gamble. "Flesh and blood. Come have tea. Talk. Let me see what Maelona thinks about you in real time."

Alanna stood up a little straighter, gears turning in her head. Silently, Raegan's hope surged—she just might have the shadewalker. She inhaled. And she might be about to lose her.

"And Alanna, you should meet the King."

The silver-shrouded woman, stately as a vengeful goddess, looked down at Raegan as if she were trying to decide whether to smite her or laugh in her face.

"Have you lost your fucking mind?" Alanna eventually demanded, though she held her ground. She could turn to the hawthorns, find that breadcrumb sigil, and disappear back through the twisting limbs. But she did not.

Emrys cleared his throat and opened his mouth to speak, but Raegan held her hand out, shooting the Keeper a look that she hoped he understood. "Actually, yes, I have," she said to the Protectorate shadewalker. "And honestly, I feel much better now that I'm out of my mind. I think you might, too."

Alanna's mouth actually fell open, and Raegan understood her youth then—a creature of barely twenty-five summers, maybe less. A girlhood stolen, a Fate rewritten, and now here Raegan was, asking her to meet the living, breathing devil.

The garden fell into a preternatural hush, the breeze stilled, as if the very place they stood was holding its breath. Raegan found herself holding hers too, her heart a runaway train in her chest. Then Alanna broke the silence, throwing her head back and laughing. It was unbridled and crackling with energy, a wildfire of a sound.

"If only my mother could see this," Alanna began, her eyes coming to meet Raegan's gaze again, the outline of the shadewalker's form against the hawthorns reminding her of a military general painted in victory repose, hung in a museum somewhere.

Deep in the garden, a fox or something worse shrieked. A chorus of cries followed, throats raw with defiance and a never-ending ache for justice. A cool breeze drifted up the back of Raegan's neck, making her shiver.

"My mother," Alanna continued, taking a step toward Raegan, mere inches separating them now, "got me out because she made a deal with the Fey. And they protected us. I don't know the details of the bargain. I just know the Protectorate only found me because they killed the Fey who helped my mother. Whoever they were, they refused to give up our location. And they died for it. The cloaking spellwork died with them, of course. My handlers bragged about it. Called me a changeling. I suppose I am. Just not in the way they think."

Suddenly, like the sacred moment the sun climbs over the horizon and casts the world anew, Raegan understood she was looking an entire revolution in the eye. She understood that for all the efforts of the Unseelie Court and her own father and the people of Hiraeth, nothing would have freed them without this woman. This shade-clad torrent whose voice sounded like the truth.

"The High King of the Unseelie Court humbly extends an invitation to you, Lady Alanna, to discuss what kind of world we might create together," Emrys said from behind Raegan, startling her. His voice rose high on the mist, regal and sure and perfect. She smiled. "Do you accept?"

Alanna grinned, a silvered dagger in the dark garden. "I do."

CHAPTER TWENTY-FOUR

Raegan's left boot sank deep into the mud at the same time the wind turned sharply, buffeting her with rain that felt more like tiny pinpricks. She pulled her borrowed oilskin closer and tried to focus on Oberon's tall form a few steps ahead. Treading the ground where Stonehenge's bluestones had been quarried thousands and thousands of years ago on an epic quest to find a hidden door to Avalon had been very exciting on paper. In reality, she was cold and covered in mud to her knees.

If there was any sign of the Protectorate, any at all, Emrys had made them both promise to leave immediately. Rainer awaited them in the Rivers and could be summoned from a raindrop, the kelpie had sworn, the very moment they needed to flee. For the first time, Raegan felt like there *was* actually something to lose: her aunt who still slept, waking for only brief moments at a time, the burgeoning alliance with Alanna that could change everything. She closed her eyes against another serrated spray of rain, her gaze falling on Oberon. And *him*. She could lose him, she supposed. Usually it went the other way, but his injury had reminded her there was no guarantee.

When Raegan came to the realization that she wasn't going to be comfortable healing such a complex injury anytime soon, Emrys had pulled a proficient Fey healer from Hiraeth's population. With the promise they'd agree to have the memory taken later, he brought them to the Temple. The damage from the Protectorate's attack was bad —worse than Oberon had been letting on. The healer had done what they could, but it would take months for the King to regain full use of his shoulder and pectoral muscles. Which meant he shouldn't be slogging about in the mud, but he had ignored any assertions of that sort.

"How much farther?" Raegan shouted through the torrent of rain. Oberon slowed, turning to look back at her, though she couldn't see much beyond his hood.

"Only a few paces," he replied as they fell into stride together. Oberon gave her the more manageable path, which forced him to wade through thick, knee-high grass.

Raegan squinted into the gloom surrounding them, finally making out what they were looking for: Carn Goedog. At the top of a slope stood a crown of stones, jutting out from the earth like broken teeth. It was a wild place, she knew immediately, and her bones hummed.

Whether it contained a door to Avalon was another question entirely, and only one they could answer with actual inspection. She threw a glance around, searching for any hint of the Protectorate. Armed with Alanna's information, they'd conspired to stage a few diversions at ancient sites across the Isles. Oberon seemed to think their encounter at the waterfalls might have just been poor luck— that the Protectorate was patrolling the area already. Raegan could only hope that was true.

The path began to incline, and she slogged forward, her knees protesting. And yet, in her heart of hearts, she'd rather be fighting through mud and hill and rain than doing what came next: meeting with Alanna in Hiraeth's old Temple. Raegan didn't think she—or magic itself, for that matter—could suffer losing Alanna. *If* the shadewalker was actually what she made herself out to be, of course.

Raegan slipped on a particularly muddy patch and let out a curse. The King caught her by the elbow and steadied her before they made the final ascent. Hopefully Maelona would wake up before this evening, when Alanna would come to Hiraeth in her own body. She'd requested time to figure out exactly how to disappear for a few hours, and they'd happily granted it to her, needing the three days to strategize and plan. And to check Carn Goedog, the next site on Emrys's list, which clung to more residual magic than should be possible.

Raegan ground her teeth, holding up an arm to shield her eyes as another sharp gust of wind threw knives their way. Emrys and the healer he'd recruited both thought actively intervening in Maelona's current state was too dangerous. Well, Emrys was not particularly concerned about Maelona herself, but he was very interested in preserving her memories and sanity for future use.

With a huff, Raegan crested a steep section of the hill. She couldn't really blame him. Hundreds of years of war and responsibility had hollowed out the parts of the ex-Keeper that might have been soft once. She wondered, not for the first time, what it was to persist in that endless way, one long line. Maybe dying all the time wasn't such a curse, not in comparison.

And then the slope evened out beneath her, depositing Raegan and the King on a small plateau ringed in giant shards of bluestone. Despite the pounding rain, Raegan pulled one hand out of her dry, warm pocket and extended it toward the nearest stone, laying her palm flat against its surface. She inhaled, closed her eyes and waited. To her surprise, nothing rose from her depths. With an exhale, Raegan opened her eyes, casting her gaze out wider. That didn't mean the door was not there.

She shook the rain from her fingers and returned her hand to the safety of the oilskin's pocket. The valley opened up in front of them, shrouded in damp blues and sodden grays, the grass browned and wilted with the approach of winter. Bracing herself against the cold, Raegan pulled both hands from the oilskin and began to walk around the blue-stone crown, her fingers searching for seams or inscriptions or doors that her eyes might not allow her to perceive.

Time stretched long and thin, though Raegan supposed it couldn't have been more than ten minutes when disappointment began to sing through her body. It was a song she knew well, the movements memorized by heart, all the sweeps and swells as familiar as her own voice. But it still stung. Another wild, fearless place, its teeth firmly sunk into the flesh of history and magic, but utterly lacking a door. Missing the vital way forward that might lead to the end of all this pain.

"Anything?" she asked the King over the rush of the rainstorm. He looked up from the stone he'd been examining, and hope spiked defiantly in Raegan's chest. But then he shook his head all the same.

"Again, I wish to spend more time," Oberon told her, bowing his body around hers to speak close to her ear so she could hear him over the wind. "But it feels unwise to linger."

"I'd really prefer you didn't get shot again," she replied. "Maybe I'm naïve. But if we find the door—even the general area, I think . . ."

"We will know," the King said, his voice firm and faraway at once.

"Yeah," Raegan replied with a nod that sent raindrops

cascading down the front of her hood, disappearing into the storm surrounding them. With the weak gray sky behind him, standing atop a broken bluestone crown, Oberon looked forlorn for a moment. She knew how much failure plagued him. They'd lost once, twice—would it be three times?

But then the moment shattered as the King turned, kneeling to brush his fingertips against a puddle of water that had gathered in the soft earth. In the blink of an eye, Rainer's deep green, scalloped ears emerged, and then the kelpie leapt from the puddle, coming to stand between Raegan and the King atop the rocky outcropping.

Rainer swung his head to either side, taking in Carn Goedog. "No door?" he wanted to know, his sonorous voice effortlessly rising above the thundering rain.

"If it were so simple," the King replied, moving toward the kelpie, "I imagine the Protectorate might have beaten us to it."

Oberon helped her onto Rainer's back. Disappointment held her tongue fast, and so she said nothing. As the King mounted behind Raegan, the kelpie went tense beneath her. Intuition prickled the back of her neck, and she turned in the direction of the wide valley, painted in rain.

"Ahh," Rainer said dryly, taking in the five sleek black Land Rovers that had appeared from nowhere and were barreling toward the outcropping. "Our friends join us at last."

"Rainer," Raegan said, leaning forward to lay her hand against the kelpie's neck. "Please. Let's just go. I can't stand to see Oberon hurt again."

The kelpie grumbled something Raegan couldn't make out, but he still turned deftly on his hindquarters, positioning himself to face the puddle from which he'd leapt into this plane of existence. Warily, Raegan eyed the Land

Rovers, not liking the progress they were making across the slippery, boggy ground, even if she and the King and the kelpie were moments from disappearing into the Rivers.

And then she watched something happen that she did not quite understand for a long moment. One of the Range Rovers faltered, like its wheels had caught in the mud. Reasonable, she thought, though her breath was caught fast in her chest. But no—a chasm was opening in the valley, the land splitting itself wide, a hungry maw.

She whipped around to look at Oberon, a confused mangle of emotions bursting to life inside her body.

"I did not ask the valley for anything," the King immediately told her, catching her eye from beneath the gloom of his hood.

Despite the thunder of the rain and the pounding of her own blood and the wretched, gnawing sound of wet earth consuming man-made metal, all the world fell silent to Raegan. The King had not bid the land of his making—the land his ancestors had imbued with their blood and their magic—to do anything at all.

And yet the valley that tumbled out at Carn Goedog's feet bucked and roiled, splitting open like a seam or a door. Not to Avalon, no. Half of Raegan winced, the other yelping in triumph, as a second Land Rover was dragged down into whatever dark, open mouth awaited it.

"The land is awakening," Rainer said, the kelpie sounding in absolute awe—a tone Raegan had almost never heard from him in all the years they'd known each other. "How could . . . It is *impossible*. The Protectorate bound the land centuries ago."

The land. There were a thousand stories of where the Twyleth Teg and the Tuatha de Danann of these lands had originated. There were Fair Folk of different kinds all across the globe, but the ones from these Isles were some of the most fabled. Tales were told of how they had long ago walked out of the sea or sailed from an unknown island in the west or arrived from another plane of existence altogether.

But those stories were human. The Fair Folk of this land had been here long before mortals were created, long before they shared their stories around the fire. The Fey were, in many ways, spirits of land made flesh by the gods, guardians of this green and abundant earth. It was why the Protectorate held the Isles so fiercely: to prevent that intimate connection, forged thousands of years ago, from being regained by the Unseelie Court. To stop the old sleeping things in this land from awakening and rattling their chains. The land, in the Protectorate's view, was a thing to be exploited, mined, colonized.

And perhaps Raegan was just being fanciful, gleaning too much from the few seconds of destruction she saw before Rainer plunged back into the Rivers headfirst.

Or perhaps the land, just like the Fey, just like the magical mortals, just like Alanna, had finally had enough. Perhaps that damp, wide mouth in the valley had also tasted revolution. And perhaps it wanted more.

CHAPTER TWENTY-FIVE

"I wish Emrys could give me back my memories of Hiraeth," Raegan said to Oberon, squeezing water from her hair with a towel from the bathroom. She hadn't even realized so much rain had snuck through the seams of her oilskin, but by the time she'd trudged up the ridiculously grand and increasingly annoying staircase at the old Temple to their quarters, she'd begun to shiver violently.

"Memory spells are difficult on their own," Oberon said from the foot of the bed, pulling his damp sweater over his head. "And Emrys removed your memories of Hiraeth *before* you asked Baba Yaga to place the Seal."

Raegan nodded, padding over to the roaring fireplace to leave her boots to dry on the hearth. "Two separate workings scrambling my brain. So even if he *wanted* to give them back . . ."

"It is unlikely they can be recovered," the King replied as she turned to face him. The dancing light of the fire deepened every dip and curve of his muscular chest and torso, now bare, black pants slung low on his hips. The rest of the world fell away in an instant.

"You'll have to remind me," Raegan said, desire throbbing unhelpfully between her legs; there had been no door at Carn Goedog, and she had a meeting with Alanna this evening, so it hardly seemed the time for such things. "Why Hiraeth? Wouldn't both Fey thrones being in the same place at the same time be an enormous security issue?"

If her mind were not so clouded with thoughts of his porcelain skin and full lips and impossibly sculpted body, she might have realized she'd answered her own question.

"That is precisely why," the King replied, one ink-dark eyebrow raised. "Hiraeth was the most secure location possible, especially considering that we were planning something neither of our advisors or courts would have been particularly supportive of."

Raegan freed her thick auburn curls from her braid, shaking them loose over her shoulders to dry. "Ah," she said, shimmying out of her damp jeans, which clung stubbornly to her skin. "I remember that, at least. We wanted to reunite the Fey courts."

From the other side of the bed, Oberon nodded, something dangerous and delicious playing on the beautifully inhuman planes of his face. His gaze slid down her body to where she was peeling denim from her generous thighs. "We have a meeting with a Protectorate informant in less than three hours," he murmured, but everything about him —the silvered rasp of his tone, the long-fingered hand clutching the bedpost too tightly—told a different story.

"Yeah," Raegan agreed, stepping out of her jeans and moving onto the bed, sitting on her knees as she faced him, clad in only her bra and underwear. "She might bring an army. We might die."

The King reached out, capturing her jaw in his powerful hand. Raegan shivered at his touch, fire roaring through her body. "Yes," he agreed, fingers tracing whisper-light down her neck. "It would be a terrible thing if I died without pleasuring you one last time."

And with that, Oberon was on her, pushing her onto the bed—though his hand cradled the back of her head, just in case she came too close to the headboard. A moan crept out of Raegan's mouth as she wrapped her legs around his hips, meeting his mouth with hers. He caged her between his arms—all coiled muscle and hard-wrought power—deepening the kiss, her name escaping his lips in a long, low groan.

"Shouldn't you be more careful with your shoulder?" Raegan asked breathlessly, tracing the bandage with her fingers. The visit from the healer had left him with only a patch of spiderweb gauze on his chest; the sling and heavier bandaging was gone.

He let out a sigh, and then without another word, pulled her against him and rolled. Raegan found herself on top, the High King of the Unseelie Court pinned beneath her on the quilt, his dark waves of hair spilling out onto the embroidered fabric. Despite the deep, rich want humming from the very center of her being, she took a moment to savor him. To memorize the beautiful mouth, the impossibly sharp jawline, the high cheekbones and ocean eyes, the heavy ridge of the collarbone and dusting of black silk across his chest.

And then Raegan could contain the desire no longer, so she brought her body to his, entangling her fingers in his hair. Oberon undid her bra so smoothly she didn't even feel it, and then his hands were roaming her bare back, sweeping around her ribcage to cup her breasts. She rolled her hips against his, all of her electrified and tender and wanting, wanting, *wanting*.

Raegan reached down to undo the closure of his pants at the same time he slid a few fingers beneath her underwear, finding where she was damp and throbbing. Her head fell back, a sigh slipping through her lips. Oberon sat up with a quick contraction of muscle, and she moaned from somewhere deep in her throat as his touch deepened at her center.

"God," she groaned, somehow still surprised at how quickly he ignited the kind of intense pleasure she'd rarely experienced with any other partner.

"Is it a god with his fingers inside you, pulling all these pretty sounds from your mouth?" Oberon asked dryly, his lips moving against her collarbone.

"No," Raegan panted, adding too many syllables to the word. When he brought his tongue to the tip of her breast in just the way she liked, she knew exactly what to say. "*Fuck,* Oberon."

He laughed softly, his body so close she could feel it rumble through his chest. "Better," he said, tilting his chin up to look at her. "I do not remember inviting a god into our bed. Or anyone, for that matter."

Raegan ground her hips into his hand, slipping her own fingers down the hard planes of his stomach and beneath his waistband. "You don't share well," she murmured against his mouth, finding his thick, wanting arousal a moment later. A strangled gasp left his lips—the Unseelie king, panting at her touch; what a thing to witness—and she kissed him, swallowing whatever he might have said next.

They tangled themselves in each other, all hungry mouths and ancient longing. When Oberon pinned her against the bed, the sensual heat of him so close to smothering her, Raegan didn't have the selflessness a second time to remind him of his shoulder. Pleasure sank its teeth into every inch of her, and there was little room left for any other thoughts.

Only how much she wanted him, how much she had

always wanted him, from that very first moment she saw him. Some invisible, undeniable thread was strung between the two of them, burning and endless. Raegan couldn't let him go even if she wanted to. Even if he asked. She dug her nails into his skin, and the King groaned her name. Then he rocked back, sliding out of the embrace of her thighs just enough to slip her underwear off her hips and down her legs.

"You belong to me," the faerie king said, his lips smoldering and insistent against the delicate skin of her thighs. He brought one hand back to her core, playing her like an instrument of flesh and bone. And Raegan sang for him—his name left her lips in a cry so loud she suddenly wondered if the room had silence or privacy wards. Too late now. She certainly wasn't going to stop what was happening to check.

"I belong to you," she agreed feverishly as his mouth drew closer to the apex of her legs. The King looked up, his dark eyes sliding to meet hers before he placed a soft, delicate kiss where she wanted it most. Her head tipped back of its own will as another wolfish sound tore itself from her lips. When she felt Oberon's tongue dive inside, Raegan's vision went white. Her want for him was all-consuming. She loved him with her entire being, so fiercely that she could barely understand it. The way she had been ripped from him a hundred times over only made every touch sweeter. Pleasure mounted deep inside her belly, growing more and more intense until she could barely stand it.

His fingertips digging into her hips, his mouth barely raised from her core, the King commanded Raegan to come for him. She did, shattering against him, knowing without a doubt that he was the only thing that could make her feel whole. Besides, Oberon could handle her jagged edges, didn't mind that she was more broken glass than woman.

He'd still run his tongue along her curves, even if it drew blood.

Moments dripped by, soft and slow as molasses. The only sound in the room was their breathing and the crackle of the fire. Raegan was flushed and still panting when she realized she wanted—*needed*—more of him. She curled deeper into his embrace, sliding her leg against the hard, long evidence of his arousal. Oberon released a breathy sigh into her hair, his arm tightening around her waist.

"Maybe you can remind me," Raegan murmured, lightly raking her nails down his chest, "of my first time?" He said nothing for a long second and she laughed, adding, "in Hiraeth, I mean."

"Oh," Oberon said, a smile that showed those long-lost dimples curving across his lips. "Thank you for clarifying. I would not have been able to fulfill the first request."

"Virginity is extremely overrated," Raegan replied, watching his every movement as he unfolded to sit up. "Just two people fumbling around and hoping for the best."

"I could not agree more," the King replied, slipping both of his large, powerful hands around her waist and dragging her to the edge of the bed. "You knew *exactly* what you were doing when we met that first time in Camelot. You did as Titania, too, when we were introduced at your coronation."

She gazed up at him, some distant part of her in complete disbelief that such an impossible, beautiful thing was hers—that she hadn't truly spoiled it, not yet. "Enough to get the Unseelie king to agree to go away in secret with the Seelie Court's High Lady to a hidden Fey city," Raegan teased. She reached forward, trailing a few fingers down his chest and the muscled planes of his stomach, and then lower, to the strong V of his hips, to where he was hard and wanting just below.

But before she could, the King slipped one arm around her waist and flipped her onto her stomach, bringing her ass to his hips. She felt the length of him slide against her skin and groaned, grabbing a handful of the quilt above her head.

"I could show you," Oberon said in a barely controlled rasp, his breath dancing across her neck, "what happened the last time we were here, if you ask nicely. Or if you beg. I would prefer, I think, if you begged."

Raegan smiled into the duvet, though the expression quickly morphed into something else when she felt Oberon's capable fingers move against the place she was most sensitive. "Please, Oberon," she moaned, grinding her hips into his hand. "*Fuck*. Please."

He did not reply, though with his other hand, he gathered her hair around his fingers at the nape of her neck, pulling ever so gently, just enough to set a wildfire spreading across her skin. How something as powerful and deadly as him, Raegan thought with a gasp, could know the *exact* pressure to exert on a creature so much more delicate and breakable . . .

"How badly do you desire me?" the King asked, the silken husk of his voice alone driving her close to madness. "Enough to betray your court?"

Despite Emrys's spell, despite the lingering effects of the Seal, despite the hundreds of years that separated her from that life, for a split second, Raegan thought she saw it —her body willingly, achingly, bent at the waist over a large writing desk, long golden hair gathered in the hand of the king who could destroy her entire world.

"Yes," she rasped, barely more than damp, desperate need. "*Yes*, Oberon."

"Say it," the King replied, gripping her hair tighter in exactly the way she wanted, crushing her hips with his.

"Say you want my cock so badly that you would betray your own throne."

The words tumbled out of her like she'd been born to say them, and all of time condensed for a moment, like everything was happening all at once and nothing had ever ended. And then the faerie king slid himself inside her and Raegan went limp with pleasure, save for her hands desperately clutching the sheets above her head.

"More," she begged, barely able to say anything else as another orgasm threatened to devour her entirely. "More. *Please*. Fuck me as hard as you can, Oberon."

He did what she asked, burying himself inside her. A feral cry thundered out of her chest as the feeling of his hand between her legs and the hard length of him deep within her took Raegan over the edge. She said his name again and again—like an incantation, like maybe if she repeated the sound of it enough, Fate would understand how badly she needed him. Oberon followed behind her, and if Raegan had uttered his name like it was a spell, then he said hers like it was the entire universe contained in only a few syllables.

He pulled her close, and they both tumbled onto the bed, Raegan's head coming to rest on his chest.

"Jesus fucking Christ," she panted. The King laughed—genuine, deep from his belly—in response, and she clung to that sound, a silvered bell in an autumn meadow.

The rest of the world forgotten, the lovers lounged in each other's arms, their breathing like the tides of two oceans meeting somewhere far from the shore, far from where anyone might know their names.

But that was the thing with the sea. Everything turned up in the shallows at some point, dragged in by the merciless tides.

Chapter Twenty-Six

An hour later, Raegan stood at the gates to Hiraeth —the last free Fey city—and hoped with every fiber of her being that the Protectorate-oathed shadewalker would not betray everything she held dear. At her side, Emrys paused before the mystifying structure of hawthorn branches and ancient metal, his body going completely still.

"What?" Raegan hissed, trying very hard not to sound frantic.

"Just this whole godsdamn thing," Emrys replied without looking at her, his gaze locked on the towering gates. She bit down on her tongue, eyes darting between the ex-Keeper and Hiraeth's doors, very much wishing the three of them hadn't agreed for Oberon to stay behind in the old Temple—a reasonable enough decision to not overwhelm Alanna, but Raegan personally would've felt a lot better with the King at her side, especially now.

But then Emrys reached forward and pulled open one of the twin gates as if it weighed nothing. He slipped through into the never-place at Hiraeth's edges. Raegan sucked in a deep breath and followed him into the shadowy chamber where the ancient, sentient city would decide Alanna's fate.

At the far end of the room, silhouetted by the gray light of open moorland, loomed two massive kelpies. Rainwater streamed down their murky green-gray coats, spilling out onto the worn stone floor beneath their hooves. Alanna stood between the two creatures, wrapped in waterproofed wool, a sword strapped to her back. When she pulled back her hood, Raegan saw that her locs were bound in an elegant twist at the nape of her neck and her spine was ramrod straight, shoulders defiant. Again, Raegan felt that tug toward the shadewalker, that preternatural sense she couldn't quite put into words.

Alanna's dark brown gaze met Raegan's, and something passed between the two women, something old and feral and lightning-charged. Raegan understood that they were not alone in Hiraeth's antechamber; she knew Emrys was busy conferring with the kelpies as he checked Alanna over for spellwork, toggling between lenses and spells on his delicate silver glasses. And yet for a long, haunted moment, Raegan felt as though the only thing that existed was the future they might create together—delicate, half-birthed, hung on nothing but a silken thread of hope above a yawning abyss.

Alanna glanced down, and the sensation evaporated. Emrys dismissed the kelpies gratefully and then led the shadewalker into Hiraeth's chamber, explaining it was the space itself that would make the final decision. He was careful not to name Hiraeth or even mention a city at all; it was safer for everyone involved if Alanna remained unaware.

Raegan held her breath as she felt the chamber constrict. As a witness this time, safe enough at the other end of the room, she distinctly felt something very much *alive* turn its all-seeing eyes to the tall wool-clad woman at the Keeper's side. To her surprise—and Emrys's, judging by his expression—Hiraeth did not deliberate long. One heartbeat, two, and then the room released all its tension, the exhale of a beast choosing different prey.

"What the hell was that, exactly?" Alanna wanted to know as Emrys guided her through the gates, her words aimed at Raegan.

"Some ridiculously old faerie magic," Raegan settled for, cocking her head, playing the irreverent mortal card. "Follow me," she added before anyone could have second thoughts about the madness of this situation—a faerie king awaiting a Protectorate turncoat, a real chance that the world could be upended and made anew.

Alanna showed no trepidation. She swept down the hallway at Raegan's side, politely clipping the length of her longer strides. The shadewalker was clearly on high alert, her eyes roving, body poised to react, but there was an ease about her that Raegan deeply envied. A sureness that she would be ready for whatever awaited her. Raegan had never been sure about anything for more than five seconds at a time.

Only when they reached the entrance to the Temple's great room did Alanna pause. "Here?" she asked, gesturing toward the tall, arching door carved out of black wood that gleamed in the low light.

"Yeah," Raegan said, expecting Alanna to hesitate, to ask more questions, to maybe make a threat about what would happen if they fucked her over. The woman did none of those things; she simply held Raegan's gaze for a long moment, tilted her chin up, and stepped through the door of her own accord.

Raegan was so surprised that she just stood there dumbly, the door swinging closed in her face. A few paces behind her, Emrys let out an amused sound. She glanced back to find him shaking his head, though he looked pleased.

"Gods, I hope we're right," he said, pushing his shoulder into the door but not opening it just yet. His gaze met Raegan's. "I like her, I think."

"Didn't know you could actually *like* mortals, Emrys," Raegan teased, following the Keeper as he moved over the threshold. The two of them spilled out into the hearth-lit great room of the ruined Temple. Any items that could possibly hold any information had been removed from the space, and Maelona had been settled into a small room on the other side of the kitchen.

The space was hushed and still. For a few harrowing seconds, Raegan was terrified that neither Alanna nor the King were there—that something had already gone terribly, horribly wrong. But then she told herself to breathe and cast her gaze around the room.

The King, in typical fashion, was leaning against the far wall, where the hallway led around to the grand staircase. Candlelight danced across his exquisite features. The long legs, the crossed arms, the powerful shoulders—all neutral, relaxed, but clearly ready to strike at any time. He said nothing, letting the silence wind itself tighter and tighter.

Alanna was just to Raegan's left. It looked like she'd only taken a step or two into the room before she spotted the Unseelie king awaiting her in the gloom. The shade-walker's body was straight as an arrow, her feet firmly planted. If not for the way her chest fluttered like a bird's wings, Raegan wouldn't have thought the woman was in any distress at all.

The King unfolded from the stone wall, a shadow detaching itself from the night, and prowled a few steps closer. Alanna flinched but held her ground. Good—Raegan knew that Oberon was testing the Protectorate woman as much as Alanna was surely testing them.

The silence strung itself tight as a noose. Raegan's heart thudded painfully against her throat. Each and every one of her veins suddenly felt overfilled, too thick with blood. And then, all at once, movement bled back into the room.

"Why," the King began, unfolding his arms, his voice deep, steady, dangerously alluring, "are you here, Protectorate-oathed?"

"Because," Alanna replied, taking a step toward the King—Raegan hid her smile of approval—and looking up to meet his eyes, "I want liberation."

The King, in that way of his, draped all of his attention over Alanna's shoulders. She did not crumble; she did not even tremble. And then he waited, pinning the shadewalker beneath the weight of his eternal gaze, waiting for her to fill the silence, to speak the words she'd left waiting at the back of her throat.

"And I want to be very clear," Alanna said, crossing her arms, refusing to look away from the King. "I will free this world of the Protectorate's chains with *or* without you, faerie king."

The quiet settled shadowed and heavy, like all the world had turned its many eyes to the stone-walled room. Perhaps in another Thread, a Fatesong would've trilled, long and low and looping.

Instead, the King smiled, a terrible, world-rending thing. "I think my court has been awaiting you for a very, *very* long time."

Hope flared hot and dangerous inside Raegan—the kind of mad, desperate hope that destroyed empires and shook despots from their thrones. A warm, strong hand suddenly grabbed hers, and it took Raegan more than a few skittering heartbeats to understand it was Emrys—the Keeper who had watched his Temple fall and built a haven from its ash. A thick wave of emotion uncurled in her throat, tears falling down her face like an unrelenting river. She squeezed Emrys's hand so hard she thought he might protest. But when Raegan glanced over, all she saw were the tears gathering on the Keeper's own lashes.

"Then should we sit," Alanna asked, breathless as she gestured toward the beeswax-crowned table beneath the leaded glass window, "and speak of revolution?"

～

A handful of hours was not enough to make a Protectorate shadewalker, Temple-less Keeper, exiled King, and deathless witch into full-fledged allies. Raegan had known that going in. But what they *were* able to agree on—it felt too grandiose to say it out loud, but it seemed like the kinds of things that changed the entire world.

Rain drummed on the window, an orchestra accented by the sound of clinking porcelain. The scents of Ceylon tea and bergamot wafted heavy and rich in the air, a tiny plume of woodsmoke sneaking beneath the Temple's front door. Raegan shifted in her seat, the antique chair creaking.

"So," Alanna began, reaching to refill her teacup. "Would the Unseelie Court be willing to include a reconstruction committee in the formal bargain, with seats split equally between Fey and humans? As well as the formation and continued support of an organization dedicated to balancing the disparity between our peoples?"

Raegan turned to her left, watching the King as he considered. He moved forward in a languid stretch, resting his elbows on the table. For a moment, he examined Alanna, no doubt weighing every word she'd spoken. And then, to her surprise, the King's gaze came to rest on Raegan.

"What do you think?" he wanted to know, eyes searching hers.

"I mean, that'd be necessary, I think," Raegan replied, gaze flicking to Alanna. "I don't know how we'd proceed without these sorts of things already in place. And whatever decisions we come to, the language of the bargains has to be plain. No wiles. No wordplay."

Alanna smirked, though it was good-natured. "Yeah, I mean, that's usually your thing anyway, isn't it? Plain language sounds great to me."

Oberon nodded, hooking one arm over the high back of his chair in a surprisingly casual gesture that highlighted the carved muscle just beneath his suit. "With that understood," he began, his attention falling back onto Alanna, "will we even get so far? Tell me, Alanna: will Protectorate-oathed humans and those mortals whose minds have been poisoned by propaganda ever be willing to work with my people?"

Emrys inhaled sharply across the table, and Raegan resisted the urge to look down at her hands. They'd been dancing around that question for a while, speaking instead of the world they might shape. But that world could never be birthed if there was no bridging the chasm the Protectorate had torn between mortals and Fey.

Alanna puffed up her cheeks with air and then blew it out slowly. The mannerism immediately—and probably irrationally—further endeared the shadewalker to Raegan.

"My cohort is ready for a coup," Alanna replied, tracing the gilded mouth of her teacup with one elegant finger. "And look, we know overthrowing the Protectorate's leadership is going to put us in a treacherous situation with a terrifying, ancient god that all of us were oathed to against our will." She paused, coiling the end of one loose loc, a darkly wry expression moving across her features.

"It's a death sentence," Raegan breathed, all at once understanding, the words coming out hoarse. The sorrow sitting deep in her marrow surged, boiling over into rage. How many people would have to die to rid the world of the Protectorate and the Timekeeper? Unbidden, her father's face appeared in her mind, and she bit down hard on the inside of her cheek. There was no room for more grief, more weight.

"Yeah," Alanna said, chewing on her lip as her eyes darted away. "Rough, innit? But gives us good strategic leeway. I can position the Unseelie Court's involvement as a way for us to . . . maybe not all die horrible deaths. My people are practical. And scared of death, like anyone else. But what about *your* people? That's some ancient grudges we're talking about."

"Yes," Emrys replied, turning to look at Alanna, who was seated at his left. "But you have to understand that both Fey courts have always had mortals among them. Most of us can count at least one human we've come to trust, or at least befriended. It's the Protectorate we hold our grudges against, not individual mortals. Besides, do not underestimate our people's loyalty to the King. Where he leads, we will follow."

Raegan sipped on her tea, finding it had gone cold. In her peripheral vision, she saw the King frown for a heartbeat. Alanna stared at him expectantly.

"The Seelie Court is in disarray," Oberon said, his eyes narrowing in thought. "My Court is powerful but small. There is some number of unaligned Fey hiding in plain sight among mortals, but I doubt any of them will participate in our plans. What I am saying, Alanna, is that I cannot promise you armies."

Alanna straightened as the rain increased its deluge outside, the roar of it deafening for a moment. "I don't want that kind of a war," she replied, sounding wise beyond her years and all the more burdened for it. "I want the singular kind of power that your people—*you*, specifically—can wield. Remember the Protectorate prophecy about you two returning to these lands I mentioned?" She paused, gesturing between Raegan and the King, one perfectly groomed eyebrow arched. "It's a doomsday prophecy."

Emrys turned sharply toward the shadewalker with rapt interest. Raegan watched him open his mouth to speak before closing it, setting his elbow onto the table and then his chin upon his palm, watching Alanna closely all the while.

"Go on," Oberon commanded. The air around the four of them sharpened with expectation and revelation.

Alanna exhaled, staring into the dark liquid swirling in her teacup. "The prophecy says you seek Avalon because there's some ancient weapon hidden there. And that you'll destroy the world with it."

The silence pulled taut as a bowstring. Raegan's heart hammered in her chest, palms gone clammy. The room seemed three times smaller than just a moment ago, the fire in the hearth burning too warm, the air filled with smoke.

"So," the shadewalker continued, raising her eyes from her teacup, examining the three ancient things seated around the table. "Are you *actually* looking for Avalon? I've asked a few times before, but none of you have given me a straight answer yet."

Raegan shot forward in her chair at the exact moment the King leaned back and drawled, "Yes." She whipped her head around to stare at him in disbelief. Across the table, Alanna was fighting to maintain composure. Raegan watched as she picked up a tiny, delicate teaspoon, her hands shaking around the fluted metal.

"For a weapon?" she asked, her eyes meeting the King's, her voice heavy and stilted. But not, Raegan realized all at once, with fear as she'd expected. No, the shadewalker's voice was laden with the treachery of hope.

"Yes," the King replied, holding Alanna's gaze with a simmering intensity.

"Would you say," Alanna asked, leaning forward to rest her elbows on the table, steepling her fingers as she gazed right back at the King as if he were not the avatar of every horror story she'd ever been told, "it's a weapon strong enough to destroy the world that we know? The world we seek to remake? Maybe even a weapon powerful enough to destroy that tweed-suited fuck of a god?"

Hope wrapped its green vines around Raegan then, too, infecting her with the same sweet poison that had led Alanna to do something as reckless and utterly unhinged as attempt to align with the Unseelie king.

"That is our hope," Oberon said, and he was smiling now, dangerous and impossibly beautiful. "We know not for certain, but the weapon we seek could indeed bring about doomsday for the Protectorate."

A feral grin overtook Alanna's features. "That's *exactly* what I was hoping you'd say."

Silence swept through the room again. Something not unlike awe unfolded in Raegan—that maybe after all this time, all this suffering and pain and darkness, the world had just been waiting for these four people to turn the key and unlock salvation.

"Not to ruin the moment," Emrys said as he rubbed his jaw, indeed ruining the moment, "but I want to be honest with you, Alanna. We don't know where Avalon is. And I'm not sure we're going to find it in time to make a difference."

Even though she knew it was true, Raegan still squeezed her eyes shut, wanting to savor that honeysuckle-sweet drop of hope upon her tongue.

Then the sudden sound of movement rang out behind her, sending the King to his feet. Alanna leapt from her chair a few seconds later, her sword already drawn by the time Raegan scrambled out of her seat and whirled around.

Of all things, there in the long shadow of evening within a ruined Temple, draped in a woolen blanket, stood Maelona Overhill. "Good news," said, her voice hoarse and wavering, her body unsteadily propped up against the stone wall. "I'm not dead. Also, I might know how to find Avalon."

Chapter Twenty-Seven

No one knew what to say, so instead, the four of them stared dumbly at the Protectorate woman who had crawled back from the grave.

Maelona scowled in response, eyes narrowing, one still shadowed by a bruise. "If someone gets me a chair," she grumbled, "I'll tell you all about it."

Oberon moved faster than any of them, so by the time Raegan even thought about reacting, he'd pulled his chair to the head of the table and held it out for Maelona. She gathered up the blanket draped around her shoulders and limped over, muttering a "thank you" under her breath. Just when she reached the high-backed antique chair, she looked up at the King.

Really looked at him.

"Are you— Fucking hell, it's *you*," Maelona sputtered, stumbling back a step. Raegan had more or less regained her senses by then and reached out to steady her aunt. "Is it all true?" Maelona wanted to know, her voice low now, gray-green eyes meeting Raegan's.

"That's a very vague question," Raegan replied slowly. "Why don't you sit down? You can barely stand."

Raegan gestured toward the open seat. Oberon had wisely stepped away, crossing his arms. With a huff, Maelona collapsed into the chair, her gaze fixed on the King standing in the dimness of the ruined Temple.

"Do you really know where Avalon is?" Raegan asked, pouring a cup of tea for her aunt, wondering if she should ask Emrys if there was any coffee. But Maelona didn't seem to mind, eagerly curling her hands around the warm teacup.

"Are you really a thousand fucking years old?" Maelona shot back, a harsh set of coughs curtailing the end of her sentence.

Raegan exhaled, sinking down to squat with her forearms on the table, as if she were talking to a small child. "Yeah, sort of," she settled on, her gaze flicking to the King's, whose expression was impassive.

"Hmph," Maelona said, reminding Raegan so much of Baba Yaga for a moment that her heart almost burst. "And he's . . ." She trailed off, narrowing her eyes at Oberon.

"The Unseelie king," he supplied, leaning back against the stone wall, the firelight making his features all the more inhuman.

"Oh, I know who you are," Maelona replied with a venom that surprised Raegan. Anxiety fluttered in her stomach. Alanna's fear and distrust of the King was one thing. But open hatred was another, and she knew she could only ask Oberon to tolerate so much. "We've met."

At that, Raegan nearly toppled over. Emrys twisted suddenly in his chair, looking at the King. Only Alanna didn't react, slowly sipping from her tea as if she were watching an afternoon play staged in a botanical garden.

Oberon examined Maelona, his lips parting slightly. And then eventually, he said one word. "Prague?"

"Prague," Maelona confirmed with a sneer, taking a huge—and likely searing—gulp of her tea. She wiped her mouth with the back of her hand and reached forward for the sugar bowl. "You almost killed me."

Oberon exhaled in an exhausted, long-suffering way Raegan recognized immediately. "I am sure it would have felt that way to you," he replied, his voice even. But Maelona only scoffed, digging a spoon deep into the sugar bowl. "In truth, I was trying to help."

"As fascinated as I am by the history between you two," Emrys said after a moment of silence, "you indicated you might know where Avalon lies. Is that true?"

Maelona's gaze briefly darted toward Alanna, who nodded, before drifting to meet Raegan's eyes. "There's a dossier of some kind. Despite being a pretty high-ranking field operative, I'm not even supposed to know about it."

"So then how *do* you know about it?" Raegan asked, folding her hands on the table. Emrys shifted in her peripheral vision; the King was barely more than a large shadow.

"Because when you suddenly reappeared after thirty years, I got pulled into a lot of meetings that I normally wouldn't have been involved in," Maelona replied, sitting back in her chair and pulling the woolen blanket tighter around her shoulders. Despite the warmth of the room, a shiver wracked her body. "I kept my ears and eyes open for Alanna. Anything that might be useful to what she's trying to do: explore allyship with the Fey in order to overthrow the Protectorate."

Raegan chewed on her bottom lip. So her aunt, despite being heavily entrenched in the Protectorate, was not necessarily bigoted against the Fair Folk—just Oberon. Just the person Raegan loved more than anyone else in the world and who had been very deep inside her only a few hours ago. Good. That was great.

"I would like to know more about this dossier," the King

said, prowling a step closer to the table. Maelona watched him carefully from the corner of her eyes.

"Very interested myself," Alanna said, settling her elbows on the table. "We didn't really get to discuss it yet."

"Didn't really have time to," Maelona replied, pausing for a few concerning coughs. "It came up in a few briefings when I was in the States looking for Raegan. But when I got back, all the beatings and interrogations sort of filled up my schedule."

"Do you have any idea of its purpose or why it was created?" Oberon asked, completely ignoring her aunt's dark humor, something in his tone that she couldn't place. His gaze was magnetic and consuming, pulling even Maelona into his orbit. Raegan studied him, her brow furrowing.

"I assume it's because of the prophecy," Maelona replied, all of her attention on the tall, inhuman being looming in front of her. "Keep possible locations heavily surveilled and guarded, or better yet, find Avalon, destroy the mother of the Fey, and take the weapon first."

Again, ferocity moved across Oberon's face. Unease stirred in Raegan's stomach; there was clearly something she didn't know, which was not her favorite feeling. She picked at her cuticles under the table, her gaze still on the King even when Maelona said something about feeling absolutely insane that she'd rather the Unseelie Court have the weapon than the Timekeeper.

And then, all at once, his eyes were on hers—haunted, hollowed, filled with that endless pain. She looked away, back toward Maelona, only so Alanna would not catch anything. But she took a few moments to refill her cup of tea, moving slowly while her mind raced.

When the realization hit her, Raegan had to disguise her reaction with a cough, as if she'd choked on her tea. Of course—Avalon. Fucking *Avalon*. Where the once and future king slumbered until England needed him to murder any and all living creatures who had made the mistake of being born with magic in their blood again. Where the man who had founded the Protectorate, orchestrated so much of Mordred's misery, launched a war against the Fey, and ordered Nyneve's execution slept peacefully, Excalibur forevermore clutched in his hands.

Because there wasn't a more secure prison on the entire planet than a goddess's realm that had long since faded into the perfect disguise: mere legend.

"Do you know where the dossier is?" Alanna was asking, sounding slightly breathless. "Because if Raegan and the King could get there, recover that weapon, then . . ."

"Then our little coup might stand a chance," Maelona said with a tight smile. "But unfortunately, it's kept in the Manor." She said the place name with no small degree of dread. Alanna's face fell in response, taking Raegan's hope with it.

"The Manor is basically impenetrable," Oberon said, moving to stand behind Raegan, his fingertips brushing her shoulder for a moment. She knew why he'd done it— because she'd been glancing at him too often and they needed to get through this meeting without raising alarms with Alanna. "I have tried more than once. I imagine this dossier is in the Undercroft, yes?"

"I'm uncomfortable with your knowledge of a highly secure Protectorate building," Maelona said with a narrow-eyed glare. "The only thing I know for sure is that there is a single copy and it's held in the Manor. The Undercroft would make the most sense, but . . . then I have no fucking idea how we would get our hands on it."

But they *had* to. Raegan fought to maintain her composure. Not just because the dossier could significantly shorten their search for Avalon but because she was suddenly very sure that the Protectorate wasn't just defending possible locations. They were searching, too. And not just to steal a weapon.

They wanted to *awaken* one. Arthur Pendragon, the Once and Future King, in particular. The thought made Raegan ill. Before she'd known him, Arthur had held ideals, or so people claimed. He'd given it all up in exchange for power. As if he'd needed more.

Her fingernails bit into her palms as her memories of King Arthur turned in their sour graves. He'd feasted while others starved. He'd barred Nyneve from healing peasants when the plague swept through, wanting her available at all times if any of his favored few developed so much as a cough. He'd used magic for his own gain while executing anyone he suspected of witchcraft with no trial, no chance to prove themselves innocent. He'd treated Guinevere— whom Nyneve had loved dearly—with such casual cruelty over not being able to produce an heir, even though he knew any issues with fertility lay squarely at his feet.

And like all shitty men, she remembered with rising rage, he'd found a way to make himself even more powerful: Excalibur. The blade was not just crafted—or altered, apparently—to kill the Fair Folk more easily. It also siphoned power from the Fey and god blood it spilled, granting its bearer magic and powers that were not meant to co-exist within one being. That's why the kelpies had tricked Bedwyr into putting his mortally wounded king and Excalibur onto the coracle with a tale about the Lady of the Lake, spun to match the story Merlin himself had concocted about the blade's origins. Bedwyr and the Protectorate had been trying to wake their liege ever since.

The heat of Oberon's touch brushing the back of her neck returned Raegan to her body. She clenched her jaw.

She must've drifted too far into her thoughts. God, she wanted to punch something and then sit in a quiet room with a notebook and untangle all of this shit. But everything would fall apart without Alanna, she reminded herself.

"No, that wouldn't work," the shadewalker was saying to Emrys with a frown, turning to look out the window. And then all at once, Alanna sat up very straight, her pretty eyes blown wide. "The Founder's Gala."

Maelona reacted immediately too, the hand reaching for her teacup stilling as her gaze shot to Alanna's. Raegan exchanged a look with Emrys, who just shrugged.

"Could you please elaborate?" Oberon asked from behind her. "I do not see how the existing wards at the Manor would be anything but thornier during an event with the Protectorate's most powerful."

"Oh, they will be," Alanna said, looking over Raegan to meet the King's gaze, a dangerous expression tugging at her full lips. "But the unfavored are always left working during the gala, tasked with sustaining a particularly nasty series of protection spells while the elite party. It's a long, taxing night that's left me unable to do magic for *days* afterward. I'm sure you wouldn't be surprised to hear the vast majority of people assigned to the holding wards are well within my little faction."

"Could that not all be by design, then?" the King asked, to which Emrys nodded vigorously. "Could your leaders not be counting on you to assume that they will be intoxicated and relaxed at this event, and use any failures with the warding as proof of your suspected treason?"

"I understand where you're coming from," Alanna said, tapping her fingertips on the tabletop as she paused in thought. "But you have to understand how oblivious the Protectorate is to threats from within."

"Really?" Raegan asked. "Because they seem . . . paranoid to me. I mean, they ordered Maelona to kill my dad for desertion."

"Only because Cormac had been a problem since he was about twelve, and they thought his motivation was opening the Gates," Maelona cut in, sounding a little stronger, her face less pale. "To acquire more magic. More power."

She paused, and Raegan shoved away any thought of her father at twelve, the tender place in his breastbone already yearning for what he could not have. Maelona spoke again, her expression wry and sour. "*That's* how they expect us to be corrupted. Bargains with faerie courts or the few gods left alive, offers from wealthy occultists hungry for the real shit. The Protectorate leadership would never expect something like this," she continued. "All they understand is power. And acquiring more of it. The idea that we would collectively band together to *give up* our power for the sake of the world would never cross their minds."

"If we betray our oath to the Protectorate," Alanna began before Raegan really had a chance to process everything Maelona had said, "the binding spell devours our magic. Not just the Timekeeper's boon—any shred of latent ability within us. Even if the Gates open, we'll never be able to do magic again."

Raegan's heart climbed into her throat as she looked between Alanna and her aunt. She hadn't known. She hadn't realized. She never would've thought they'd be willing to give up so much. With a long, shuddering inhale, she considered what it all meant.

And then, for the second time during this meeting, she had an ill-timed revelation. No wonder her father had been forced into bargaining with agents of the Timekeeper. The second he broke his oath by not offering Raegan up to the Protectorate as a baby, all his magic would be gone. How else would he have gotten them out of the country and successfully hidden away? Of course he wouldn't have been able to see the long game—that he was just delaying the inevitable, that whoever he thought might be his savior was just the Timekeeper in sheep's clothing.

Raegan curled her hands into fists beneath the table. All of her father's aching, that open wound he'd hidden beneath whimsical smiles—he had yearned for the same thing she always had, too. And he'd given it up completely for her.

She realized suddenly that she'd need to tell Maelona about Cormac. But for now, Raegan just cleared her throat. "And you're both willing . . ." She looked between Alanna and Maelona. The two exchanged glances and then nodded.

"The gala is Saturday evening. Tomorrow," Alanna said, sitting up straight and folding her hands on the table. "Let me speak with my collaborators. I might be able to get you in. But that's it. It would be on you to navigate the Manor's inner wards, whatever hellish defensive magic is lurking in the Undercroft, and grab the dossier."

Alanna paused, looking between them, her expression deadly. "And then, of course," she added, "you'd have to manage to get out alive without a bloody ounce of the King's magic. You understand that, right? *Any* Fey magic will trigger the wards, and then the Protectorate will have something they desperately want right in their hands—the Deathless Witch and the Unseelie king."

CHAPTER TWENTY-EIGHT

Raegan yanked open a battered steamer trunk that looked like it had survived at least three wars. "Blue velvet box, blue velvet box," she muttered under her breath, reminding herself to be gentle as she sorted through the contents of the trunk.

"Not here," she called, sitting back on her heels. Even though he was far off in the reading room, Emrys's loud curse was still very much audible.

"Nor here," Oberon announced from the other side of the aisle, closing the double doors on a clumsily painted hutch that could have been in any suburban mom's kitchen. He turned to look at her, one eyebrow raised.

"I know," Raegan said, holding up her hands in a peace gesture as she got to her feet. "If we can't find the glamour relics, we won't go."

Oberon opened his mouth to reply, but then Emrys's voice came drifting through the library, shouting directions for another location. "This way," the King said instead, turning on his heel and exiting the aisle. He took a sharp left out of the stacks, leading them deeper into the library. Rain pattered pleasantly on the greenhouse roof, and warm light spilled from the hanging lanterns bolted to the last bookshelf in each row. Emrys had lit a fire in the reading room, and they'd even brought a fresh pot of tea down from the kitchen with them. A perfectly cozy scene in which to desperately search for the one thing that might keep her and Oberon from dying during an ill-advised heist.

Letting out a sigh, the King turned to look at her with an arch, sideways glance. "We should not go at all," he said, slowing as he scanned the shelves on either side of them. "For Modron's sake, Raegan. Will we allow the Protectorate to lure us so easily to our doom? Or perhaps worse, are we willing to locate Avalon *for* them?"

"I know, I know," she muttered in the low light, grabbing the sleeve of his shirt and gesturing to the aisle he'd nearly walked by. "Here, I think."

"Thank you," he replied, stalking into the row of bookshelves and antique display cabinets. "Do you recall what he said?"

"L-142," Raegan replied, gesturing for Oberon to keep going. "Yeah, trust me. This whole thing seems like a really great set-up to imprison you and cut off my fucking head again or get us to do their work for them. Probably both. And I'm not ready for something like this, either. I know. I just—"

"You think it is worthwhile," Oberon began, giving her another sideways glance, one eyebrow raised again, "because of your aunt's involvement?"

"Not just that," Raegan huffed, stopping in front of a small metal cabinet. She turned the key that was already in the lock and began hunting, yet again, for a blue velvet box that stored two matching rings. "I think Alanna is being honest with us, too. I mean, did you pick up on anything?"

When the King didn't answer, Raegan looked over her shoulder. In the shadows of the stacks, his eyes were black hollows, the impossibly sharp points of his cheekbones and jaw like daggers beneath the pale skin.

"No," he admitted, though unhappily. "Not anything significant, at least. Truth and intention spellwork is difficult. You know this."

One of the conditions Alanna had for meeting them in the Temple was a bargain promising no harm to either party, including interfering spellwork. She had worded it quite well—at least, for a twenty-something-year-old human with little direct experience with the Fey. But Alanna was dealing with the Unseelie king, and it hadn't taken him long to find a way around the bargain to perform a series of workings intended to gauge her trustworthiness.

"I know," Raegan muttered, holding up a box. "What color is this?"

"Purple," Oberon replied immediately despite the low light.

"If she *thinks* she's telling the truth, the spell counts that as truth," Raegan sighed, putting the box back and pulling out another drawer. "If she doesn't *think* she intends harm, the spell counts that as neutral or positive intentions."

"It would be a clever plan," he murmured, stretching above her to check a top shelf that was well out of her reach. "It is easy to view her actions as incredible risks for a cause she believes in, but if all this was orchestrated by the Protectorate, those risks significantly decrease."

Raegan slammed the drawer with a huff. "Okay, but not really? Like, hello, being around you is a huge risk? No offense."

"The Protectorate, despite their preaching, know I do not kill indiscriminately," he said, pulling out a container before tucking it back into place. "Not typically, anyway."

She rolled her eyes, opening the last drawer. "Even if this *is* all a ruse, the motherfuckers are dumb enough to let us inside the Manor. I think we shouldn't waste that opportunity. Because Oberon, you and I both know that they're . . . they're . . ."

The words caught in Raegan's throat, old memories stirring up like a sudden sandstorm, clouding her vision and stinging her eyes.

"Trying to wake Arthur," he finished for her, stepping back from the cabinet. "Yes, I imagine they are." He met her gaze, and their shared pain stirred between them.

She opened her mouth and then closed it; there was little point in digging up the past. They'd both been there. They'd both been hurt time and time again by Arthur's cruelty, which had grown more ingrained each year. They'd both tried to pull him back from the brink. Arthur hadn't been born evil, but she'd always thought that only made everything worse. They'd both watched a city full of people they loved crumble into despair and war because of one man's choices.

"Why wouldn't Danu or whoever else is on Avalon just kill him? I mean, we're talking about the Mother of the goddamn Fair Folk," she demanded, closing the last drawer —no blue velvet box—and turning to face the King, just in time to see the bitter curve of his mouth.

"He amassed so much power through taking life with Excalibur," he replied, his tone empty. "He would need to be dispatched either by Excalibur itself or something very similar. Another hungry weapon, another blade that siphons the powers of its enemies to its bearer instead. But I do not think there is another."

"And the Fair Folk and gods can't wield Excalibur because it was created to destroy them," Raegan breathed. Then anger surged in her, white-hot. "Jesus fucking Christ."

And sure, she knew a mortal might be able to handle Excalibur like a regular sword, but they wouldn't have the power to actually *wield* it. To open the blade's hungry maw, to take all of Arthur's stolen power back through its tangled web of vicious enchantments.

"Unless you and I can return the faerie blade to its true nature," Oberon sighed. In the orange-hued lantern light, Raegan watched him pinch the bridge of his nose. "Come. Emrys just shouted the next location instead of using any of the multitude of sound projection workings at his disposal."

"Go easy on him," she suggested, following the King out of the row. "He's freaking out."

"I had not noticed," he replied, turning to look over his shoulder, one of those ink-dark eyebrows lifted again, a wry smile on his face. He paused, levity bleeding from his expression. "It does not help that the library's cataloging was Sylvionne's design, which means Emrys is currently searching through a card catalog handwritten by his dead lover."

Raegan paused as the weight of his words caught on her limbs, threatening to drag her down. Though Emrys had devoured her memories of Hiraeth, a series of short but rich images flickered through her mind: blackberry-hued ink, an elegant brown hand dripping in gold jewels, a melodic voice explaining the best way to apply kohl eyeliner.

"Should one of us go through the catalog instead?" she asked in a hushed voice, even though Emrys was far off, breaking into a jog to catch up with Oberon.

"No, I think not," he replied as she drew even with him, gesturing toward the aisle on the right. "It likely allows Emrys to feel close with Sylvionne, which may be needed after he invited the Protectorate into the home they once shared."

"*Sylvionne's murderers*," Oberon did not say. Raegan let out a long breath, her mind still tossing memories she shouldn't even possess onto her shores like the remnants of a shipwreck.

"Why do I feel like I remember him?" she asked, her throat raw, as Oberon led them deeper into the stacks.

At that, the King glanced back, worry creasing his brow in a way that made her heart pang. "You and Sylvionne became quite close in your short time here," he replied, slowing his pace as he began to scan the shelves. Raegan couldn't make out much this deep in the library, the lights dimmer with each row. "He cared for you, and you for him. Strong emotions can tamper with memory spells, no matter how proficient the practitioner. Emrys is the best memory-eater I know, but you feel more intensely than most."

The King came to a halt in front of a slim, towering cabinet. Raegan did her best to shove the unfolding memories of the Temple's murdered Oracle back behind whatever door they'd come tumbling out from. It felt like a dishonor to his memory, but she couldn't carry anything else. No more grief. No more fuel to the fires that already burned too hot in her ribcage.

Oberon ran long-fingered hands down the front of the cabinet in a way that made her irrationally jealous of a piece of furniture. He murmured something under his breath and then conjured a small sphere of light. Déjà vu threatened to devour Raegan—he had done this before, back in the archives when she knew nothing of herself. And another time, somewhere else . . . the memory slipped through her grasp like river water.

"Ahh," the King muttered, pressing a rectangular section of the cabinet, its face heavily carved with stylized berries. A small slot popped open.

Fascinated, Raegan leaned closer, finding a compartment lined with rich blue velvet. She exchanged glances with Oberon, her heart fluttering in her chest. There, nestled in the shimmering fabric, was a key—long and slender, its bow so ornate that Raegan couldn't make out the details in the low light. Oberon gently plucked the key from its resting place, revealing that it was strung on a loop of pale blue silk.

"If this isn't it, I will lose my mind," she announced. His shoulders shook with a short burst of laughter as he leaned in and unlocked the main compartment. A soft hiss and then two doors fell open, revealing a shallow cabinet shrouded in shadow. Oberon reached in, and time seemed to stand still.

Then he pulled his hands back out, and resting within his palms was a blue velvet box. Like the cabinet itself, it was elegant and slender with a domed lid. Oberon looked over at Raegan, who nodded excitedly. The box opened with only the gentlest touch from the King, revealing two silver rings resting on a bed of silk.

"Fuck," she breathed, leaning closer. Under the faerie light, Raegan could see the rings were indeed silver, but in the same way a chameleon would be silver while crawling in front of a sterling chalice. The edges of the rings bled into the pale silk of the ring box, even pulling in the golden warmth of the King's conjured light in a few places.

"I did not think these still existed," Oberon breathed, one hand hovering, though he did not touch the rings themselves. "Somehow I am not surprised Sylvionne stashed away old Fey relics for safekeeping. The rings are sleeping, and I am unsure if they can be awoken. But if they can—"

"—we might be able to do this." Raegan laughed with a wild-eyed glee. Physical glamours—like this set of rings— were impossible to create anymore with so little residual magic left in this half of the world. But that kind of working was the crème de la crème when it came to concealment and espionage.

Physical glamours subverted defensive spellwork because the wearer didn't actually alter their appearance the way most glamour magic worked. Instead, Raegan and Oberon would still look like themselves—nothing would actually change in their physical appearance—but anyone who looked at them would think they were someone else entirely. It was more mind-spellery than anything else, and that was one of the most difficult kinds of magic to detect. And best of all, only the most sensitively attuned wards would read physical glamours like these rings as *active* magic and trigger a response.

The air shifted, the back of her neck prickling as a shiver trailed down her spine. Oberon said something, his long fingers entangling with hers, but Raegan did not hear his words. Something obscured his voice, spiriting it away on bronze wings. All at once, the room filled to the brim with a golden thrum she'd never thought she'd hear again.

Despite the crushed Prophecy she'd seen with her own two eyes in the Oracle's grasp back in Philadelphia, a Fatesong looped through the half-sunken library. Oberon's hand tightened around hers. The hymn was ancient, orchestral, humming with so much want and ache that Raegan wondered if she had not composed the song herself in another life. That tender place in her chest opened wide as if she had never stitched it closed with shaking fingers.

Movement stirred in the corner of her eye, and her mind churned sluggishly, half-expecting Emrys to come barreling around a corner, his eyes wide and wild with the impossibility of it all. But instead, a paper-winged creature floated out of the gloom and down the aisle. It was neither luna moth nor griffin, not falcon nor pegasus, but some terrifyingly beautiful combination of them all. Raegan watched it sail on the looping and lonely notes of the Fatesong, the twin moons at the bottom of its wings blinking in and out of existence.

Her Threads quieted to a low hum as the paper beast landed on the velvet box in the King's hand, perching on the open lid. Its wings beat once, twice, three times. Then the creature floated off into the shadowed gloom of the library, taking the Fatesong with it and ending—as always—with the same haunting note on which it had begun.

CHAPTER TWENTY-NINE

"That is impossible," the King murmured, his head tilted back, the lovely expanse of his neck exposed as he searched the ceilings of the library, like he might find Fate Herself there, held aloft by dove wings.

"How fucking *dare* She," Raegan seethed a heartbeat later, that place in her chest empty now with the Fatesong gone—no, emp*tier* than before. As if each time Fate rang Her fingers along Raegan's threads, the primordial goddess stole something else.

Oberon swung around to face her. Just as Raegan met his eyes, footfalls at the mouth of the stacks rang out and she turned, finding Emrys standing there.

"Did I just hear a Fatesong?" the ex-Keeper shouted, a few card catalogs still clutched in his fist. "There's only dead Prophecies here, tucked away in the drowned halls. I do not understand how this is even—" Emrys cut himself off, his gaze falling on the blue velvet box in Oberon's hands, eyes going wide.

"Yes, you *did* hear a Fatesong," Raegan said, her voice

strangled as she remembered the cabinet in the abandoned chamber all at once. "Earlier, when I was researching, I found a cabinet with old Prophecies in it. And—and there was a luna moth, like the Prophecy back in Philadelphia." She paused, looking between Oberon and Emrys, bracing herself for their reactions. "I opened the cabinet because . . . because I'm a piece of shit, I guess, and they all came to life and, like . . . ate each other?"

In the low light of the library, both the King and the Keeper just stared at her, no expression on the ancient planes of their faces. So Raegan took a deep breath and kept going. "I closed and locked the cabinet, and it all stopped. I was coming to tell you, Emrys, but then Maelona was here."

The Keeper's eyes closed and he massaged his temple. "I am no Oracle. The drowned halls of the library can be . . . strange. And if Fate is toying with our Threads, I imagine She *wanted* you there." He shifted his weight, leaning against one of the heavy bookshelves, his metal frames slipping down his nose. "I don't understand it. But I don't think you did any harm. My Temple feels the same as always. And I know my Temple well."

Silence hung heavy in the towering, dark stacks where a Fatesong had just trilled. Raegan swallowed hard, glad that Emrys was not angry. She had no intention of keeping the cabinet and its creatures from him; with all the other bullshit she was busy dealing with, she'd honestly just forgotten until the damn thing had fluttered out in front of them.

"I do not believe we ever will understand," Oberon replied, his voice heavy with exhaustion. "Frankly, I have no interest in cabinets of dead Prophecies or Fate's winged things. Let us see if the glamour relics can be awoken. We will pay no mind to Her abuses."

Raegan set her jaw and, her hand still entwined with Oberon's, began to make her way to the mouth of the aisle.

He was right. What point was there in unwinding what this all meant? They had no Oracle, no Seer—they'd left all of that behind in Philadelphia for a quest to end this once and for all. What interest did Fate have in endings? She seemed only to enjoy bringing Raegan back from the grave, waiting just long enough in between each life to drive Oberon mad.

"For a million reasons," Emrys said as they reached the main aisle, "I wish Sylvionne were still here."

Raegan reached her free hand out to brush Emrys's shoulder. "I know. Me too. I remember . . . a little. More than I should."

Emrys examined her in the light of the aisle's lanterns, his deep, dark brown eyes glimmering. He opened his mouth and then closed it with a small shake of his head. "I won't entangle your memories further. But I am glad someone else remembers him. He deserves to be carried into the future."

Then the three of them made their way back to the reading room, shoulder-to-shoulder, yet again returning from the deeper, darker places with a sacred jewel in their hands that might just change everything. Maybe this *was* possible—maybe magic could be returned to the world, and maybe it could stitch the earth back together again. Raegan's heart swelled at the thought as she sat herself in a leather Chesterfield chair at the far end of a large table, watching Oberon's every move as he set the box down.

Across the gleaming surface, their gazes met. Emotion crowded her throat. And maybe one day, she and the faerie king could just *be*. She imagined looking into his eyes over the bursting jewels of their garden, over a candle-laden table surrounded by friends, across a meadow they walked every evening at dusk.

Anything but another battlefield, another graveyard of shattered hope.

Emrys muttered something, breaking the hush of rain and crackling hearth, toggling lenses on the side of his silver metal glasses. Raegan watched him closely, wondering exactly how the magic worked; there were no visible additions to the frames until Emrys touched his fingertips to metal. She supposed it didn't matter, but that was always how her brain operated—inquisitive, curious, always wanting to understand.

"Yes," the ex-Keeper said, the single word rich with triumph. "Yes, I think there is enough magic to awaken these relics." He pushed his glasses down his nose, looking at Raegan and then the King. "But whether that means we should send you two into the belly of the beast is another thing entirely."

"They want to wake Arthur, Emrys," Oberon replied. "I fear that was always the plan. Put down the initial rebellion, build the Gates, use our resistance as a reason to restrict the flow of magic further and further. Then, once the Gates were closed and all the residual magic gone from this half of the world, they would descend on Avalon to awaken their once and future king."

"And I doubt they'll just be interested in this side of the Gates," Raegan said as the realization dawned on her, sending dread creeping through her veins. "With Arthur, they could finally subdue the Otherlands in their entirety."

"Because Arthur was the only thing that came close to destroying the Unseelie Court," Emrys whispered, squeezing his eyes shut. "I mean, we knew this was possible."

"Yes," Oberon replied, placing both palms on the table and then leaning onto the dark, rich surface. "But we did not realize how quickly the residual magic would bleed out."

"I don't think we have a choice," Raegan said, chewing on her bottom lip. "How many sites on your list, Emrys?"

The ex-Keeper shifted uncomfortably, looking down at the glamour relics instead of at Raegan. "Thirty-three on the shortlist. Almost a hundred on the longlist."

Oberon heaved a sigh. "I can go to the Manor alone."

"How the hell would that even work?" Raegan spat, more harshly than she meant. "No magic, Oberon. Fuck, even your aura will have to be rolled up so tightly you'll hardly be able to breathe. How, exactly, are you going to get through the Undercroft's wardings without any Protectorate blood and no magic?"

"You are not oathed," the King reminded her, drawing himself up, his features all the more inhuman in the skittering light of the hearth. "The wards may read you as much of a stranger as me."

"But she's mortal," Emrys chimed in, though he immediately shrank under the intense look Oberon shot him. "The Overhills are an old Protectorate family, Oberon. Even unoathed, she may be able to slip by the wards with a little clever glamouring. But you? Alanna will get you in, and then what?"

Raegan watched as Oberon's jaw clenched, muscles jumping beneath his moonlight skin. His hands gripped the edges of the table too hard, powerful tendons flexing. "I will continue to think it over. I have not made a final decision."

A short rush of fury burned through Raegan, and she slammed an open palm on the table, loud enough to make Emrys jump. "Why do you get the final decision? It's about *me*."

His shadowed, heavy gaze landed on her then, the long column of his body angling toward her. "I have told you before, Overhill," the King snarled, as if they were not lovers, as if she had imagined everything since that night at Gossamer, "a Fey court is *not* a democracy."

She shot out of her chair, a few steps bringing her directly in front of him. The King towered over her, a wall of muscle and ancient power. "And I'm not a member of your fucking court, Oberon! I don't know why I have to keep telling you that. You're not my king. I do not bow to you."

He closed the meager distance between them, a storm brewing on the planes of his face. But Raegan wasn't afraid of him—she never had been. Wasn't that the reason they'd ended up tumbling into each other's beds in the first place? Because the Druid girl sent to Camelot wasn't afraid of the king's bastard son with a heavy Prophecy on his shoulders, who turned out to be something much worse—an embedded Unseelie changeling?

"Why do you *insist* on endangering yourself?" Oberon demanded, his eyes narrowing, though his words were husky around the edges now, soft and raw.

"Why do you think your grief is more important than my agency?" Raegan asked in return, her hands balling into fists at her sides. Anger snaked through her, prodding at the locks of its cage. At that, the King flinched, his weight shifting away from her, eyes dropping to the boxed rings.

"May I offer an observation?" Emrys asked meekly from the other side of the table.

"No," Raegan and Oberon snapped at the same time. The King dragged a hand through his hair and then pinched the bridge of his nose, eyes closing briefly. Raegan stepped away, straightening the hem of her sweater, the anger cooling inside her. Emotions were bound to run high due to the intensity of their situation, she reminded herself. He wasn't trying to curtail her autonomy; he just loved her more than anyone else ever had, and sometimes that scared the shit out of Raegan.

"I will work on awakening the relics," Oberon said, reaching a hand out, his fingertips brushing the rings for the first time. She palpably felt the relics pulse in return, like an old thing rolling over in its grave to rise again—a sensation she was well familiar with. A glance at Emrys told her that the ex-Keeper felt the same call-and-response of the King's magic to the relics. Raegan let out a long breath.

"I'll see if any couturiers are available last-minute," Emrys said, stuffing his hands into the pockets of his chore jacket. "I assume neither of you have evening wear? Maelona said the Founders' Gala is black-tie."

Across the table, Oberon shook his head, the weight of his attention on the slim filigree rings.

Raegan glanced at Emrys. "Nothing black-tie, no. I'm assuming we should limit our glamours beyond the relics, right?"

"Thank you, Emrys," Oberon replied without looking up. "Raegan is correct. Appropriate attire would be helpful, as our appearance should be as unaltered as possible. The relics work best on their own without interference."

For a moment, anger nipped at Raegan's insides—was he trying to make some kind of a sly comment about not needing her for the gala? She opened her mouth and then closed it. She could not push him away by twisting his words and assuming ill intent. She didn't *want* to, not actively—but her survival mechanisms were strange things with a life and bite of their own.

"Emrys," the King added, glancing up. "Could I borrow your glasses for a moment before you go?" The Keeper nodded, handing Oberon the slim metal frames, briefly explaining how they worked. Raegan grasped at the information, her curiosity sparking, but the second the glasses settled on the King's face, all intelligent thoughts went out of her body. Fuck. Why did he look so *good* in his casual suit, no waistcoat, the white shirt unbuttoned at the collar, and those glasses perched on the end of his aquiline nose?

She chewed on the inside of her cheek. Didn't he realize she didn't want to leave him either? That every time she tangled her body with his, she knew she was only cutting deeper and deeper into his wound? The fierceness with which she desired him was a double-edged sword. Every moment they were together, Raegan was asking the King to love something he knew he was going to lose.

Oberon handed the glasses over the table with a few words of thanks, and then Emrys disappeared down the long hallway that connected the library to the great room and living quarters. A heavy silence descended, squeezing her insides.

"I apologize. I do not seek to curtail your autonomy," the King said just when Raegan felt like she might burst. He looked up from the rings, both palms flat on the table, his hips hinged over the edge. Hunger stirred low in Raegan's belly as she took in the way his suit jacket strained against his broad shoulders.

"I know," she replied in a low, raw whisper. "I'm sorry for saying that."

One of his powerful shoulders moved in a shrug at the same time a smile ghosted his lips. "No need. I admit there is a part of me that enjoys it when you are angry with me."

She leaned away from the table with a grin, crossing her arms. "Is that so?"

"Not when it is serious, of course," the King clarified. Raegan was delighted to see a pale blush blossom on his face. "Only in these minor disagreements. Few dare to argue with me, and there is a certain . . . thrill, I suppose."

"That's good," Raegan said, uncrossing her arms and

prowling toward Oberon, chin tilted up to meet his eyes. "Because I'm going to do whatever I want. I don't care what you say. You're not my king."

She raised a hand and flattened her palm on his chest, giving what would've been a solid push to anyone else, but the King did not budge at all. He did, however, gaze down at her, those oceanic eyes all-consuming, the hard lines of his body gone predatory, his breathing rapid.

"I'm not afraid of you," Raegan whispered, curling her fingers into the front of his shirt, holding his gaze all the while. "In fact, you can be as terrifying as you want. I'm not going anywhere."

The words barely felt like they had finished leaving her mouth when the King seized her in his hungry grasp. In one fluid movement, he pulled Raegan against him and lifted her onto the worktable. Woodsmoke and autumn rain surrounded her as desire beat a drum between her legs, faster and faster.

"Still not afraid of you," she breathed, even as she felt the might of his magnificent body, even as his large hands took the back of her sweater in fistfuls.

"No," the King echoed, breathless, "you are not." And then he swooped low and kissed her, the taste of him like folklore and revenge. She wrapped her thighs around his hips, welcoming the way he pressed her into the table, the weight of him sending damp want howling through her core. He kissed her like it might save them both, like he wanted to devour her whole, like his love could hold off her always-waiting grave.

Raegan wound her fingers into his hair, pulling him closer. The hard evidence of his own desire pressed against the apex of her legs, and she let out a strangled moan.

"Fate can sing whatever songs She wishes," the King

murmured, his mouth trailing down her neck, the heat of his words like a flame against her skin. "You are mine."

"Yes," Raegan gasped as he slid one hand into her hair, his palm cupping her skull, his other arm wrapped around her hips. Then the King dragged her closer, her thighs opening wider for him of their own accord.

In the hush of a forgotten library where a Prophecy had awoken from its grave, he leaned close, a promise falling from his tongue. "And I am yours forevermore, my love."

CHAPTER THIRTY

Raegan sucked in a breath, desperately trying to avoid the cold pinch of steel. She felt like she'd been trapped here for hours, every muscle in her body screaming for release. Her arms trembled from being held at an uncomfortable angle, hovering above her sides like broken wings.

"Okay," the couturier, Monette, said as she stepped back, running her critical gaze over Raegan. "That'll do it. Take a look and tell me what you think."

With a sigh of relief, Raegan let her arms fall against her sides and turned toward the full-length mirror on the opposite wall.

"Well, fuck me," she sputtered, her mouth falling open. The gown that the Fey seamstress had just finished pinning was *glorious*—almost too beautiful for its purpose. She ran her hands across the sumptuous fabric, wishing she could be wearing such a heart-stopping creation to attend a faerie fete instead of infiltrating the Protectorate's Founders Gala.

Whisper-light storm-gray silk swept across her body, gathering in a tauntingly low neckline before looping over her shoulders, providing plenty of support for her full bust.

A dramatic slit displayed one generous thigh, the rest of the long skirt fluttering to the floor in artfully uneven pieces. An ethereal train floated down from her waist, soft as mist. Across the bodice, just under her bust, tiny blood-red jewels dripped down irregularly like a bloodstain. The gown was terrifyingly and impossibly beautiful.

"Do you like it?" the couturier inquired, rearranging the pieces of silk that made up the short train.

"It's incredible," Raegan breathed, turning slightly to take in the low dip of the garment's back. Leave it to the Fey to figure out how to make a dress with a low back *and* deep neckline that somehow still provided enough internal support for a large bust. "You're extraordinarily talented."

The Fey couturier beamed in response. "I wish I could know more about my very beautiful mystery client," Monette said with a sly smile, coming to stand beside Raegan to consider the dress in the mirror. "But you are hardly the first to request such discretion. So alas, I shall keep quiet about one of the most lovely things I've ever made."

Monette had meant the words playfully, but a pang of guilt still sounded in Raegan's chest. Much like Oberon, she hated hiding from the residents of Hiraeth, even if it was for their own good. She hated the short, sparse missives from Philadelphia that grew more alarming every day. The Protectorate's siege there had only intensified in an attempt to draw the King out of hiding. The Unseelie Court had expected that eventuality and prepared for it, but Raegan hated knowing her friends and comrades were fighting for their lives across the ocean while she languished in relative safety.

Well, at least for the moment.

She turned, pleased with how easy the dress was to move in, as the couturier spoke an incantation to finalize the stitching on the garment. In just a few hours, she and the King would attempt to steal the dossier on Avalon. Trying to keep her suddenly clammy palms away from the silk, Raegan thanked the designer again and dismissed her. Downstairs, Emrys would pay Monette and then devour her memory.

Raegan allowed herself another moment to take in the way the dress hugged her curves like a lover. She hoped with all her heart that it was not the garment she'd die in.

~

An hour later, thoughts of death still circled her like buzzards. Raegan shifted uncomfortably, rolling her shoulders as she watched her aunt take a seat at the Temple's heavy wood table. She probably should've told Maelona about Cormac already. But when had there been a moment to tell Maelona that any hope she might secretly hold for Cormac was wasted? That Raegan had watched her father dissolve into nothing, the Timekeeper devouring everything he'd ever been? As if he'd never been anything but a corpse ripe for harvesting?

"Your last meal, as requested," Emrys said, jarring Raegan from her thoughts as he slid a beautifully prepared bowl of ramen in front of her. But she just stared blankly, her mouth not quite able to form words. "I suppose that was funnier when you weren't less than an hour from leaving for the Manor."

"Something like that," Raegan replied, picking up a chopstick and poking at a thin slice of beef. "Thank you, Emrys. Seriously. I really appreciate it."

Maelona leaned closer, sniffing like a bloodhound. "Well, if you can't eat it, I certainly will."

"No nerves around your last living relative possibly

being murdered tonight?" Raegan asked, looking up at her aunt, who frowned.

"When you put it like that," Maelona began, twisting her mouth, "I suppose my appetite is a bit shit, too."

The side door to the Temple opened, and the King appeared with Alanna at his side. They were so clearly not comfortable with each other, Alanna looking like she was walking beside an enormous predator who hadn't eaten her yet for reasons she could not begin to comprehend, the King trying too hard to hide his inhumanity, lest it send her running. Raegan gave a snort. It was kind of amusing, actually.

"Alright," Alanna said by way of greeting, coming to stand at the head of the table. She gently pushed aside a plate piled high with bean sprouts and artfully sliced pickled eggs. Maelona snatched up the bowl of ramen Emrys had wordlessly handed her. Then Alanna unfurled a large piece of parchment on the table. Raegan leaned closer, peering at the charcoal lines in the dancing candlelight.

"There are no blueprints of the Manor, for obvious reasons," Alanna said, using a candlestick to pin the sketch down. "So this is what Maelona and I came up with from memory."

Alanna—with interjections from Maelona—walked them through the single entry point for the gala, as well as all the security measures. None of that was particularly of concern. If the Unseelie king and the Queen of the Hill simply wanted to slip into a Protectorate gala to fuck around, it wouldn't be hard, particularly with Alanna's help. But getting into the Undercroft and the secure vaults was another thing entirely.

"Besides the general gist, I can't tell you a ton about it," Alanna said, frowning. "Our wards are complicated. Actually, probably not that different from your own—protective spells added to again and again over the ages to the point they're nearly sentient. They will sense Raegan's bloodline and the intention of any magical acts. You'll need to be clever. But that's all I can tell you."

"I wish I could say I knew much more," Maelona added woefully. "But it's above my paygrade. I'm a special ops soldier, essentially. Commanders tell me to jump, and I ask how high. That's it. Alanna's right about the wards, though. And they're more intense in the Undercroft."

Alanna gestured at a section of harrowingly long and circular corridors that burrowed deep into the earth below the Manor. "There's checkpoints all throughout. Sentient spellwork, glamour-eaters, gods only know what else. My oath would prevent me from going past the research archives—that's on level two—and I think Maelona's would halt her somewhere around level six. You need to get to the very bottom floor of the Underbelly. Level twelve."

"Great," Raegan replied, her mouth dry, the whole thing much more dizzying when sketched out in charcoal and paper, taking up nearly the entire surface of a massive table.

"I still don't think you should go," Maelona said, looking at Raegan.

"On that, we agree," Oberon replied without hesitation. Her aunt and the King exchanged glances of pleasant surprise, naturally bonding over telling Raegan what to do, of all things.

"Too bad," she said through gritted teeth. "Not even the Unseelie king is getting through all of this shit with zero magic. And I'll be able to do *some* magic in there."

Beside her, Oberon let out a long sigh but did not refute her statement.

"My people are in place and know to expect you, though of course, most are unaware of the details," Alanna said, stepping back from the table and clasping her hands behind her back. She looked formidable, dangerous, but in the shifting beeswax light, Raegan could see the worry on her too-young brow. "Maelona will be on standby, hidden in the wooded parkland across from the Manor, just in case everything goes to hell. She can help you navigate the compound if it comes to it, but ideally, you'll leave with the kelpies' help through the Rivers. You'll have a few minutes —at most—after triggering the wards to get out. Use them wisely."

The five people bound together by a shared audacity that they might be capable of killing a god sat silently around the table. Raegan's blood thudded in her veins. She picked up her spoon and tried to shovel some broth into her mouth, but her stomach revolted.

"I have attempted to follow much more foolish plans before," Oberon said, looking over the parchment sketch.

"Yeah, well, not all of us were made by goddesses and the night sky or whatever," Maelona grumbled, poking at her ramen. "Mortals are a bit more fragile."

Oberon flinched and then tried to hide his reaction by straightening the collar of his shirt. But Raegan caught it and her heart clenched. He knew precisely how fragile mortals were. He'd watched her die more times than she wanted to count. He knew *exactly* what he was risking. The King looked at Maelona and then Alanna. Raegan recognized that feral, predatory glint in his eyes and opened her mouth to speak, but it was too late.

"Yes, mortals *are* more fragile. Understand that if Raegan is harmed tonight due to either of your actions," the Unseelie king said softly, a palpable chill taking root in the air, "I will tear the flesh from your bones and feed you to the kelpies."

Maelona froze, her jaw grinding as she glanced at

Alanna, who had also stiffened. There was a part of Raegan that wanted to placate or make a joke out of Oberon's fierceness, but she couldn't deny the heat unspooling low in her belly. She let out a long, shuddering breath and crossed her legs.

"Trust me, I don't want to see Raegan hurt any more than I want to be fed to kelpies," Alanna said, all business, ignoring the tense hush that had settled over the table. And then she softened, her eyes meeting Raegan's. "We can pull this off. And when we do, we'll have a map to a weapon that can finally take the Timekeeper from his unearned throne."

Raegan smiled and gave Alanna a firm nod, but when the shadewalker turned to leave to make her own preparations, she felt a shred of relief. They needed Alanna's assurance and steadfast fierceness that the world could be changed. But the four left at the table—Emrys, Maelona, Oberon, and her—understood too much of the toll that hope took from her victims. To imagine a newer, better world was a beautiful thing. To have it taken away before it even had a chance to bloom was a gut wound that never quite stopped bleeding.

But time was running out, magic was dying, and there were no better options. So Raegan forced some bok choy and noodles into her mouth before getting to her feet.

"I'm going to get dressed," she said. As she expected, the King stood beside her, forever the shadow to her defiant flame.

"I should as well," he said, slipping his hand around hers. They left Emrys and Maelona at the table and headed for their chambers. A charged silence hung between them as they climbed the stairs, Raegan's mouth dry and her heart racing all the while. The anticipation was the worst part, she repeated to herself. Soon, her mind would be dedicated to real-time calculations, split-second decisions, and nothing else.

But for now, as they entered their quarters, the nature of what Raegan and the King were about to do strung the air tight around them like a spiderweb. The gorgeous room—all dark, gleaming wood, rich velvets, and wide windows—suddenly felt like a coffin as they changed into their gala attire. For a moment, she fussed with her curls as the King awaited her silently, the blue velvet box clasped in one hand.

"I'm ready," Raegan finally said, though she had never felt less ready for anything in her life.

Oberon turned toward her, the moonlight breaking through Hiraeth's clouds dipping him in silver. He was statuesque in an all-black tuxedo, the tailoring of the garment absolute perfection.

"You look magnificent," Raegan breathed, her heart racing. Oberon offered her a slight smile, the gentlest curve of his shapely mouth.

"And you are a vision," he murmured, one hand reaching out to trace her jaw.

"How do these physical glamours work?" Raegan asked instead of saying that maybe they should just disappear and leave the world-saving to someone else for a change.

"Quite well, actually," Oberon replied, lifting the domed lid. He'd been adding to the existing spellwork and testing the rings most of the morning while Raegan attempted to get a few hours of sleep. "They are designed to function as a pair, which is fascinating. It is best if I recite the activation rite for yours and vice versa.'

"Sure," Raegan said with a shrug, not really grasping exactly what he meant. So she just took another step toward him, clenching her jaw and trying to force her heart to beat slower, calmer, to find that river deep within.

They stood facing each other, heads bowed over the domed box, as Oberon told her the rite. It was short and sweet, though she had to repeat the Old Feyrish a few times to make sure she had the pronunciation correct. Then the King went first, reaching for her hand as he recited the words.

And all at once, Raegan realized—here she stood in the most beautiful dress she'd ever worn, Oberon before her in a garment that showed off all his sharp, inhuman angles instead of hiding them away, speaking ancient words and slipping rings onto each other's fingers. A violent flood of sorrow roared through her chest. They'd tried to marry, more than once, but Fate always called Raegan back to the soil before the words could be exchanged, the vows made.

Oberon slid the ring onto her finger—not her left hand, no, but it hardly fucking mattered—and shifted away slightly. She choked on the sorrow, on the ache, her dress suddenly weighing a thousand pounds, as if the silk had been spun from her own heavy grief. Raegan forced herself to look up at him. The King's expression softened the moment he saw the tears brimming on her lashes.

"Oh," he murmured, so much feeling in a single syllable. "Nyneve. I—I did not think—"

"It's fine," she replied in a hoarse whisper, patting the tears away, not wanting to smear her eyeliner. "Let's just finish."

Raegan reached into the blue velvet box—fuck Fate and the gods, it was literally borrowed and blue—and palmed the second ring. She said the incantation, doing her best to remove the actions from any kind of meaning. Just words, just a ring, just a glamour. Not another stinging reminder of what they couldn't have.

When she'd finished, Raegan shrank away from Oberon, stumbling back to sit on the edge of the bed. She forced herself to breathe. "How does it look?" she asked, biting down on her tongue as soon as she finished speaking.

The King only sighed. Silence overtook the room, thick and oppressive. And then, finally: "Excellent. Emrys will be the final test. He knows our actual identities, of course, and the diplomats' identities we have chosen to borrow."

"Okay," Raegan said, misery latching hooks into her chest. She couldn't breathe. She couldn't see. She couldn't think. "I just need a minute. I'm sorry. I know that's ridiculous."

"It is not," Oberon murmured, suddenly kneeling before her, the heat of him washing over her like the first rays of spring sun after an endless winter. "Not at all." He took her hand in his, bringing it to his chest, where he cradled her palm like a wounded bird.

She looked at him through watery eyes, and her heart only broke a little more. She'd wormed her way into his heart and created an empty space he could never fill. The Unseelie Court would be so much less compromised, their King more focused, if only all those years ago she hadn't fallen in love with someone who did not think he could be loved.

And yet, Raegan was a selfish creature as much as Oberon was a monstrous one, so the only words that came out of her mouth clung to a future that would never come to pass. "If we survive this—all of it, I mean, not just tonight— if the Gates fall and we live to see that world, would you, High King of the Unseelie Court, do me the honor of marrying me?"

She wanted to take the words back as soon as she said them. God, was there no end to her cruelty? Raegan stuttered through her tears, trying to walk back what she'd said, but the King only held her gaze. Then he let go of her hand and reached up to trace his fingertips over her mouth. The all-consuming sensation of his touch distracted her, and the words died in her throat.

"My love," Oberon murmured, studying her, "do you so fervently wish to make a widower of me?"

A sob gathered up like a storm in Raegan's chest, but she forced it down. Her hands shook. "No. Gods, *no*, Oberon, that's—"

"Every part of me aches to say yes," the King said, that inhuman ferocity prowling onto his features. "But you know the weight of a Fey union. I—I do not know if I am strong enough to endure losing that, Raegan."

"Right," she stuttered, her face bright red and hot as a flame, looking down at her hands. "I know. Fuck, I know. I know it's a bond for life, and I know how horribly it affects the Fair Folk when their spouse dies."

She absolutely did, all of her knowledge deciding just now to release itself from the recesses of her mind. Commitments among the Fey were not unusual, but marriage was. The ceremony was intense and binding for the Fair Folk— much more than a pretty dress and nice dinner and a signed piece of paper. Raegan exhaled, digging her nails into her palms as she forced herself to look up and meet the King's gaze again.

"That was fucking stupid of me. I'm sorry. I didn't— I just mean that I love you with everything that I am."

"I appreciate the sentiment," Oberon murmured, one eyebrow arched. "And I return it threefold. You know that, yes? That all of me belongs to you. That I was not even created with the capacity to love, and yet I love you eternally."

"I know," Raegan said, not managing to raise her voice above a whisper. She roughly shoved tears off her cheeks and moved to do the same on the other side before the King caught her wrist. With his free hand, he pulled an inky black handkerchief from his waistcoat pocket and dabbed her tears away in impossibly, absurdly gentle movements. She shivered.

"I'm fine," she said a few moments later, straightening. "We need to go."

"We do," Oberon replied, fingertips brushing the underside of her jaw. "Let your sorrow sharpen you. Let it feed that flame in your belly."

His words danced like a lightning storm across her skin, and Raegan pushed herself to stand. "You're right," she said, as if she were not little more than broken pieces. "If they won't grant me peace, then I'll take my revenge."

CHAPTER THIRTY-ONE

With each heavy, anxious thud of her heart, Raegan reminded herself of the glamours. She and Oberon had made it through the first two checkpoints into the Protectorate compound. In all likelihood, they'd make it through the third. After all, Emrys hadn't recognized them when they came into the great room, even though he'd been expecting the glamours and they still very much looked like themselves. None of that mysterious toggling of his lenses revealed anything—except that the latent magic in the rings had been fully awoken and bent to Oberon's will.

But fuck, every glance from the people milling about sent a spike of fear through Raegan's chest. She bit down on her tongue, wrapping the King's overcoat tighter around her body. November's approach had turned evenings into cold, shivering things, but her leather jacket looked absurd with the dress. A fine wool overcoat about four sizes too large draped over her shoulders, clearly belonging to the beautiful man at her side—now *that* was more acceptable.

"I was having a little more fun last time we dressed up," Raegan murmured, knowing the King's sharp hearing would catch her words. He chuckled and looked at her sideways, something ravenous in his gaze. For a moment, it transported her back to that evening at Gossamer, which felt as though it could've been another life entirely.

"I must agree," Oberon replied dryly, taking a few lazy, long-legged steps forward as the queue of gala attendees moved. The gravel crunched under his footfall, pulling Raegan from her memories.

She frowned, staring down at her feet. "Why do rich people always have gravel?" she wondered under her breath.

"There are many things I do not understand about these people," he replied, his voice right in her ear, tone edged in something hard.

She didn't either. The compound was located in the Lake District, a breathtakingly gorgeous area of England. But as she peered around the queue and took in what she could see of the estate, Raegan noticed immediately that the natural beauty of the land was hardly emphasized, let alone respected.

Beyond the courtyard they were standing in, the Manor awaited like a camouflaged beast, crouched in the shadow of the mountain behind it. The massive stone building hummed in a way that made her head hurt. The wards, the battle magic surely embedded into the walls and grounds—all of it stolen and twisted. Barely magic at all, really. The entire compound seemed to be made of sweeping, imposing stone and cutthroat angles. A low-lying series of manicured hedges interspersed the gravel, their long, sharp lines creating a labyrinth—or a killing field.

Only the Manor stood tall, its turrets clawing into the night sky. Raegan had a soft spot for antique buildings. But not this one—not even dressed up for festivities with twinkling lights and red banners draped across the boxwoods.

The queue shifted ahead of her, and she was treated to a much more pleasing sight.

"Oh, there's Alanna," Raegan said in a tone that she hoped sounded like someone spotting a work colleague. But gods, what a relief it was to see Alanna—stern-faced, her hair flattened against her skull in a severe braid—at the main security checkpoint. She'd do her part and get them through, glamour intact and undetected. It was also a comfort that she and the Unseelie king were standing in a large crowd of high-ranking Protectorate and no one had given any indication they'd noticed a glamour in their midst. People had hardly looked their way.

Well, no, that wasn't true. More than one man had stared long and hard at Raegan's body, to the point she had become concerned Oberon was going to expose them before they even got inside. The King had plenty of admirers, but they were mostly women and took their pleasures in smaller morsels, sneaking glances at the tall, lithe, dark-haired creature in his perfectly tailored tuxedo. All preferable to someone pointing at them and screaming about enemies infiltrating the Manor.

The queue moved sluggishly, and Raegean took another step forward, catching the scent of expensive perfume on a fur coat. Otherwise, the night air was crisp and cold with late autumn. She chewed on the inside of her lip, tracing the ornate details of the silver ring that took up her entire middle finger on her right hand. It was jointed in the middle and strongly reminiscent of armor, delicately inscribed with ancient spellwork. The rings had been small bands in the box, but once awakened, became something else entirely. She could relate.

"Pity Alanna has to work so hard this evening," the King said into her skin, his mouth moving against her neck, skin exposed by the simple yet elegant hairstyle she'd coaxed her curls into. Raegan shivered, leaning closer into him. Then the line moved again and they were nearly at the last security checkpoint. So far, so good—unless, of course, they'd already been detected and the Protectorate had decided to let them dig their own grave. Raegan swallowed that thought down.

"A pity indeed," she replied, feeling like that might be how the French ambassador she was impersonating would talk. It didn't actually matter; the physical glamour would change the way everyone perceived her, including her speech patterns and accent.

A large group was waved through ahead of them. And then Raegan and Oberon were standing face to face with a line of heavily armed Protectorate operatives, as well as a few dressed like Alanna who seemed to be doing the inspections for glamour and weapons. *And* holding the wards. No wonder all of them looked a little unsteady on their feet, dark circles stamping their eyes. That was just like the Protectorate, wasn't it? Exhaust the people keeping them safe for the sake of exerting more power.

"Good evening," Alanna greeted, her voice at least an octave higher than usual. "I'm just going to look you over for any unauthorized spellwork while my colleague checks for weapons, alright?"

Oberon nodded his consent, and Raegan did the same, realizing Alanna didn't recognize them—an absolute mind-fuck considering their appearance hadn't actually changed. But then Alanna's gaze connected with the glamour ring on Raegan's finger. For the briefest of moments, her eyes widened, but Raegan was sure she only caught it because she was already looking. The rings were the tell they'd agreed on. Alanna had no idea what the rings actually were, though she now certainly understood more about the kind of magic the Fey still had at their disposal.

She watched them a little too intently as she completed her spellwork, but scrutiny of foreign ambassadors from another country's paranormal and magic regulation organization was probably not going to raise any red flags. And then she waved them through. Oberon slipped his arm back into Raegan's and followed the flagstone pathway through severely pruned hedges to the mouth of the Manor.

Raegan found herself digging her fingers into the King's arm. All of her instincts told her to flee. The closer she drew to the building, the more she felt the wrongness of it leach out into the ground—the stolen magic, the god-granted oaths, the perversion, the power. The enormous front doors were thrown open wide. With the cold air nipping at her, Raegan should've wanted to pass over the threshold into the brightly-lit and undoubtedly warm foyer. But she'd weather any chill if it meant staying away from this goddamn manor.

"I know," the King murmured in her ear. "Steady, love." Then he pulled back and smiled at her as if he'd just offered a flirtation instead. She tried to match his expression but worried it looked too garish, so she settled for what she hoped was a soft smile and not a grimace.

A tangle of black-tie-wearing bodies thronged around the entrance. Despite the chaos, a doorman greeted them and offered to take Oberon's coat. Raegan exchanged words briefly with someone who complimented her dress, and then they were moving through the foyer. The ceilings were absurdly high, a marble staircase snaking around the sides. She squinted in the light of the enormous chandelier and noticed about twenty gunmen lining the staircase, stock-still in the shadows.

"Lovely," she muttered, directing her gaze in front of her instead. The floors were wide, flat stones, worn down over centuries. They moved through a hallway with a few doors—all white with dull gold gilding—and then followed a length of red rope to a ballroom. As they walked, hopefully long-dead Protectorate men leered down at her from ten-foot-tall portraits. Wall sconces with spindly candles brought their features to life, shifting in the illumination.

"Well, I hate it here," Raegan whispered, her tension easing a little when Oberon laughed, turning to look at her with an amused expression.

"Ahh," he exhaled, pulling her closer against him. "Cannot say I am surprised."

For a moment, Raegan watched him, equally impressed and disturbed by the ease with which he moved about the stronghold of the people who had been trying to kill him for a thousand years. Yes, when she looked closely, she could see the notch between his eyebrows, but she knew him better than anyone and it took even her a moment to find. Otherwise, the King was all fluid grace, drawing appreciative glances, moving about the space as if it belonged to him. She swallowed. His rage had always been different than hers, simmering in his depths, only released when he knew for sure that everyone would drown in his tide.

"Welcome to the Founder's Gala," greeted a woman in a shimmering dress at the double doors that led to the ballroom. She stood behind a small table laden with what appeared to be ribbons. After looking closely at both of their faces, she waved her hand over the table and then handed them a pair of blue ribbons. Brass tags at the top were engraved with the names of the married couple from Contre La Sorcellerie, France's magical enforcement agency, whose identity they were borrowing. The kelpies had promised to ensure the mortal couple "would not be permitted to depart their hotel." Raegan had not taken the time to question by what means.

"Same color system as last year," she explained sweetly.

"Just so we all know each other's roles! Always so many faces on the night of the gala. Have a great evening!"

Oberon thanked her and affixed the ribbon to his lapel. "Hold on," Raegan said, struggling to find a good place to pin hers. What a stupid idea—tell people to dress in black tie and then ask them to shove a pin through their garments?

The King swept Raegan to the side of the ballroom, near more of those off-white and dull gold walls. "May I?" he asked, leaning over her in that way she liked so much.

Raegan glanced up at him, briefly distracted by his mouth before nodding. "Thanks." He nodded, sliding the pin around the strap of her dress without actually piercing the silk. "Oh," she muttered. "I guess I should have thought of that."

"You are nervous. I am always happy to serve you," Oberon replied, his gaze hot and intense on hers before he swept his eyes around the ballroom.

Raegan quelled the warmth low in her belly and followed suit, hoping to get a feel for their surroundings beyond what Alanna and Maelona had sketched out in charcoal. A waiter passed by and offered them champagne, which Raegan took mostly so she would have something to do with her hands while she looked around.

Despite the glittering chandeliers and the sashes of blood red fabric draped everywhere and the rococo moldings and the white tablecloths glimmering with fine silverware, it felt more like a cavern than anything else. Like the deeper she went into this place, the more terrifying the creatures sheltering within its walls would become. She knew the entryway into the Undercroft was farther down the hallway from the ballroom's entrance, and she'd seen the line of soldiers standing stock-still, blocking any passage. For a moment, panic fluttered helplessly between her ribs, nervous sweat pooling on her lower back. Raegan had no idea how they were going to get this done.

"Steady," Oberon reminded her a heartbeat later, his thumb stroking the back of her hand. "Let us get our bearings first. One task at a time."

Raegan nodded, smiling as if he'd said something amusing, taking a swig of her champagne. With a long inhale, she swept her gaze across the room. Maelona's summation of the meanings behind the colors and styles of the ribbons pinned to everyone seemed to track with what Raegan saw.

"It looks like Maelona was right," she said to the King in a low murmur. "Blue for outside but friendly organizations. Red for Protectorate. The small swags are for spouses, the larger ribbons for oathed members. The golden crossed sword ornament is for titled officials. The wide black stripe is for top leadership."

"Seems accurate," Oberon replied, slipping his arm around her waist. The feeling of his fingers splayed across her belly eased a knot of tension in Raegan's chest. She tried to breathe deeper, looking around as if she were enjoying the view and not calculating how to destroy everything this place stood for.

With both relief and a dash of anger, Raegan noticed that only a few women had the gold ornament on their ribbons; none bore the wide black stripe. The majority of the women milling about the room in glittering gowns bore ribbons marking them as spouses or members of other organizations. The few women with the gold swords reminded her of Maelona, actually—not so much in appearance but more so the way they moved about the space, stiff and alert, eyes darting this way and that. By contrast, the men with similar ribbons laughed and slumped, grabbing a third or fourth champagne flute from a passing tray.

Protectorate guards dressed like Alanna—tactical black

clothing, weapons on their belts, combat boots—prowled the ballroom, arms clasped behind their backs. The first time one came near, Raegan thought the pounding of her heart would give her away. But the operative only offered them a nod before moving on.

Even so, Raegan's anxiety didn't cease. This place was well-organized, well-resourced, and remarkably well-fortified. What kind of magic would they have to work to actually get from the ballroom to the Undercroft? Would she even be capable of it? Yes, she was getting stronger every day, but her progress was infuriatingly slow—and she did not want to let Oberon down. Again. Or worse, get them both killed.

"We talked a lot about getting into the Manor and navigating the Undercroft," Raegan muttered, leaning into Oberon, tilting her chin up so the crown of her head rested on his chest. "Not so much about how we get inside the Undercroft in the first goddamn place. How much magic and spellwork are we talking? Because . . ." She trailed off, embarrassed.

"Oh, *cariad*. Be sensible," Oberon replied with a lazy smile, his expression gone heavy-lidded as he met her gaze. "We are going to seduce our way in."

CHAPTER THIRTY-TWO

A thrill slunk through Raegan, banishing the anxiety. "Oh," she murmured, raising a brow as she slid out of his grasp to turn and look up at him. "I'm quite capable of *that*. Why didn't you tell me earlier?"

The King's full mouth parted. The gray of his eyes was all molten heat, amusement rolling across his expression in a way that made her feel light-headed. He reached out a capable hand, cupping her jaw in his palm. Her knees went weak.

"What was there to discuss?" he murmured, closing the distance between them, gazing down at her with the intensity of an inferno. He tilted his head to one side, studying her. A flame ignited in Raegan's core, white-hot. The King—this beautiful, impossible thing—found her so irresistible that the idea of anyone not falling under her spell was absolutely foreign to him.

"Won't you be jealous?" she asked playfully, pulling at his jacket lapels. Instantly, Oberon's palm flattened against her ass, pulling her hips against his thighs.

"Extremely," he replied, his mouth brushing hers.

"Espionage as foreplay," Raegan said, trailing her fingers down his chest. "I'm in." And with that, she disentangled herself from his arms and began to stalk farther into the ballroom.

She moved slowly, like it was a dance, stopping to compliment people on their outfits, asking what *exactly* was in that canapé, greeting other attendees with blue ribbons. And she watched. Raegan cataloged the way people grouped themselves, whose features grew hungry when she passed by, who lingered on the fringes and who stood at the center of adoring circles. The King moved like a shadow, a few paces behind her. Raegan knew all too well what kind of men were in this room; in all probability, they'd love to feel like they'd stolen Raegan from someone who looked like Oberon. But she'd need to play it just right because she also knew men respected another man's property more than anything else.

And despite the Timekeeper's power surging in their veins, the bloodline they'd been born into, the oath they'd been laden with at birth, that's all they were: men. And Raegan could handle some goddamn men.

The ballroom seemed to stretch on forever. She peered into the rafters, eyeing the excessive number of chandeliers, the exposed beams draped in more banners—tasseled, embroidered with Latin phrases she had no desire to translate. And then up ahead, when a large group of people broke apart, she spied something much more interesting.

A tented bower of red fabric loomed in the distance. She imagined it was meant to seem mysterious and elegant, but it looked quite a bit like the tent-top of a circus. Raegan prowled closer. The open panel at the tent's front revealed a circular bar in its shadows. The bar was handsome, she could admit—Art-Deco-inspired, which did not match the rest of the atmosphere. But the burl wood veneers on the bartop and the inset fans of glass were nice to look at.

As she and the King drew closer, skirting what looked like an art auction, Raegan noticed the lights were dimmer beneath the tent top. She wavered, pretending to read the sign with information about the artwork offered for sale, but her gaze slid back to the shadowed, red-hued space. She noticed small seating areas dotting the floor around the bar. Tucked into a banquette-style booth was a man wearing a black-striped ribbon, four women draped over him like ornaments.

Raegan glanced to her right, making eye contact with Oberon, who was a few paces away. When he caught up and came to stand beside her, she slipped her arm through his.

"Certainly looks like the place where naughtier things go down," she said, stretching up to speak into his ear, battling the sound of the mediocre jazz band playing somewhere in the ballroom. "Want to see if we can hook ourselves a black-stripe? I doubt these guys will do a threesome with both of us, so we'll have to make it look like I'm sneaking off with him."

"I will be just behind you, even if you do not see me," the King replied, his hand open on the small of her back. "But please take care if you pass through security or warded doors, as that may limit my ability to follow you."

"Of course," Raegan replied with a wink. As they approached the blood-red tent, a man of middling height moved toward them. He was dressed in a drab but probably expensive suit, his hair slicked back so harshly that it gleamed like a burnished shield. He didn't block their way, not exactly—but he waited expectedly, like there was something they were meant to do or say before slipping into the darker recesses of the evening's offerings.

"Last year was our first Founder's Gala," Oberon added, feigning nervousness that Raegan knew he almost never felt. "We were not aware until afterward that there were additional . . . *activities* to explore."

Raegan shrank back against the King's solid bulk, looking at the ground as she wrung her hands nervously in a pretty little motion that made her bust strain at the neckline of her dress. She glanced up and found the man immediately distracted. Too easy. He managed to drag his eyes away, gaze skipping to the King.

"Of course," he replied with a leer, stepping aside.

Oberon slipped his arm through Raegan's, and they strode into the tent's mouth. Inside, small lamps were scattered throughout the seating area and a few chandeliers dangling down beneath the tent top cast everything in shades of red. Perhaps it was meant to look carnal, seductive —and it probably did, Raegan realized, to the kinds of men who saw women as nothing more than conquests. A bloody, vicious hunt ending with a delicate neck between their teeth.

Oberon led the way now, reading her mind regarding how she thought they should adjust to the tone of this space. In this high-danger, high-pressure situation, she felt so attuned to him, like she could make the slightest suggestion with a shift of her weight or a tug on his hand and he'd respond immediately.

A delicate warmth spread through Raegan. She'd wanted this for so many years—a kind of magical, intuitive understanding between herself and a romantic partner. At a certain point, she had convinced herself it was only the stuff of fairytales, of myth.

With a smile, she looked over at her faerie king for a moment, realizing she hadn't *exactly* been wrong after all.

As they reached the bar, he pulled her into him, arms

sliding possessively around her waist. Good—making her look claimed and untouchable would probably only heighten interest. Raegan glanced around the bar as Oberon ordered drinks, trying to get a read on as many people as possible.

They'd arrived fashionably late to the gala, so it was a bit past nine PM, but she was still surprised by how drunk a lot of attendees seemed. She was *not* surprised to see the way the majority of Protectorate men interacted with women. They either left their spouses behind before striding into the tent, or dragged their wives along to look pretty on their arm as they bellowed in laughter at other men's piss-poor jokes.

The bartender slid two drinks onto the corner, and Raegan scowled into her glass. Maybe she could summon a tidal wave of river water and just drown all of them. She sighed and shifted her weight, turning her mind to more practical forms of action. Should she be meek and demure, like she hadn't realized how hot she was, like her husband had purchased this dress to show her off? Or should she be more herself—coy, sharp, wild? Something already broken or something they could tame and mold into the docile, domestic thing they desired?

Yes, she decided. The latter would probably work. It was the Protectorate, after all—they'd demonstrated a long history of breaking wild, magical things. So she took a long sip from her drink and then reached over, playing with the King's silken black pocket square. He'd wisely struck up a conversation with a middle-aged man next to him, giving Raegan the opportunity to play as though she had to fight for his attention. She did just that, turning to face him, her back arched, tilting her head to look up at him.

Oberon turned and glanced at her, one eyebrow arched,

face impassive. "Yes, dear?" he asked in a tone she'd never heard out of him. "The men are talking."

Oh, he was *good*. Not just how quickly he'd picked up on her play, but also the way he said something completely different with his body. The heat of him bled through that fine suit as his fingertips trailed up her thigh, exposed by the slit of her dress.

Raegan pouted, all of her fear and anxiety sweeping out of her on a rushing current, leaving only the dark, slinking thrill. "You've been talking to colleagues *all* night," she whined, pitching her voice higher.

"Just a little longer," Oberon replied distractedly. One hand brushed away one of the curls framing her face as if she were an exasperating child, but the other slipped farther up her thigh. "Be a good girl for me, yes?" He timed the words with a brush against the apex of her legs. Raegan inhaled sharply in response, her chest heaving against his torso. She'd thought a lot of things about how this night would go. At no point did she think she'd be heady with arousal, fear long forgotten in the rush of desire.

"I will," she agreed with a sigh, dipping her lashes. She slid over so she could turn around and face the bar, fiddling with the orange peel on the rim of her glass. Oberon angled his shoulders away from her, but she had the strong sense he was doing the same thing she was—subtly surveying the room, seeing who might take the bait on the hook.

Raegan glanced up, finding that a young blond man's eyes were already on hers. She met his gaze, coy, but when the light shifted, she saw he wore a plain red ribbon. With a huff, she turned away, looking over at Oberon for a long moment.

She took another sip, propping her elbows on the bar, perfectly aware of what it did to the neckline of her dress. Shifting her weight as if impatient, Raegan glanced over her shoulder to her left. Again, someone had already been looking at her—this time, a man probably in his late forties with blunt, severe features. A possessive sort of hunger that she knew too well clung to his expression. The ribbon pinned to his tuxedo had a wide black stripe, accented at the top with golden crossed swords.

Raegan bumped her hip into the King's so he would glance over. He did with an irritated exhale, meeting her eyes before his gaze skipped over her head. When he looked directly at her again, she nodded, ever so slightly. Oberon frowned and then checked his watch, making sure the movement was visible to the man at the other end of the bar.

He swore, just loud enough, and made his apologies to the Protectorate operative he'd struck up a conversation with—who would probably never know who they had actually been talking to. Then he downed his drink and turned back to Raegan. "Late to speak with the chamberlain," he told her, pressing a hasty kiss to her hairline. "You can stay here. Enjoy yourself. See you in a bit."

And then Oberon pulled away, hesitating for almost a moment too long before he turned on his heel and stalked out from under the tent, leaving Raegan alone. She watched him go, twisting her mouth into a mopey expression before collapsing a bit dramatically against the side of the bar.

"From the gentleman across the way," the bartender said, interrupting her thoughts, sliding another drink in front of her as he gestured to the young blond man. That was quick. Raegan raised the glass and smiled prettily at him, hoping it would spur the black-striped ribbon she actually wanted into motion.

It did—like poetry. A minute or two ticked by, and then the severe-featured man appeared at her side. His harsh mouth moved into something like amusement, but she didn't think she was in on the joke. "Your husband?" he asked, gesturing toward the mouth of the tent, where Oberon had gone.

Raegan paused, reading the man before her—the expensive but classic suit, no wedding ring, but also no pretty young thing on his arm. Yes, she surmised. He would do just fine.

"Yes," she replied, turning to face him, her glass in one hand. "Doesn't always keep up with his husbandly duties, though." A test. The man—Commander W. Rochester, according to the shining brass tag on his ribbon—frowned, but she saw the interest flicker in his gaze.

"Oh my goodness," Raegan amended, covering her mouth with her hand for a moment. "Apparently I've had too much to drink. I can't believe I just said that. And to a stranger!"

That's what he wanted. His body slid closer to hers with an exhale. He wanted her desire to be real, and he wanted her to feel shame for it.

"Would it make it better," he asked, leaning toward her, one elbow on the bar, "if we were no longer strangers?"

Raegan laughed and then took a sip of her drink. "That might help, I suppose."

With that, the commander formally introduced himself, offering her that limp fish handshake that men like him for some reason always gave women. She supplied the French ambassador's name as her own and pulled Rochester into further conversation.

She didn't wait long to start with the delicate, fleeting touches—his forearm, his wrist, and then a swat at his shoulder when he told her how beautiful she looked in her dress. "Do recall I *am* a married woman, Commander," Raegan said, though she shifted another few inches closer to him anyway, running her eyes down the length of his body.

She couldn't make it too easy, so she followed up by

immediately leaning away, letting silence build between them for a long moment. "Your compound really is something," Raegan added when she saw just the right amount of tension in the commander's body. "Much nicer than where we work from in Paris. The neighborhood's lovely, but the offices? Terrible little spaces."

Rochester grinned at her for the first time, all teeth, all hunger. Raegan swallowed, missing the feel of Oberon right at her side. She twirled a lock of curls, leveling all of her attention at the commander. He was slim though well-built, likely fit, certainly brimming with the Timekeeper's boon. She had access to some Protectorate magic by virtue of her blood, but she hadn't been inducted as an infant, so she wasn't vested with full power. If she had to fight him, she'd have to maintain the element of surprise, or else she'd probably be fucked.

"You have some time to spare, don't you?" Rochester asked, leaning too close, his breath heavy with alcohol, his gaze devouring her body. "Would you like to see our offices? I could give you a little tour while your husband finishes up his business."

Raegan hesitated, looking over her shoulder as if Oberon might reappear. Then she glanced back at the commander, biting her lower lip. "Oh, I don't know . . ."

Rochester closed the small space between them and plucked a curl from her collarbone, wrapping it around his fingers. She clenched the fist he couldn't see at her side.

"I can see how badly you want to," the commander muttered gruffly, his hand roughly grabbing her hip. "Besides, if he doesn't give you what you need, I'm doing you both a favor, right?"

She forced herself to smile and nod. When Rochester's hand closed like a vice around her wrist, Raegan barely managed to let out a giggle instead of a growl.

CHAPTER THIRTY-THREE

"**A**nd don't worry about your husband," Rochester said as he pulled her along, slipping through a side opening in the tent's blood-red fabric. "He's out front. Won't even see us."

"Oh," Raegan cooed. "Done this before, have you?"

"Women are simple creatures. You see the alpha of the pack and can't help yourselves," he said over his shoulder with what he seemed to think was a charming grin. "But lucky for you, I'm generous."

Raegan had been planning to use a sedation spell—it was an old, little-used healer's incantation, so wards and defensive workings almost never registered it—but now she was considering slitting his throat. Surely he'd have some big, phallic letter opener in his office. The thought settled her as she glanced around him, trying to figure out where they might be headed. But the slim opening in the tent seemed to only lead to a dead end a few paces away.

"Commander, perhaps you've been blinded by my beauty," Raegan said when he came to a halt. "But this is a wall."

Rochester winked at her. "Like I said. Simple creatures." And then he laid his hand on the white wall, just between two drab, chipped gold ornamentations. He applied pressure with his fingertips at seemingly random intervals, and then the wall opened into darkness.

"Oh, a secret door?" Raegan asked as if it delighted her, letting her voice drop low and husky.

"Obviously," Rochester scoffed, somehow becoming even less charming—an impressive feat—the closer he came to getting what he wanted. Instead of holding the door open for her, the commander plunged into the darkness, his hand still wrapped around her wrist. His lack of manners was actually good, though, as it gave Raegan the opportunity to shift her weight back and catch the door with her heel. She had no doubt Oberon would've seen where she'd gone, but it would mean nothing if he couldn't get through. So she did her best to ensure the door remained cracked open just a hair, but with Rochester moving quickly down the corridor, she couldn't risk pausing to be sure. That'd only cause him to notice what she'd done.

The shadowed passageway opened up in only a few steps, spilling out into the massive main hallway she'd come down earlier. Raegan tried not to smile with glee when she saw this secret little passageway exited *behind* the line of soldiers that blocked anyone from leaving the ballroom and moving deeper into the Protectorate manor.

"See, look at this," she said, keeping her voice low, trotting a few steps to fall in line with Rochester. "Architecture, antiques, art! Much better surroundings than my gray cube."

She and Oberon had memorized information about the French organization whose representatives they were impersonating, but there had only been so much time. Raegan knew for sure that the offices were quite gray and modern, but she wasn't positive that the ambassador she was masquerading as didn't have a nicer, cushier workspace somewhere in the building.

Rochester didn't answer because he obviously didn't think women were people, so Raegan paid careful attention to the space around her, straining her ears. Sounds spilled out from behind the closed doors that lined the imposing stone walls. What she heard gave her two impressions: Protectorate officials using their offices for such dalliances during this gala was not uncommon, and they did not seem interested in the female orgasm. No surprises on either account. She swept her gaze from side to side, counting her footsteps. The entrance to the Undercroft should be visible at any moment.

Rochester muttered something filthy and not even remotely hot into her ear, almost making Raegan miss the gleaming iron door. She barely caught sight of it in the flickering light of the candles, appearing just as Maelona and Alanna had described. The Protectorate thought Fair Folk would have no chance of opening it—on account of it being made of iron and enchanted to throw any Fey magic directed its way back at the user threefold. But the Fey they'd locked on this side of the Gates were more resilient than that. Sure, iron *did* hurt—but pain was fleeting.

The commander, though, would have a swipe-card for the estate's outer gates and a set of spelled keys for the more secure parts of the Manor's innards. Raegan would have to get the keys from him without offering something she did not want to give.

"Here we are," Rochester said triumphantly, stopping at a massive oak-hewn door. As if on cue, he pulled a set of antique skeleton keys from his pocket—left side, likely an interior pocket of his waistcoat.

Raegan summoned her strength. It would be too hard to get those keys back out once he stowed them away again;

she was no pickpocket. So as Rochester unlocked the door and pulled it open, Raegan grabbed the front of his tux jacket and stretched up to kiss him. In the same moment, she slid her thigh between his, pushing him backward and off-balance.

It worked. The commander stumbled inside, and Raegan kicked the door closed behind them. She cataloged a quick impression of the office—lavish, stone-walled, a massive antique desk, leather armchairs in a sitting area near a fireplace, locked metal cabinets—before Rochester grabbed her by her hair. Adrenaline exploded in her blood.

"Not so fast," the commander said in an ice-cold tone that didn't really surprise her. Raegan had been expecting something like this; after all, it was always easier to fool the men who had no doubt they were the top of the food chain. Rochester yanked her to the front of the desk by her hair. Maybe those weeks of training with Andronica had been useful in more ways than one, because Raegan *let* him do it as opposed to being overpowered.

Rochester shoved her forward. The edges of the desk bit into her hips. Then he closed in behind her, reaching around to pin her hands to the desk. But he let the keys fall onto a neat pile of folders to do so. With her back to him, she was free to smile with glee.

"Fucking Contre La Sorcellerie," Rochester spat in her ear. "Are you stupid enough to think you can get your hands on that report so easily, just with a bit of whoring?"

Raegan pretended to freeze, going completely still against him, which he seemed to enjoy.

"And also stupid enough," he continued in a snarl, "to follow a man you know to be dangerous into a location where your partner will never find you?"

Raegan rolled her eyes and then realized she should be afraid. Shouldn't she? She knew what men were capable of more intimately than she'd prefer. But she wasn't what Rochester saw when he looked at her—ass and tits, a bitch to conquer, just a girl. She never had been. But particularly not anymore. With an intact Seal, she would've been afraid. Angry but afraid.

But Baba Yaga herself had removed her Seal. Then Raegan had walked the wasteland of a thousand lives and returned not only intact but stronger than ever. So for regular, mortal women everywhere, she decided to make him pay.

"But I hope you're smart enough," Rochester panted, his fingernails digging into her skin, "to not make this harder than it has to be. You're going to be spending the night for some questioning." He paused and she waited, prepared to react. "And don't worry. I won't be taking *advantage* of your precarious situation here. You're lucky I'm a better man than that."

God, she fucking hated this guy. She said nothing, making a series of quick, dagger-sharp calculations. She knew that defensive spellwork or even something as subtle as a disorientation working would trigger the wards, particularly this deep into the Protectorate's compound. Her sedation spell wouldn't help; he'd need to be relaxed for it to take.

"Unfortunately for you," she said, her voice so low and dark she almost didn't recognize it, "I'm not Contre La Sorcellerie. I'm much, *much* worse."

She snapped her head back hard, slamming her skull right into the commander's nose. He barked out a loud curse and stumbled back. Raegan turned, staying low, knowing that he would reach out for her with clawing hands—which is exactly what he did. She slipped under his guard and placed a hand over his heart, digging her fingernails into his chest. Relief and victory flushed through her when the spell took root immediately, rushing out of her memory like whitewater rapids. The wards did not even tremble.

Rochester did, though, when Raegan shoved him. He stumbled back against the wall, rattling a metal cabinet, clutching his hands uselessly at his throat. As if that would save him.

"You know," Raegan said, looking up at the commander with what was probably a manic smile, "I'm familiar with some ancient Druidic medicine practices that most have forgotten. Very advanced for the time, you see. It was men like you that outlawed it as devilry."

Rochester gasped, groping at her forearms for purchase, but in his weakened state, it was easy enough to shrug him off with her free hand. His eyes bulged out of their sockets like fat, ripe grapes she could pluck and devour.

"You might know from modern medicine that some-times it's necessary to briefly stop the heart so repairs can be made," she continued, laughing now, her head thrown back. "And that's exactly what I'm doing now, you stupid fucking asshole. I'm stopping your heart."

"Th–the—wards," Rochester stuttered, blood draining from his face, "w-won't l-let you—"

"Oh sweetheart," Raegan said with a feral grin. "I'm not *hurting* you. I can see how badly you want it. I'm just being *generous.*"

On some level, she recognized that she was taller than him now, her feet leaving the ground in a swell of magic and rage. She leaned in close, as if for a kiss. "After all," Raegan sneered, "why would you go to a secluded place with the Queen of the Hill if not to die?"

Chapter Thirty-Four

Rochester went slack, sliding down the wall into a gray pile on the floor. Anger and victory coursed through Raegan's veins, heady as ambrosia, but the intensity of the working left her a little woozy. With her feet back on the ground, she staggered to the desk, steadying herself. Black dots danced across her vision. She would feel better in a few moments, she told herself, and besides—she was safe for at least a little while here.

Sheer horror electrified her insides as Raegan watched the heavy wooden door swing open. She shoved herself upright, unsteady in her heels, calling desperately to the rivers that wound long and terrifying within her.

But it was the Unseelie king who slipped into the office, closing the door behind him with a soft click. Despite the headache beginning to drive nails into her head, Raegan couldn't help but notice that he looked ridiculously good. He must've shed the tuxedo jacket at some point, pushing the sleeves of his black dress shirt to his elbow. His waistcoat remained, and *gods*, was it fitted beautifully around his powerful frame.

For a moment, the King's eyes took in Raegan and then

tracked to the dead man on the floor. In the next heartbeat, he moved in a sweep of shadow and grace, pulling Raegan off her feet and into his arms.

"My villainous thing," the King murmured, holding her tight against his chest, "are you quite alright?"

"A little woozy," she replied, trying to meet his gaze instead of staring at the curves of his sculptural mouth. "But there's one less asshole in the world. Oh, and the Undercroft keys are on his desk."

Oberon's gaze didn't falter. He looked only at her, didn't even take a split second to glance at the spelled keys that might lead to his people's salvation.

"Would you say," Raegan began, giving up and tracing a few fingers along the bow of his full lips, "that I was a good girl tonight, like you asked?"

Amusement shimmered across the inhuman angles of his face. "Yes," he replied, cradling her skull in one large hand. "Even better than I could have expected."

And then Oberon pulled her close for a kiss that made her feel as though perhaps the world had stopped spinning on its axis. Perhaps there was a Thread where he was helping her harvest honey from their bees. A Thread where she was just sitting down next to him by the ocean and nothing had ever been taken from them. It was the kind of kiss that shivered with possibility, that cracked the future open wide and glorious.

When they broke apart, Raegan found the dizziness had dissipated, her limbs feeling more like muscle and bone instead of jelly. "I think I'm okay," she said. "If my knees give out, it's only because you're a hell of a kisser."

With a laugh like an autumnal bell, the King gently set her down. Only then did his gaze wander to the dead commander.

"Oh," Raegan said with a wave of her hand. "Had to be

crafty with the wards. I stopped his heart. Archaic Druidic healing spell."

"You are terrifying, my love," he replied, tracing her collarbone with the lightest touch. "Do you need another moment, or are you ready to press onward?"

In response, Raegan snatched the keys from the desk and jingled them. "Let's go steal a dossier or die trying."

The side of his mouth curved upward, but she saw the anxiety draw his brows together. All for her, Raegan knew. The King had made his peace with dying for freedom centuries ago, but losing her seemed to be something he could not live with.

"Come," Oberon said, his fingers wrapped around hers, pulling Raegan closer to the body of the man she'd killed, not toward the door. In the movies, people usually vomited or had existential crises or passed out after their first kill. As she looked down at the gray, empty corpse, Raegan felt none of those things. Perhaps her soul remained tainted with every new body, each resurrective life, carrying the weight of death always.

Oberon released her hand, kneeling beside Rochester's corpse. "Do you think you would be able to lift some echo of the Protectorate oath from this man and craft it into a glamour?"

Raegan stared at him, her mouth going dry. The exercises Oberon had given her and the spellbooks Emrys had lent her fell firmly in the category of practical magic. It was, of course, nothing like the magic she'd so frequently seen depicted in television and movies growing up in this life. Still, it had a formula, a logic, that made sense to her because she was mortal.

Oberon was suggesting she attempt faerie magic. Humans pulled magic from the world around them with set rituals and incantations charged with will and practice.

The Fey *were* magic; they could shape the world as they saw fit.

"It is alright if you cannot," the King said, reading her like a book. "I would do it for you, would it not trigger the wards."

"It's an excellent idea," Raegan said, spreading her hands wide. "I just don't think I'm capable."

"You were born Fey, once," the King murmured.

"Exactly," Raegan scoffed. "Only *once*."

"You taught Baba Yaga witchcraft," he added, one ink-dark eyebrow arching. "Morgana le Fay said you were the most brilliant witch she'd ever worked alongside. You may be human, Nyneve, but you have *always* worked magic like the Fair Folk."

Raegan swiped damp palms on her dress before remembering it was a beautiful, exquisite thing. She sighed, squeezing her eyes shut. If she tried and failed, they'd have wasted time and possibly tripped the wards in the process. Too much time could pass and someone might come looking for Rochester. The French operatives they were impersonating might evade the kelpies and alert the Protectorate. She opened her eyes, watching the King stand in one long, fluid movement.

"How can I do that without upsetting the wardings?" Raegan asked, meeting his gaze. She felt the workings palpably as she spoke, like a hundred spiderwebs stuck to her skin, suddenly aware of her.

Oberon tilted his head, considering. "We do not categorize magic in the way mortals do," he said slowly, "but it would be a . . . transfer of sorts, yes? Neutral magic, as humans sometimes call it."

Raegan tongued the inside of her cheek, picking at her cuticles. "Okay," she said, nodding. And then she crouched down beside Rochester's cooling corpse and the currents surged—a thousand jaws with a million teeth scuttling scavenger-like across the riverbeds.

"Steady," the King murmured, a gentle warning, his voice like a hot cup of tea on a cold, wet day.

Raegan nodded, sinking to her knees beside Rochester, her thighs cramping. She pushed aside the rivers with a firm, gentle hand, fighting to stay within the boundaries of her Protectorate magic instead. Sweat began to pour down the back of her neck as she sent her magic through the commander's body, pulling back on the coursing river of her older power. She put herself in that healer's mindset—like she was searching for what had hurt him, or perhaps what might pull him back from that dark, final place.

Alanna and Maelona had stressed how much the wards sensed intent. Raegan had to believe she was helping Rochester or risk triggering an immediate reaction. She *was* helping him, though—lifting that heavy burden of an oath not asked for, letting his body rest for the first time since he'd been born.

The moment she thought about it that way, something floated to the surface—gossamer-thin, pearl-gray and lightly iridescent. It was not, Raegan knew, the full oath. Such a thing would be deeply embedded in Rochester's skin, in his heart, chained around his lungs. But this thing she'd conjured was a reflection, a simulacrum of it, almost like a grave etching. If she extracted it correctly, it would look like evidence of the Timekeeper's oath, at least on a magical level.

Raegan let out a long exhale. Best not to think about the complex theory. That was something she enjoyed over dinner with Oberon, tucked in a cozy chair beside a fireplace. Not in the belly of the beast, attempting a spell that mirrored faerie magic in a place where faerie magic was forbidden.

"Holy shit," Raegan whispered, the words leaving her mouth entirely by accident as the gossamer-thin veil drifted toward her on the currents of her power. She snatched it before it could float away and let it settle onto her body. For a horrible moment, she thought it was going to disappear—that her Protectorate blood would betray her, seeking the oath like a moth to a flame—but it just sat on her skin, damp-looking like a newborn thing.

"You clever witch," Oberon breathed, looking at her wide-eyed, the corners of his mouth upturned with wonder.

"It won't last," Raegan said, knowing intrinsically that whatever she had conjured was delicate as a butterfly's wing. "But it should at least get us through a few levels."

"Allow me to field dress your kill," the King said in a low, husky tone, "and then we may be on our way."

"Into the Undercroft," she said, trying to mentally prepare herself.

Oberon's eyes left hers, dragging around the room as he searched for something. "Ahh," he said, moving toward a large bottom drawer of the metal cabinet. He pulled it open, revealing about ten thousand manila folders.

"They should really digitize," Raegan said, wrinkling her nose.

"The Protectorate are paranoid about modern technology," the King replied, grabbing a pile of the folders and moving to the desk, where he yanked open drawers with his free hand. Finding an empty one, he began ferrying folders. Raegan understood a little too late, apparently still recovering from the spellwork. But when she caught on, she moved to the desk drawer, shoving folders in as Oberon handed them to her.

When the large lower cabinet was empty, the King knelt in front of Rochester and wrapped his hands around the corpse's leg. And then he snapped it, bending the limb at an angle it should never be bent. A novel combination of queasiness and arousal bloomed low in Raegan's stomach as Oberon continued to break a grown man's bones as if they were toothpicks. Once he had folded the corpse into a more suitable size—her stomach did roil a bit then—the King stuffed Rochester into the cabinet and closed it.

He turned to look at Raegan. "A bit distasteful, I know."

"I mean, he deserved it," she said with a shrug. "Kinda gross to watch, though."

"Onward, then," Oberon replied, closing the distance between them with a few strides. He took her hand with the same fingers that had just committed so much violence, and yet he touched her with unyielding tenderness.

They slipped out into the hallway, a pair of shadows. Beneath the skittering candlelight, the space was silent. In the distance, the hum of the gala was detectable, but it felt a thousand years away.

"This way," Raegan said, pulling the King toward the door she'd spied on the way in with the commander. She counted her steps again, just to be sure, but she saw it looming and her heart quickened.

"This is dwarven made," Oberon observed in a low murmur, his tone sour. "Undoubtedly stolen."

"What a surprise," Raegan replied, standing directly in front of the massive iron door, sweeping her eyes across it. "All of the Protectorate's power is stolen."

She took a hesitant step forward, spying a keyhole in the middle of the door, which was curious. Raegan reached for the oath's veil and felt it like threads of silk across her shoulders. Her fingers ghosted the ring of keys in her hands. She didn't need to look; it would be the dull iron key, the one nearly the size of her hand, that would open the Undercroft.

It was a strange thing, she realized, to stand in front of a door that did not call to her with all the sweetness of a lover.

This door did not repel her, not precisely, but when one only knows songbirds, a silent winged creature is unsettling.

Raegan took a deep breath and held the enormous skeleton key just above the lock, her body grinding to a halt at the last moment, stiff with hesitancy. But then she remembered something she couldn't believe she had forgotten: hadn't she, all her life, been looking for a door?

So Raegan put the key in the lock and turned.

CHAPTER THIRTY-FIVE

When the twelve-foot-tall iron door opened without a sound, there was no time to celebrate. Raegan and the King disappeared into its mouth. The door sealed shut behind them with the quietest of sighs.

Once her heart no longer felt as though it was going to burst out of her chest, Raegan took a look around. The Undercroft's interior was a cruel space, at least to Raegan's eye. The echo of the rest of the Manor was there, all the old, dark stone and high ceilings, but steel and glass sutured it all together. A blood-red runner stretched down the center of the stone floors, the dragon rampart stamped in yellow every ten feet or so. Conference rooms seemed to make up the majority of the chambers off the main hall. They were dark and empty, their glass-pane-eyes staring back lifelessly. Sickly fluorescent light poured down from the ceiling.

"I don't understand how this would be *less* creepy if it were some stereotypical dungeon," Raegan hissed as she forced herself to move forward.

"The wards appear to be reading me as your guest," the King said in lieu of a response to her statement, his gaze roving the space. Good. So far, they were neither dead nor captured.

But the space was eerie in its utter silence. Oberon moved forward, his footsteps soundless on the carpet. She trailed behind, her heart still somersaulting. It was not helpful, she kept reminding herself, to think of the Undercroft as a sleeping beast that would awaken the moment they put a foot wrong. They passed by more glass rooms with heavy, immoveable tables, then a small space for document storage, though the pigeonholes were empty.

Ahead, shadow devoured the blood-red runner and the hallway curved sharply to the left. In front of the yawning darkness of the corridor stretched a gold-washed gate. It reminded Raegan of old-fashioned accordion elevator doors, except instead of open diamonds of metal, chainmail stretched between the hinges. In the middle of the gate were two enormous scythes, crossed at the middle, a strange-looking keyhole fitted into the place the weapons met. She palmed the keys she'd stolen from Rochester and walked closer.

"The scythes are glamour-eaters," the King said from a few steps behind her, his footsteps silent on the stone. She nodded, glancing back at him. They'd expected this from Maelona and Alanna's reports, but the magic built into the barrier shouldn't register the physical glamour spells in their rings, let alone devour them.

The metal keys clung to her fingers, which were damp with anxiety and nerves. In the gloom of the dark corridor, Raegan found a key that appeared to be the right size and had a scythe etched into it. She put it into the lock and twisted. For a long and deeply horrible moment, there was nothing but silence and the heavy weight of Oberon at her side, like the electrified rush of an incoming thunderstorm.

But then the scythes hissed like snakes, sliding apart

and granting them passage. Raegan let out a breath, her heart still hammering away at her ribs. "So far, so good," she said as she walked through.

"We should probably close them behind us, yes?" Oberon asked, eyeing the tall stretch of golden chainmail. It was a risk to have the literal Unseelie king touch anything here, so Raegan reached forward and pulled the two halves of the accordion gate back together. The scythes slid closed.

"Right," she said in a huff, pushing a curl out of her face. Then she reached for the King's hand, and once their fingers were firmly intertwined, she continued down the corridor. Lights clicked on as they went—like industrial fluorescent bulbs in a warehouse. Up ahead, the corner rounded sharply, creating a blind turn. It would be like this on the approach to every level, Raegan knew, but seeing it in person was unsettling. The Undercroft's structure felt too much like following the trail of a massive serpentine beast that had burrowed beneath the earth. Every step felt as though she might disturb a great sleeping thing.

Oberon moved out ahead of her to round the tight corner, but she kept close, wanting to feel the solidity and security in his bulk. When she saw what was awaiting them around the bend, she regretted her choice. Like a sentinel with its back against the wall, a grandfather clock stood there. It was quiet, no ticking hands, no chiming pendulum, but the aura of the thing was vile. In fact, Raegan realized, it felt very much like the Timekeeper's train platform, the place her father had—

"Steady," Oberon said, slowing to a halt, his bicep brushing her shoulder as he drew close. Though his nearness eased her tumbling thoughts, her body still very much wanted to panic.

"We can't destroy it," Raegan hissed, eyes darting between the King and the clock. "Not yet, at least. We wouldn't have enough time to get out before the whole damn gala knew we were here."

"Luckily," the King said, his gaze narrowed as he examined the clock, not drawing any closer, "I believe it sleeps. For now."

Without letting go of his arm, Raegan searched the ground around her uselessly, looking for a rock or something similar she could throw out past the grandfather clock to see if movement would make its teeth appear. But then she realized the workings on this abomination were probably much more sensitive and fine-tuned.

"Guess there's only one way to find out," she sighed, her jaw clenched. At her side, Oberon nodded his agreement, though it was clear from the expression on his face he was not any happier about it than she was.

Together, they stepped forward tentatively. Closer now, more lights clicking on, she saw the clock did not possess simple carved feet made of mundane wood. Instead, tentacles curled at the bottom, gray and fleshy. She swallowed hard, trying not to stare at the thick, slimy-looking appendages.

"We're just going to walk right past it," Raegan said, looking up at Oberon. His mouth moved into a firm line. "It's a fucking *clock*. I'll stomp on its tentacles or something."

Up close, the thing was horribly tall, rivaling Oberon's height, its skin a burnished walnut, its face lacking any kind of numerals, only two spindly arms still on the blank white. In her peripheral vision, she noticed unmoving pendulums hanging down into its hood, something about them not quite right.

Three, two, one—and then they drew even with the awful thing. Raegan shoved down the anxiety boiling in the pit of her stomach, clenching her jaw. She prepared herself to punch a sentient piece of furniture, which would be a new experience, even for her.

But the clock, like the rest of the Undercroft, was silent. Raegan didn't dare release a breath or relax until she and the King were at least ten paces away. Only once her head began to swim with a lack of oxygen did she unclench her jaw and suck in air.

"I do not wish to see one of those awaken," Oberon observed archly.

Nervous laughter bubbled up Raegan's throat. "Absolutely not," she replied, focusing on the dark, narrow hallway ahead.

The corridor turned sharply again ahead. She half-expected something horrible waiting in the gloom of the hallway's sharp turn, but there were only plain stone walls and that plush carpet the color of dried blood stretching down into shadow. It was empty and quiet, save for the humming of the fluorescent lights that cast everything in a pallid shade of gray-green.

When the hallway deposited them into a circular room that looked like it had been dug out of the earth two thousand years ago, Raegan slowed to a halt. Her heart thudded noisily in her throat, her legs trembling. It wasn't exhaustion —it was fear. Something about this place reduced her to prey, a rabbit hopelessly digging deeper into its warren even though a wolf had its hind legs firmly between quickly closing jaws.

"Okay, we made it to the second level," she breathed, sweeping her gaze around the space. This room had stone walls, too, lined with wrought iron benches that were too familiar. They were just like the ones in the In-Between. Raegan grit her teeth again, refusing to fall into the pit of despair and grief that waited for her with open arms.

"You are a force of nature," the King murmured, pulling

her close, fingertips tilting her chin up to face him. "I am in awe of you."

Raegan smiled, that look of admiration on his angular features chasing away the darker feelings clamoring in her chest. "Save it 'til we've got the dossier in hand," she said with a wink. "Then you can properly admire me."

He bent his brow to hers, hand flattening against the small of her back. The endless heat of him rolled across Raegan's skin, banishing the chill of the Undercroft. "I look forward to it," the King said, a gruff rumble that sent anticipation unfurling low in her belly.

Raegan stood on her tiptoes, suddenly grateful for her high heels, and kissed him for good measure. Then she turned, reached for his hand, and snuck deeper into their enemies' burrow deep below the earth. The second level reminded her of a college library, but more evil—more glass and steel, that blood-red carpet running down the stone floors, documents and books piled high on plain shelves. It was frustrating to leave it behind without rifling through to see exactly what the Protectorate knew, what they were putting effort into researching—but with the dossier, none of that would matter, she told herself.

The next few levels passed in much the same fashion. An accordion gate of chainmail with its scythe keyhole, the tentacled grandfather clock waiting at the turn of the corridor. Tight, winding hallways with steep inclines. It was *working*—the physical glamours and the veil she'd made of Rochester's oath. And yet Raegan couldn't relax, feeling as though their lives were hanging on a knife's edge with every step, the Undercroft a living beast watching their every move.

But as they went farther into the dark, she discovered the horrors contained within the Undercroft were so, so much worse than the deep, damp wound in the earth that held them. The Protectorate held far more reserves of sainted iron—metal specifically forged through an intensive, time-consuming ritual to better kill the Fair Folk—than the Unseelie king himself had even known existed. The Fey had thought the ritual no longer possible, the weapons low in number.

"They are preparing," was all Oberon said as they passed another armory filled with shining, yet-to-be used weapons hungry for Fey blood.

From there, it only got worse as they followed that carpet—too much like a blood-trail shining in the fluorescent light—down into the shadows of the Protectorate's most secure holding. An entire library of books bound in human skin. Kelpies in too-small tanks, their eyes plucked from their skulls, a thousand tubes running from their sickly hides. Rarer magical creatures kept like test animals, skin pinned down by vicious hooks—an aged griffin, a tank of water leapers with clipped wings, a cockatrice, a cage of Coblynau. A handful of Fair Folk and magical mortals, some of whom Oberon knew by name. All of them dead to the world, unaware that the Unseelie king himself stood just feet from their enclosures.

Raegan didn't have the strength to look at him directly. She saw the powerful hands curled into fists at his side, felt the dark rage he kept hidden deep within him begin to stir.

"We could look at the spellwork, see what's keeping them in stasis and whether we can get them out," Raegan murmured, reaching out to sweep a hand down his back.

"There is no need," the King seethed, his eyes flat and black. "I already have. The stasis working is tied to remaining in this level of the Undercroft. I cannot remove it. Only the Protectorate mage who placed it can. I cannot even ask them if they wish to live or die. So instead, I must abandon them. Fail them. Again."

"My love," she replied, though any words died in her throat as she felt her rivers begin to rise, a call and response to the faerie king's rage. She gritted her teeth and shoved the currents down, forcing them back under the veil of Protectorate magic.

"We should keep moving," the King said, though his voice broke.

Raegan roughly wiped away the tears that gathered in her own eyes. "That's all we can do," she replied, her tone gruff as she held back the torrents of blackened water and emotion.

They didn't speak as they continued to the next level. In the massive cavern they found there, full skeletons of the Fair Folk were proudly displayed with their names and place of death, shining gold plaques ensuring the reader that these Fey had been murdered and skinned like animals, not simply found and harvested. Out of the sixteen skeletons, Oberon had known seven of them when they were alive. Two of the displays were children, the details on the plaque too gruesome for Raegan to manage reading more than a sentence or two.

"Sometimes," the King said, his voice hoarse, breaking the silence that had descended heavy and hot between them, "all you can do is witness."

Raegan didn't know what to say, all the words withering in her throat. What was there to say in the face of such meaningless cruelty?

She reached over and took his hand. "And keep going," she reminded him as they continued down the corridor.

The Undercroft was more than Alanna and Maelona had managed to convey. Their sketches weren't incorrect— there was just no way to conceptualize or prepare for one long hallway winding itself deeper and deeper into the earth like a poison, horrors lining its walls.

Strangely, the Undercroft looked older as they descended; Raegan would've expected the surface-level to be the oldest, the Protectorate digging deeper as time went on. But it was the reverse, nearly all traces of metal and glass disappearing, save for antique display cases and more modern enclosures. The majority of the space was ancient, unflinching stone, filled with that rigid, masculine kind of grandeur—marble and gold and animal skins.

Down at this level, the fluorescent lights overhead disappeared. Instead, candelabra burned on plinths, wax dripping down like melted flesh. Another grandfather clock guardian and slinking hallway loomed ahead, but Raegan was more than happy to leave the hall of death behind. At least until the King stiffened. She flattened herself against the wall without a second thought, the position providing her the best sightline in either direction.

"We are no longer alone," Oberon said, his eyes flicking to hers before he turned to face the direction they'd come from. Raegan tried to slow her breathing and waited for more information; she knew his hearing was far superior. Time dilated, viscous and rotten as it passed too slowly, those few seconds stretching into an eternity.

And then the King grabbed her hand and moved into an urgent, long-strided walk. "At least twenty people just entered the Undercroft," he explained, his eyes darting to hers, a flash of white in the darkness as they rounded the too-sharp corner. "It does not sound friendly. It is safest to assume we have been discovered."

Raegan nodded, grim, panic twisting her stomach. In the scenarios they'd run earlier in the day, this one was the worst: that they'd be in the depths of the Undercroft when the Protectorate came for them. Burrowed deep in the earth where no kelpie could reach them and Oberon's magic was a dangerous liability, not a god-like power among mortals.

"Not to pile on," Raegan said with a steadiness she did not feel, "but the past two levels . . . the wards have been getting tighter. I don't know how else to explain it."

"I feel it as well," Oberon said. "The corridors are becoming narrower, too."

"I thought I was just claustrophobic," she muttered. They rounded the last turn, coming to the opening of level eleven. Just like the other levels, a hallway twisted and opened up into some kind of receiving room. All were the same, though they had become more luxurious the farther down—plush cushions lining the wrought iron benches, marble statues of past Protectorate leaders standing tall, chandeliers hanging in the center of rooms.

This room was much the same, except for one significant difference: a massive grandfather clock stood at the far end.

And this one was awake.

Its tentacles were easily the width of her body, already writhing about, twisted in their direction. In the hollowed-out trunk, a mace hung instead of a pendulum, its razor edges winking in the light. She and the King exchanged a long, tense glance. But there was no other choice. No other options. There was only forward into the devourer's mouth where salvation might await if they could just stay alive long enough.

They approached the too-large abomination. Oberon had to tilt his head up to look at the thing, the arms on its face scuttling about like beetles. And then a chime—deep and resonant, a shrill train whistle buried in its depths. Raegan's breath caught in her throat. The filigreed brass handle of the clock's trunk turned, and it swung open.

A slot unfurled from beneath the clock's face, looking too much like the tongue of a python flicking into the air, tasting its prey. Raegan settled her racing heart as best she could and leaned forward, peering at the small, wooden tray that extended from the now-still grandfather clock.

Resting upon the slim slab of wood was a scarab beetle, its thorax etched with a scythe. Every movement of its legs released a ticking sound. The beetle stood on its back legs, its jaws flexing. Anxiety thundered through her body, all her muscles trembling, every good sense buried in her mind screaming at her to run and never look back.

But Raegan just set her jaw and, with a deep breath, extended a finger toward the beetle. As she expected, the insect lurched forward and sank its jaws into her flesh.

CHAPTER THIRTY-SIX

A prick of the finger, a bead of blood, the drop devoured by the not-living, not-dead thing that emerged from the grandfather clock. The stifled air of the Undercroft hung low and weighted. Raegan stopped breathing, her heart raging against her breastbone. Then the scarab retreated, its jaws closed, and the wooden tongue slipped back into the clock's maw.

Tentacles shifted across the stone floors, the sound sending a shiver down Raegan's spine. The clock swayed to the side, allowing her to pass into the dark hallway that waited beyond. Tentatively, she moved forward, gripping Oberon's hand firmly.

"Raegan," he warned, but he followed her anyway. Disappointment sang through her body when the clock shot between them, blocking the King from following. Raegan's hold on him was broken as she turned, her heart in her throat, watching as the scarab beetle slid expectantly from the dark, waiting mouth open again.

From around the pillar of the clock, Oberon met her gaze, his brows knit together.

"You can't," Raegan whispered, terror slinking through

her chest. With the glamoured oath and her very real Protectorate blood, she'd passed the test. But a faerie king? It was a miracle he'd made it this far. Which meant there'd be two floors of the Undercroft's horrors to navigate on her own, the King waiting in the vestibule, caught between the advancing Protectorate and the monstrous mechanical thing.

"How close are they?" she asked, blood thundering through her veins.

The King tilted his head, a wolf honing in on the pack of deer moving through the forest. "Be quick," was all he said, a dangerous smile moving across his inhuman features.

"I—I can't . . ." Raegan's tongue felt too large for her mouth.

"You can," Oberon reassured her, stepping back from the threshold into the vestibule. The clock retracted its tongue, the tentacles ceasing their writhing. "If anyone can, it is you. It has always been you."

Raegan hesitated, knowing she was wasting time but feeling incapable of leaving him behind. How far would her rage alone carry her into this place? Every level down felt more oppressive, the hair crawling on the back of her neck, unease coiling thick in her stomach.

"I am well-accustomed," the King began, his expression gone tender, "to awaiting your return." Raegan's heart broke a little, tears pricking the back of her eyes. "Go, so you may return to me all the quicker."

"I love you," she said, fierce as an oath, her fingers curling into her palms.

"I love you," Oberon returned immediately, his oceanic eyes locked on hers. Then he nodded, just once, and before she lost the nerve, Raegan turned on her heel and shot down the hallway.

It was the same as the last—a short, curved corridor that

deposited her into level eleven. To her surprise, no horrors awaited her in glass tanks. Instead, something not unlike a gentleman's club surrounded her. Carved marble fireplaces, the heads of magical creatures mounted above the mantle, whisky brown leather armchairs, shining marble floors, a wine cellar.

It had only recently been emptied, she saw—a tumbler with half-melted ice sat on one side table, the condensation spreading in a circle on the wood surface. Raegan swept her gaze through the rest of the space, looking for movement, for a slip of tweed or the dull glint of a gun. But she found nothing, though she stuck to the carpeted runner down the center, wanting as much cover for her footfall as possible.

"Rich ass fuckers," she grumbled as she passed a second cellar, this one filled with casks and barrels that were probably worth enough to feed a small family for years. Briefly, she toyed with yanking out the corks and spilling liquor all over the stone floors, but she decided against it. Better for it to seem like no one had been here at all, if possible.

Raegan unlocked the accordion gate and passed through it. No grandfather clock awaited her at the turn of the hallway, which filled her with relief for a moment before the abnormality stirred dread deep in her stomach instead. She tried not to think about what might happen on the way back up, instead plunging forward.

The air was damp but chilly in the corridor, and she noticed in the dancing light of the candelabras that the walls here were earthen instead of gray stone. Single candles lined shallow shelves in the wall as she turned the corner to the straightaway. It felt more like a mausoleum now, any remnants of the gentlemen's-club-feel long gone.

The corridor deposited Raegan into a simple room. It was positively ancient—arching walls, well-swept dirt floor, no seating area or fancy chandelier. She turned, expecting another horrible clock-monster. But the short hallway was empty. At its end stood an iron door—certainly a sibling to the one at the Undercroft's main entrance. She stepped closer, her heart pounding ceaselessly against her ribs all the while. Raegan was tired and cold, her nerves completely frazzled. But this was the most important part, what *everything* was hinged upon. So she took a deep breath and snatched a candle from one of the built-in shelves on the wall, examining the door.

On its face was some kind of a cipher. Twelve concentric rings of metal, fitted within each other like a Russian doll, sat in the middle of the door. Esoteric etchings covered them in equal increments, absolutely none of them familiar. Unease slid through Raegan's veins. What if she wasn't good enough, smart enough, strong enough to see this through?

She tossed the thought aside angrily, passing the candlelight over the rings. Possibly, she thought, each individual Protectorate member granted access to the twelfth floor had their own combination. Like a particularly brutal high school looker. Raegan bit the inside of her cheek, leaning closer.

But nothing made any sense. There was no dial where the etchings could be lined up to mark a combination, and besides, all the symbols were nonsense, anyway. She found a few almost-alchemical symbols easily enough, but each was altered, rendering it meaningless. Why the whole dog and pony show with the terrifying clock and the scarab beetle if all that could be accessed was a room with nice alcohol and some fireplaces?

"Why would it need a lock at all, then?" Raegan muttered out loud. "And what self-important prick is going to dial in a twelve-symbol code every time they want access?"

She reeled back then, her mind turning. "*Oh.*" Hoping she was right, intimately aware of the wards stretched like cobwebs across the Undercroft, Raegan raised Rochester's keyring and held it up to the middle of the door like a swipe card.

And just like that, a soft click sounded and the door opened. She'd been right—the cipher was a trap. The real way to get through was to hold one of the magicked keys up to the door. Raegan resisted the urge to whoop in triumph and crept forward, peering around foot-thick iron.

On the other side, she saw a setting much like the last floor's. But instead of empty space for entertaining or sacrifices or whatever the fuck the Protectorate did, there were rows and rows of bookcases. She slipped inside, deciding to keep the candlestick in her hand for now.

Raegan's heels clicked loudly on the pristine marble floors, so she set the candlestick down for a moment and pulled them off, shoving the keys into the bodice of her dress while she was at it. Then she padded deeper into the space, finding display cases filled with scrolls and worktables piled with books, as if someone had stopped mid-research. Large corkboards attempted to trace her and the King's whereabouts. Worth a detour from the main aisle, she decided, so Raegan slipped over and examined the papers pinned to the cork. She smiled. It didn't seem the Protectorate knew shit about Hiraeth besides the fact that a hidden Fey city existed somewhere on the Isles. They also seemed to think hanging a cross blessed by a bishop over a doorway could keep Oberon out of the building, which was positively laughable.

The dossier. Letting out a long breath, Raegan strode deeper into the archive, trying to get a sense for organization. She even doubled back to look for a card catalog at the front of the room but to no avail.

"Of course you motherfuckers don't know how to properly catalog a collection," she grumbled, abandoning another disordered bookshelf. Minutes ticked by. She was undoubtedly aware of them thanks to the grandfather clocks lining the walls every twenty feet, all ticking away, mocking her inability to find the *one* thing she, the King, Alanna, and Maelona had risked everything for.

At least she found a light switch. Once flicked on, the archive was illuminated by plain white light bulbs, encased in industrial wire cages, that studded the ceiling above her head. Much easier to navigate an underground room full of flammable objects by artificial light than the naked flame of a candle.

Finally, at the very back of the archive, stood an antique display case—shining ebony and sloping glass. Raegan noted the locks on each compartment, as well as the complicated protection spells that would prevent a simple smash and grab. Elation flitted in her lungs.

She darted toward the case, starting on one end and working her way over. Her entire body stilled when she saw it—a document case labeled "Avalon: Possible Locations & Theories." The case was slim, brown leather with ornamental brass accents on each corner. The label was written in a spidery hand and faded. Her blood hummed, and she fumbled through Rochester's keys, looking for one that might fit the clever little lock on the front of the case.

When she found it, she slid it inside and popped the top of the case. And there it was—the fruit of their labor, one last mad hope. Gently, Raegan flipped the case open, skimming the first few pages. An introduction outlining the Protectorate's search from the early days until the present. Lots of raving about being tricked by the kelpies and how at the very least, they had the right to bury their lord's body. Raegan scoffed. As if they just wanted to honor their dead, not raise Arthur Pendragon from his grave.

And then, there it was—a page stitched in between two much older ones. "CURRENT LOCATIONS OF INTEREST AS OF MARCH 2024."

Her hands shook. For a long moment, her eyes refused to comprehend any of the words below the title, as if her mind couldn't fathom actually getting this far. But then it all fell into place, and Raegan found herself looking at seven place names. She scanned hungrily, her limbs still shaking violently—exhaustion or elation or something else entirely, she didn't know.

- *Tintagel Castle*
- *Sgwd Yr Eira*
- *Defynogg Yew*
- *Forest of Borth*
- *Pen Pyrrod*
- *Maes Gwyddno*
- *Carn Goedog*

Raegan's mind swam. Only seven locations—so many less than Emrys's list, making this search almost manageable. She studied each name carefully; something about seeing each location written out in ink tugged at her marrow. She steadied herself against the edge of the glass case. From the depths of the long, ancient tapestry of her mind, she felt a strange, lilting hum—like there was a lost thread she could pull and bring the truth tumbling out.

Raegan considered. They'd been to Carn Goedog and Sgwd Yr Eira already. Tintagel was on Emrys's secondary list, as was Defynogg Yew. Which ones could she remember visiting in other lives? But the tides of her memory stubbornly offered her nothing, so she quickly flipped through the rest of the dossier, finding extensive notes on each location—more fieldwork than they could ever hope to get accomplish without dying—as well as transcriptions of interviews with Fair Folk the Protectorate had captured, tortured, and executed. She grit her teeth. In the back, stamped repeatedly as "TOP SECRET," were timetables and schedules for ongoing patrol at each location.

"Time to think later," she muttered, setting the candle down onto the floor. The plan had been to memorize the locations and leave the dossier itself. But there was too much valuable information she couldn't squander, and she certainly couldn't hope to memorize it all. So Raegan steadied herself and tried to slip into her second sight so she could search more thoroughly for any warding that might prevent her from taking it with her, or perhaps worse, any location spells attached to the document case.

"Oh, fuck you," she grumbled at herself more than once, frustrated that she could create a glamour out of a Protectorate commander's oath but still struggled with something so basic.

Ultimately, though, Raegan found nothing. So cautiously, her heart pounding against the inside of her throat, every muscle in her body coiled and ready to spring, she lifted the slim, leatherbound dossier from its glass case.

Time stretched long and thin. Clocks ticked. Raegan's blood raced. A bead of sweat trickled down her brow.

Silence. Nothing.

"Okay," Raegan whispered, her voice hoarse, as she gathered up her shoes, slipping her wrist through the straps, and tucked the dossier under her other arm. She grabbed the candle and moved as quickly as she dared to the front of the archives. None of the grandfather clocks along the wall suddenly sprang to life. The Timekeeper himself did not appear—though that was mostly a given, as he rarely left the

In-Between and the Otherlands, the same way no king went into his own vineyard for grapes, so long as his servants kept bringing them directly to his mouth.

Raegan shoved the candle back into the alcove, almost dropping it. She swore, righted the candlestick, and then ran through the vestibule and up through the hallway. Back to the King. Always back to him.

The look on his face as she emerged from the corridor sent tears rushing down her face. Her heart burst into a thousand pieces. How often he had to let her go, expecting her to never come back, but here she was, running out of the darkness barefoot and undone. Only a few paces to go, the one person she had deeply, truly loved waiting for her across all eternity.

Raegan surged forward, eager to touch him, to kiss him, to feel like maybe this time things would be different. But instead of the powerful weight of the King's arms closing around her, something slippery and strong wrapped around her ankle. And then it pulled.

CHAPTER THIRTY-SEVEN

R ough stone floor rushed toward her face. At the last minute, she managed to tuck her arms and roll. Her bare legs banged hard into the wall, but she hardly felt the pain. Not with the tentacle of that massive clock-guardian wrapped around her ankle, dragging her toward its writhing nest of limbs.

She struggled for purchase on the floor, unwilling to let go of the dossier, which she imagined was what the creature wanted. Now it came all too clearly into Raegan's mind: it was very likely that nothing from that room was permitted to leave the two lowest levels. The thought would've brought more relief—that it wasn't Oberon's Fey blood or her glamoured oath responsible for enraging the thing—if more tentacles weren't hungrily slithering toward her.

With a grunt, Raegan snatched one of her high-heeled shoes by the vamp and slammed the heel down into the tentacle clutching at her ankle. To her surprise, the clock *screamed*—the sound of universes ending and civilizations falling and a snake eating its own tail. It did, however, let go of her, if only to send a smaller, more agile limb snaking out at her, grabbing the shoe she'd stabbed it with and flinging it to the other side of the hallway.

"Fuck you, I have *two*," Raegan snarled, scrambling to her knees, raising the second shoe in preparation to strike.

It was, however, entirely unnecessary. The Unseelie king was magic-less, not defenseless—and he strode right up to the clock, hauled his fist back, and punched the beast in the face. No, more than that, Raegan realized as she struggled to her feet, breathless and covered in scrapes. He'd knocked the monster off-balance with a direct hit, then reached his other fist into its trunk. With a snarl, Oberon drew his hand back, pulling the clock's pendulum and other innards with it. The creature let out a mechanical whine but fought hard against the King's hold, its tentacles still reaching to clutch at Raegan.

"What *is* that?" she demanded, still out of breath, stumbling backwards out of the beast's reach, avoiding the broken glass now scattering the floor. Oberon was clutching what looked like a pocket watch between his fingers, but it was *moving*. Raegan leaned closer, finding a writhing maw of tiny tentacles housed the watch face.

With disgust, Oberon tossed the thing hard at the stone floor, then crushed it beneath his heel. It disintegrated into dust, and a moment later, so did the enormous clock-monster. One second, they'd been trapped in a tunnel with an eldritch beast, the next, only silence and ash.

"Raegan," Oberon murmured, moving lithe as a panther and seizing her in his powerful arms.

"I'm fine," she mumbled into his shirt, relishing the feeling of being crushed against his broad chest. For a long moment, neither said anything. The tide of each other's breathing was enough—alive, for now, gloriously alive.

His grip loosened slightly, and Raegan pulled back,

smiling up at him. "Look what I got," she said with a grin, pulling the dossier from where she'd had it clamped under her bicep. "There's a lot more in here than just locations."

The King's eyes sharpened with interest for a second but then slid to the pile of ash where the creature had once towered. "I wonder if the rest of the guardians will react similarly to you trying to leave with the dossier in your possession."

"Fair point," Raegan admitted, something reckless and wild and giddy with abandon surging through her. "But I *will* very much enjoy watching you gut them all." She grabbed one of her high heels off the floor and went to maneuver around Oberon to grab the other, which had been thrown across the corridor by the clock.

But he grabbed her, his long fingers devouring her forearm. "Too much broken glass," he said, gazing down at her, the candlelight rendering his face in half-shadow. "Stay here."

And then the heat of his touch faded as the King stalked to the far wall and picked up her shoe in one continuous, elegant movement. He returned to her in a few strides of his powerful legs and lowered himself to one knee before her without a word. When he glanced up to meet her eyes, muscular thighs visible just beneath the fabric of his trousers, desire unfurled at the apex of her legs.

Oberon held out a hand expectantly, wordless, and Raegan took too long to react, happy to drown in the endless gray of his ocean eyes. But then she placed one open hand on his broad shoulder to steady herself before lifting one leg. He curled his fingers around the curve of her ankle and guided her foot to his knee. From there, he slid her shoe back on, his touch a gentle caress as he redid the tiny buckles.

"This shouldn't be so hot," Raegan laughed, a blush warming her cheeks as he repeated the process with her other shoe.

The King glanced up at her again, his full mouth parted, one eyebrow arched, the perfect portrait of playing with fire. "You enjoy this?" he asked, his voice a low thrum in the earthen corridor, fingertips sliding up the back of her calf.

Raegan shivered, clutching at the fabric of his shirt. "Yes," she whimpered.

"Interesting," Oberon replied, his hands gripping her by the waist as he got to his feet. Then, without hesitation, he propelled her back into the wall, his much larger body an unstoppable force that she'd happily be destroyed by. In the candlelit gloom, his fingertips brushed her jaw, tilting her chin upward. His lips parted as he cocked his head to the side. For a moment, she thought he might say something. But then he just kissed her, fully and completely, stealing the breath from her lungs. Raegan melted against him, not wanting the moment to end but knowing there were miles and miles left to go before this night was over and done.

"Should we face the remaining horrors?" he asked her, lips moving against the delicate skin of her neck in a way that made her entire body tremble.

"You know," she said, hooking a leg around his hips, nails raking down his back, "almost *anything* is foreplay with you."

He laughed then, a sound too crisp and rich for this dead place. "Is that a yes, my villainous thing?"

"Absolutely," Raegan replied, weaving her fingers into his. And then they turned and began the ascent, moving in careful steps up the corridor. Generally, she enjoyed being right, but Raegan was quite dismayed to find their theory about the grandfather clock guardians proved correct when the next one lurched at them, tentacles unfurling.

The King wasted no time, shattering its trunk and yanking the writhing pocket watch from its depths. He threw it at the floor, and Raegan slammed her heel down onto its face. The next moment, there was no proof either had existed except for the dust that piled in the middle of the walkway.

The level itself was quiet, and for a moment, Raegan hoped that Oberon had been wrong about hearing a large number of people enter the Undercroft earlier. Or maybe it'd just been for a completely different reason—some kind of fucked-up viewing party of a Fey skeleton or people looking for a good place for an orgy. Any other reason than because the Protectorate knew their secret warren had been raided.

But as they destroyed the next guardian and slipped out onto level nine—an armory, mostly—she realized that hoping was just as worthless as it'd always been. The King paused at the mouth of the corridor, motioning for her to be quiet. Then he pulled her close to him and slunk along the wall, darting behind a rack of axes the moment he had the chance.

Maybe twenty feet away, coming from between them and the corridors to the surface, a voice called, "Clear!"

Raegan nearly jumped out of her skin. She felt Oberon bow around her, his lips nearly at her ear. "Could you work a subtle silencing spell for your footsteps?"

The request sent anxiety pulsing in her blood. With Protectorate soldiers so close, she'd have to be incredibly precise to avoid detection. But the other options were just as poor—carrying her would slow Oberon down and add more bulk to their movements. There wasn't time to try to yank the high heels back off again, and even if there was, the full black tie outfit was essential if they were discovered. When all else failed, lying just long enough to create an opening could save them.

But Raegan could do this; she'd done about ten much harder things already this evening. Instead of reaching for the older, darker powers deep in her marrow, she skimmed the surface, purposefully playing in the shallows of her Protectorate magic as she worked a common silencing spell. With luck, even if the working was detected, the soldiers in the room would assume it was one of their colleagues.

She felt the charm sink in and looked up to nod at Oberon. He met her gaze, concentration written clear across his features; he was likely tracking every single person in this room by sound alone. Anticipation wrapped itself thickly around Raegan's body, stealing the air from her lungs. And then the King squeezed her hand once, giving her maybe half a second to prepare, before slinking around the corner and darting across the aisle. He pulled her behind a row of towering display cases, her heart careening out of her chest. But her spell had worked—she'd been completely soundless even when moving across the stone floors. Small victories, Raegan told herself.

"All the way to the door this time," the King whispered, gathering himself up. Raegan nodded, trying to prepare herself.

"Wait," she replied, barely even speaking the word aloud. Oberon turned to her, movement sharp as a raptor's. She held up the dossier and motioned for him to tuck it into his waistcoat. Delicately, Oberon took the slim leather document case from her and slid it beneath the rich fabric. It was testament to how stressful the situation was that he hadn't done it himself when she'd first returned with it. For a second, her mind wandered, recalling how the Unseelie king had been most concerned about making sure she didn't step on broken glass.

Raegan's face heated again, just as he closed his fingers around her arm and slid away from the display cases, barely more than a mundane shadow. Together, moving as one animal, they slipped around bookshelves and crouched behind large crates, evading soldiers armed to the teeth. When they darted out of the floor and into the next hallway, Raegan almost fainted from relief.

Shouts echoed through the cavernous space when they were barely a few feet up the corridor. Her body threatened to freeze.

"They do not understand what happened to the guardians," Oberon told her in a low voice. "Which may work in our favor as long as we keep moving."

Raegan steeled herself and pushed onward, sticking close to the King's bulk. As they rounded the corner, she gave him room to disembowel the next clock guardian. Level eight was clear and quiet, the Protectorate soldiers clearly sticking together, hunting like a pack. That was their mistake, wasn't it? They always saw themselves as the predator, not the prey. And yet their warren had already been robbed.

The thought of the dossier tucked into Oberon's waist-coat carried Raegan through the ascent to the surface. Her heart never quite returned to a normal pace, but her thoughts crystallized and her muscles obeyed her without question. It felt good to be stealing through her enemy's stronghold with her faerie king at her side, salvation snug against his skin.

On level three, they paused for Oberon to see what he could hear from the two floors above them. Raegan knew the soldiers had likely reached the bottom archive and were searching to see what had been taken. She had little doubt they'd go for the case the dossier had been in first, and then all hell was going to break loose. So she slowed her breathing and steadied herself as the King took a few steps away, his head cocked to one side.

She watched his brow furrow, tracking his gaze as it slid to a closet off to the left. Unease slid through her, catching at her insides with serrated teeth. This level was fairly bland, appearing to mostly function as a debriefing space for higher-ranked officials. But Oberon moved toward the closet all the same, his footsteps utterly silent despite the weight of his muscle and solid bone. He looked up and motioned for her to stand behind him, putting her out of sight while he opened the door. Raegan inhaled sharply and shot across the hall, glad she had maintained her silencing spell for her high heels.

The King glanced over his shoulder at her, and she nodded. The door was locked from the outside, and he slid the latch over with the barest of sounds. The next moment, he'd pulled the door open before Raegan even processed his movement.

"Sir?" stuttered a voice that she distantly recognized. "Sir Tristan, is that— Oh fuck."

With a look of disbelief, Oberon gestured her over, pushing the door all the way open with a sigh. Trepidation skittering in her veins, she obeyed, coming face to face with Reilly, the soldier she'd spared at the river.

They'd been nearly dead when she'd seen them last, but frankly, they didn't look much better. Their tangle of limbs indicated someone had probably thrown them in the closet. Their hair was matted, caked in blood by the left temple. Dark circles deepened their eye sockets. Their clothing— only an undershirt and sweatpants despite the chill—was stained and torn.

"Reilly?" Raegan asked in surprise, remembering too late to keep her voice low.

"Who are you?" they demanded, scooting farther back in the closet.

Raegan looked at Oberon in confusion.

"The glamours," he explained, gesturing to their rings. "Twist it very lightly to the left. That should dial down the glamour for Reilly to realize who we are without deactivating it."

Raegan did so, glancing over at the King so they could make the movement in unison. She was pretty confident it had worked when poor Reilly barely choked back a scream.

"How are you in the Undercroft?" they demanded, their voice hoarse. "The damn Unseelie king. In the *Undercroft*."

"Reilly," Raegan interrupted, pushing Oberon back gently. "I didn't let him kill you, remember? Can you tell me what happened? Why are you here?"

Reilly looked at her like she'd lost her mind. But then something in them shattered, like everything was just too much, and they opened their mouth to speak. "I—they were transferring me to somewhere else in the Manor w—when one of the lower levels' alarms went o–off," they stuttered, a shiver wracking their body. "Sir T-Tristan threw me in here. Told m-me to wait while they looked."

Raegan and Oberon exchanged a glance.

"Absolutely not," he said, his expression darkening.

She inhaled deeply and let it out slowly before turning back to Reilly. "Wanna get out of here?" Raegan asked, crossing her arms.

"L-like this closet?" Reilly asked, bewildered. "I mean, yeah. It smells weird."

"Like the Protectorate," she replied, amusement tugging at the sides of her mouth when she heard Oberon disguise a laugh at Reilly's reply as a cough. "All of this shit you had no choice in."

Reilly scrambled to their feet, knocking their head on a shelf and cursing. "So Alanna really did it, huh?" they asked, wrapping their arms around their torso, something not unlike hope gleaming in their eyes. "They haven't gotten anything out of me, just so you know. On my honor."

The King sighed, pinching the bridge of his nose. "Are you coming with us or not, little traitor?"

CHAPTER THIRTY-EIGHT

Reilly paled and retched, stumbling back against the wall, clamping one freckled hand over their mouth. "Oh my gods," they choked out. "That's the worst thing I've ever seen."

Oberon let out a scoff as he pulled Rochester's crumpled corpse from the filing cabinet. Raegan pressed her ear back to the office door, listening hard. Outside in the hallway, it was more or less chaos. The three of them had just barely made it out of the Undercroft and into Rochester's office before the regiment of soldiers broke through the upper levels.

Another flurry of shouts and barked orders resounded through the corridor. Raegan's gaze flitted back to the King. He was stripping Rochester's corpse of the expensive tux, now fighting against rigor mortis—not that he was particularly struggling.

"You want me to put that on?" Reilly gasped when Oberon handed over Rochester's jacket.

"Do you want to live?" he shot back, narrowing his eyes at Reilly. When the young Protectorate soldier didn't answer, Oberon flexed his wrist and sent the jacket flying through the air, landing squarely on Reilly's chest. They let out a little shriek but caught the garment and held it, watching Oberon as he pulled the starched white shirt from Rochester next.

"We're not even close to the same size," Reilly sniffed. "And this fabric is hardly appropriate for a late fall event."

To her surprise, Oberon laughed, shaking his head as he pulled the corpse's legs out straight, which released a horrific tearing sound. But Reilly donned the dress shirt all the same. Raegan watched their hands shake as they did up the buttons.

"We're lucky Rochester wasn't wearing anything more distinctive," she muttered, sagging against the door. She'd already put the commander's keys back on his desk, hoping to make it look like nothing had happened at all. Provided no one opened the cabinet drawer, of course.

Reilly finished dressing, adjusting the waistband on the pants, while Oberon rocked back onto his heels. He took a long look at the corpse, let out a sigh, and then began to fold Rochester's limbs back up again.

"Oh God, that's awful," Reilly sputtered as they turned away from Oberon and the corpse, kneeling down to tie up the brogues that were at least one size too small. "Almost as awful as brogues with a *tux*. For Kronos's sake."

Raegan snorted, feeling an immediate sort of warmth toward Reilly—the same way she had with Alanna. It must mean something, she told herself, especially since she usually had difficulty forming attachments. Or maybe she was just grasping at straws, reaching into the dark and hoping for something she could hold on to for more than a moment or two.

"How are we going to just waltz back out there like we had no idea what was going on, anyway? I mean, your glamours are damn good, but still," Reilly asked as Oberon finished with the corpse, pushing the cabinet closed.

She felt the King's gaze on her and looked up to meet his eyes, finding a sliver of that molten heat she knew so well. "Well," she said, taking a step away from the door, drawing the word out long, "there's one obvious option. Probably the most effective."

Oberon raised one muscular shoulder to his ear in a shrug. "Agreed." He glanced down at his outfit, untucking one end of his waistcoat, moving to unbutton one of his cuffs. Raegan followed suit, pulling the neckline of her dress to be slightly uneven, sliding one sleeve off her shoulder. Reilly looked at them both like they had lost their minds.

"What are— *Oh*," they said, their heart-shaped face turning red.

"May I?" Raegan asked, approaching them. "And are you okay with our idea?"

"No, no, it's fine. It's smart," they replied. "It's okay with me. Thanks for checking."

Slowly, Regan undid their collar another few buttons and pulled their shirttails out a bit. She chewed on the inside of her cheek, trying to figure out how to use her Protectorate magic to alter their appearance enough to slip out of the Manor. Healing, she decided, figuring that something familiar in her exhausted state was best. She sent her magic to soothe the dark circles, ease the chapped lips, mend the scabbed wound on their temple. But Raegan added a little more meaning beneath that first current, altering the shape and color of their eyes, making the lips thinner, lightening the distinctive freckles—subtle changes were all she could risk. Hopefully it would be enough.

"Okay," she said, standing back. "Oberon, you're sure there's no location spellery on the dossier?"

The King nodded. "I do not believe so. It would be too

easy for an enemy to use such a working as a beacon, so the Protectorate seems to rely on preventing entry and theft in the first place."

"Great," Raegan beamed. "Right. So, probably best if we all spill out the door together, acting drunk. Remember, we're in that post-orgasm haze."

Reilly, if possible, turned even redder, the color creeping up into their hairline as Raegan hooked her arm through theirs. Oberon slipped his hand around her waist, throwing his other arm over Reilly's narrow shoulders. With a deep breath, she moved their little convoy to the door, throwing it open without giving herself the chance to hesitate.

They tumbled into the hall. It looked exactly how it sounded—commanders screaming orders, soldiers sprinting up and down the hallways. The wall sconces burned brighter, as if they'd been dialed up to highlight exactly who didn't belong. Raegan plastered a confused look on her face, dropping her mouth open as she looked left and then right.

As a soldier rushed by—so young, *too* young—Oberon called out, "You there. What in the name of Kronos is going on?"

The soldier halted, immediately turning to face the three of them. The King's deep, authoritative voice and towering height no doubt made the soldier square their shoulders and formulate a reply. "Sir. The Undercroft was infiltrated. We are searching for the perpetrators."

"Oh," Raegan said with a giggle, twirling a curl around one finger. "Guess that's why Rochester had to cut out early. A shame."

The soldier turned to her, interest sparking on their long, thin face. "You've seen Rochester? No one can find him."

"He was with us," Reilly piped up, swaying back against

Oberon's muscular frame as if they were too drunk to stand. "Maybe, I don't know, twenty minutes ago?"

"More like thirty," Oberon corrected, amusement seeping into his tone. "This one's a bit out of it. Apologies, soldier—Rochester worked a privacy spell on his office, so we did not hear the commotion. We are only visiting diplomats, but we would have offered assistance sooner if we knew the gravity of the situation."

"He just said he had to check on something," Raegan added, stifling a very real yawn, putting her head on Reilly's shoulder. "Can we help at all, though?"

The soldier took in the three of them. "We're asking everyone to head out onto the front lawn for now. There will be officials there with more details."

"Copy that, soldier," Reilly said with a lusty wink.

Oberon, acting as if he were the most sober, shepherded the two of them through the long corridor. No one stopped them. Raegan fought to keep her movements relaxed and loose, her face muscles hurting from the silly girlish smile she kept plastered on her face.

She could hardly believe it when they exited the cavernous foyer onto the front lawn. There was a long queue of guests undergoing careful examination by Protectorate security. It didn't appear that anyone was being permitted to leave. Raegan gritted her jaw and looked over at the King. He met her glance with an equally worried expression. The physical glamours *might* hold, but Reilly would certainly be caught. She doubted Oberon wouldn't set off an alarm, and all they'd need to do was look a little too closely to see he wasn't human at all.

"We will not be able to sneak away," the King said to her, his voice low, one hand blatantly sliding to her ass, making the comment seem like a flirtation. He was right— soldiers with large, unnatural-looking dogs were beginning to circle the property. Floodlights burst into life across the gardens.

"Can Rainer get through the wards?" Raegan asked, tilting her head to look up at Oberon, letting her chest heave as she leaned toward him. Ideally, they'd get off the Protectorate compound, or at least out of the highest security zone, before summoning the kelpie.

"Who is Rainer?" Reilly asked, looking a little shaken before they pushed it away, playing up their intoxication.

The gravel crunched under Raegan's heels as she pivoted toward them, cupping their jaw in her hand. "A kelpie," she replied with a forced giggle.

"Probably," Reilly said with faux drowsiness, leaning into her touch. "It's less about getting in and more about getting *out*."

"We will be able to fend off the wards," Oberon said in a low, sonorous tone, running one hand down Reilly's arm. The Protectorate soldier trembled, making Raegan choke back a laugh. No one, it seemed, was immune to the Unseelie king when he turned his attention their way. "It will be a short opening, though. A few moments. There can be no hesitation, no mistakes."

"Still want to come home with us?" Raegan asked Reilly, straightening the lapel on their jacket. They nodded, their expression gone solemn again.

Her eyes slid to Oberon as he reached into the pocket of his waistcoat and pulled out a small vial. In the floodlights, the river water contained beneath the glass glimmered viciously. For a moment, her mind wandered—back to that moment in the alley in Philly when Oberon had summoned Cath Palug, the faerie cat who'd kept the Protectorate distracted. She remembered the heat of his body against hers, those brief seconds held to his chest among the weeds and debris. She'd thought that would be all she'd ever get to taste of him. And now she'd had all of him since then, time and time again—yet she still wanted him as fervently and as achingly as she had in that alley. Her yearning, it seemed, was as insatiable as the tides, ebbing in and out, but never able to stop reaching for the rugged beauty of his shoreline.

The King held her gaze, something dark and ravenous moving in the ocean of his eyes that made her wonder if he knew exactly what she was thinking.

"Take me home," she murmured, the words barely breaching the real world, intended only for the ears of the faerie king.

His elegant fingers curled around the vial. The glass shattered, sending black water trickling down his hand like tiny tendrils of ink. And then the King called to Rainer, not the summonings Raegan knew but a communion between two inhuman beasts that time could not touch. She felt the wards constrict, a bear trap clamping down, and then she let those winding rivers within her rise to meet it. The glamour she'd created from Rochester's oath fractured and broke, a fine weave of silk to a shard of glass and finally, to nothing at all.

From deep within the abyss of the Rivers that could not be dammed or denied, a kelpie shimmered into existence, fully-formed, at the King's side. Gasps went up from the crowd around them. For a moment, all the world hung still —a handsome guest at a gala shedding his humanity, a fabled creature dissolving from thin air. Someone screamed.

And then a hundred Protectorate soldiers were rushing toward them, incantations hurtling through the air. The King tossed Reilly onto Rainer's back as if they were a child, reaching for Raegan next. She summoned the rain that had fallen earlier—river water once, river water again—and soldered it into a shield. The working gleamed like a scythe, stopping that teeth-rattling magic in its tracks. The Protectorate wards howled and tore into the shield, but it held despite the horrific pull Raegan felt on every ounce of her flesh.

Then she was astride Rainer's broad back, Reilly in front of her, the King behind, his shadows devouring the weave of the wards, panther-like in their ferocity. Rainer leapt forward, his scalloped ears moving this way and that, as he charged for the opening Oberon had created. It was going to *work*. Elation burst golden in Raegan's ribs, banishing that ever-present doubt.

Oberon had chosen a gap in the Protectorate's guard, lessening their chance of injuries inflicted by more mundane, but just as dangerous, weapons. As the kelpie raced toward the growing fissure in the wards, hurtling around a boxwood sculpture, Raegan saw something that made her heart stop.

Three soldiers—armed to the teeth, their faces covered by helms—violently tackling a tall, beautiful, dark-skinned woman. *Alanna.* A nightstick slammed into the Protectorate woman's stomach, and she doubled over, shouting something Raegan couldn't hear above the thrum of blood in her ears.

"Oberon!" She turned to face him, finding his eyes already trained on Alanna. Their gazes met. The next second, Rainer slammed to a halt, swinging his head around to look at them in frustrated shock. Arrows landed like stones against a window on Raegan's shield.

"Get Reilly out of here," Raegan yelled, sliding off the kelpie in unison with Oberon. "Then come back for us if you can."

Rainer followed the King's gaze beyond the shield of river water and shook his head. "What a terrible time to have honor," he scoffed before he turned, gathered himself up, and leapt into the door the King's shadows had carved into the wards. It closed behind him like a cauterized wound.

And then it was just her and Oberon against the entire might of their oldest enemy, in the very seat of all their horrible power.

CHAPTER THIRTY-NINE

Oberon raised a hand, sending a plume of silver-laced smoke bursting into the air—a signal for Maelona to get out and meet at the rendezvous point. Raegan watched as dull black armor began to slink into existence across his body: arm bracers with elongated, violent edges, blackened chainmail, and of course, that terrifying blade spun of shadow and unearthly power.

The King gripped her bicep with his gloved fingers, pulling her behind a tall, sculptural hedge as battle magic tore through the air around them. "Do not let them separate us," he told her, his gaze steady. "Hold your shield. Do not stop unless I do."

"I'm with you," Raegan said, offering him a grim smile. She risked a glance out around the side of the hedge maze. The festive—if heavy—atmosphere had been rent in pieces by the appearance of the Unseelie king. The Protectorate's guests were scattered, some cowering behind heavy gray planters as if that might save them. Many, it seemed, had retreated into the Manor; it looked to be mostly soldiers out on the killing field of the front lawn.

"Ready?" the King asked, gazing down at her, mischief pulling at the sides of his mouth as if this were all a game.

"Why not, I guess?" Raegan replied, trying to quell the explosion of anxiety eating away at her insides.

He arched his brow at her, obscenely playful given the battle magic rocketing through the air, and then strode out into the open. He did not slink or sneak or even dart. Instead, the King moved in deliberate, graceful strides. Raegan kept pace with his bold movements though her heart felt like it might burst out of her chest. As attack workings rolled in, she fought to extend the shield, her teeth bared, sweat trickling down her back.

"Hey," she managed, "just wondering, are you fucking insane?"

"Yes," Oberon answered her, batting away a particularly nasty battle spell with the flat edge of his blade. "But you enjoy that, do you not?"

It was absurd that even in the middle of a battlefield, he could reduce her to little more than half-mad need. The way he spoke those words—his tone husky with promise—as he moved in a beeline toward Alanna, the moonlight cascading across his black armor, impossible and deadly and beautiful all at once . . . She'd die for him, Raegan realized, and he'd die for her, and there was something intoxicating about strolling so close to death the way most couples strolled around a leafy park.

Exhilaration shot through Raegan as a small group of soldiers came bursting from a hedgerow, blocking her sightline of Alanna. The Protectorate were armed to the teeth, covered head to toe in dull plated armor that hummed with protective workings. None of it mattered; Oberon summoned a bank of shadows and sent it coiling toward the soldiers, where tendrils of darkness shoved themselves into throats and noses and eyes. They dropped to the ground, gloved hands clutching at throats, and Raegan tried not to feel glee.

Instead, she stepped over the prone Protectorate, the dirtied train of her dress sliding across their bodies like a funeral shroud. Only twenty feet or so left to reach Alanna. Shoulder-to-shoulder with the King like this, adrenaline and fury rushing through her like river waters, Raegan felt like she could do anything.

But the more rational part of her brain recognized that she was drenched in sweat, droplets running into her eyes, her hair plastered to her skull. She didn't know how much longer she could hold her shield so resolutely, not with the intensity of the attack workings increasing with every moment. One slammed into her defensive wall so hard that every bone in her arms rattled. She clenched her teeth, ignoring the pain.

"Hey!" Raegan managed, the word coming out strangled not by pain or fear but by long-suffering rage. "In case you can't see, we're your nightmares made flesh. We're fucking primordial. But we only want the girl. Give her to us, and you live."

Two more steps forward, and the King's blade clashed with a spear of sainted iron someone had expertly lobbed their way. Raegan hadn't seen it. She swallowed hard. They were running out of time. Alanna was still a ways off, the soldiers who had restrained her dragging her backward for every step she and the King took forward.

Through the chaos, Alanna's eyes met Raegan's. Something sparked in the rebel's brown gaze, hope so fierce it turned furious. Without a moment of hesitation, Alanna spun to face the soldier pinning her arms to her back and headbutted them hard. The two other Protectorate scrambled to restrain her, but they'd been understandably focused on the two eldritch terrors advancing on them. Alanna ducked out of the larger one's grasp, grabbing their nightstick in the same movement and swinging it up to slam into the shorter soldier's jaw.

Then she ran, crossing the open, dangerous space, trusting Raegan and Oberon to keep her alive. Raegan gathered up everything she had, a scream tearing from her throat, as she sent the edges of her shield to extend to Alanna. Bullets ripped through the air but found no purchase. The woman tumbled into them, Oberon catching her with one outstretched arm and pulling her between himself and Raegan.

Now for the retreat. Like a soundless orchestra, everything fell into pace—the King pivoted to tear a path through the forces that had snuck up behind them, Raegan holding the shield at their backs. Despite the blood pouring down her face, Alanna yanked an impressive amount of knives from her belt and threw them with alarming accuracy. There was gore and screaming and the rending of bone. Raegan focused only on her shield and the feel of the King at her back, all of her instincts attuned to chasing the heat of him, just as she always had, across time and space and continents.

And then her vision blurred, the world broken into pieces by black splotches. "No," she grunted, biting down on her tongue. "No. Not yet."

But her shield faltered all the same and someone stole up close to her, all carefully trained movement and calculated attack. The King flipped his hold on the pommel of his sword and swung it in a backwards arc toward the attacker. They just missed being cleaved in two, taking the brunt of the sword's power at their shoulder. But it was enough—they screamed and plummeted to the ground.

Raegan staggered back another step, her mouth painfully dry, only dimly aware of Alanna at her side, who also seemed to be tiring. She risked a glance over her shoulder. The sweat and warmth coating her body chilled, terror slinking down her spine at what she found awaiting her. A well-organized group of thirty or so soldiers blocked the garden's exit in a solid half-moon, pinning them in place to be destroyed by the Protectorate forces advancing from the Manor.

Every step felt like her ankles were breaking. She should've fainted by now, Raegan knew, but it wasn't an option, it couldn't happen, so she clung to consciousness. The King slowed his pace, no doubt calculating what to do about this encroaching net of Protectorate. The Manor's wards dug deeper and deeper into Raegan with every passing second—the worst agony she'd ever endured, like meat hooks had been driven into all her joints and now she was being pulled in every direction all at once.

Her shield flickered, and a bullet grazed Alanna's thigh. A gossamer-thin wash of darkness cloaked Raegan's shield—Oberon, lending some of his power to reinforce her working, even though he felt the wards just as she did. No, Raegan realized. He must feel the defensive spells *much* more than she did.

"Isn't it time," a voice called, "to surrender already?"

"Fucking Bedwyr," Raegan spat, knowing she shouldn't expend energy so uselessly but unable to stop herself.

"Aren't you tired of all this?" the knight continued, speaking from somewhere Raegan couldn't see him—likely at her back, facing the King. "Aren't you—"

Bedwyr's words cut off in a guttural sound, followed by a small commotion.

"What's happening?" she hissed to Alanna, though her words, too, were cut short. Hooves on gravel, she realized—Rainer returning to them. She grinned through the pain, tasting sweat on her tongue, and poured everything she had left into the shield. And then the King's arm was around her waist, Alanna laughing in her ear, the broad, muscular back of a kelpie between her thighs, the wind in her air. And then, predictably, even though she fought it, nothing but darkness.

～

Fervently whispered words, a cool hand on her clammy forehead, a bloodcurdling scream, her name in the wind, the scent of fire crackling hot and hungry.

"Raegan," someone said, hoarse and urgent, "you gotta wake up."

"Okay," she grumbled in response, pulling herself from the downy dark of the void. She blinked her eyes open, finding Maelona crouched before her. "You're okay," Raegan gasped, rocking forward to toss her arms around her aunt.

Maelona froze at the contact and then relaxed, gripping Raegan hard in return. "Alive for now," her aunt said with a fierce smile as they broke apart. "We need to go. We all made it to the rendezvous point but with a lot more heat on us than we had planned for. We're in the hawthorns now. But they're . . ."

Raegan understood the thick scent of fire and smoke in her nose. Her heart plummeted to the bottom of her stomach. "They're *burning* them," she whispered. She pulled herself to her feet with a groan, dismayed to see dead leaves and forest debris had marred the storm-gray silk of her dress. The wound on her shoulder had been field-dressed with a strip of starched white fabric—Rochester's shirt that Reilly had been wearing, she realized.

Biting down on her tongue and praying her head would

clear, Raegan took in her surroundings. She saw Oberon and Rainer a few paces off, deep in a hushed conversation. A twinge of tension in her chest gave way upon seeing they were both safe. But then her gaze drifted toward the night sky and her stomach twisted again. Smoke billowed in noxious plumes, thick as a stormfront and far too close for comfort.

"We can't go back to Hiraeth," Raegan said in a whisper, meeting Maelona's eyes. "Not with the Protectorate so close. There's too much risk they might be able to follow us."

"No, we can't," her aunt agreed. She brushed dirt from her palms—she must've been keeping watch over Raegan until she regained consciousness. "There's an old faerie fort not far from here."

"A *Seelie* faerie fort," Alanna chimed in, materializing from the darkness of the hawthorn wood that surrounded them. The blood had been cleaned from her face, the wound on her thigh wrapped in more of that starched white fabric. Oberon, Raegan remembered all at once, did not have the power to heal. Not magically, at least. He'd been created to destroy. Nothing more, nothing less.

"Protectorate's been trying to get into that fort for a while," Reilly said, appearing from Alanna's far side, desiccated leaves crunching underfoot. They pulled Rochester's tux jacket tighter around their body, shivering. Their dress shirt had clearly been sacrificed to tend to wounds. It was sort of a look, though, Raegan thought deliriously.

"They can't breach it," Maelona said, her mouth a grim line. "They've been throwing some of the younger folks— like Alanna and Reilly—at it. The perimeter's secured. We just can't get *inside*."

"And you think I . . ." Raegan pulled on the door in her

mind that led to Titania's life—her time as the High Seelie Queen. She wished fiercely and fervently for Blodeuwedd.

"There are few other options," Oberon said, moving closer to her, Rainer at his side. The King's gaze turned skyward, watching the approaching curls of flame.

"Well," Raegan said, coughing, "I suppose we've tried stupider shit tonight."

"Can't argue with that," Maelona grumbled at the same time Rainer tossed his massive head in triumph, sending the heavy waves of his mane rippling in the smoke-choked moonlight.

A few moments later, Raegan and the King were leading the way through the hawthorn woods, mounted on Rainer. The kelpie had been able to call a few of his comrades. Maelona was astride a silvery mare with white crowfoot blossoms wound into her long braids, while Alanna and Reilly rode double on a stocky, stoic kelpie the color of black floodwaters, his mane roached short on his thick neck.

Smoke billowed into Raegan's eyes as Rainer surged through the wood. Tears tumbled down her face—partially because of the fire, but also because this ancient copse of hawthorn trees was burning to the ground. All because they'd needed a safe harbor for a few moments. Hatred boiled low in her gut for the Protectorate, but she hated herself, too—for not being strong enough to end this so many years ago.

Up ahead, the hawthorns grew sparser, giving way to open moorland and lichen-covered rocks just visible in the moonlight. A whisper-thin sphere of shadows blinked into existence around their entourage. Silently, Raegan thanked Oberon. She didn't think she had very much left in her, which sent guilt spiraling up her throat. She forced it away, focusing on the rhythm of the kelpie beneath her and the faerie fort she only hoped she could open.

Forts had once dotted the landscape—underground dwellings with a small cache of rooms and supplies. They'd been essential to the Fair Folk's ability to move about the land unseen and organize against the Protectorate. Most of them had been cracked open like geodes in the past few hundred years, their glimmering insides raided and harvested by the enemy. If someone knew precisely what they were looking for, they might find a skeleton of a fort somewhere in the rural, tucked away places of the Isles.

But Raegan had no idea one still stood intact. Oberon was going along with an idea formed by three Protectorate-oathed humans, so she assumed he'd had some prior knowledge that a fort might still exist. She took a deep breath as Rainer burst out into the open moorland, nothing but the hawthorn berries they'd all shoved in their pockets offering a shred of protection against the heavy, burning eye of the Protectorate.

The kelpie moved like a shadow, his heavy hooves silent as he galloped. Raegan resisted the urge to hold her breath, scanning the horizon line. Instead of a gray-suited soldier or a faerie fort's beacon, she felt the sweep of a river somewhere, her sisters of the water calling out gently, lending their strength.

"Is there a river nearby?" she asked the King.

"The Derwent," he replied, the English name spilling from his tongue.

The night wind whipped through her hair, stinging her face with its cool kisses. Raegan grinned into the pain. "Derwennydd," she whispered into the air. Somewhere in the distance echoed a rush of tides—a roar, a battle cry. She felt the King go still at her back.

"Around the next bend," Alanna called from Rainer's

left, pointing toward a craggy knoll. A cairn crowned the top of its rise—from when mortals had understood the power of the old places and respected them instead of harvesting the guts of what remained.

Rainer swung around a large flat stone pockmarked by a thousand years of rain, the moorland tilting down beneath his hooves. By the glow of the moon, Raegan took in her surroundings, realizing that the site of the faerie fort was atop the banks of the Derwennydd. She grinned, feral and vicious.

"Stay astride," the King instructed Maelona, Alanna, and Reilly as he dismounted, holding a hand out to assist Raegan. She took it gratefully, sliding down to the peaty soil of the moorland. The faerie hill's knoll rose up before her, the river—barely more than a wide stream this far north—stirring at her presence.

"Do you have any idea how to get inside?" Raegan asked, wading through the knee-high stalks of heather, a difficult exercise in high heels.

Beside her, Oberon shook his head, the wan light of the moon just allowing her to see the movement. "No," he told her, stepping closer to the rise of the knoll. "You never allowed me to watch you open it."

She threw him a sideways glance, just for a moment, before turning her attention to the wide piece of broken shale at the hill's base. The dark stone devoured the moonlight. Raegan squinted, looking closer—was that an etching in the rock? She parted the heather and gorse gently, crouching down to examine the rock that was looking more and more like a threshold stone. It was cracked down the middle, but the carving was deep and deliberate. A spray of wheat, maybe? Oh no—feathers.

An owl.

Raegan's mind pulled her beneath the currents with

one sharp tug, showing her images of Blodeuwedd at her side, of this grassy hill when it had been young and sweet, of lanterns strung on the earthen walls of its interior, of the river creeping up from the shores and—

A howl of rage from the mouth of a kelpie tore Raegan's attention back to the present. She spun around, the knoll at her back, to find a wall of Protectorate soldiers coming at them from across the moorland. Their chainmail glinted dull and artificial under the moon's gaze, the muzzles of their guns pointed from gloved hands like hunting dogs straining at the leash.

"Do something before they get a time spell finished!" Alanna shouted, drawing a dagger from the top of her boot and throwing it into the night, where it hungrily embedded itself into the neck of a tall woman in a dusty navy suit. Alanna slid off the kelpie's back despite Oberon's request for her to do exactly the opposite. She yanked Reilly down behind her, shoving them toward the mouth of the fort. A few large stones circled the knoll, and Reilly crouched behind one, their face pinched.

Raegan's heart raced. Reilly was in no condition to fight. Maelona and Alanna were only human and had to be tiring. All no longer had magic, their oaths to the Protectorate broken.

She scanned the hills, watching black hounds materialize from the tall grasses. For a moment, Raegan's heart stopped in her chest—until one of the beasts tore into the thigh of a Protectorate soldier. She glanced over at the King, watching a bead of sweat glide down his temple, the muscles in his jaw feathering.

Raegan gritted her teeth. No more. No more iron littering the hillside, no more fingers of hungry men digging into the heather, no more chipping away at the bones of the old world. She curled her hands into fists and called to the river.

Power surged in her, the flame fed by her undying rage, and a shadow rose from the water, taller and taller, taller than even the King. A woman, or something that people might call a woman, a column of river water and ruin, arms like a spider, her fingers long and ravenous.

As Raegan watched, the massive creature unhinged its jaws. A damp, dark maw yawned wide. Then the river-woman's arms shot out into the Protectorate ranks and the screaming began.

Chapter Forty

"You will take no more from us," Raegan snarled, advancing into the meadow, little more than the dark river that rushed in her lowest places. There was nothing but that blackness, that cold and endless fury. She threw her head back and shrieked, banshee-like on the moonlit moors, feeding the river-woman all of her anger.

"You have taken my father," Raegan shouted, passing Rainer, who looked on with something like awe in his black toad eyes. She couldn't feel the ground beneath her feet. She should be unsteady, she thought distantly, walking in high heels on peaty ground, navigating clumps of thick grass and moss-covered boulders. But she floated, deity-like, sanctified, across the ancient ground. The woman-shaped column of river tore into the Protectorate ranks, soldiers clutched in her many hands. She drowned shouts and bullets as she drew them into her mouth, devouring and devouring and devouring.

"You have taken my aunt's freedom," Raegan continued, the wide stream at the bottom of the slope swelling into something too large, too thick with dark currents and silver eyes. "Alanna's autonomy. Reilly's choice. *No more.*"

The black hounds crafted from little more than spite and shadow were herding Protectorate soldiers toward the river creature's spindly-fingered hands, tearing apart anyone who fought back. Raegan reached for the Threads that spun all around her—magic, or what was left of it, tattered lines of silk sagging in the air—and stilled the ravenous column of water.

"If you, too, were never given a choice," she said, her voice hushed and yet still singing across the moor like a hymn, "leave now. I won't stop you."

The words had barely left her mouth when a number of soldiers—younger, from what she could see—dropped their guns and maces and spears. Time hung tense and still. And then one took off into the gloom of the moors, the woodsmoke from the burning hawthorns closing like a door behind them. Two more followed, then four, then ten. The force that remained was halved, reduced to rocky-faced mortals clutching tightly the sainted iron and the grips of their guns.

"So be it," Raegan said, and then she let the Threads go —released her hold on them entirely, letting the violence sing out true and unrestrained. The column of river water threw its head back and shrieked, more limbs sprouting from its sides, its jaws unhinging even wider.

"Raegan!" Maelona's voice came on the wind, whipping through her hair. Raegan turned and found her people at the door of the faerie fort. She watched the river slink toward the knoll, soft and gentle in its movements, so unlike the thing that ate Protectorate men hand over fist at her back.

She blinked, and then the next moment, she was standing beside her aunt. "The river will open it," she said, her voice not quite her own, staring down at the owl she'd carved into the threshold hundreds of years ago. It was cracked, yes, but its wings were still spread wide and proud, its beak still half-opened, that vicious cry building at the back of its throat.

Raegan watched, impassive and filled with peace, as the water slowly filled the owl etching. Once the carving had disappeared from view, golden bells rang in the distance like a homecoming. The hill face split down the middle, a seam opening for the first time in centuries, soft yellow glow spilling out into the gray velvet of the moorland night.

"In you go," Raegan said, ushering Maelona, Alanna, and Reilly into the forgotten faerie fort until only she, the King, and the kelpies remained on the other side of the door.

Rainer said something, long and low, the words from a language long forgotten, and then turned to dive into the surface of the river water, his comrades at his side.

The King stood resolute and still in the shadow, the moonlight tracing silver strands in his midnight hair. Raegan gazed up at him, a thousand feelings tangled in her chest, the love she felt for him so overpowering that she thought she might faint.

"You know," she said instead, gesturing toward the river-woman behind them, "there's a reason I've been called a maneater."

The faerie king swept low, his long, elegant fingers gripping her jaw in a way that made Raegan feverish and half-mad. Those ocean eyes met hers, the tide of him all-consuming. But his body was too far from hers; her skin craved contact, to consume the heat of him, to be consumed in turn.

"A terrible day to be a member of the Fair Folk and not a man," he murmured, his head cocked to one side, a dangerous gleam in his eyes, "for I would gladly be devoured by the likes of you."

Raegan seized the front of his tuxedo jacket and hauled her mouth toward his—no elegance, no whisper-light touches, just the depth of her hunger ruthlessly on display. The Protectorate flesh her river-avatar had devoured would not satiate her. Not the way the faerie king did with his ivory skin and coiled muscle and elegant hands.

He met her with an equal hunger, fingers curling into her hair, drawing her close to his broad frame. A moan escaped Raegan the second his tongue slid into her mouth; there were so many other places to invite him inside, so many other ways he could slip beneath her skin and claim her. The patched dusk quilt of the moor, the rush of the river, the final cries of the Protectorate soldiers, the baying of the King's hounds—it was all swept away on the currents of her desire. Her hands slid down his sides, moving to the front of his hips, fingers splayed across the sharp V of muscle.

"We have houseguests," Oberon reminded her, trailing his lips down her jaw, though his hands cupped her breasts, her body painfully aware she wore no bra beneath the structured silk dress.

"Let's get them settled," Raegan said breathlessly, but her hands also wandered, finding hard and tightly wound proof of the King's desire—though she'd heard it loud and clear in his hitched tone.

"They've had quite the night," Oberon murmured against the shell of her ear, his arm winding around her waist, palm open on the soft slope of her belly.

Raegan looked up at him, amazed that he was still hers and that maybe this time it might stay that way. "Follow me," she said, interlacing her fingers with his. And then, with one last glance at the now-quiet moors behind her, Raegan stepped into the seam of light. Like most old doors, there was a moment in-between, a long and skittering heartbeat where nothing was real at all. But then she stepped out into the hall of the faerie hill, the King's hand still in hers.

Memory burst like ripe orchard fruit, the juice running between her fingers, sticky and sweet. The faerie hill's main hall was a large, earthen chamber—the bones of it so much like the Undercroft that for a second, she wondered if they'd even made it out alive at all. But no—this place was different. The Undercroft's design was theft; this forgotten faerie hill the Protectorate could not breach was another thing entirely.

Thickly knotted vines—wisteria, she was quite sure—were latticed across the walls, holding the soil in place. Delicate glass ornaments hung from the bare vines, scattering rainbow kisses this way and that. The ground beneath her feet was a creamy stone shot through with veins of gold. She smiled up at the King and moved forward, headed for the hallway reaching off the entrance room.

Willow-o-wisp lights studded the corridor like strange sapphires, curling around the shadows. Each willow-o-wisp was contained in the metal-worked mouth of a swan, its elegant neck curving away from the wall, beaks open to emit light. Despite the cobwebs stretched across the lights, Raegan marveled at them—their cobalt-teal hue, dancing with wild abandon in a way no natural flame should.

At the end of the corridor, three hallways branched off a small chamber. In the middle of the space stood an elegant round table with three impossibly delicate skeleton keys upon it. The golden metal winked in the light. The air smelled like wisteria and cool spring water and osmanthus, the deep, rich smell of petrichor and dark earth lingering beneath.

Wordlessly, Raegan and the King stepped down the hallway with light spilling from its mouth; the other corridors were silent and dark. They emerged into a great room.

Dark carved wood graced the walls, the cream marble joined by deep blue accents that created mesmerizing patterns. At the far end, an enormous marble fireplace drenched the space in a warm orange glow. The hearth was shaped like an owl—stone wings stretching out along the walls, the mantle formed by powerful shoulders, its head and beak just above, another willow-o-wisp glittering in the depths of its open maw.

Sitting in front of the fire, wrapped in woolens likely retrieved from the open cedar chest beside the hearth, were Alanna, Maelona, and Reilly—all safe, their bodies curled around one another. A moth-eaten silk settee had been dragged off to the side, its legs broken off, likely to feed the flame. A large table sat in the middle of the room, looking like it had also been carved from marble. Raegan walked past it, running her finger down its side, creating a stark line in the dust that had gathered over the years.

"I cannot believe it's all still here," she murmured, startling Maelona, who turned sharply, worry written clearly across her features.

"We're all alive," her aunt whispered, one brow arching. "I'm astounded." Despite her low tone, Reilly and Alanna stirred, and then Raegan had three sets of wide, mortal eyes staring up at her and the King.

"This faerie fort was mine," Raegan explained, clasping her hands in front of her. "When I was Titania, the Seelie Queen."

"The Queen of the Hill," Alanna murmured, her gaze going even wider.

"Yes," Raegan confirmed, gaze darting toward the King, who watched her with his usual dark intensity. "We are safe here. I don't think they'll have much luck breaching the walls."

"But we will be under siege," Oberon said when she fell

silent. "We should rest, but then we need to catalog our supplies and calculate how long we can reasonably stay here."

"This place is, like, hundreds of years old and covered in ten centimeters of dust," Reilly said, a yawn cutting their words in half. "How could there possibly still be edible food or anything of the sort?"

Oberon and Raegan exchanged glances. "There's a lot of magic in this place," she settled for, catching Reilly's yawn—her body still mortal, after all. "I'll explain later. I'm exhausted. Remember the table in the hall? You'll find keys on it. The lights will lead you to your rooms. For now, will the three of you be okay if I go take a bath?"

Alanna and Reilly nodded easily, but Maelona's gaze locked onto hers. "I have questions for you, niece," Maelona said, and Raegan might've thought they pertained only to the workings of the fort had her aunt's eyes not strayed to the King.

"Later, I promise," Raegan replied, offering a smile that took too much energy to muster.

Maelona didn't relent with the steel in her gaze, but then she nodded, waving her niece off. Raegan wavered, watching as Maelona gathered the woolen blanket around her and curled up on her side. Raegan exchanged a long glance with Oberon and then turned to investigate the quarters the fort offered.

She remembered the hill being eerily close to sentient with all the magic she and Blodeuwedd had poured into it—a necessary expenditure considering the political machinations of the Seelie Court. Moving slowly, Raegan took in the tapestries hung on the walls. Their stories were incomplete, half-devoured by moths as the strength of the housekeeping spells she'd woven into the space had weakened over the years with the loss of residual magic. She left the great room, sliding her arm into the King's.

She plucked a key from the center table, gesturing toward the hallway that bloomed with soft, wisteria-toned light the moment her fingers brushed the metal. "Have you been here before?" Raegan asked, parts of her memory still fuzzy.

"Yes," the King replied, moving soundlessly at her side toward the mouth of the corridor. "I think with some rest, you will remember quite vividly."

Raegan frowned, digging for the memory. Then, a beat too late, her brain registered the slinking heat in his tone. "Ah," she replied, leading them to a doorway at the end of a short hallway, sliding the golden filigree key into the lock. "I brought you here for that first discussion about uniting the Courts."

Before she could open the door, Oberon reached above her, his open palms against the earthen walls, pinning her in. "And I tasted you for the first time here, too."

Warmth unfurled low in her belly, but Raegan rolled her eyes, reaching over to push the door open. "You were trying to seduce me. You saw an opportunity," she said playfully, ducking beneath his arms to enter the chamber the faerie hill had conjured for them.

The space was, unsurprisingly, breathtaking. More dark wood stretched across the walls, carved with all manner of ornamentation and medallions. The flat panels in between the intricate moldings were painted with breathtaking scenes—a unicorn, decorated in gold leaf, before a verdant meadow; a dragon curled at the bottom of a river, mother-of-pearl shimmering on its scales; a griffin flying low at sunset, the sky studded with amber jewels. In one corner, the floor sloped downward, a spotless clawfoot tub lounging across the creamy marbled floor.

A large canopy bed towered at the far end, its linens thankfully fresh. She and Blodeuwedd had tied a few of the more important housekeeping spells to the river instead of relying on ambient magic. They'd focused on the necessities, like clean bedding, preserved food and fresh water, though now Raegan wished they'd taken the time and energy to protect things like the tapestries, too.

"Yes, I saw an opportunity," Oberon admitted, his voice a low, deep, sonorous sound just above her ear as he stalked in behind her. He paused, pulling their luggage tags from his pocket and setting them down on a carved wooden chest by the bed's footboard. The dossier followed, retrieved from beneath the fabric of his waistcoat. "But I desired you as well. Much more than I had any right to. Much more than good sense and all my careful plans dictated."

Despite its grandeur and the way it felt like home in a way almost nowhere did, the faerie hill's chamber faded away. The world condensed to the beating, wild-hearted love conjured by the Unseelie king. Raegan turned to face him, ensuring the door was closed. He swooped low, arms encircling her, and kissed her until she felt like the world had stopped turning.

Then Oberon lowered himself to one knee before her again, even though she saw the way his body caught in painful places, and undid the buckles on her high heels. "You did say I could undress you if we survived," he murmured, his hand skimming up the back of her calf to her thigh as he recalled a playful conversation they'd had during one of their many planning sessions. Goosebumps blossomed across her flesh, the ache winding tighter in her core.

"And you said," Raegan panted, curling her fingers into the silken strands of hair at the back of his neck, "if I got the dossier, you'd fuck me with more than your tongue."

"And I," the King replied, helping her out of her shoes

and then rising to stand, his large hands spread wide over her hips, "always keep my promises."

"No, you don't, faerie king," Raegan laughed, unbuttoning his waistcoat, delirious and incandescent with belief and joy they were alive.

"For most souls, no, I do not," he agreed, slipping the silk straps from her shoulders and then bringing his mouth to her collarbone. "But for you, my love? *Always*."

Chapter Forty-One

"I told them I was taking a bath," Raegan laughed as Oberon pressed her onto the bed, his body an unrelenting weight she would happily be crushed beneath.

"You will," he replied, tone gruff as he gathered up the floating train of her dress—mostly torn to pieces, a few scattered pieces of dead leaves caught in the silk.

"To be clear," she replied, her voice shooting up three octaves as he ghosted her shoulder with kisses, "I'm not complaining."

She felt the deep rumble of laughter in his chest, their bodies fitted together like a locket. He undid the zipper on the side of her dress, exposing her skin to the warm, humid air of the room. Raegan tipped her head back with a sigh, admiring the patterned canopy top over the bed for about two seconds before the King slid the bodice of her dress down to her waist. The ache between her legs wound tight and pleading as she met his gaze, shimmying her hips so he could pull every stitch of clothing from her body.

For a moment, he stilled, gazing down at her in the same way Raegan had seen people look at art in museums. The

King's full mouth parted slightly as he traced the fan of her auburn hair, haloed around her head, his fingertips brushing her jaw and then her collarbone. Both of his capable hands closed around her ribcage, a feather-light touch, sliding down her waist to her hips and then her thighs. His name tumbled out of her mouth, dampness gathering in her core.

"You have all of me," Oberon murmured, his palms at the back of her knees, guiding her thighs around his hips.

Raegan's chest heaved with thick, suffocating desire as she closed her legs around him. "I'll keep coming back," she panted—even though he'd hardly touched her. "Bury me shallow *every* time, Oberon. I'm coming back for you."

An endless sorrow blossomed in the ocean of his eyes, but then he bowed over the edge of the bed and kissed her. She fisted the starched fabric of his dress shirt in one hand, fumbling for the waistband of his trousers with the other. But as much as she wanted his skin against hers, she also loved being exposed to him like this: the King still dressed in his fine, dark clothing, all power and menace, backlit by the willow-o-wisps on the walls, while she ached and panted naked on the silken sheets below his broad, muscular frame.

"I belong to you," Oberon said, his lips moving against her skin, one hand sliding to the apex of her thighs. The other lightly pinched the tip of her breast, sending a moan careening out of Raegan's mouth as her back arched, pushing her chest into his. Even with her head tipped back in pleasure, she felt the heat of him shift as he knelt at the edge of the bed between her thighs.

"You promised," Raegan managed as he kissed the inside of her leg, long fingers caressing her ankle.

"I did," he agreed, eyes sliding to hers, mouth drifting closer to her center. "Burying my face between your thighs is *my* reward for our survival, not yours. Unless you object?" He'd already begun soft, slow circles on her core, his touch unreasonably pleasurable, his precise understanding of her body an absurd, beautiful thing.

"Take what you want, Unseelie king," she murmured, meeting his gaze with one brow arched, opening her thighs wider for him.

Oberon tilted his head back and sighed—a velvet sound, lush and luxurious. "What I want," he said, deepening the pressure of his fingers, pulling a cry from her lips, "is to die like this. *Just* like this." And then his mouth met the wet, wanting heat at her center and Raegan's vision went white. All the tension curled low in her belly exploded. She felt frenzied and wild, rolling her hips against the King, desperate for more. Every time, she knew, could be the last.

She captured one of his long-fingered hands, bringing it to her breast. He obeyed without question, toying with her in the precise way she wanted, bringing Raegan closer and closer to the edge.

"Do you enjoy how I play with you?" Oberon wanted to know, his voice hoarse and husky, barely lifting his mouth from her core.

"Shut up," Raegan panted, gripping a handful of the bed linens in one fist. "Obviously I do. Don't stop."

The King's laugh rang out like a bell, and then his darkness closed all around her—his mouth at her center, hands roaming her body, all of it dedicated to her pleasure, her wants, her cravings. She fell apart for him, crying out his name like a declaration. Distantly, Raegan registered when he slipped out from between her thighs and lifted her into the center of the bed. As her breathing returned to normal, the daze of pleasure morphing into a quiet, satisfied peace, she realized she heard the sound of water running.

"Right," she mumbled, pushing thick curls away from her face as she rolled to her side. "A bath."

At the far end of the room, steam curled in wisps from

the mouth of the clawfoot tub. It was large, big enough for two, but somehow not ostentatious, its porcelain a mild-mannered cream, though its feet were darkened silver and decorated in dagger-sharp claws.

The King crossed her vision, reappearing at the end of the bed as he began to unbutton his shirt. She sat up, long hair tumbling across her shoulders. She shimmied onto her knees and moved closer to where Oberon stood. His dark gaze dipped to her—the expanse of her generous thighs as she sat on her knees, the hills of her soft belly, her full, heavy breasts, partially covered by her hair.

"You drive me mad, witch-queen," he whispered, hand stilling on his shirt buttons.

Raegan grinned, tossing a length of hair over her shoulder. "That's the *only* response I'll accept when I take my clothes off," she replied, hungrily eyeing his exposed skin, the dusting of dark, silken hair across his chest visible below his undone collar.

"You drive me equally as mad when you are fully clothed," the King said, his hands sliding into her hair, mouth meeting hers.

Raegan's body keened in response, the ache between her legs returned already, sharp and wanting. He trailed his lips down her neck, taking the tip of one breast into his mouth as he cupped the other, fingertips light across sensitive flesh. She moaned, digging her nails into his back before reaching for the front of his shirt.

She realized he'd been struggling to undo the buttons— the small, mother-of-pearl things were lovely and a gorgeous finish for the fine garment but not practical for the pain she knew he must be feeling.

"Let me," Raegan said. He pulled away from her slightly, hands returning to her hair. She bit down on the inside of her lip as she worked her way down the buttons, eager to feel his skin against hers. "And if at any point, you're in too much pain, please tell me."

A shimmering kind of warmth spread across his angular features in response to her words. Raegan's heart leapt. "I think," the King replied, his voice thick, "you may be able to bring me enough pleasure to override the pain."

"It would be an honor," she said with a laugh, looking at him again. Then she came up on her knees, threw her hands around his neck and kissed him like it might make up for everything. For all the suffering, all the pain, all the ache. She slid her fingers up the back of his neck, pressing her breasts to his chest, pulling him closer and closer.

"I'm yours," Raegan whispered fervently against his mouth. "Every part of me, every life, every door, every name I've ever had. Yours. Always."

She didn't stop saying it as he pulled her into his arms, his shirt discarded on the floor below, trousers half undone. Not even as he carried her to the bath, not as they both slipped into the silken waters. And though she could barely form words when he buried himself deep inside of her, every ounce of his power and alabaster skin and intricate musculature focused solely on her, she tried to say it again. Again, again, and again.

Just in case.

~

Raegan slipped out through the heavy door, pulling the soft dressing gown tighter around her waist. Her stockinged feet were quiet on the stone floors, the willow-o-wisp lights devouring her shadow in their strange dances.

She'd woken up and hadn't been able to fall back asleep. It should've been peaceful—the high earthen ceilings of the faerie fort, the gentle tide of the King's breathing at her side, that bone-deep ache quiet for the moment. But her thoughts had run wild and sharp-edged, so she'd tried to rummage through her bags as quietly as possible. Oberon had appeared to be in a deep sleep—a rare thing—and she hadn't wanted to wake him.

Part of Raegan was not surprised when she passed through the connective chamber, finding that Alanna and Reilly had taken their key—the fort must've guessed they wanted to room together—but Maelona's still sat on the table, the filigreed gold winking in the cobalt light. Raegan sighed as she passed by, making her way to the great room.

"Hey," Maelona greeted without turning around as Raegan slipped over the threshold. Her aunt was still wrapped in an ancient woolen blanket, seated in front of the fire.

"Hey," Raegan returned. She slowed her pace across the mosaic tile, her heart starting to thud thick and heavy in her chest. It was time—past time, actually—to tell Maelona about Cormac. "Is it okay if I sit down with you?"

"Sure," Maelona said, looking over her shoulder now, her eyes bloodshot and weary.

Raegan took a deep breath and sank down on the cool floor next to her aunt. For a long time—an impossibly long time—she just stared at the grand fireplace. The towering marble, stylized as an owl, made Art Nouveau designs by mortals seem trite. The hearth also made her ache for Blodeuwedd. Like her love with Oberon, her and the owl-woman's friendship transcended time, refuted all the attempts at separation and despair. Raegan yearned for the feeling of talons on her shoulders, to watch Blodeuwedd take off into the golden autumn sunlight. For tables piled high with orchard-fresh fruits to share with her people. She swallowed and blinked back tears. The Seelie Court—at least, what it had been when it was hers—was gone. Like most things she loved.

"Why did my dad know the Unseelie vow?" Raegan asked, her words barely louder than the crackle of the fire, everything muffled by the sloping ceilings of soil and wisteria vine. "He taught it to me. Why?"

Maelona sighed, dropping her head into her hands. An odd feeling came over Raegan—that she might not even care about the answer. That it might not even matter. She wondered whether it was due to exhaustion or the immensity of everything she had thrown herself into, or maybe a combination of both. She supposed that didn't matter, either.

"When we were young, younger than Alanna and Reilly, even," Maelona began, the words hoarse and thorn-edged, like the bramble at the edge of a meadow before it turned into dark and deep wood, "your father and I handled a small raid of some mortal witches in North Wales. A good operation for us to run, to prove ourselves a little, but without real stakes."

Maelona shifted, the firelight making it so painfully clear she was Cormac's sister. "Ended up with a little more than we could handle. The witches must've been tipped off, because nobody was at the cottage when we seized it. We sent part of our detail to pick up a trail while we went through the place. Wouldn't be unusual to find a secret compartment or a hidden door. Most witches with enough power to attract the Protectorate's attention have prepared for such inevitabilities."

Maelona's tone went dry as she raked one hand through her hair, hitting a knot and pulling her fingers away with a curse. Raegan fought to stay in her body as she watched a few strands of her aunt's hair drift through the air, silver shimmering in the firelight.

"Cormac touched a divination object without gloves," she continued, still staring straight into the hearth. "We always wear iron-lined gloves when we review the contents of a raid. Don't ask me why he wasn't wearing them. It's protocol. I don't know. He said he thought he had been, but then he heard a voice and went into a back room. The place was all rambling hallways and tight turns. I guess 'cottage' isn't really the right word, but you know, thatched roof, muddy pastures outside, paper-thin walls. Anyway. It was a scrying glass with active old magic, which is rare to stumble upon, even on a raid. Looked like a shitty glass bowl to me, so I gotta admit I might've picked it up to see the spellbook underneath it, too."

Raegan's heart hammered against her ribs. She picked at her cuticles, drawing blood. She dared not say anything to interrupt Maelona's flow of words; she knew too well how easily her aunt could clam up. But, she supposed, that was when Maelona had thought she'd been protecting Raegan. Her aunt had just watched her summon a giant river monster who ate a bunch of people. So maybe Maelona wasn't so concerned about that anymore. Either way, at least for now, they weren't talking about Raegan watching her father die in front of her eyes.

"The light from someone's torch caught the glass, and Cormac saw a vision," Maelona continued after a long pause, saying the words as if they tasted sour in her mouth. "Your father was always sensitive. He either struggled with Protectorate spellwork or nearly killed someone by accident in training. No in-between. But old Feyrish magic? He had a . . . knack for it, I guess. Right before he left, we could bring him a box of objects from a raid and he could tell just by looking which one had Fey magic still active in it. He followed a kelpie through the Brecon Beacons once just based on where he *felt* the magic go."

Raegan chewed on her lip. "That's all very interesting. But, uh, the vision?"

"Sorry," Maelona huffed. "He saw a woman—curly red hair, wearing a black leather jacket, bursting through a door and standing in this shadowy room with dark floral wallpaper. At the other end of the room, he saw a tall, black-haired Fey on a throne. He knew the woman was in danger. He also knew—and even your father didn't understand *how* he knew—that the woman was the daughter he'd not even conceived yet and that the Fey on the throne in the corner was the Unseelie king. And he knew she'd need the right words. He knew that more than his future child's life depended on it. He said, right after he put the glass down and stumbled back to me, that the entire world depended on it."

Maelona paused, the atmosphere winding tight and thick beneath the earth, deep in the faerie hill. "He said that if the woman said the right words, a secret, unseen Thread could unspool, and it would change everything."

CHAPTER FORTY-TWO

Awe and nausea, then the feeling of Fate's gaze—heavy, dove-winged, treacherous as quicksilver—bloomed in Raegan's body. She shuddered, pulling her dressing robe tighter, and seriously considered throwing one of the folded woolen blankets Alanna and Reilly had left next to the fireplace over her head like a child hiding from a nightmare.

"That's fucking insane," she managed, her lips feeling numb. "You know that, right? That's absolutely fucking insane."

"Well," Maelona said, turning to look at Raegan, pulling her knees to her chin, "was he right?"

She swallowed. "Yeah," Raegan breathed, holding her aunt's gaze. "Yeah, he was. Down to the goddamn wallpaper."

"And now we're here," Maelona replied drily. "In a forgotten faerie fort the best of the Protectorate couldn't open. With the Unseelie king. Trying to find the door to Avalon to retrieve a weapon that could end the world. But, like, in a good way, because fuck the world as it currently stands."

It was definitely the exhaustion that made Raegan throw her head back and laugh, and the same reasoning could probably be given for why laughter bubbled out of Maelona's chest. The last two living Overhills dissolved into a puddle of giggles, wrapped in woolen and antique cloth. When Raegan caught her breath, she looked up to find Maelona wiping tears from her eyes.

"You met Oberon, you said," Raegan asked, amusement drying up like a summertime riverbed, all the thoughts spiraling around inside her skull again.

"Oh," Maelona said, waving her hand. "Prague. The 70s. It was a whole thing. I . . . Despite the nightmares I still have, I always . . . I don't know. I got sent to investigate, and while I was away, someone sacked my and Cormac's apartment. He was followed around the compound the whole time I was gone. I won't bore you with what the politics were like back then, but . . . there were worse fates for me than having an admittedly terrifying encounter with the King."

The fire crackled loudly, a log crashing down from the cradle, making both of the women jump out of their skin. They exchanged sheepish glances and laughed, the vast room swallowing up the sound.

"I think," Maelona said after clearing her throat, "maybe he actually helped me. Made me and Cormac look less suspicious by going after me. And I mean, he didn't hurt me. Just trapped me in some shadowy half-realm for a day or so. If we both live, let's ask him about it."

Raegan agreed with a nod, the words about Cormac still strangled in her throat.

"Speaking of the King . . ." Maelona began, turning to look at Raegan, her brows etched with suspicion.

Anxiety twisted in Raegan's stomach for another reason. "I know," she replied, letting out a long sigh. "Am I being fooled by an immeasurably powerful faerie king? Have I been aiding and abetting the end of mankind for a thousand years?"

"Well," Maelona grumbled, her eyes darting away, "I wasn't gonna start there. But . . . Yeah."

"I can't rule it out, technically," Raegan said with a shrug, settling her chin on her knees, staring at the dancing flames in the hearth. "But no, Maelona. I understand you're looking at me as your niece, the last thing left of your little brother. And I *am* those things, sure. But I'm also a lot more. More than you can comprehend."

"Why would the Timekeeper allow you to be reincarnated into a Protectorate bloodline?" Maelona asked hoarsely, still not looking at Raegan. "Considering all that you are?"

"So I could be raised like a fattened calf to be devoured," she replied with a dark, caustic grin. "Long story. Fate's a cunt. She and the Timekeeper, they're constantly setting up for about a hundred different plays. But they wait until the last second to make their move. To twist the knife."

Maelona finally glanced at her then, eyes wide. "Sure. Fine. But look, could I . . . could I check you over for coercive spellwork? I'm actually really good at this, examining someone's Threads and seeing where they've been rewoven or tweaked."

Anger rose in Raegan like a tide, teeming with sharp-toothed things, all the rage of a storm surge. How *dare* she? This mortal creature of not even a century, thinking she could pick apart Threads stretching across a millennium, believing she could deliver some truth on whether the King's love was true or false?

Raegan sat up straight, poison gathering in the back of her throat. She opened her mouth to spit venomous words at Maelona but then closed it, pressing her lips together.

Yes, it was insulting, belittling, and completely absurd. And yet, it would make Maelona feel a lot better, wouldn't it? There was little way for her aunt to look and not see Cormac, not see a young niece who'd been thrown to the wolves. Maelona couldn't possibly look at Raegan and see the Queen of the Hill or the Witch of the Water. She just saw Cormac. Whom she didn't know, not with absolute certainty at least, was dead.

"Sure," Raegan said with a shrug, settling into a cross-legged position.

"Really?" Maelona asked, looking surprised, pulling her hands out from beneath the blanket. "Alright. Just don't fight me. Apparently it hurts if you do."

"I have felt the brutality of Protectorate magic," Raegan said, the words coming out of her stilted and ancient. "Many times, in fact. Rest assured I am familiar with its bite."

In the low glow of the firelight, Maelona examined her, as if she finally understood something about the woman seated before her. She exhaled and raised her hands—spindly and barely more than bone, the fingers shaking. And then she paused.

"Go ahead," Raegan said once more, relaxing her shoulders. She closed her eyes, not wishing to see Maelona's expression; she wasn't quite sure why. For a long moment, there was only the warmth of the hearth on her right side and the scent of osmanthus and petrichor. And then there it was; Maelona *was* actually fairly proficient, particularly for a mortal. Her aunt's magic was deft, though far from delicate, as it crept along her Threads. The sensation was still uncomfortable—her chest a filing cabinet that someone was rifling through with cold, sterile hands.

"Okay," Maelona said some time later. When Raegan opened her eyelids, her aunt was slumped, the blanket pulled higher on her shoulders. "Your Thread pattern is intense. You're definitely not mortal, not really. But no coercive spellwork that I can see. Just . . ."

"What?" Raegan asked, faint panic blooming in her chest.

Maelona let out a huff, raking her hand through hair, leaving the dark locks even more disheveled. "I thought it was a myth," her aunt said, looking up to finally meet her gaze. "This thing called a Godpath. It's a specific kind of knot in people's Threads that indicates some grand entity— Fate, in this case, probably—interfered with the weave of your essence. I've only ever read about them. You . . . you actually *have* Godpaths."

"Godpaths," Raegan repeated, her mouth dry, information racing through her mind from previous lives, though nothing really stuck.

"I mean, it could be something else that we just don't understand," she said with a shrug, looking absolutely exhausted. "Ask the King. Maybe it's just some Fey shit. But yeah. Godpaths. You have a lot of them, Raegan."

She looked away from Maelona, chewing on the inside of her lip. Hadn't she always known? Even with the Seal intact, even before she'd had a shred of evidence besides the books her father had left behind. Her mother had burned them, anyway—likely compelled by Cormac's protective spellwork, though certainly aided by her very real emotions —and left Raegan with only a mad, desperate hope. Some kind of deep-rooted certainty that she was destined for paths unseen.

It had been there all along, knotted deep in the fiber of her very marrow. Godpaths. The touch of the divine, of the grander things that made the universe turn. Raegan hated it and loved it at the same time. She didn't know how to say any of that to Maelona, though, so she just stared into the fire and picked at her cuticles. The memory of her father on the train prowled to the front of her mind, threatening to devour her if she didn't release it.

"I went into the Timekeeper's realm," Raegan blurted out, tears already choking her words. "There were a lot of things I didn't tell you. Thought I *couldn't* tell you. Probably best I didn't, I guess. Anyway, I found him."

Beside her, Maelona straightened, her knuckles going white. "Cormac?" she asked, a ghost in the firelight.

Raegan nodded, looking for the words. "The Timekeeper . . . Dad made a deal to get me out. It had nothing to do with the Gates. He wasn't chasing magic. Maybe he told you that to keep you safe or to keep us safe. I don't know. Maybe that was just easier to believe. He didn't want me in the Protectorate. And I guess . . . I never knew about the vision he had. But that's part of it all, obviously. So he made a deal. It kept me and my mom safe. He had to perform a spell after twelve years and a day. He did, and it set this whole fucking thing into motion because he'd been tricked."

Maelona said nothing, but the way her eyes held Raegan's was feverish, hungry. She'd said more than once she had accepted Cormac was dead, but as Raegan looked at her, it was very clear that even practical, stoic Maelona had held a shred of hope.

And Raegan was about to crush it. "Look, I'm a thousand years old, and so much of this doesn't make sense to me, either, because I'm not a primordial entity beyond comprehension." She fought for her words, for the right way to explain.

"Tell me, Raegan," Maelona rasped, leaning toward her, an arrow nocked.

"He's dead," she replied. "The Timekeeper used my dad like a fucking worm on a hook to get me where he wanted me, to be sure the King wouldn't be a problem. And then he killed him. Just like that. Turned him into dust as I watched."

Silence barreled into the wood-paneled great room, heavy as a freight train. Raegan's breath shortened, her chest hitching, dismayed to find out exactly how desperately she needed Maelona to not hate her.

"But you escaped?" her aunt asked, not a shred of emotion on her expression.

"Barely," Raegan replied. "Dad was caught in the bargain. His skin was . . . it was stitched to a train seat. He'd already been drained of so much. But I—I had meadowsweet in my pocket from Blodeuwedd, and I blew the dust into the Timekeeper's eyes, and then I ran. Because Dad told me to run. Because you have to understand, Maelona, that the only revenge at that point was living long enough to destroy everything the Timekeeper ever built."

Her aunt watched her, those familiar eyes glittering in the gloom. Raegan's heart climbed into her throat, and she thought of ten different things to say, to soften the blow or make herself look better, or maybe to plead with her aunt not to leave her, because everyone always left. Because Raegan was too hard to love.

But despite all the thoughts rattling in Raegan's head, the only thing Maelona did was pitch her body forward and wrap her arms around Raegan. One of them started crying, and the other followed with sobs of their own. Raegan buried her head in her aunt's shoulder and wept. She cried until her throat was sore, until she could barely breathe, and Maelona sobbed like a child, curling her body into Raegan's, tears dripping onto the tiled floor.

Good. Because she'd promised the Timekeeper a flood, hadn't she?

CHAPTER FORTY-THREE

Inside the faerie fort, day was indistinguishable from night. The willow-o-wisps cast the same eerie, pale, blue-lavender light, the earthen ceilings and near-black wood paneling unchanged by shifting slants of morning sun.

"You saw the ocean, right? Or some body of water?" Maelona demanded, the sound of her exasperated voice pulling Raegan from her thoughts. "So how the fuck could it be the yew trees?"

She chewed on her lip, refocusing on the items spread across the great room's massive table—a thick slab of dark wood settled on ornately carved legs. The end of the table was covered with the fort's foodstuffs—dried mushrooms and salted beef, dusty jars of pickled vegetables, sacks filled with flour, crocks of jam. Enough to last three mortals about a week, maybe more if they rationed conservatively. Raegan thanked the gods she'd listened to Blodeuweddd all those years ago when the owl woman had suggested an eternal food preservation spell, powered by the river, like the house-keeping workings.

The rest of the table's surface was taken up by the

pages of the Protectorate's dossier, a map with dried beans marking locations, and Raegan's notes made on delicate parchment Reilly had found in the storeroom. The nib of the pen, which had been tucked inside a roll of parchment, had bitten through the thin paper in multiple places.

"We're talking about a door to fucking *Avalon*, Maelona," Alanna sputtered, spreading her hands wide. "You might be thinking too literally."

"I wish we could just check all of the sites," Reilly offered, scratching their head. Their hair sprang out in unruly directions, sleep transforming their locks into a frizzy halo.

"It's too risky," Maelona snapped, massaging her temple with a few fingers. "They'd be opening themselves up to more battles with Protectorate forces. How many before the Timekeeper decides to leave the In-Between and come have a look for himself?"

"He won't," Raegan said, surprised by the sureness in her voice. "It's the same reason why Fate, in all Her truly terrible power, doesn't just move us around like puppets. Well, not exactly. She and Kronos—they're functions of the universe. She can fuck up my life, he can send all his armies raining down on this faerie hill, but neither can directly interfere with their own hand."

"He is too vulnerable in this realm as well," Oberon added, leaning onto the table, his weight on one palm. "I would not rule it out completely, but it is highly improbable."

Maelona threw her hands in the air. "A year ago, I would've thought it highly improbable I was going to be in a fucking faerie fort with two other traitors and the goddamn Unseelie king. But here I am."

"Why are you so fucking bitchy?" Raegan snapped at

her aunt before she could stop herself. "Usually it's endearing, but you're pissing me off right now."

"Oh, my apologies, your highness," Maelona replied, sweeping into a mocking bow, the blanket draped over her shoulders fluttering like a cape. "Despite all of your insane magic, the faerie fort that seems alarmingly sentient, and your incredibly powerful faerie king boyfriend, the fact remains that there are no cigarettes and *no goddamn coffee*."

Raegan blinked, absorbing Maelona's words. In her peripheral vision, she saw Alanna and Reilly exchange a glance of amusement. "He's not my *boyfriend*," she settled on, spitting the words out. To her outrage, she heard the rich sound of the King's laugh, followed by Reilly's giggles and a strangled sputter from Alanna.

"Glad to be of amusement," Raegan grumbled as she circled the table, trying her best to ignore the flush of embarrassment creeping across her face. She stubbornly refused to meet the King's gaze. He wasn't her fucking boyfriend. But he wasn't technically her husband, either, though the thought sent butterflies loose in her stomach.

Besides—she wasn't exactly in a laughing mood. She and Oberon had both expended themselves considerably to survive the fallout from the gala the night before. She'd barely been able to heal everyone's wounds without losing consciousness. The King wasn't faring much better—she could see his movements were heavy and stiff, lacking his usual grace. But they didn't have the luxury of rest. The Protectorate might not be able to get inside the faerie fort, but they'd retaliate—likely against whatever vulnerable places they could find in the Philadelphia court. Raegan winced at the thought.

She stared down at the dossier, running her eyes over the list. Frustration bared its teeth and she curled her hands into fists, relishing the sharp pain of her nails biting into her palms. Maybe they had no choice—maybe going to the remaining five locations was their only option. Raegan resisted the urge to fling the dossier across the room.

Instead, she forced herself to go through each page again. From the head of the table, Maelona sighed dramatically. Raegan didn't take the bait; besides, it *was* about the hundredth time this morning that her aunt had watched her do the exact same thing. Feeling the weight of everyone's eyes on her, Raegan tried to pick up her pace, only scanning for things she and the King might not have noticed before— notes in the margin, symbols, a hidden enchantment. With their broken oaths and no magic, there was only so much the three mortals could really do to help.

"Wait," Maelona said, nearly shouting the word, her hoarse voice brightened with excitement. "Alanna, do you have a knife?"

"Sure," the younger Protectorate operative replied, her dark brow furrowed as she plucked a small dagger from her belt and handed it across the table. Raegan's head snapped up to look at her aunt, the sudden bolt of understanding electrifying her entire body.

"Shit," she sputtered, snatching the dagger. Raegan's blood had let her pass the clock sentinel in the Undercroft, so there was at least a chance it might work on the dossier itself. But before she could do anything, a pair of large, powerful hands closed around hers.

"Would you permit me to help you?" Oberon asked, woodsmoke rolling over her senses as he drew closer. "Your hands have been shaking all morning."

Raegan turned to look at him, the feral angles of his impossibly beautiful face etched out in blue-black by the willow-o-wisps. "Good idea," she said, laying one hand flat on the table, palm up.

Oberon nodded, testing the sharpness of Alanna's

dagger against one of his own fingertips. Satisfied, he leaned over the table, his eyes meeting hers. Raegan nodded and then, with the heavy weight of the future settled on their shoulders, the King cut a tiny wound into her flesh. With a deep breath, Raegan turned her hand over, squeezing the cut finger above the dossier. A single glass bead—wine-dark, crimson-jeweled—tumbled toward the dossier.

Time held still, and Raegan might've watched the bloodrop's journey for a thousand years, something in the world stretching wide, a forgotten door opening. The paper drank up her blood, the spot disappearing in a heartbeat. Then the pages turned of their own accord, flipping to the back of the folio. Where there had once only been smooth leather, there was now a slim, flat pocket.

Raegan's heart stopped. Holding her breath, she desperately shoved her hand inside the pocket. A piece of heavy, thick parchment met her fingertips and she pulled it free, eliciting a gasp from Reilly.

With shaking hands, Raegan unfolded it, laying it flat on the table. For a moment, her vision swam and she was sure there was nothing but strange, looping symbols. After a few harrowing seconds, she understood that she was looking at magical passkeys to the surveillance spells embedded in all seven possible locations. She inhaled. Helpful, maybe, but not the kind of revelation she was looking for. Exhaling, Raegan turned the paper over, hoping beyond hope. And there, written in faded, old-fashioned calligraphy, she saw:

THOSE WHO KNEW THE LOCATION OF AVAL-ON'S DOOR, *to the best of our knowledge, both living and dead, contemporary and historical:*

- Danu, Mother of the Fair Folk {*beyond our reach*}

- Nyx, Goddess of Night {*slain by Kronos*}
- Rhyfelwr, leader of the kelpies {*slain by Bedwyr*}
- The Witch in/of the Wood, mortal sorceress {*dead of natural causes*}
- John Dee, mortal magician {*slain by the Unseelie king*}

Raegan's knees nearly gave out, hands trembling as her mind swam. "In our vision, the Morrigan said all doors once open to me remain open," she sputtered, struggling to find the words. "Fuck. And the Witch in the Wood said that to me when my Seal was removed." She swung to look at Maelona, her eyes wild. "Does the Protectorate *know* I was the Witch of the Wood?"

Her aunt stared at her, mouth falling open, gaze narrowing as she took in her niece. "No," Maelona whispered hoarsely. "The Witch in—*you* evaded the Protectorate almost entirely during your life. We really only understood how dangerous you were after your death. During all the briefings in the States, only Nyneve, a few lesser rebel rousers, and the Seelie queen were attributed as your identities."

"Why would her blood even work?" Oberon asked, his tone tempered, though Raegan could see the hope glimmering in his eyes. "All the living Overhills are now traitors. Can Protectorate wards not be adjusted in case of defection or betrayal?"

"Of course they can," Maelona said, raising her gaze to meet the King's. "But she was never inducted in the first place, so the workings can't identify her personally. The old wards on the Undercroft, on this dossier—all they're gonna see is one of the oldest Protectorate families. I mean, the Overhills contributed to their *creation*."

Maelona paused, looking around the room, the notch between her eyes deepening. "It's hard to lock out a founding bloodline. Trust me, when Cormac deserted, it was all anyone talked about for months. I mean, it's easy enough to designate a person-non-grata within an existing modern spell, particularly when they're oathed and known. The old workings, though? Too many layers. Much harder to do without breaking the whole damn thing. And in what world would we foresee someone getting past fifteen layers of modern, updated protective wards?"

Silence swept its wings around the great room of the faerie fort. Raegan squeezed her eyes shut, trying to think, to *remember*.

"You killed John Dee? Like, you know, the greatest English magician?" Reilly asked in a small squeak, breaking Raegan's concentration. She opened her eyes and glanced over to find them looking up from the parchment, considering the Unseelie king. A slow, dangerous smile graced the curves of Oberon's mouth.

"Okay," Raegan said frantically, trying to get her thoughts marching in a straight line. "So I just need to remember. It's in me, somewhere."

As she glanced in his direction, concern etched the King's expression. "We discussed this with Baba Yaga. Allowing your memories to resurface on their own is best. Attempting to force anything through spellwork is incredibly dangerous."

"More dangerous than any of the other shit we've done?" she snapped, her frustration with the situation—not so much with him—wearing her patience thin. The King took a deep breath, and she had the distinct feeling he was counting to ten.

"This is a really stupid idea," Reilly said, fiddling with

the blanket they'd swaddled themselves in after retreating to one of the heavy chairs pushed against the wall.

"I'm all ears," Raegan said when no one spoke. "At this point, there's no stupid ideas."

"I wouldn't go that far," Maelona muttered, crossing her arms.

"Reilly, please, if you will," Oberon managed, his gaze dipping toward Raegan. "What was your idea?"

Reilly glanced cautiously around the room, chewing on their lip. "Okay," they began, looking a little sheepish. "So, there were quite a few of us obsessed with civilian stuff as kids. We found all the woo-woo spiritual shit particularly amusing, for obvious reasons. One night, there was some important dinner or whatever, and a couple of us were fucking around on YouTube."

"Oh man," Alanna said, brightening considerably, suddenly looking so young it made Raegan's heart ache. "Those were the days. Before the council realized how expansive the internet was and yanked that away from us, too."

"Yes!" Reilly said, reaching out for Alanna's hand. She tucked their short, freckled fingers into her palm, smiling. Raegan's ache intensified. It was a terrible thing to find Blodeuwedd again only to be yanked apart mere hours later. "Okay, do you remember when we tried the past life regression video?"

Alanna's amusement fled, her eyes darting toward Raegan. "Right, but like, that didn't actually work, Reilly."

"Maybe only because we don't *have* past lives," they replied, looking up at Alanna from their chair. "I think I remember enough of the video. It's worth a shot. It's not spellwork, so it might be safer."

"What," the King began, his hand opening on Raegan's back, "would this entail, exactly?"

CHAPTER FORTY-FOUR

Raegan slipped deeper into the water, adjusting the makeshift blindfold she'd made from a dressing robe's belt. Even though it was confined by the surrounds of the clawfoot tub, this element was still hers. Water was her home. She took comfort in that, spreading her arms out wide.

"I think there's enough salt this time," she said, not sure where to direct her words. "I feel pretty float-y."

"Good," came Reilly's delighted voice from an indistinguishable direction. "Okay, just a reminder that I'm going off a video I saw a few times nearly a decade ago. So temper your expectations."

Words came slinking across the tide of the darkness she floated on, soft and deadly: "Understand that if this harms her in any way—"

"Oberon, leave the kid alone," Raegan snapped, resisting the urge to yank up her blindfold and glare at him. She curled her fists, hearing only the gentle lapping of water for a long moment.

"Thanks, Raegan," Reilly said, their tone significantly

meeker than when they'd last spoken. "I'm going to guide you through the meditation. Just listen to my voice."

Raegan nodded, trying to let the feeling of the room around her go; they'd done their best to approximate a deprivation tank. She was wearing only a sports bra and high-waisted underwear, her hair braided tight against her skull. At first, she'd been aware of the tub's edges, of the people standing around her, of the tag at the back of her bra. But now, the set-up did seem to be working. There was little more than water and breath.

And then Reilly's voice, opening with a meditation exercise that was standard enough from the smattering of yoga and breathwork classes she'd taken, usually at the behest of a girl she was fucking. Raegan pushed away thoughts of her current life and focused all her energy on Reilly's words—as they instructed—until the time came to "cut the cord," so to speak.

Only water, only breath, the osmanthus and petrichor gone, the slanting cobalt light of the willow-o-wisps a distant memory. But then Raegan's fingers brushed the edge of the tub, and she jolted back into her body. Exhaling, she squeezed her eyes shut—fuck, now she could feel the blindfold again—and tried to relinquish control. Reilly was already trying to guide her through the "rooms of her lives," which might have worked if she wasn't damp and pissed off in lukewarm bathwater.

"Reilly," came Oberon's voice, only lightly edged in steel. "A moment, please."

"Thanks," Raegan said, lifting the blindfold off one eye. She squinted against the sudden light, finding Oberon gazing down at her. "I actually think this could work. The deprivation part of it. But I need to concentrate. Could you three leave? I need Oberon to stay. Baba Yaga said he was my tether. I think if I get lost, he'll help me come back."

Raegan tucked her chin to her chest, looking at Maelona, Alanna, and Reilly in turn. Her aunt's jaw flexed, gaze darting suspiciously to the King. But she relented, nodding, and then the younger Protectorate operatives followed suit. The three of them filed out of the bedchamber, Alanna pulling the door closed behind her.

"Lower, please," Raegan said to the willow-o-wisps, which immediately dimmed. "You, come here."

Oberon closed the distance to the edge of the clawfoot tub with a long, gliding step. Without any further prompting from Raegan, he knelt down on the tiled floor beside her, draping his beautiful hands over the porcelain lip. On instinct, she reached out of the water and wrapped her fingers around his.

"Right," she breathed, looking up at him. "I'm going back in." With her free hand, Raegan slid the blindfold back down and let herself sink into the water holding her like a mother. Without Maelona's nervous energy, Alanna's gentle corrections, and Reilly's general anxiety, she found herself able to breathe deeply and float. There was no reassurance like the Unseelie faerie king at her side, fingers interwoven with hers like an ancient thicket. He would not let her stray too far into her own currents. He knew her tides, her ebbs and flows, the drop-offs in her deep waters. He would keep her safe, just like he always did.

And with that thought, she slipped out of her body and into the rivers of her mind. She'd expected something like the room of doors that Reilly had mentioned, or maybe just doors in general, because she'd spent so long aching for one to appear. But instead, she found a thick, rushing current of black water. Raegan moved toward it gently, carefully, seeing how easily it could whisk her away. The currents called to her—here, she could be free and wild, shed her

402

humanity, tangle her hair with the kelp, and sharpen her teeth.

"Thank you," Raegan murmured, wavering at the current's edge. "But I'm looking for a door, actually. From a long time ago, something tucked away for safekeeping. Could you help me find it?"

The currents tumbled around her like a nest of angry hornets, and for a long, tense moment, fear pounded in Raegan's chest. Or no, something much worse—she had no chest, she had no fingers interwoven with the King's, she had no body at all. When she turned, wanting to look over her shoulder or maybe down at the tub below her, she found nothing at all but dark waters.

"Listen," she said, grateful she at least had her voice, which still sounded like her—accented with Philadelphia, a little rough around the edges, low and rich. "Do you want me to save magic or not?"

But the waters just continued to churn, frothing with silver whitecaps. She ground her jaw, or maybe she would've, but she had no jaw of which to speak. Raegan eyed the swift currents, holding her place in the milder tide. And then she realized—she'd have to surrender. She'd have to pitch herself into the blackened waters and let the tides take her where she wanted to go.

Raegan took a deep breath and repeated her request to the waters—the door, the slip in time when Danu had left this realm, the corridor that led to Excalibur. And then she tumbled into the heart of the rushing waters, where the currents twisted vicious and unforgiving, praying she wouldn't drown.

It was not unlike when Baba Yaga peeled her eroded Seal away. Entire lifetimes danced beneath the tides, presenting themselves in no particular order that Raegan could decipher. She wasn't in control, not quite—the currents swept her through this strange world of dark water and glimmering depths, and she could do little to impact their speed or sway. She did, however, have the distinct impression that upon finding the right place, she could choose to dive deeper. There were dangers there, too, she knew—not enough air, too little light, of going so deep she wouldn't know which way was up or how to get back.

But she was strong enough. She knew that now. For a moment, she felt something simple, physical—cool, strong fingers between hers, the power lingering just beneath moonlit skin. Raegan smiled and slipped farther down the river, her eyes on the depths below, where the people she'd once been peered up at her like a strange passing cloud.

At a certain point, she stopped trying to move with the current and simply became the water instead. Her Threads eagerly molded into the shape of the river, moving more quickly now. Down below, she saw the life she'd dreamt of back in Philadelphia, of running into the King at a coffee shop in the 1940s in London and feeling like her heart had been broken into a million pieces. Even now, lacking physicality, she still had the sensation of her throat closing, of tears pricking the back of her eyelids with hot, sharp needles.

Lives she hadn't remembered slipped by on the waters, too. She watched the King—much younger, though he still wore sorrow like a crown—arch his brow at a tall, powerfully built man with thick, sun-bleached hair gathered in a loose braid. For a brief moment, she remembered what it was to have that body—the weight of a battle ax, the sway and creak of a longship beneath her, the tender fierceness with which she tangled with Oberon between sheets—but then it was gone, rushing away like floodwater.

The lives where she hadn't gone looking for doors were barely dull glimmers at the bottom of the river, the scales of a fish long since gutted. But they were terrifyingly numerous, and she found herself averting her eyes, not wanting to know how many she had wasted. Just when she dared to look back, something caught her eye: a woman with a single silvery-blonde plait down her back, hands curled tight around a walking stick as she walked through a meadow.

Acting on some half-remembered instinct, Raegan dove deeper, chasing the flash of silver-blonde like a minnow, resisting the current that wanted to pull her forward, forward, always forward, only to come back around and devour her own tail. She strained, reaching for the depths, suddenly aware of the King's hand in hers again. She curled her fingers around his tighter, steadying herself, and then she was tumbling through black-water rapids, falling through space, coming undone.

"Why are you showing me this?" a voice—her voice—asked, clear as spring rain. No answer came, just the jeweled chorus of a late summer orchestra humming all around her. The light slanted low and golden, as if the afternoon were fading into a balmy evening.

"Because one day, it might matter," came the answer, unsteady, spoken from a voice she recognized but could not place. She strained to find the speaker, but her gaze stayed stubbornly on the soft mound of earth rising from the meadow. It was covered in the green down of moss, and from it grew a tree. She knew she was many, many years in the past—and yet the tree was already ancient, its roots encasing the mound.

"That is hardly an answer," she huffed in reply.

"You should know better than to expect one," came the reply, sharp as mugwort tea.

Her memory-body finally turned, peering into the shade of the towering tree. A woman—no, something much more—stood there, draped in the glory of golden hour. Her face was lined, but her eyes danced with intelligence as swift as a river. A long, thick braid of silver hair fell over her shoulder as she leaned forward, gazing deeply into Raegan's eyes.

The Witch in the Wood. But she was the Witch of the Wood, wasn't she? She glanced down, finding roughspun clothes and worn leather boots. Confused and beginning to panic, she reached for the nape of her neck, finding a braid similar to that of the woman before her, though with less silver and more youth. Raegan stared at the woman, stumbling back a step, thistle and gorse tangling around her ankles.

"Ahh," the witch said, smiling now, reaching up with one hand to shade her eyes from the slanting sun. "You found this little jewel I buried for safekeeping. For the day when all the Prophecies become one. Well done. Now, tell me—what kind of a tree is this?"

"How is this even possible?" Raegan demanded, her mind reeling, particularly after the thousands of currents she'd tumbled through just to get here. "I—we?—hid a memory in ourselves?"

"Yes," the witch replied, straightening, her expression gone sober. "And we're the only ones who can find it. I did it for a reason. Because no one else could know. And we could only know the truth again if we were strong enough to go looking for Avalon. Which apparently you did."

"Jesus Christ," Raegan groaned, feeling faint. She leaned hard on her walking stick, wondering if she should put her head between her knees. "Sorry. This is a bit of a mindfuck."

"We taught Baba Yaga herself the craft," the witch replied, cocking her head, a vicious grin spreading across her thin, weathered lips. "A bit of complicated memory work is hardly beyond our limits. It's all just Threads, Raegan. And we are quite good with a needle."

Raegan's head spun, but she held the witch's gaze even

*as the currents began to tug her on again. She dug her staff
into the soft earth, scrambling for a foothold.*

*"Ahh," the witch said, sly and shimmering like a beacon
in the late summer light. "No need to tire yourself out. Just
have a look at this tree, if you would. Speak its name. Then
you may return."*

*Her head spun hard, and Raegan barely managed to tear
her eyes away from the person that was her but not her to
look at the tree growing proud and defiant from the soft,
vulnerable mound in the earth.*

*"Oh my God." And then she spoke the name of the tree,
the syllables rolling off her tongue like thunder.*

She broke the surface sputtering, her Threads barely
returned to her current body. Water droplets spewed in
every direction, sapphire-like in the willow-o-wisp light. She
yanked the soaked blindfold from her face, twisting to the
side of the tub. Resting her elbows on the lip, she reached
for the King, pulling both of his hands to her heart. She held
them there, ravenous for his heat, for the feeling of his touch
to bring her back to this world.

He knew, somehow, because he *always* knew. The King
bowed over the clawfoot tub and pulled her from the porcelain pool as if she weighed nothing at all, bringing her close
to his body—never mind the rivulets of water running down
her shoulders, the way her hair surely soaked his shirt
straight through.

But that's how it was—she was forever diving into the
deepest, darkest places, and he always awaited her on the
shore, always pulling her out when she no longer had the
strength to surface. Raegan felt his hand cradle the back of
her head and melted into the feeling. Delicately, she
searched for words—for the language of this time and place,
for the energy to explain. Exhaustion crowded her, sending
black splotches dancing across her vision.

"Are you unharmed?" Oberon asked, gently pushing away the curls plastered to her forehead.

"Yew," Raegan gasped, praying she'd found the right language, beginning to shiver.

The King furrowed his brow, cocked his head in that way she always liked, but the way she yearned for him was just another depth, and she needed the shallows right now.

"Yew," she repeated, coughing up water. "It's the Defynogg Yew."

CHAPTER FORTY-FIVE

Gray moorlands flashed overhead, and the wind tore ferociously at her hair, ripping it from the tight braid Maelona had coaxed it into. The mist seemed intent on sinking into her bones. But at least they weren't being followed. Not yet, anyway. The kelpies had agreed to distract the Protectorate, luring them away from the mouth of the faerie fort, while Rainer ferried his cargo in the opposite direction—toward the yew trees in an unassuming church graveyard, on the outskirts of the Brecon Beacons.

Raegan tightened her hold on Rainer's mane as the kelpie's long, powerful legs carried them up the face of a craggy hill, his hooves seeming to just barely skim the ground. Anxiety and terror swarmed her insides, and even the reassurance of Oberon's muscular frame at her back couldn't banish the feeling. What if she was wrong? What if the door wouldn't open to her any longer? What if she failed the entire world the same way she'd failed her father, the same way she'd failed the King a hundred times before?

"Steady," Oberon murmured, his lips brushing her ear, the word just audible over the roar of the wind. For a moment, Raegan smiled into the mist like a fool, marveling at how two syllables spoken from his tongue could settle the tides thrashing inside her. She felt his hand open wider on her waist, fingers splaying. The heat of his touch reached her, even through the thick oilskin coat.

It should be carefree, barreling through the moors on the back of an ancient creature born of the same murk and depth that she knew so well. But it felt like going to the gallows, taking the train to the last stop on the line. They were out of time, out of options, out of chances. The snake had already taken its own tail into its mouth, Raegan knew, and it was only a matter of time before it began to devour.

"Up ahead," Rainer called, swerving around a rocky outcropping.

Through the mist, Raegan saw the beginnings of a village, the wild, heather-ringed lands giving way to civilization. A power line stretched up into the gray skies, and narrow lanes twisted this way and that, lined in short stone walls draped with vines. And there, farther down the hillside, was a white steeple. It was all a regular kind of pretty, nothing impressive—certainly not a vista that would inspire awe or wonder.

"How could this possibly be the place?" she murmured to herself, eyes searching the landscape. Then she finally found their quarry, tucked into the center of the churchyard between weathered gravestones. The yew trees. They curled in around themselves, an oasis of deep green in a world of smoke and umber.

Maybe it was all going to her head, maybe she just wanted to believe, but Raegan's breath caught in her throat all the same. Even from across the village, power lines and blacktop bisecting her vision, the pull of the yews was undeniable. They pulsed, not unlike a door, but quiet, subtle, a thrum in her blood instead of the soaring loop of a Fatesong.

Rainer tucked his knees and neatly jumped over a low hedge, bringing them closer to the churchyard. Anxiety roiling unpleasantly in her stomach, Raegan looked both ways, eyes sharp for a flash of chainmail or dusty suiting, but she only saw regular people going about their business. Their glamour seemed to be holding, though Oberon had been forced to weave something that wouldn't draw too much attention from the Protectorate. Which meant there was a chance that any mortal more sensitive to the way of things would likely see a kelpie with a deathless woman and a faerie king on its back, careening toward an ancient churchyard as if everything began and ended within its stone walls.

Rainer's hooves clattered over the blacktop, and the world hung so still and slow that for a moment, Raegan panicked, thinking they'd been caught in the web of a time spell. But it was only the dilation of adrenaline, of every moment leading up to this one. Her heart climbed into her throat as Rainer leapt over the wall of the churchyard, carrying them across soft, damp earth to the cluster of yew trees.

Raegan all but flung herself off the kelpie's back, scrambling for the trees; it felt like she was moving through water, or like she was having one of those dreams when all she needed to do was run away but her legs just wouldn't work.

The King hooked his arm through hers, pulling them beneath the dark, soft shadow of the yews. "Keep watch, please, Rainer," he called before letting out a long breath, turning his attention to the trees.

Raegan's attention fell in a similar direction. The yews towered above them, their trunks clustering together at the roots before reaching up toward the sky, interlacing their hands to form a sphere of eternal green. Their trunks were a reddish brown, covered in tiny branches of growth. The mound the yews grew from pulsed, its energy washing over Raegan like ocean waves, leaving her trembling and gowned in salt.

As they stood there, side by side within the yews, something golden and orchestral slipped through the air, delicate as smoke and humming with want. It split her down the middle, digging fishhooks into her intestines, the cruel beauty of it pulling on every fiber of her being. Of all things, a Fatesong looped above them.

Raegan tilted her chin back, looking up into the sky, hating the way she felt like a vine reaching for the sun. The thrum of the song filled up all the empty spaces that stretched wide and aching inside of her. Traitorously, that yearning within her silenced, slipping quietly beneath the mead waves of the Fatesong. With a final trill, the ancient melody ended the same way it had begun, the snake devouring its own tail.

Still in the thrall of the Fatesong, Raegan stepped toward the yews, hand outstretched, reverent as a sinner. The moment her fingertips brushed the bark, the entire churchyard roiled, like something ancient turning over in its grave. Hope keened in her chest, spreading wings as it awaited the headwinds on which it could finally, after so many years, fly home.

But then nothing, not even when she pressed her palm against the trunk. The churchyard silenced, and the yews stood expressionless again. No key appeared in overturned dirt atop the mound. No maw opened with the sound of a half-forgotten lullaby. The hope in her chest turned to ash and nearly choked her.

Despair coiled in her ribs as she looked over her shoulder at the King. As always, he met her gaze evenly, his features all the more feral and inhuman in the deep green gloom. His oceanic eyes held a vastness she still didn't understand, power and prophecy moving like shadows in the depths.

"All the Prophecies become one," she muttered, her mind racing—luna moths and doves and river-conjured swords and crumbling citadels and the skies turning to black and the ground to stone and the mortal king sleeping on the other side of the door in the yews. And most of all, those bloodstained words scrawled across the Prophecy beast she'd awoken in Hiraeth's depths, repeated by the Witch in the Wood.

"Oberon," Raegan said, speaking his name like a vow. "Come here." She held out her free hand, reaching for him as she always did—across time and space, across graves and cradles, endlessly and defiantly.

The King did not hesitate. He placed his hand in hers, the intensity of his attention settling over her shoulders like a mantle. She let out a shaky breath. Then she guided his hand to the yew's trunk, laying his palm flat against the bark. Less than a second later, she layered hers on top, hoping with every fiber of her being that together, they might finally be enough.

The yews shivered. The ground rumbled again. From behind the hush of the trees, Raegan heard gravestones clatter like broken teeth, a great wave of energy rising up like a storm surge, the force of it ringing the church bells. The mound at their feet shuddered and then slid open, revealing a set of stone stairs leading into sparkling waters. Though the sun stood directly overhead, shrouded in clouds, another light source shone from the opening in the mound, spinning the space between the yews with golden thread.

"Welcome home," Raegan said, choking on tears as she turned to face Oberon, "once and future king."

He gazed at her like she might be the sun. "Nyneve," he

murmured, expression filled with awe. Despite the door to Avalon—to *salvation*—at his left, the King only had eyes for her. He looked at her with a love so fierce and wild that her heart skipped a beat. "Though two goddesses created me, it is you, I think, who is truly divine."

She laughed, delirious, her entire body shaking. She opened her mouth to say something, but whatever words she might've spoken were devoured by the shrill shriek of a kelpie's war cry. There was barely time to process anything before bullets tore through the air, threatening to snatch this victory right out of her hands. Out in the churchyard, Rainer shrieked again, though this time he was answered by a chorus of shrill, deadly kelpie voices that echoed down the surrounding hillsides.

A gossamer-thin shadow began to encompass the space between the yews, slinking through the air like silk. Before the sphere could close, a spear sailed through the air, tearing the protective working in half. Raegan reached for her own power, but they were far from the shores of any river and opening the door to Avalon had taken its toll on her. Beside her, the King pivoted, his back to the door in the mound.

"Stay close to me," he warned, his blade of shadow blinking into existence in his free hand.

Raegan nodded, steadying herself—and then a wall of muscle and cloth knocked her onto the damp earth below, stealing the air from her lungs. She rolled, reaching for the knife on her waistband, but large hands pinned her wrists above her head. With a howl, Raegan struggled, kicking and thrashing, hunting for flesh to sink her teeth into.

The world rolled again, and she took a knee to the stomach, stealing her breath. She gagged, nauseous from the intensity of the blow, only to have her arms yanked behind her back. With horror, she realized the bitter cold of the metal meeting her wrists was of a very specific make—

sainted iron. She screamed, the sound bloodcurdling to her own ears, and reached for the water running through her imprisoner's body. But the cuffs had already closed, and the old magics in her quieted. Furious, Raegan reached for the currents within her, but they slipped from her clumsy grasp.

"So close this time, weren't we?" a voice sounded triumphantly in her ear.

Raegan clenched her jaw. *Bedwyr*, yet again carrying on the cruel legacy of his king. She thrashed again, throwing her weight into the body of her murderer and the Time-keeper's favorite pet. But his powerful, mountainous build at her back didn't give an inch. In the thin gray light leaking in from the churchyard, she watched a gloved hand appear in her vision and grip her jaw.

"If you do not release her," the King roared from across the space between the yews, out of Raegan's sight, "I will slit you open from throat to navel and feast upon your intestines."

Bedwyr threw his head back and laughed. "His feelings for you are such a weakness, don't you think?" he purred in her ear. "Oh, and don't stop fighting, Nyneve. I *like* when you fight. You fought so much the first time I killed you. You're prettiest when you're struggling against things too powerful for you to ever come out on top."

Raegan opened her mouth to spit obscenities until she saw something much worse than anything Bedwyr could do or say to her. Just a few paces away, in front of the door to Avalon, the King fought against a net of sainted iron. At least ten heavily armed Protectorate soldiers swarmed him like vultures, battering him with battle magic that rattled Raegan's teeth as it sailed through the air. Her heart stopped.

And then time stopped, too. A powerful working exploded into existence—far too quickly, too easily; those spells were *immense*. It caught the King in its wake, leaving the Protectorate surrounding him to move in real time as he struggled against air that had turned to molasses.

"We would've never been able to open the door without you," Bedwyr murmured in her ear, the feeling of his lips against her skin vile. "But you led us right to it and cracked it open. Really, I'm in your debt, witch."

Something in the time working bent in on itself, and suddenly, the soldiers surrounding Oberon were moving faster than they had any right to, dealing blows and magical attacks with terrifying speed. Raegan screamed, struggling against Bedwyr. He laughed, dangling a pocket watch—much like the ones inside the grandfather clock guardians in the Undercroft—in front of Raegan tauntingly. Its face was cracked down the center, the arms of the clock trembling.

"I've been saving this for a very special day," Bedwyr said, yanking her arms back at a painful angle. She bit down on her tongue, refusing to give him the pleasure of her pain. "Even in the Otherlands, ambient magic's not what it used to be, so these are hard to come by. But using such a special thing to kill your Fey lover in front of you? Well worth the expenditure."

Raegan's rage knew no words, no languages, only an endless, keening howl as she struggled against her murderer. The King's left shoulder—where he'd already been injured—had torn back open and was bleeding profusely. He'd summoned more of those shadow hounds, but their jaws couldn't snap closed quickly enough around the Protectorate soldiers.

Even if they couldn't kill him here—they *couldn't*, Raegan told herself; they'd tried before and failed—all of it was happening again. She choked on rage and sorrow, her entire body going limp. No matter what they did, no matter how hard they fought, it always ended the same. She'd go to her grave wearing a burial shroud of failure, and the King would face endless torture until maybe they finally figured out how to kill him. A sob tore from her lips, drenched in a thousand years of misery.

"Stop," Raegan begged, fighting against Bedwyr, fighting to gain a hold on the dark river inside of her, the sainted iron dampening her feel of its currents. "Stop."

Her voice hardly broke over the din of baying hounds and shrieking kelpies and battle magic rattling through the space.

"Stop," she said, louder now, something rising in her like a tide. Not the river, not even water at all, but something else entirely, unfamiliar and bitter on her tongue even as she gave into its swell.

Desperate and mad as a wolf, Raegan fought against Bedwyr's iron hold. For a moment, she nearly broke his grasp, but he just shoved her to the ground, the hard-packed damp earth biting into her knees.

"That's more like it," he laughed a moment before she felt a boot on her back, almost pushing her to the ground before fingers caught her by the hair and yanked her back up to her knees. "Careful. Wouldn't want you to miss anything."

Raegan locked eyes with Oberon. There should have been disappointment, there should have been hatred, there should have been the grief that she had once again failed him. But she found none of those things in the ocean of his eyes—just a gleaming, defiant love that would've brought her to her knees if she weren't there already. His face was bleeding now, a gash opened across one of those sharp cheekbones, and he was barely fending off attacks, taking most of the battle magic full-on, swaying under the intensity of the spells.

Something in Raegan broke. "Stop," she commanded,

her voice rising above the cacophony this time, a battle cry hemmed in grief.

Did the Protectorate's movements slow, or was she just filled with a chemical hope flooding her brain in the final moments of life? She didn't care—she clung to it, let the tide fill her with the kind of rage she had always thought she needed to keep under control.

Raegan let the anger stampede through her body. It was pure and vicious. It cared not for the sainted iron around her wrists or the immortal abomination that held her fast. A thousand years of fury bled into the air, and the soldiers around the King slowed another half-step.

"What is happening?" Bedwyr barked in the voice of an army commander, though she felt the fear slink through him, and she feasted upon it.

Raegan snarled a response, but even her own words were lost to the flow of boundless rage. No more. No more of this misery, no more watching from her knees in the dirt, no more of this man's hands on hers.

"Stop," Raegan commanded, her voice orchestral and golden like a Fatesong, ringing through the churchyard louder than any bell. "*STOP.*"

Silence, yearning wide and endless, and then all the world went still.

CHAPTER FORTY-SIX

R aegan and the King stared at each other for one,
two, three full seconds before she managed to
stagger to her feet. Bedwyr was frozen behind
her, his mouth open in a snarled shout, hands clasped
around where her body had been. A clanging thump broke
the silence—Oberon shrugging off the net of sainted iron,
letting it fall to the ground below. The soldiers surrounding
him were motionless, attack spellery hanging still and
powerless in the air.

Raegan dragged herself to him. Despite his injuries, the
King pulled her into his arms without hesitation, his mouth
meeting hers as if it were the antidote to all he had suffered.
She surrendered to the faerie king's kiss, his dark tide
rushing to meet her river like brackish water.

"Steady," he murmured as they broke apart, his hands
coming to her face, examining her for injuries.

"I'm fine," she protested, running her eyes over the singe
marks where the sainted iron had draped over his frame, the
blood seeping from his cheekbone, the too-pale ivory of his
features. "You're not, though."

But the King was already moving, searching the motionless Bedwyr's pockets for a key to Raegan's cuffs. "We do not know how long this will hold," he said, gaze darting to meet hers, the closest he'd ever come to frantic.

Movement outside the canyon of yews set Raegan's blood on fire. But it was just Rainer, barreling through the small opening, nearly slamming into the King. His bulk filled the minimal space left between the trees, making it feel more like a crowded elevator than a sacred place where the earth's bones showed through.

"How?" the kelpie asked, the weight of his gaze falling onto Raegan like a hundred river stones.

"I have no fucking idea," she replied, her voice shrill. "Does it matter?"

"Not at this precise moment, I suppose, but in general, yes," the kelpie said.

"Thank the Morrigan," the King muttered, pulling a keyring from Bedwyr's pocket. Without a further word, he strode to Raegan and released her from the cuffs, tossing them onto the ground with a curse. She rubbed her wrists, the skin bruised and smarting from contact with the sainted iron.

"You found the door," Rainer said, his tone filled with awe as he noticed the opening in the mound, sunlight spilling out of it like spun gold. Then he sobered, his flat black eyes looking between Raegan and the King. "Go. You must go."

"She did a time working," the King said, taking a ragged breath as he shifted his weight off his left leg. "None of the Protectorate can return with that information, Rainer."

Raegan did not feel sorry for the soldiers frozen around her, and neither did the kelpie, apparently. The light from the door glimmered, catching Rainer's viciously scalloped ears and ancient eyes. He arched his thickly muscled neck, the long waves of his mane turned iridescent in Avalon's illumination. "That, my friend, can be arranged. After all, I must consume."

His gaze tracked to Raegan at those last few words, and if kelpies could wink, Rainer certainly did.

"That one," she said, pointing to Bedwyr. "Make sure he's awake first."

Rainer bowed his head, his coat shimmering silver-green-black with the movement. "It would be my honor, high lady. Now go. We will ferry the mortals at the faerie fort to Hiraeth as soon as it's safe."

"Thank you, Rainer," the King said, emotion thick in his low, hoarse tone. Then he turned to Raegan, and without hesitation, he swept her into the place beneath the yews where the world opened wide. She felt the door close behind her—a wound stitching itself out of existence, leaving no scar and no trace. The sunlight on her face was warm and soft, the air cool, scented with sea salt and creamy feathers and damp stone.

The stairs led down, just like the vision had shown her, weathered and ancient, disappearing into the lapping waves. The King's hand tightly grasping hers, Raegan looked around, finding nothing but the sea. It seemed to stretch forever, its colors like nothing she'd ever seen—a deep, impossibly rich lapis lazuli turned to sapphire where the sun touched it, whitecaps dusting the tops of waves like chiffon. Dark, drenched stones broke through the surface in a few places, gleaming tide pools pockmarking their surface.

She turned to look over her shoulder, finding a sheer wall of stone so tall that vertigo lurched in her chest. Like the stairs, it looked positively ancient. Beside her, the King swayed, and she reacted in an instant, turning to grab him by the forearms.

"Let me heal you," she said, reaching up to brush a wave

of ink-dark hair away from where his temple still bled freely.

"You need not tax yourself further," came a voice from behind Raegan at the same moment an immense presence washed over her.

Slowly, not taking her hands from the King, she looked up to find a goddess floating inches above the ocean's surface, just a few feet from her.

The deity had violet-gray hair rippling down her shoulders, part of it bound in intricate plaits that circled her head like a crown. Her skin was a mossy hue, her features sharp and inhuman—the knife-like cheekbones and sharp jaw that Raegan had come to know so well, the planes of her face feral beneath the kind expression. She was dressed in a diaphanous gown the color of a storm, its hem damp with water, the sleeves billowing about on the breeze. Above the elegant drape of a cowl neckline, the goddess's neck was as long and elegant as a swan's. Her eyes were large, deep-set, a color that was impossible to name. Like a kaleidoscope or a rainbow or perhaps an oil spill, but all of those descriptors were too gaudy for the unyielding beauty Raegan was gazing upon.

"Avalon was a place of healing and knowledge before the rest," the goddess said, her voice like crashing waves and blooming flowers and spring rain. "We can help. Come."

Raegan and the King exchanged glances. He gave the smallest of nods and straightened, brows pulling together in pain. She did her best to support him as together, they sloshed down a few more steps.

"Danu?" Oberon rasped, barely audible over the sway of the sea, but the goddess caught his words all the same.

She smiled, a dangerously lovely thing. "Yes, child," the goddess replied. "I am known as Danu. And Anu. And Modron. And more, I would imagine. I shudder to know what the mortals have attributed to me as of late. Much about motherhood, I am sure, though if they perceived me differently, they might call me a creatrix instead."

Raegan just stared at the divine being in front of them, her body trembling with exhaustion. Had she really spun a time working out of sheer rage? Had Oberon truly survived all those brutal attacks to stand here in the surf and the sun, a goddess making little backhanded quips about gendered human society?

Before she could convince herself that she wasn't still trapped in Bedwyr's arms beneath the shadow of the yews, the water pooling up onto the stairs slipped away. Raegan watched with awe and some degree of unease as the ocean slunk backwards, as if Danu were the mistress of the tides in this place and not the moon. The water's retreat revealed a stone causeway leading through the sea. The goddess turned and began to follow the path, moving in long, elegant strides. Her feet were bare, dainty jewelry around her ankles winking in the sunlight. The back of her dress dipped in a low V, offering a glimpse of the goddess's muscled form, woad tattoos in strange shapes dripping down the line of her spine.

There was nothing to do but follow. So cautiously, her chest tight, her mind still struggling to comprehend everything before her, Raegan held tightly to the King and began the journey. No creatures struggled in the wake of the receded tide—there was only weathered stone and long-dead bones and clumps of glimmering kelp.

"Do you . . . see anything up ahead?" Raegan asked after a long silence. They'd followed the goddess far into the ocean; it would be an easy thing for the tides to sweep them to their death. She didn't dare look behind her—knowing how far away the shoreline of rock and narrow stairs was would offer no reprieve.

"I am hoping that Avalon is glamoured," the King replied in her ear, his voice hitching with pain.

Raegan grit her teeth. Danu might possibly be their savior, but she was the creator of the Fey—of course she would see little wrong with making one of her own limp along an uneven, rocky causeway. Casual cruelty was not so different between humans and the Fair Folk.

"And that it's not much farther," she replied under her breath. She should be too tired for it, but anger rose in her chest regardless, sparking between her lungs.

"I do so adore your rage, little deathless thing," the goddess in front of them said as she turned to look over her shoulder, coy, though her pace didn't change. "But no magic is permitted here in the buried sea beyond the causeway enchantment. Another line of defense, you see. The way is not much longer now."

Raegan held Danu's gaze and then nodded, turning to look up at the King.

"I will be alright," he assured her, though his breathing was still too heavy. "Thanks to you, my brilliant witch, I will be alright."

A different kind of warmth spread across her chest, and she smiled to herself as she continued down the stone path.

She couldn't say how long they walked. The sun never wavered in the sky—too bright to locate, though there *was* a sun, unlike the unnatural light of the In-Between. All she knew was that one moment, she was about to protest, to gesture wildly at Oberon's wounds and demand to know how a creator could be so cruel, and the next, something flickered into existence on the horizon.

An island of mist, just like all the stories said. Ethereal white spires reached into the blue-gray sky, piercing the roving clouds like daggers. When the silvery veil parted, Raegan caught glimpses of rocky cliffs crowned in heather, a half-moon of pearlescent sand beach and dark, thick woods stitched onto the horizon line. Sea-drenched stones hemmed the land like sentinels. Her breath caught. That coiled root of yearning deep inside her keened.

"It's really Avalon," Raegan breathed, tears streaming down her face before she even realized she was crying. Wordlessly, the King gripped her hands tighter. She looked up at him, and despite all the pain, she saw a wild kind of hope in his eyes that made her heart leap. Maybe this time . . .

"A carriage awaits you on the shore," Danu said, stepping off the causeway and onto the beach, which was suddenly ten times closer than Raegan had dared to imagine. She followed, nearly delirious as the breeze pulled at her braid, bringing with it the scent of mist, black currant, and violet leaf—impossibly green and spellbinding.

A carriage did indeed await, like something out of the fairytales Raegan had long since forsaken for darker stories with sharper teeth. It looked as though it had been carved out of pewter and mother-of-pearl, fashioned after the ribs of some long-dead creature, glimmering every time the sun broke through the banks of fog. She climbed the delicate, silvery steps, doing her best to help the King along. Once they were settled, she looked up to see Danu lingering before the carriage doorway, though the goddess did not move to join them.

"A visit with the pharmakon first, I think," Danu said, arching a thin brow, her mouth twisting with humor as if she were addressing naughty children. "And then we will speak."

"But Excalibur," Raegan blurted out, her anxiety thudding too loudly in her veins. "It's here, right? And is it true what the Morrigan said—about it being a Fey blade?"

All these years around the Fair Folk—she *knew* the right

way to deal with them. But sometimes she just didn't have it in her to cater to their whims. Sometimes the burning question slipped out without a stitch of that stupid Fey-mandated politeness.

"Of course," Danu said, her brows furrowed as if more taken aback by Raegan's doubt than her direct inquiry. "And the Nameless One is the only Fair Folk it could not kill, because he was made in my image but not by my hands. Fey, yes, but different enough that the spellwork imbued in the blade is not as potent against him."

Rage lurched in Raegan's body, her nails digging into the aubergine velvet seat cushions—all this strange and otherworldly beauty be damned if any of it came at *his* expense. She was intimately familiar with the vicious scar on his chest where Excalibur had tried to lay claim to him a thousand years ago. "In other words, you'll heal him just so the sword can harm him again? Because it won't outright kill him like the rest of you, but it'll still really hurt him, won't it?"

Danu's eyes flashed, the universe turning in their depths, anger flattening her expression into something that looked too much like Fate's had back in that forest clearing. "It is just as you said at my door—he is the once and future king. Such a glorious destiny comes with pain."

The goddess's gaze slid to the King, who was resting the back of his head against the carriage's mother-of-pearl inlaid interior, the proud line of his shoulders collapsed, his breathing too much like rasping for Raegan's comfort. She reached across the space and took his hand gently into hers, the long fingers and calluses achingly familiar.

"He was spun from the night sky and milked from blood," Danu continued, her voice softer now, a single tear balancing on her silver eyelashes. "His Threads are barely more than grief spooled into yarn. He is a weapon. And all good weapons are cross-hatched in scars."

Oberon's heavy breaths filled the carriage, the whisper of the sea distant, Raegan's blood ringing loudly in her ears. She could raise a tsunami, she thought. She was a witch of the water; anything that flowed, that moved in tides and currents, was hers to harness. She could drown this entire island—for the King's older brethren certainly didn't deserve such bliss on the back of his suffering.

"Creatrix," Oberon breathed, his eyes holding Danu's—two oceans meeting in some forgotten place shrouded in mist. "Will we one day, perhaps, linger in the sun?"

That centuries-old ache throbbed in Raegan's chest, and she nearly choked on the grief. She looked away from the King, taking in his shaky exhale, only to notice that tears were streaming down the goddess's face, more gathering in her kaleidoscope eyes. Sorrow spun around the three of them, thick and heavy as a stormfront rolling in.

"My child," Danu murmured, moving as if to reach into the carriage before thinking better of it. "I fear not all of us are meant for the sun."

CHAPTER FORTY-SEVEN

Raegan wrapped her hands tighter around the gilded teacup and stared blankly into the fire. She was going to scream. She was going to throw something. She was going to march down to the pharmakon —a ridiculously beautiful glass solarium bursting with lush foliage—and ask what the fuck was taking so long.

But she had already done all of those things at least once in the past hour, and the kind coordinator had resorted to begging her to wait for an update on Oberon's treatment in their guest quarters. Having a mortal wandering about, the coordinator repeated for the umpteenth time, would draw attention, and Danu would very much prefer to avoid such things. Apparently even a utopia still had politics, and many Avalonians found Danu's desire to interfere with happenings outside of their safe haven alarming at best.

That, at least, Raegan understood. Of course the Fair Folk in their towering spires the color of bone china and their supposedly endless libraries and city center that had been built *with* nature instead of against it didn't care what was happening outside their walls. They were safe. They were happy. Doing anything about the Timekeeper would risk all of that—and besides, hadn't they seen all of this bull-shit coming? Wasn't that exactly why Danu had led them away all those years ago? In their eyes, anyone who chose to stay behind got what was coming to them.

She seethed, biting down on her tongue. If not for the sound of the whitewashed double-doors opening, she might've bitten all the way through. Instead, Raegan turned in her chair, heart fluttering. And there he was—the Unseelie king, his wounds vanished from existence, his button-down rolled to the elbows, collar open, the black-ened remains of his suit jacket slung over his shoulder.

She didn't hesitate. Raegan leapt to her feet and ran to him, slowing herself only at the last moment. "Is it okay if I—"

She didn't manage to get the words out before Oberon wrapped his arms around her so tightly it squeezed the air from her lungs. A sob of relief clawed its way up her throat as she returned his embrace, burying her face in his chest.

"You have been attended to as well, yes?" he asked in a low murmur, tucking her head under his chin.

"Yeah, but I didn't get the shit kicked out of me like you did," Raegan replied, breathing in the scent of him, all damp stone and woodsmoke and black pepper.

"Hmmm. The pharmakons were impressed I was still alive," he observed dryly, fingertips brushing her hair.

"Did you tell them that spite is a very powerful tool?" she asked with a laugh, pulling away to gaze up at him. That notch in his brows said he was still in pain, but his color was no longer that sickly pale hue, his breathing returned to the long, even intakes she'd come to know so well.

He smiled at her, a curve of his beautiful mouth, cupping her jaw in one large, powerful hand. "As are you," he murmured, the pad of his thumb brushing her lower lip. "It is worth staying alive just for you."

Raegan closed her fingers around the collar of his shirt, standing up on her tiptoes. The King met her halfway, kissing her until she was dizzy, until all the horror of the day had been banished for a moment or two. Then she slid her fingers through his before leading him past the hearth and into a narrow side room with high ceilings. Avalonians preferred to do their soaking in large, communal bath spaces, so the washroom only had two shower heads with a low wooden bench, but that worked fine for Raegan's purposes. A thin window of frosted glass at the far end of the room sent sunlight scattering across the stone floors, the shadows of tree limbs dappling the bright, warm space.

"I thought you might need help," Raegan said, her mouth twisting into a smirk as she began to unbutton the King's shirt.

"Very generous of you," he replied in a low, husky tone that made all her nerve endings curl in on themselves, desire unfurling low in her belly.

"Selfless, you might say," she said, bringing her mouth to his exposed collarbone. A deep sound of approval thrummed through his muscular chest, stoking the flames of Ragean's arousal. "If you're in too much pain . . ."

"After everything that occurred today, I ... I *need* you," he replied, mouth moving roughly against her neck as he bowed around her smaller frame, hands sliding under her sweater. She tilted her head back, giving him more access, a soft gasp escaping her mouth. Everything about him drove her absolutely mad, even a thousand years later.

"I love you," she murmured, pushing his shirt off his shoulders.

He tugged her sweater over her head, powerful palms skimming down her sides, meeting at the zipper of her jeans. Raegan arched into him, begging for more, and he acquiesced. Once all of their clothing was piled unceremoniously in the corner, Oberon caught her mouth in his and pushed her against the wall. The rough stone was delightfully cool on her skin, particularly in contrast with the dark heat of his muscular frame.

The shower head beside her switched on, water streaming from its sprout raindrop-like, already the perfect temperature. She pulled the King beneath it, marveling at the way water gathered on his ivory skin, how it sluiced down the hard, powerful lines of his body. They kissed each other feverishly, his rough groans mingling with her hitched gasps.

Oberon pulled back, cupping her face in his hands, resting his forehead against hers. Hot water streamed down around them like a rainstorm, soothing Raegan's tired, strained muscles. She could've lived in that moment, nothing but the water and her faerie king.

"The closer we come to the end of this," he murmured, tracing the line of her jaw with his fingertips, "the closer I fear I come to losing you."

Raegan's breath caught in her throat. "I wish I could tell you that wasn't true."

He dropped one hand to her side, curling his fingers possessively around her waist. "How can it be," he said in a long exhale, forehead still against hers, his large body blocking out all the rest of the world, "that I feel as though I was born to save you?"

Sorrow surged under her breastbone. "You can't. You know that, right?" His breathing stilled, muscles coiled and tense. Grief thrashed against her hurricane-glass heart. "Mordred. You can't hold that against yourself."

"So why," the viciously beautiful changeling rasped, his fingers tracing the curve of her hip, "does that desire beat harder in my chest than anything else?"

He shifted back from her, and she gazed up at him—his

black hair flattened by the water, caught in spirals against his skin, long eyelashes framed by water, or perhaps tears. An inferno burned in his expression, all the fury and promise of a predator gone too long denied.

The next moment, that mouth was on hers, breathless and insistent, the evidence of his arousal pressed thickly against her belly. Raegan moaned against his lips, threading her fingers into his hair, the drenched black strands curling like ink around her fingers.

"Prove it," she gasped, her hands moving to the nape of his neck. "Prove that you want me more than anything."

His gaze slid to hers, the angles of his face gone vicious and feral. His body was as preternaturally still as the long, dark form of a panther about to seize prey between its jaws. Then he moved all at once—his hands cupped the generous curve of her ass, pulling her from the ground. The King's broad, powerful body pinned her against the cool tile from all angles. She greedily wrapped her legs around his hips, trailing fingertips down his chest, tracing that delicious line of downy, silken hair that bisected the pale expanse of ivory muscle.

Damp with a blistering need, Raegan rolled her hips against his, digging her fingernails into his shoulders. He caught her lower lip between his teeth, dragging a throaty groan from the depths of her body. Every inch of her skin demanded more of him. One of his long-fingered hands slid between their bodies, teasing at the apex of her thighs. She said his name in a voice that barely sounded like hers, keening with endless ache.

"I would burn the entire world in your name," the King rasped against her mouth, the pressure of his touch increasing. He shifted her up higher on the wall with one deft movement, bringing his tongue to the tip of her breast. Raegan couldn't stand it—to feel all of this pleasure, to be

432

surrounded by all his glorious darkness, without him inside of her.

"Oberon," she gasped, digging her nails deeper into his skin. He glanced up at her, a dangerous smile gracing his beautiful, full mouth even as he continued his ministrations.

"Is there something in particular," the King murmured, his words slow and sweet, "you require of me? As proof of the devotion you seek?" Humor lilted his tone upward, but his deep voice was still husky with the same desire she felt.

"Fuck me with your cock, you goddamn monster," she managed to get out.

They both broke into laughter, the sound ringing out in the space. She wouldn't have thought it possible, but that sweet look of levity on his expression . . . it filled her with a yearning that might've broken her, were his hands not in all the right places, his hips already lined up with hers.

"As always," the King replied, lips ghosting hers, one large hand sliding up to toy with her breast in exactly the way she liked, "your wish is my command."

He buried himself inside of her. He offered none of the gentler movements he typically did to ensure she was prepared for him. Instead, he filled her entirely, completely, ferociously, his teeth grazing the side of her neck. Raegan let out a sound she was worried all of Avalon might've heard, going near-limp against the wall with the thick, devouring wave of pleasure that rolled over her.

As Oberon drove into her, one hand still working in circles at her core, Raegan could barely tell where she ended and he began. They moved against each other with wild abandon, like if they only proved how desperately they wanted to be together, Fate may just allow it.

But no such provisions existed in this cruel universe, Raegan knew, so she told herself to savor every moment of it: the look of ecstasy on his impossibly beautiful face as he slid inside of her, the way he said her name as if it were a wish, the pleasure so thick and sweet that she wasn't sure she could contain it. How he took her like a creature half-starved, how he chased her pleasure like it might save them both.

"Mordred," she begged, the ages and the world outside slipping from her grasp. "More. Fuck, I need more."

With a low, deep sound of acquiescence that rumbled in his chest, the King increased his pace into something near-punishing. Raegan moaned his name, her head tilting back against the wall, gaze tracking toward the ceiling. In a movement so quick her pleasure-addled mind could hardly trace it, Oberon lifted one hand from her body, grasping her jaw between his fingers with a steel-like grip. He lowered her chin, his oceanic gaze meeting hers.

"Eyes on me," he commanded in a tone so darkly devoted that it almost sent Raegan over the edge. She nodded, holding his gaze, her mouth parting to release another strangled cry.

"Just don't stop," she replied, her chest heaving against his.

One of those black brows arched, sending a thrill through her body, though she didn't understand how a sensation so perfect could keep feeling better and *better*. He kept his word, driving into her hard enough to send her heavy breasts bouncing, even with her back pressed against the wall. Through the falling droplets of water and her own thick haze of desire, she watched the King's gaze drop to the swell of her breasts, his eyes devouring her every curve.

Raegan didn't hesitate; she let go of his shoulder with one hand and took his sharp jaw between splayed fingers. "Eyes," she began, the word coming out a guttural groan. "On. *Me*."

Obediently, he raised that fathomless gray gaze of his,

water gathering on his long, dark eyelashes as he gave her every single ounce of his attention. With no interruption to the rhythm of their hips coming together, he took one of her wrists above her head and then the other, pinning both her arms against the wall.

"Come for me," he commanded in a voice like dusk, like every shadow sweeping in from the dark and lonely places.

Raegan held his gaze. "Fuck me harder, then."

After, they dried off and stumbled into the large sleigh bed of pale wood, dressed in soft linens and a thick quilt in a sea of blues. Judging by the light —if such things were the same in a place like Avalon—it was only late afternoon. And yet drowsiness pulled at Raegan pleadingly, her eyelids as heavy as her burdens. She curled her smaller frame against the King's, and he tucked her head under his chin, arms encircling her. They weren't safe, she knew. How could they be? Even if they retrieved Excalibur, destroyed the Gates, and vanquished the Timekeeper, their ouroboros would still march on, would it not? She would always slip from his grasp like river water. He would face the centuries ageless and mostly alone.

"Why do you keep returning to me, my queen of lovely rage?" Oberon murmured, fingertips tracing the spiral of curls spilling down her back.

Raegan hesitated, flattening her palm against his chest. "Because it's you," she finally said. "It's always been you. No one else looks at my anger like a sacrament."

His breathing stilled against her, slow as the morning tides. "And yet I can never manage to hold on to you for very long."

"That's not a failure on your part," Raegan protested,

lifting her head to look him in the eye. "I'd never ask you to take on that burden."

His smile was wan, awash in the rich golden sunlight streaming in from the large window that overlooked the city. "Good. Take care what you ask of me. I cannot say no."

"You probably should," she replied, raising a brow. "I'm fucking insane." His resulting laugh rumbled through her own body, and she hung on to the sound—sweeter than a Fatesong.

"As you said," he replied as she lowered her head back to his chest, "your madness, your rage, whatever you wish to call it—I would drown in it. Be consumed by it."

"You need to stop saying such incredibly attractive things," Raegan said with a yawn, nestling closer to the hard angles of his body. "I'm not going to be able to walk straight tomorrow as it is." Before he could respond, she patted the long length of his side and added, "That's a joke—you didn't hurt me."

Silence stretched downy wings over the quiet chambers at the center of Avalon. Another impossible city, a place relegated to myth and lore, and yet Raegan had walked within its walls and been greeted as a friend. For all the suffering, it was hard not to feel as though Fate's punishment was in some ways, at least, a gift. An offering. Otherwise she would've gone to the soil a thousand years ago, never to return. Instead, she rose from her grave again and again, searching the wide expanse of the world for her faerie king.

She took a deep breath, his woodsmoke and damp stone filling her senses. Not so much a gift for the King, of course. He'd be better off without her, and to pretend otherwise was just fondness on his part.

"I hope you understand," Oberon murmured, his voice soft and quiet in the massive room, "the ways you have mended me. From the first day we met, you have never been afraid of me." His hand slid over hers, and she turned her palm, their fingers interlacing. "I have been feared and loathed and desired. But rarely loved, not truly. I cannot even save you, Raegan. And yet you love me still."

Tears choked her. She wondered if she could raise a tide high enough to wash away all his suffering, to take all his pain out to sea where it could sink into the depths and be forgotten. She could not, she knew.

"This time," the King continued, pulling her tighter against him, "please. I beg you. "Outlive me. I love you too much."

CHAPTER FORTY-EIGHT

T he sea lashed at the high rocky cliffs of Avalon. Beneath the mist, the waves roiled in undulations not unlike some ancient sea monster. Raegan swallowed, pushing away a stray curl that the wind had pulled loose from her braid. The path leading down the cliffside was dizzying, barely more than steps carved into the crumbling chalk rock.

"The caves below have served us well," Danu said. Though the goddess did not raise her voice over the wind, Raegan heard her just fine. She turned to examine Danu, who stood at the top of the stairs, her grayed violet hair undisturbed by the same breezes that were currently unbraiding Raegan's curls. Divinity seemed nice. Lots of power, no real responsibility.

"Where in their depths will we find Excalibur?" the King asked, narrowing his eyes at the goddess. It was hard to believe he'd barely been able to limp into the city just the day before. The healing arts at Avalon far exceeded Raegan's thousand years of experience. Part of her itched to stay here, to pore over ancient texts and study every leaf in the greenhouses and permaculture orchards. But as Danu had said, some are not meant for the sun.

"Arthur's chamber is toward the back of the caverns," Danu answered serenely. Both Raegan and the King flinched at the name, even after all these years. "The places below have a mind of their own. Your resolve may be tested."

"Are you fucking kidding me?" Raegan snapped, nearly shouting to be heard over the wind. "What do some goddamn caves know about *resolve*? We've been surviving in a world with no magic."

Danu's otherworldly, impossibly clear eyes met hers. Amusement danced on the goddess's mouth. "I can see how you have vexed Fate so," she said, clasping her hands together in front of her. "Though I find your rage a good match for the last of my children."

"Oh, I'm so glad your deadbeat of a mother who just met you for the first time approves of me," Raegan quipped, looking up at Oberon, whose lips twitched at her words no matter how much he tried to wipe his expression clean. Danu's mouth pressed into a firm line, but one of her eyebrows arched with something that looked like amusement.

"How might our resolve be tested?" the King asked, crossing his arms. The borrowed overcoat was a little too small for his broad shoulders, pulling the fabric tight in a way that made Raegan think of the previous night.

"Some wander a labyrinth, others confront memories, some see their beloved dead," Danu said with a shrug, as if these were small, simple things.

"Great," Raegan said. "And someone can't just like . . . go get the sword for us, right?"

Danu's pale silver brow arched again. "The reason the places below may want to taste your intentions is because nothing sealed into those chambers is ever meant to come back out. Thus, the caves must be sure. Besides, I dare say few of us would fare well touching Excalibur."

Raegan eyed the winding stairs, the swelling waves, the entrance to the caves that they wouldn't even see until they reached the bottom of the cliff at exactly low tide, during which they would have approximately two hours to find a half-dead mortal king and his stolen faerie blade.

"You're a goddess," she said, drawing out the words. "So couldn't you—"

"Child," Danu interrupted, her expression unguarded, the crow's feet around her eyes crinkling as she squinted into the sun. "You know there is a way of these things. I can only interfere so much in this Thread. Even here. Even with all my power."

The wind scaled the cliffside in a rough exhale. The heather and gorse around Raegan's feet trembled, the standing stones a few paces off whistling as the wind raced past.

"When, precisely," Raegan began the moment it died down enough to speak, "was anyone aware that Excalibur used to be a faerie blade? And how did the Morrigan know?" Her mind swam as she shoved her hands into the pockets of the wool cape she'd been lent.

"Does it matter?" Danu asked dryly, staring off into the horizon—just ocean, endless swathes of sea in every direction. When neither Raegan nor Oberon responded, she heaved a very un-goddess-like sigh and turned back to face them. "Understand, my information is secondhand. I used to send spies into the Otherlands before it became too dangerous, before I buried the sea-door. Myrddin intended to take Excalibur's secret to his grave, I imagine, but Arthur knew, and at some point, Morgana le Fay learned of it. Arthur executed her for witchcraft to silence her, but as a priestess of the Morrigan, she told her goddess on her funeral pyre."

Wordlessly, Raegan reached out to take Oberon's hand. Morgana—Arthur's half-sister—had been the one to raise the King as a child, teaching him the ways of human nobility. He'd loved her, as had Raegan, and they'd done everything to stop the burning. It had, of course, not been enough. Rarely, it seemed, were they ever enough.

"I conspired with the kelpies to bring Arthur to Avalon so he could not rise again. I knew nothing of the blade's past and have squandered its potential for so many years," Danu continued, something not unlike grief etching her divine features. "When Kronos captured the Morrigan at the Battle of Camlann, the truth of Excalibur was locked away. It stayed that way until she escaped in the Otherlands, but by that point, the Gates had long been sealed in their entirety and the only people who could possibly do anything about it were trapped on the other side. I imagine she has been trying to reach you for hundreds of years. I too was only able to briefly communicate with her because of the temporary door you tore through the worlds with your tears."

Raegan felt exhausted, too much like the cliff at her left, which had spent thousands of years under the ocean's constant assault. She wanted to sleep. She wanted to have tea with

Oberon in the mornings and have nowhere to be. Clenching her jaw, she closed her eyes and tried to remind herself of how badly she'd wanted all of this once.

But she'd hardly remembered anything then. Now she carried the weight of the centuries, her spine trembling with the energy to stay upright, to stay alive, at every moment.

"You're right," she said to the goddess. "It doesn't matter. It doesn't matter that the Morrigan has been trying to reach though the Gates for hundreds of years and only because everything went to shit and Fate played me like a fiddle was there even a tiny tear for her to reach through at all."

The words had barely left Raegan's mouth when a realization shot like lightning through her body. She jolted to stand ramrod straight, her mouth going dry. She looked at the King, whose wide eyes were already on hers, and then at Danu, who looked significantly coyer.

"Did Fate . . . Was this all . . ." she breathed, resisting the urge to tear her hair out at the root.

"When it comes to the primordial forces, even a being as old as I hesitate to comment," Danu said, staring out at the sea again, her tresses fluttering around her bare arms, which didn't appear to prickle with goosebumps despite the chill of the wind. "But it is possible. Do not trust Her, mind you."

A mass of shadow slunk past Raegan's side. She watched, confused, as the King stalked toward the mouth of the chalk rock stairs, his silhouette slicing into the mist that crowned the island.

"Oberon," she called, breaking into a jog, trying to be mindful of the fog-damp vegetation and loose rock.

"The goddess is right. None of it matters," the King half-shouted, turning on his heel, his eyes dark. "I do not care if Fate is secretly helping. I do not care about the machinations by which the knowledge of Excalibur's true nature reached our ears. I care about my people and you, Nyneve. Nothing more, nothing less. So let us go retrieve this godsforsaken blade."

His eyes slid to Danu and narrowed, his chin tilted arrogantly. "If your island's low places give us undue trouble, know that my witch could drown this place, Old One."

Heat, of all things, slunk through Raegan's core at the

way he referred to her. She caught up to him, sheltering against his bulk from the gnawing wind.

Danu grinned, her teeth just a little too sharp. "And if not for the love of my own people, nameless child, I should like to see her try." And then the goddess was gone, only tendrils of mist writhing in the place on the headland where she'd stood just seconds ago.

Raegan looked up at Oberon, and he met her gaze. "The only way, I think, is through," she said, studying his expression. He had just as much rage as she did—Raegan had always known that. He only controlled it better, had a wider and darker chasm within him to imprison it. She was not sure, not even after all these years, which way was actually better.

"Together," he said, bringing his forehead to hers. He planted a kiss against her skin and then turned to make his way down the crumbling stairs. Raegan followed at a safe distance, and they fell into a pattern, relying on the King's agility and quicker reflexes to forge a path ahead. It might've been beautiful, the impossibly sheer cliff face, stretching its white wings before giving way to the roaring gray ocean below, if not for the way all of destiny hung on the shoulders of the two people crawling across its expanse like ants.

By the time about a quarter of the stairs remained, according to Raegan's extremely rough estimation, the tide had begun to retreat, revealing a rocky beach awash with tidepools that shimmered like gems whenever the sun managed to reach through the crown of mist that circled the outer edges of the island. It was pretty, but her ankles and knees hurt. Getting back up would probably be worse, she reminded herself.

"If we come all this way," Raegan began, huffing as she navigated a particularly steep section, "just to die in a fucking cave, I swear to God, Oberon, I'll be so pissed."

He glanced over his shoulder at her, amusement tugging at the corners of his mouth. "I do not think any body of water would force itself into your lungs. And I cannot drown. The Protectorate tried."

Raegan's heart skipped a beat. She had attempted—unsuccessfully—to banish the thoughts of what the Protectorate had done to him following his capture. It had been her fault. They'd tried to kill him for *years*. All that pain and suffering, more than even she could imagine. And yet here he was, smiling up at her, making a joke of the horrors he'd endured, the wind ruffling his dark waves of hair.

She carefully made her way toward him, stopping on a step that brought her eye-level with him. "How we endure," Raegan murmured, reaching out to trace her fingertips down the side of his face. The King leaned into her touch like a love-starved alley cat, closing his eyes as she held his jaw in her hand.

"Forward, then," he said, so softly the wind almost grabbed his words and spirited them away. Upon the chalk-white cliffs of Avalon, Oberon reached for her hand and then brought his mouth to her knuckles, brushing her skin with a delicate kiss, gentle as a butterfly. Raegan's mind reeled, pulling her back to Camelot and the dark-armored knight with a gaze that seemed to see right through all her lies.

"Onward," she agreed, following the King as he turned to continue forging a safe path down the cliffside. The wind, thankfully, died down the lower they trekked, becoming little more than a strong breeze tugging them toward destiny.

At the bottom of the carved staircase, a wide plane of sandy rock breached the surface of the sea like a whale's back. Raegan scrambled onto it with Oberon's help, gripping his forearm tightly. It wasn't fair—nothing about anything was. They were both sufficiently healed, yes, but an exhaustion that no pharmakon could address lingered in their bones. And yet here they were, delving deep into the earth, praying that this place would not be their end.

"Shit," Raegan said as she took in the wide mouth of the sea caves: a door—it was always a door, wasn't it?—of a tall, narrow shape cut into the expanse of the white cliffs. They moved toward it, steps careful and measured. Raegan looked over her shoulder, back toward the ocean, and saw that this location would be woefully inaccessible any other time of the day. Experimentally, she pushed at the seawater with her magic. It did respond, but its answer was sluggish, irritated, unused to this taskmaster with mortal blood in her veins.

"I have a little sway with the ocean," she informed the King as they approached the mouth of the cavern. "Don't count on anything, though. It'd be a Hail Mary."

He looked at her sideways, mouth grim as he nodded. "Better than nothing, I suppose," he replied with a shrug, turning back to gaze into the open maw awaiting them.

The higher tides had left lines on the cave's walls, far above their heads. Raegan eyed them uncomfortably, her heart thudding a bit too hard against her ribs.

"How far does Avalon's sea go?" she wanted to know as they skirted a large tide pool with a lavender-spotted black octopus lingering within its waters.

"Forever, as far as I know," he replied, gazing up at the cavern's ceilings as it closed in on them, the mouth of a predator snapping shut. "From what I've gathered, when Danu pulled this realm out of ours, it did not happen quite right. Avalon should have been, perhaps, a larger, more magically fortified pocket realm. It is not. It is its own place entirely, with its own rules and wonders and terrors."

Raegan swallowed, nodding. It was easy to forget.

Avalon was undeniably beautiful, and not terribly different from the Cornish coast, but Raegan was the first mortal to step foot here in thousands of years, if not more, and it would not do well to slip into complacency simply because the environs held some familiarity.

The air stilled farther inside the caverns, smelling of seawater and stones gowned in brine. They continued down the main walkway, silent, eyes roving this way and that, relying on the sputtering torches of lilac flame bracketed to the walls. All at once, the atmosphere changed—there was a deep, bone-rattling hum of terrible, eldritch magic. The awareness of it skittered down Raegan's spine like a chill, and she sharpened her eyes. Some doors, she remembered, are hungry.

But it was hard to keep an eye open for doors as the terrain grew more difficult. She stuck close to the King, scrambling up tight, slippery inclines and shimmying through claustrophobic passages. At one point, they had to descend a sheer drop into the darkness, bringing them into an inner cavern riddled with stalagmites. Neither spoke during their trek; the air filled instead with their footsteps and the drip of seawater, holy as a hymn.

Time, as it does in places such as these, dilated and shrank, passing in an unknown amount, before they saw the first cave. It opened like a mouth in the gray, stretching abyss of the walls. One of those eldritch workings reached over the opening, pale and iridescent in the fading light. The surface of it rippled like a living thing, so similar to the oil-spill surface of a porticus.

Raegan approached it slowly, peering inside as best she could. The space was filled with shelves, laden with plants stored beneath bell jars, seemingly in a form of stasis. It was hard to identify anything in the low light and through the shimmering, spiderweb barrier of the working, but even so, she could see flora that had never grown on earth in the thousand years she'd been walking it.

"Likely biological stores, in case anything suffers a blight on the island," the King observed, his eyes tracking down farther into the cavern. Where Arthur slept, where Excalibur awaited a faerie king to release its true, feral nature.

Wordlessly, Raegan nodded and continued into the lilac-tinted gloom of the sea caves, aware of the presence that seemed to rove the space. She was growing a bit tired of sentient locations. It felt too much like being surveilled—judged and sentenced by a being she couldn't even *see*, let alone understand or reason with.

They wove deeper into the caves, Raegan worrying about the return of the higher tides, but the clock on her phone had been frozen since they'd entered Avalon. No service, either. Its battery was getting low, and she doubted anyone in the hidden Fey city had a charger. She wasn't sure why it was even still in the pocket of her leather jacket. Habit, maybe, or perhaps guilt about the people she'd left behind.

Farther, farther into the darkness they went, clinging to each other. Fear pounded in Raegan's veins, anxiety spiking at every distant wave crash she heard. But forward she went because there was little the deathless witch was not capable of with the nameless one at her side. The gossamer-thin, iridescent mouths of more sea caves opened as they journeyed, offering glances at impossible-looking archery bows and strange creatures gone still. Most were empty. She tried not to think about that too much.

"Raegan," Oberon murmured, the heavy silence of the cave carrying his voice right to her ears. She turned on her heel from the cave she'd been examining; it was filled with strange, bloated jars. The hair on the back of her neck prickled.

"You found it, didn't you?" she asked, her voice so small, every fiber of her being aware and terrified and filled with the treachery of hope.

Across the narrow corridor, Oberon nodded. Carefully, like she might be in a trance, like all of the future was balanced on the edge of a knife, Raegan navigated the pock-marked rock and came to stand beside the King.

There, beyond the oil-spill mouth of the door, lay a man on a slab of rock. His eyes were closed, the wrapped leather pommel of a longsword clutched tight between sleeping hands. He was—at least to look at—nothing at all remarkable. A man of middling height and build, of middling pale brown hair, of middling features.

Once, Arthur Pendragon had held the fate of the world in his hands. But it had never belonged to him in the first place, so it was well past time, Raegan thought, to take it back.

Chapter Forty-Nine

She reached out and brushed the working stretched like spiderweb silk over the mouth of the cave. It gave slightly, bending around her touch. When her skin made contact with it, Raegan's head swam violently.

"I do not think I can disarm it," Oberon told her, pacing in front of the cave's mouth, his dark brow furrowed. He was so far from the young, heartbroken, and outraged knight he'd been the last time he and Arthur Pendragon had walked the same halls, stalked the same fields of war. And yet, an old feeling rose in her chest—she wanted to get him as far away from Arthur as possible. She so badly wanted him to be free of this sword and this horrible man. But like so many things she wished for, it could not be.

"I think it's the test," Raegan said with a sigh, eyeing the eldritch magic. "I think we have to walk through it and let Avalon's low places judge us."

The King's frown deepened, but he did not contradict her. "I wish we had the time to be sure," he sighed, his attention roving back the way they'd come. The lilac fire contained in the simple metal torches dimmed for a second. A warning, probably.

"Together, then," Raegan said, trying not to sound terrified.

Instead of reaching for her hand, Oberon closed the distance between them and wrapped his body around hers, pulling her into a kiss that drove her madder than an ancient spell ever could.

And then, before she could think or hesitate, the King clutched her in his arms and dove into the glimmering maw of Arthur Pendragon's resting place. For a moment, the working stretched against Raegan's weight and almost gave —she was so close to the sword she'd crossed realms for, the King's arms still around her.

And then everything was gone, the cave and the rock-hemmed darkness and the rush of ocean waves blinking out from existence. Instead, there was a nothingness so downy and sweet, as soft as being wrapped in furs by the fireside. But she could not feel her faerie king—could not feel *anything*—so she pushed through it, swimming without sight or hearing. At least she knew the darkness half as well as she knew herself.

Raegan awoke slowly, gently, blinking her eyes open to find the molasses-thick light of autumn streaming down all around her. She sat up, finding she was sprawled out on a cozy wool blanket, a book forgotten at her side. The breeze danced across her skin, smelling of woodsmoke and damp stone and fallen leaves. She turned, not understanding, finding herself at the edge of a meadow. Beyond it, a forest grew dark and lovely. In front of her was a stone cottage, smoke curling out of its chimney. A fox roved the far edge of the meadow. Raegan stretched, feeling adrift. A distant buzzing met her ears, and she looked for the source of the sound—beehives, she saw, clustered between the house and the meadow.

Confusion knit thickly on her brow, she stood, finding

nothing but mundane tiredness in her limbs. In fact, Raegan felt light—lighter than she had in years. But her body was the same, she saw with a quick glance at her soft flannel pants and oversized wool cardigan. She slid her feet back into the leather boots at the edge of the blanket and walked toward the cottage.

Some voice in the back of her mind warned her to be wary, but that made no sense. She was home, wasn't she? Her bees were busy in their hives, her vegetable garden still offering a few lush herbs even this late in the season. She walked up the moss-lined stone stairs at the back of the house and pushed open the heavy door. The scent of black tea and a hearth fire immediately greeted her, wrapping around her body like a blanket. Moving through the small entryway, lined with coats she recognized as her own, Raegan found herself in a small kitchen.

The cabinets curved in a half-moon with a large sink set below the garden window that looked out into the backyard. Less hardy herbs grew there in thick, colorful clumps, filling the cozy space with a deep green perfume. And there, at the stove, turning to face her with a kettle in hand, was the person she had loved through the ages.

"Oberon," Raegan murmured, enjoying the way his expression brightened when he saw her.

"I was about to come check on you," he replied in his deep, husky voice that she loved so much, that she had chased across the world. "Did you fall asleep?"

"I must've," Raegan laughed, her heart bursting with a joy so fragile she worried one wrong move might crack it down the center. "Is the water hot?"

Oberon nodded, gesturing with an elegant hand to the pair of teacups on the counter, already garnished with sugar and loose leaves of a dark, malty blend. "I planned to gently awaken you with a cup of hot tea," he said, one eyebrow arched as he poured hot water into both mugs.

"I think you just wanted to fuck out in the meadow again," she replied teasingly, memories flooding her mind of the day before—no, maybe not the day before. Hadn't they been somewhere else? She shook the thought from her head, instead lingering in the scene her mind offered up: autumn sun silhouetting his ivory skin, gilding his black hair with gold, how he'd moved above her, the weight of him pinning her to the blanket, the cool breeze caressing her bare skin.

His eyes slid to hers, all molten heat, the ocean turned to inferno. "You question my honorable intentions?" he asked, placing the kettle back on the stove.

Raegan laughed, picking up her mug and wrapping her hands around the steeping tea, warding off the chill from being outside. "I had a weird dream," she said, fighting to recall. "We were somewhere dark. A cave, I think? Looking for someone."

The King sighed and leaned on the counter on his fore-arms, the muscles of his chest and shoulder standing out beneath the thin shirt. "We have lived a long time, my love," he murmured, stirring his tea. "I have no doubt we were there, once."

"But we're here now, yes?" Raegan asked, suddenly doubtful, feeling like a rabbit in a snare. "We've been here?"

Any amusement in Oberon's face fled, and he reached for her, wrapping his larger hand around hers. "For six years," he said, his brow pulling tight in concern. "Some-times you slip backwards in time. There is no danger in doing so, but it distresses you."

"Oh," Raegan said, relief bubbling up in her, though she didn't feel convinced, not with the remnants of the dream still clinging to her. "Right. I'm sorry."

"There is nothing to be sorry for," he replied without hesitation. "As long as you are alright."

"I think so," she promised, looking around the kitchen. The open cabinets were piled with mismatched dishes and bowls that felt like hers. She knew the utensils were in the top drawer of the counter, remembered cutting the fabric for the gingham tea towels by the sink. Trying to let go of the strange anxiety pulling at her, Raegan let out a long breath and looked up at the King.

He was hers. The lines around his eyes, the silver threaded through his hair—just a little more than there had been in the strange dream—the full, sculpted mouth, the knife-like cheekbones, the notched scar bisecting the outer corner of his left eye. Yes. This was her love, and this was her life.

"We made it," she realized, tears brimming in her eyes. "Through all of it. You didn't lose me, and we made this little life. The Jersey cow in the pasture is named Acorn. I saw that big fox in the meadow again. We should name him, too, I think."

Oberon watched her, his gaze so full of endless love—love that finally had somewhere to go, to stay and grow—and she resisted the urge to weep. They'd fucking done it.

"We can cancel our dinner plans if you need more rest," he said to her gently. "The weight of your mind is heavy, and some days you find yourself tumbling out of time."

"Dinner?" she echoed, distracted as a crow landed on a tree outside the garden window, its feathers turned blue-black in the rays of the sun.

"Reilly, Alanna, and Maelona are coming by," Oberon told her, gesturing to the backyard. "You wanted to drag the long table out there and decorate it with apple blossoms. And then I believe you wanted to, and I quote, 'become blisteringly and stupidly drunk.'"

453

Raegan laughed, so much sweet, wondrous joy bursting in her chest, though unease bloomed sour somewhere in her stomach. "That's right," she said, half-remembering it. "I think I'll be okay if it's just them."

"You can always change your mind," he reassured her. The crow at the garden window suddenly pecked the glass hard, startling Raegan. Oberon glanced over his shoulder, frowning. "Perhaps we are feeding them a bit *too* much."

The crow drove its beak hard into the glass again, louder now. The King stalked the three steps to the window and waved his hands to shoo the crow off. It only pecked harder, almost ferocious enough to break the glass. That tendril of unease coiled around Raegan's gut.

"I'll go give it a talking to," she said, trying to maintain her light tone.

"I am sure it will leave soon," Oberon replied, knocking hard on the inside of the glass. The crow pecked back in return, not stopping now, jackhammering its beak into the window. Without another word, Raegan turned and fled out the back door, coming around the corner to face the large black bird.

"Could you stop, please?" she demanded, waving her arms. "Glass costs money. I don't think crows have capitalism, but we do, unfortunately."

Raegan paused, suspended in the murky light of late autumn that stretched across the meadow like honey. *Did* they have capitalism? Or had they changed all of that, too? Why couldn't she remember? Her hands curled into fists, fingernails biting into the flesh of her palm as she bit down on her tongue. She had to focus. What had she done this morning? Nothing but blankness arose in her mind, and she looked at the crow. It spread its wings and took off in flight. For a moment, her heart unclenched—maybe that was it, maybe its pecking meant nothing at all, maybe this really was her home and everything had worked out perfectly.

Raegan glanced around the space—the brown cow and speckled goat in the large, rolling pasture, the apple trees rooted in the forest, the swaying grasses of the meadow, the perfect little cottage, the King now standing in the open door frame. All hers. And yet fear clutched at her, a sob tearing its way up the back of her throat.

"Nyneve," Oberon called, stepping down into the yard. "It is alright. I promise."

Instead of taking off for the trees in the distance, the crow began to circle her with desperate caws, its wings nearly brushing her shoulders.

The seed of doubt broke open beneath her breastbone, taking root. Tears spilled out from her eyes as she drank in the dreamscape, wanting to believe so badly, so desperately. But nothing this sweet and simple would ever be hers, she knew.

The darkness of the crow grew wider around her, the yawning mouth of a cave. She watched it, dizzy, her heart breaking into a thousand pieces. Not only was none of this hers, she knew, but there was the real King and a faerie blade and the future of magic awaiting her somewhere else.

"Stay here," the not-King pleaded, walking toward her with all the predatory grace she knew so well, his hands spread wide. "We could stay here, Raegan."

She gazed at him, eyes wide, brimming with tears, and wondered if this *was* Oberon. Was he trapped in this same working, and was he encouraging her to lay it all down? No, it might not be real—their bodies would rot at the entrance to the king of men's resting place.

But it would *feel* real. Did anything else even matter? She could have the thing she'd always craved: a future with the people she loved, bright and sweet as a honeycrisp apple. Yearning unspooled from the caverns of her body, thick with ache and unyielding in desire. She wanted this. She did not care, maybe, how she got it.

"No," Raegan gasped, tears streaming down her face. "Fuck, I want to. I can't even tell you how much I want all of this. The cottage and the apple blossoms and the afternoon cups of tea and most of all, you. You without Fate's Threads gouging lines in our skin. You without the rest of it. But we can't. Not yet. Maybe never."

The flap of the crow's midnight wings began to rip wounds in the world around her. Raegan could nearly feel the welts opening inside her own body. She would've rather not tasted this fantasy at all. She didn't want to know what it could be, what it could feel like—she wanted no part in something that she knew deep down she could never have. Some people, like Danu said, are not meant for the sun.

"I love you," she whispered to the King, the words choking her. And then she gave into the darkness forming around her, the shadow that devoured this beautiful little dream. Raegan squeezed her eyes shut, clenching her jaw to stem the sobs building like a storm in her chest.

Nothingness threw its arms around her, quiet and void of anything at all. Part of her thought about staying in the dark, but it was where she'd always return—ready or not—so she pushed through it, seeking the damp of Avalon's caves and the heat of the person she loved with everything she was.

CHAPTER FIFTY

"Raegan." Someone spoke her name, their voice like heather on the hills and dusk over the lake. She stirred, stiff and cold, the wool cape wrapped around her not enough to ward off the chill of the damp stone beneath her. With a start, she bolted upright, nearly smashing her forehead into the King's.

"Are you alright?" he asked, worry curled around his voice. He was on his knees at her side, one hand interlaced with hers.

"Yeah," she muttered, a tide of sorrow still lapping at her being, threatening to pull her back into that daydream. "Did you . . . the cottage?"

The way his angular features collapsed told her everything she needed to know. "I . . . I thought about remaining there."

Her heart clenched. "So was it really you?"

He tilted his head, eyes searching hers. "I do not know. I worry I cannot dwell on it, lest the gravity of it pull me back into its orbit." His gaze slid away from hers, coming to rest on something at her back—the mortal king wrapped in a thousand years of sleep, she realized.

Raegan took a deep breath and with the exhale, did her best to expel the rest of that beautiful vision that she'd almost happily allowed herself to be trapped in forever. Instead, she pushed to her feet, aided by the King, and took a few trembling strides to stand beside Arthur.

The man looked much as he had all those years ago. Raegan's stomach churned with distaste. Arthur had held ideals, once. He'd had honor, once. And all of it had been twisted and leached away by the taste for power. And, she realized now in retrospect, probably Excalibur, too.

"Caledfwlch," Oberon breathed, his eyes ghosting the length of the blade, speaking its older name in his native tongue. Something ancient and aching stirred in Raegan as she stared down at the sleeping king, at the tunic she'd watched a servant mend, at the once-broken right ring finger she'd healed. Bittersweet memories rose up from her depths, playing across her vision with a biting clarity.

She spun to look at the King, words tumbling from her mouth. "Why didn't you let me take you away from there?" she choked out. "I offered. I would've done it, Mordred. I would've left my people behind. What difference did it make that we stayed? Camelot still fell. The Druids of old are still gone, their traditions with them. The Gates still rose. The Timekeeper still happened to all of us."

He gazed at her, the Unseelie regent melting away entirely. Suddenly, in the dim glow of the torches, watered down even further by the working at the cave's mouth, Mordred stood in front of her. He was too young for the worry that sat on his brow, heavy as a crown.

"If you wanted it," Nyneve said, tears cutting into her words, "I would've saved you."

All of the faerie knight's attention fell onto her, heavy as the sweep of night, delicate as a moth's wings. He turned from Arthur's plinth—from the last chance at salvation they might have—to take her face between his hands.

"Nyneve, you fool," Mordred murmured, his gaze little more than an ocean of grief, "you *did* save me." His mouth met hers, hot and demanding, hands sliding into her hair, fingers weaving into her curls.

Grief and regret and ache exploded in her chest. She clung to him like a lifeboat in a terrible storm, tears still running down her face as she returned the intense need of his kiss.

"You did save me," he repeated, his breath ghosting her cheek, forehead resting against hers. Despite all of her instincts, despite the way a voice told her it would make everything else hurt too much in the end, Raegan let herself lean against the comforting, solid bulk of his muscular mass. She buried her face in his coat, inhaling the black pepper and woodsmoke that would surely haunt whomever she came back as next.

With a deep breath, she righted herself, aided by the powerful arm slung around her waist. She dragged the back of her hands across her face, shoving away the tears; it was not the tide she needed now. Instead, she looked past the King and at the sword.

"It used to hurt you to be in the same room," she said, her heart panging with the weight of memory.

"It still does," he reported, bitterness creeping into his voice. "But pain is an old companion now."

A flash of fury tore through Raegan. Why should he suffer more? Why did it always have to be *him*, the person she loved more than anything in the world?

"You're not going near it," Raegan declared, swallowing hard as she curled her hands into fists. Oberon looked at her in clear surprise, his brow knitting in confusion and then concern.

"Who else but a faerie king to turn a faerie blade back?" he demanded in a scoff, his voice thick with that easy, casual arrogance she knew damn well was just a bluff.

Raegan paced in front of the plinth, her thoughts running too fast for her to keep up with them all. "Exactly. You're only supposed to turn it back," she pointed out, raising her gaze to him. Defiant, she held her body between the King and the blade. His dark eyes tracked her like a predator, clearly aware of what she was doing. "The Morrigan didn't say anything about you being the one to steal it out of a damn cave."

His brow arched, the angles of his face growing sharp and dangerous. "Nor did she say anything about *you* doing it. Raegan, be sensible. We have no idea what Excalibur will do to a mortal vessel like yours."

She ground her teeth, shifting to the left as the King did, again blocking him from moving closer to the plinth. "You know that I have never been sensible a day in my goddamn life," she snapped, throwing up one hand. "Why the fuck would I start now, in an undersea cave with an evil sword?"

He said nothing, so Raegan took a step backwards, closer to Arthur's plinth—a test. Oberon closed the distance as she thought he might. She watched him carefully, noticing the catch in his movements, the furrowing of his brow. Even a single step closer pained him. She wasn't surprised. The power that radiated from Excalibur was immense. If not for those strange, glimmering workings stretching over the caves' mouths, Raegan surely would have felt the blade's presence at the entrance to Avalon's low places. Or possibly on the headland itself, the ancient, twisted magic reaching tendrils up the sheer cliffs.

"Raegan, my love," the King pleaded, that feral glint leaving his eyes. "Please. Let me do this. I cannot bear to see you injured."

"But that's not even *why* you want to do this!" Raegan replied, surprising herself by shouting. The words rang out in the cavern, and for a moment, she was terrified Arthur would somehow awaken. A quick glance over her shoulder told her that the king of men's sleep continued with more peace than he deserved. "You think you earned the pain. As punishment. For failing. You think this is some kind of fucked-up penance."

Oberon stilled, his chin moving in an arrogant lift, the words to deny her statement undoubtedly brewing eloquent and cutting at the back of his throat. But when he opened his mouth, he only closed it again, squeezing his eyes shut, too.

"You don't," Raegan protested, her voice rough with the tears she found herself holding back. "You don't deserve to be punished."

"And neither do you!" Oberon replied in a desperate, strangled tone, opening his eyes to meet her gaze.

Her nails bit half-moons into her palms, frustration and long-simmering rage threatening to boil over in this small cavern. Holding his gaze, she began to reply, but then a sound met her ears that filled her with horror.

Heart in her throat, Raegan looked toward the corridor running through the cave system and found sea water. The tide was returning, already ankle-deep and rich with swirling currents. The protective workings kept the ocean out of the cavern, at least, it seemed.

"Oberon," she said, nervousness spilling into her tone. "We can't get trapped down here. But I'm not letting you do this. I'm *not*. It will literally feed on your magic and use that to hurt you. We both know that."

The King's gaze averted from hers, falling to the king and the sword at her back. His full lips pressed into a firm line, a dangerous determination in the line of his shoulders.

"And it's already tasted your blood," Raegan reminded him, trying to ignore the water rushing through the corridor just beyond the cavern's seal. "At Camlann. It is much harder, Oberon, to hold back a wolf once it's scented you. Let me do this."

"No," the King said, the words hoarse, his jaw clenched. "I cannot ask that of you. We can make better plans with the information we have gleaned and return with the next tide."

Despair seeped into Raegan. She glanced back at the corridor to find the water had come to knee-level, rushing fast and hard past the mouth of Arthur's cave. The lilac torches pulsed again, a few seconds of frantic fluttering similar to what she felt in her own chest.

"The cave is only accessible *one* day under the new moon," Raegan replied, fingernails biting into her palms. "We got stupid lucky with arriving right before it, but we'd be forced to wait another entire month to come back. And God only knows how fucking long that would be in our world."

"I know," he murmured, looking back at her.

Bile churned in her stomach. She hated to see that look on his face—that such a magnificent creature, carved from shadow and blessed in blood, the most breathtaking thing she'd ever seen in her entire life, would be made to feel small and useless in the swell of Fate and destiny.

Water rushed mercilessly at his back. When Raegan pulled on it experimentally, it answered reluctantly, acknowledging what she was but not her authority. She wanted to scream. She wanted to slip back in time and kill Arthur before he could do all the horrible things that had landed them in this underwater cavern, desperate and running out of time. Always running out of time.

Even if Avalon's sea did not answer her, Raegan's rage

still rose in her like a tide. She turned to look down at Arthur, and all the memories came surging to her shores: the meaningless cruelty, the rough way he had treated Guinevere, and the iron fist that had defined the last few years of his rule. All because some Gods-touched sorcerer had given him a sword that could rend the world in two.

"Fuck it," Raegan said, reaching for the plinth. The pain Excalibur caused the King slowed his reaction, so when her hand wrapped around the sword's pommel, he had only just grabbed her shoulder.

Time hung still. Even the sea rushing in outside faded away. Raegan's entire world condensed to the slab of rock, the sleeping king, and the blade in her hand. She let out one breath. Two. Three.

Nothing at all was happening.

Perhaps her rage wrapped around her like a shield. Perhaps her anger was its own sacred thing—a sacrament, like the King had said. With a shaking exhale, Raegan pulled Excalibur from Arthur's grip. His pale, sleeping fingers slipped away much more easily than she would've thought. She turned, the most legendary sword in the entire world gripped between her palms. It was heavy—much heavier than it looked—and she felt it reaching for her, looking for a way inside to feast. If she tried to actually *wield* it—to activate its power, to siphon away the power of whoever's flesh she cut into with its blade—Excalibur would probably tear her to shreds. But for now, it seemed, she could carry it out of this tomb.

Oberon looked at Raegan like nothing else had ever mattered to him and nothing would. Then he threw his head back and laughed, feral and glorious, the baying of a hound with its teeth bared. "It knows not what to do with you," he explained, a light shining in his eyes that she hadn't seen in so many years. "You are both mortal and magic, dead and living. Your contradictions seem to be rerouting its power, turning the sword back in on itself."

Raegan hefted the blade with both hands, nearly dropping the heavy object. "A snake eats its own tail," she observed in a soft murmur, chills cascading across her skin.

"You are a miracle," the King said, his grip on her shoulder tightening. "And we should take our leave. Now. Can you carry it?"

"I'll do my best," Raegan replied with a grunt, her biceps and forearms protesting as she lifted the tip of the blade from the ground again. The only reason she could lift it at all, Raegan knew, was because of Andronica's training back at the Philadelphia Temple.

Oberon kept his eyes on hers, moving backwards to the cave's mouth. Fuck, she hoped that Avalon's low places didn't insist on testing those who walked its depths on the way in *and* out.

Raegan had almost made it to the veil stretched over the cave's maw when she remembered. Excalibur could kill the sleeping yet-not-fully-mortal king. She froze. But surely it wouldn't let her wield it. The blade would never open its mouth for the likes of her, would never unleash its enchantments on the man who had borne it for so many years. But the sword was—like her—hungry. How long had they both languished in the shadows, away from the heat and light of the world they knew, dreaming of what they used to be? Perhaps Excalibur's loyalty had waned in the dark, damp dim beneath the buried sea.

With a snarl that didn't even sound like her own voice, Raegan turned on her heel. She raised the sword, and the weapon registered her intent to wield it. The spellwork closed around her like a vice, but her magic—that wild, keening thing embedded in her ribs—was neither Fey nor mortal nor god-granted. And she was neither living nor dead. Excalibur's power reached for Raegan, tearing at her insides, but it found no purchase. There are, after all, no handholds in a river. And what is a river if not a devourer?

So with a feral cry, the pain lancing through her, Raegan scrambled onto the slab, scraping her knees on the sharp, rocky edges. And then, straddling Arthur Pendragon's waist, she raised Excalibur high. In a way she would never be able to find the words for, the not-quite-mortal, half-mad woman felt the ancient, storied sword's mouth open wide, its teeth sharp and long and so, so hungry.

"Fuck you," she snarled, her spittle flecking the face of the king of men. "This is for Morgana. For Guinevere. For Mordred. For *me*."

And then she plunged Excalibur into his heart.

Chapter Fifty-One

"**D**o you need to trade off?" Raegan called down to the King as they scrambled back up the chalk cliffs, the ocean closing in behind them. On the way to the sea caves, neither of them had noticed the darkened horizontal lines across the sheer drop, marking how far the tide reached. The ocean appeared to be fighting to beat its highest record, and Raegan thought that *might* have something to do with the fact she had killed one of Avalon's sleeping wards.

The protective working across the mouth of the cavern had all but exploded the moment she drove Excalibur into King Arthur's heart. Somehow, despite the pain and the power it took to ward off the blade's hunger, Oberon had thrown a protective spell around them both. They were battered and bruised, but the spellery had fought off the worst of it.

And then, of course, the ocean had surged in anger, the water suddenly writhing and steaming. Raegan had barely coaxed it into parting just enough for her and Oberon to run through the cavern's corridors. The wide plain of rock and sand that connected the sea caves to the stairs had diminished to a tiny spit of land, but it was enough.

She huffed, steadying herself with one hand on the side of the cliff. There hadn't been time to examine precisely how or why, but something about feeding Arthur's blood to Excalibur had altered the sword. He hadn't tried to wield it, but Oberon could carry it now, albeit wrapped up in Raegan's salt-soaked wool cape. Surely all the ageless knowledge in Avalon would be of use, if they could just make it to the top of the sea stairs in time.

"I am fine for now," Oberon replied, a few steps behind her, the word tugging at his voice. As if in response to his statement, the sea roared beneath them, crawling up the cliff with open, white-capped fingers. "Hold on."

Raegan felt the King grip the back of her sweater, and she turned in surprise, panic crowding out the air in her lungs. "We need to *go*," she protested, trying not to look at the boiling ocean below.

"Precisely," Oberon replied, his eyes sliding shut, body going still. She briefly considered screaming, but then she watched as the scant shadows on the sheer drop of the chalk-white cliffs slunk toward his hands. The darkness curled around his arms like snakes, reaching up for the back of his broad shoulders. Her heart in her throat, Raegan watched—with one eye on the alarming progression of the sea's surge—as the shadows stitched themselves into an impressive set of wings at the King's back.

"That's kind of hot," she said, taking him in, the contrast of his pale skin and dark hair all the more intensified by the backdrop of the cliffs. His shadow-wings were too wide to open fully on the cramped space of the stairs.

"Come," he murmured, reaching out a hand, the curve to his beautiful mouth telling her he knew exactly what he was doing. Desire thrummed between her legs, and she obeyed, stepping into his arms. He handed her the wool-wrapped sword, which she clutched to her chest, before sweeping her off her feet.

"Ready?" Oberon asked, shifting to face the sea, his back against the cliffs.

"Oh, absolutely not," Raegan replied cheerfully.

In reply, the King pitched them both off the cliff. For a long, horrible moment, there was nothing but the sea rushing up to meet her and fear clamoring loudly in her chest.

But then his shadow-wings caught the air and they soared higher, leaving the angry ocean to crawl up the sea stairs in pursuit of them. Oberon banked to return to the island, fighting all the competing headwinds that buffeted them, trying to tear Excalibur from Raegan's grasp. All she had to do was hold on, she told herself—he was doing all the work. The heat leaking from his body spoke of the pain he must be feeling. Raegan's heart panged, and then her stomach flipped when she saw the quickly approaching ground.

But the King landed on the rocky, heather-hemmed land with a feather-light agility that should not be possible for bipeds, no matter how many goddesses created them or what kind of magic ran in their veins.

"Jesus fucking Christ," Raegan said weakly, lowering herself to the sweet, blessed ground. She didn't care that the gorse was still damp with dew or that uneven edges of stones bit into her thighs.

Oberon heaved an exhale, leaning against a tall boulder next to Raegan. "I have not done that in hundreds of years," he told her, his breathing quick.

"You look absolutely *delicious* with wings," she told him, gazing up at him from the ground, "but I hated the actual flying bit."

He let out a laugh like a silver bell, languid and free, and Raegan found herself joining in, laughing until her stomach hurt. They'd actually done it. Excalibur lay next to her leg, wrapped up in woolens. She stared at it, half-delirious. Hope soared in her chest, an unwelcome brush of dove wings against her insides. She squashed it, grinding her jaw. It was too dangerous to hope, to think, *maybe this time . . .*

"You have done it," came a voice to Raegan's left.

She startled, scrambling to a seated position, finding that Danu had returned. Despite the damp chill of the fog bank that crowned Avalon, she was still dressed in one of her diaphanous gowns, a tiny garter snake curling around her bicep like a jewelry cuff. The wind barely tugged at her waist-length violet-gray hair.

"Yeah," Raegan agreed weakly, reaching over to pat the bundle of wool. "If this is the part where you betray us or take the sword for yourself or whatever, could you give me a second? That was exhausting."

Oberon laughed again, crisp as an orchard-fresh apple, and butterflies fluttered in her stomach. God, all these years later, and just the sound of his laugh had her blushing like a schoolgirl.

"Can you wield it?" Danu asked the King, and only then did Raegan register how grave the goddess's voice was. In her peripheral vision, she watched Oberon stiffen, drawing himself up to his full height.

"No," he replied, his expression growing wary, "but Raegan has shown much promise."

Danu's strange, too-light eyes sharpened as she glanced Raegan's way for a moment. Her lips formed something quick and sly, and Raegan might've said the goddess looked pleased. But then a heaviness came over her expression and she crossed her slender, muscular arms. "I have received word that your Philadelphia court is under quite a brutal attack, worse than what it has already been facing. Much worse, I fear."

The air stilled in Raegan's lungs, any levity or triumph seeping out of her in only a heartbeat or two. She pulled herself to her feet, her joints catching. "How do you know this?" she demanded, watching the goddess suspiciously. "You're locked away from the world, aren't you?" She was suddenly very aware of how still Oberon had gone at her side.

Danu's mouth twisted. "I keep a few choice scrying glasses. They are old, formidable things, and their eyes rove only in one direction."

The words were barely out of her mouth before the King was moving, striding across the gorse-dappled earth as if his body had not nearly failed him just moments ago. He was standing before Danu in an instant, and though they were roughly the same height, the fury on his face and the mid-morning shadows spooling at his feet made him look twice the goddess's size.

"How long," he began roughly, "have you watched, *Mother*, and done nothing at all?"

"Child," Danu replied, tears falling down her face as she clutched her hands at her heart, "for too long. It is my greatest shame."

Raegan and Oberon both stared at the goddess wordlessly, unsure what to make of her response. Was it simply a ploy? Or was it the truth? Was Danu's great and powerful force held back in ways they could not understand? The wind rattled through the clearing, the hem of the goddess's dress flowing out behind her.

"Tearing Avalon from the fabric of reality and creating a new realm to house our people took nearly everything from me," Danu explained, her eyes tracing the horizon line, as if in every stitch of this place, she could see her blood staining the seams. "I slept for a long time. When I awoke, I was not the same. Other leaders had moved forward, and they hold more sway than I do. I am a sacred relic at best, a forgotten and useless deity at worst."

Something flashed in Danu's eyes that made Raegan believe her—that kind of unhedged fury that only came with mistreatment. The King seemed to read the goddess's response in much the same way, as he retreated back a step, the angles of his face suddenly no longer so sharp and feral.

"Can you get me to my court, Danu?" Oberon breathed, barely audible over the orchestra of the wind. He reached for the goddess's hand, timid as a child, but she closed the distance immediately, gripping his fingers in hers.

"There is only one door left in Avalon," she said, her gaze skipping to Raegan. A fierceness lingered there that felt like looking in a mirror, no matter how primordial the goddess was. "It is only meant to open in one place."

The wind stood still, the fog banks parting for a moment so the sun could flood down upon the three of them, rendering the faerie king, the deathless witch, and the ancient goddess into something out of myth.

"But," Danu said, that arrogant tilt to her raised chin a clear hallmark she'd handed down to her children, "it is *my* door and I am no relic. Not just yet."

"We'll follow you, goddess," Raegan said, stepping closer to the two of them, her arms wrapped around the wool-cloaked sword. "Take us to your door."

The goddess nodded and turned on her heel, striding off across the headland. Though there was no magic on the waters of Avalon's sea, Raegan watched in awe as the island folded itself like an accordion, shortening the long trek to the beach, supplicant beneath Danu's feet. With a sideways glance at Oberon, Raegan hefted the sword against her shoulder and took off after the goddess. The land allowed her and the King to cross it in the same way, but they stayed close at Danu's heels, just in case.

In moments, they stood on the beach, the rise of the fog-crowned cliffs behind them, the otherworldly spires and lush solariums already moving into Raegan's memory. She'd hoped they might have more time here, that perhaps someone could help her sift through her mind. Or better yet —though she didn't dare voice the desire out loud—to see if anyone upon this grand and sacred isle had discovered how to extend a mortal life. So that perhaps she might know peace at the King's side and he wouldn't need to dig a grave or light a funeral pyre twice a century.

But for now, there was only the crash of the foam-tipped waves and the far horizon line that she knew held a door, though she certainly couldn't see it from here; at this distance, it didn't call to her, either. The ocean wind whipped her hair into a wild frenzy of auburn as Danu turned to face them.

"If you cannot wield it, I fear you may not be able to turn the Protectorate forces back," the goddess warned.

Obediently, Raegan laid the sword on the ground and unwrapped it from the woolen cloth. Oberon approached, his mouth in a firm, grim line. She didn't think it hurt him as much to be near to the blade, but then again, he was excellent at pretending.

"It *is* altered," Danu said from her position about ten paces away. She craned her neck, peering down at the unremarkable-looking sword lying on its bed of gray fabric. With an inhale, she walked closer, her bare feet carrying her to stand beside Oberon. There, she peered down at it, her eyes narrowed. "How did you accomplish this?" she asked, something not unlike awe seeping into her expression when she looked back up, her gaze landing on Raegan.

Nervous energy coiled in her gut. She didn't know what

the goddess would think of what she'd done, and when she glanced at Oberon, she saw he wasn't sure either. Before he could take the blame or try to slip out of the conversation, she settled her shoulders back and met Danu's eyes.

"I killed him," she said, finding herself savoring the words. "I killed Arthur Pendragon, son of Uther Pendragon, the once-king of Camelot, while he slept. For what he did. For *all* the things he did."

Danu's lips parted, and she regarded Raegan, her head cocked to one side, one pale braid sliding off her shoulder. "You killed the Bear?"

"Yep," Raegan agreed, though her palms were clammy now, her blood pounding in the veins of her neck. Regardless of how diminished Danu's power supposedly was, Raegan had no interest in being on the receiving end of the goddess's wrath. "He had it coming."

"I suppose he did," Danu said, sounding the words out slowly. "Raegan, you do understand he is nearly impossible to kill? It is why we have kept him in a sleep stasis all these years, unable to disentangle the mortal king from the blade."

"So I heard," Raegan said, not sure she understood the goddess's point.

"There are no worlds in which you should have been able to wield Excalibur to take Arthur's life," Danu said, her tone calm, definitive. "And you, child," she continued, turning her attention to the King, whose mouth curved into something dangerous that sent heat diving low in Raegan's body, "are meant to be the only one who can change the faerie blade back into what it once was."

"Perhaps it is her," Oberon replied, though he looked at Raegan as if no one else was standing on the beach. "Perhaps it has always been her."

Something about his tone—deep and regal, like the decree of a king—made her reach down for Excalibur. She

473

didn't pause this time as her fingers wrapped around the leather pommel. She felt the sword respond to her, its power sweeping through her, looking for a place to exploit. When that didn't work, the blade changed tactics, offering up some of its stolen, bloodsoaked power, sly as a bribe. Raegan scoffed.

"Unfortunately," she said to the sword, which she suspected could understand her in one way or another, "I am none of the things you were taught to devour. I'm too vast and terrifying to fit between your jaws."

She hefted the storied blade from the ground, some part of her not surprised to find the weight of it was no longer a strain. The wind whipped around the beach, scattering sand like ash, the ocean roaring at her back.

And then, reaching down from the heavens, thick as honey, rich as mead, came a Fatesong, looping around the woman who refused to die, the sound of it like a snake devouring its own tail.

CHAPTER FIFTY-TWO

On the other side of the causeway that stretched across the shimmering sea, Danu began to open a door. It might've sung to Raegan the way doors always did if she were not so tired, so terribly aware of how far they still had to go. The path to Avalon had been long.

As Danu whipped the ocean mist into a frenzy with an ancient working that made Raegan's head hurt, she pushed down the rising panic. Would she and the King even survive a winding, arduous journey back to Philadelphia?

But then Avalon's mists settled at their goddess's command, revealing a door in the towering cliff face. Raegan barely choked back a gasp. Instead of ancient yew trees and the white church spire, she found herself face-to-face with the Keeper of the Philadelphia Temple. His pinstripe navy suit was as immaculate as always, glasses tucked into his breast pocket as he peered through Danu's door. Behind him, the long, blue-velveted hallway of the Temple stretched wide and empty.

"Keeper," Raegan breathed, her body frozen in disbelief.

"My liege and my lady," the Keeper replied, clearly startled. Suspicion settled onto his expression. "It should not be possible to open this door. Not like this."

"At ease, my child," Danu said, coming to stand at Raegan's side. In her peripheral vision, she saw the flutter of the goddess's gown, the way her long, violet-gray braids floated around her shoulders instead of lying flat the way physics dictated.

A hundred emotions swam across the Keeper's features at the sight of his long-lost creatrix: awe, terror, the sweetest sorrow. His dark eyes darted back and forth between the goddess and her two charges before settling on the sword in Raegan's grasp.

"You— Did you . . ." the Keeper began before tears choked off his words.

"Yeah," was all Raegan could manage, holding Excalibur aloft. Her forearms strained, but she steadied the shaking muscles. "We got it." She averted her gaze from the Keeper's, tears pricking her own eyes, instead watching Avalon's mists curl around the world's most storied blade.

"This cannot be," the Keeper protested softly, one hand clasped to his chest. "We . . . we never know such kindness from neither the gods nor the universe." His words landed like a storm on Raegan's shores, pulling a sob filled with as much sorrow as anger from deep within her. She gritted her teeth, shoving the knuckles of her free hand into her eyes.

"Anakletos," Oberon said, his voice rich as the wind grabbed for his words with greedy fingers. "I understand your doubt. I assure you we are quite real. Otherwise, how would I know that you keep the best whiskey in the false drawer of your desk? Please, let us pass. We hear you are in great need."

Raegan pulled her hand away from her eyes to find the Keeper looking faint with relief. With a nod, he stepped to the side, opening one arm to offer entrance to the Temple.

Raegan turned to Danu, unsure what parting words would suffice. In the end, she let Excalibur's point rest on the rocky ground and threw her free arm around the goddess. A bittersweet vine tangled in her throat, chest burning with the effort to hold back tears.

"You are more my child, I think, than any other creator's," Danu murmured into her hair, clutching Raegan's much shorter frame in return. "Should you ever wish to rest, know Avalon is as open to you as it is to your faerie king."

Raegan pulled back, stunned. Danu only smiled that faint, sad smile of hers and reached forward to brush a single escaped tear from Raegan's face.

"Thank you," Raegan said to the goddess, her throat tight, unable to summon any further words. Perhaps—Raegan dared not hope too fervently—Danu's offer meant one day she and Oberon might linger in the sun.

The goddess released Raegan and turned toward the King. The two ancient beings examined each other, Oberon's chin raised at that haughty angle, his jaw feathering. Danu seemed at a loss for words.

Then, like a stalemate broken, the King sighed. "There is little sense," he offered, his tone measured, "in sowing discord among those of us who nurture the same fruit in the same orchard."

Raegan watched a thousand pounds of weight release from Danu's shoulders. "I appreciate your understanding," the goddess said. "In turn, I will try to better tend the entire orchard, not just the sections I can see."

The King reached for Raegan's hands, his fingers slipping between hers. "Thank you, creatrix," he said, bowing his head. Then, before either of them could hesitate, the deathless witch and the faerie king stepped through the goddess's impossible door.

Raegan looked back just once. Danu's tall, willowy frame was still there, shrouded in mist, and then she faded out of existence as if the goddess and her hidden realm had never really existed.

Instead, the familiarity of the Temple flooded Raegan's senses with marble floors and running water and the scent of cool vanilla laced with lilac. She wanted to feel relief, or perhaps some kind of tender homecoming. But she noticed too quickly that many of the blue velvet wall hangings were torn, others blackened and scorched. Something that looked too much like dried blood stained a section of marble behind the Keeper. Her stomach churned.

"The Morrigan was right," the Keeper whispered, though in the quiet of the corridor, his words nearly echoed. Raegan tore her eyes from the wounded Temple to examine the Keeper. The small besuited man's gaze was locked on Excalibur. His hands shook at his sides.

"She was right about most of it," the King said, his tone dry. "Raegan, it seems, is the one who wields the sword."

The Keeper's attention snapped to her, head cocked to one side as he examined her. "Well," he began, pulling his glasses from his pocket, "I believe the Morrigan's vision did indicate it was the *two* of you who might accomplish this task."

Raegan frowned, looking down at the sword, its length reflecting the deep blues of the Temple. "I don't think we really turned it back," she said, even though she wanted it to be her, wanted it to have always been her. "It's just . . . confused by me. For now."

A muffled shout echoed from somewhere down the hall. Alarm snaked across the Keeper's face, sending Raegean's heart thudding against the cage of her ribs. "While you were gone, half the Temple was destroyed," he told them. "The kelpie gate, which you used to safely enter the Rivers, is gone. We are far past the capacity that this pocket realm can handle. We cannot feed everyone. We need to evacuate our people who cannot fight, but there is nowhere to go."

"The archives?" the King asked.

"I will not risk it," the Keeper replied immediately, standing up straighter. "Too much of who and what we are is held there. Keep it safe. Our people that remain need to know who they are. What it means to be Tylwyth Teg."

"Anakletos," Oberon said, his tone soft in the heavy stillness of the corridor, "the archives will not matter if there are no Fair Folk left to enjoy them."

Raegan chewed on the inside of her cheek, her mind racing. "So we could safely evacuate to another pocket realm?" she asked, looking at the Keeper and then Oberon.

"Yes," the King replied, his head tilted to one side. "What are you thinking?"

Raegan grinned. "Keeper, can you get me a scrying glass? Sometimes it helps to have friends in low, strange places."

Beside her, Oberon's sculpted mouth curved up at one side, his dark gaze glimmering with a kind of admiration that set Raegan's entire body on fire.

"Of course," the Keeper replied, looking between the two of them like they were a riddle he could not quite parse. "Follow me."

The Keeper turned on his heel and began to walk down the cavernous corridor. Raegan moved to follow him, the King at her side. She had taken a few steps when a thought prickled across her skin, breathing down the back of her neck. Without breaking her stride, she turned to look at the place Danu had opened her door—the place in a well-fortified Oracle's Temple that had parted at the touch of a goddess.

There, in the dim, diffuse glow, stood the door to the

Vaults. Its ornate ironwork was precisely the same, its frame humming with something that could not quite be attributed to an inanimate object. The last time Raegan had walked through that door, she'd returned with a delicate Prophecy encased in glass, cradled between her shaking hands.

This time, a sword that might topple a god from his throne.

～

"Is Baba Yaga ready for that kind of onslaught?" Andronica asked, her face pinched as she examined the plans laid out across the large table.

A muffled boom erupted in the distance. Raegan jumped, but Andronica hardly reacted.

"It's fine," the Unseelie knight said with a wave of her hand, responding to Raegan's startled look. "The Protectorate's not getting through that way and they know it, so they make a lot of noise hoping it'll draw us away from their true entry point. Anyway. Can she withstand what they're going to throw at her?"

"She seems to think she can," Raegan said, looking across the table at the King. He should have been resting, but instead, he'd called an emergency war council. The sleeves of his button-down were rolled up, a shining ink-black lock of hair untucked from its usual place. Both large hands were palm-down on the table, the corded muscles in his forearms standing out like those of a marble statue.

"Baba Yaga and I have historically disagreed on a few things," Oberon said, straightening, one hand raking through his hair. "But if the witch says she can hold her pocket realm, she can hold. She wouldn't agree to house those of our Court who cannot fight otherwise."

"I agree," Raegan said, looking toward Andronica. The

Fey woman's thin eyebrows were pinched tight, her mouth screwed up in concentration.

"Okay," she said, looking up at the both of them, her gaze skipping to Kamau, who stood at the other end of the table. "Kamau, can you start the evacuation? Orderly, please. Calm. If everyone was out of the Temple by tonight, that would be ideal."

The Keeper exhaled long and low, cradling his forehead in his hands. Raegan glanced over at him, sympathy blooming in her chest. He'd all but collapsed into the chair at the head of the table when Andronica had relayed her idea.

"We're really going to do this, then?" he asked, looking around at all of them, those nebula-brown eyes brimming with tears.

Kamau reached over and tenderly took the Keeper's hand in their much larger one. "Is there another way?" Kamau asked, their booming voice impossibly gentle.

"Not one that I can see," the Keeper replied after a few moments of silence that threatened to choke the air out of Raegan's lungs. "We sacrifice the High Temple of Pythia, home of the Oracle Octavia. For our people."

"For our people," Kamau echoed, crouching before the seated Keeper and cupping his small face in their hands. "We will mourn with you, friend. You are never alone."

"Never alone," the Keeper managed, his voice hitching, before Kamau brought their brow to his.

"For all of this to be worth it," Andronica said, her head tipped back as she examined the domed ceiling above them, covered with those celestial blue illustrations Raegan had admired so much her first time in the Temple—at this hour, the constellations had gone shimmery, more mother-of-pearl than gilt, the background a deep midnight, "Oberon must wield the blade. I see no other way. Raegan, it's not as if we had even six months to train you for combat. We had, what, fifteen sessions together before you left for the Isles, if that? Besides, the Morrigan said it is a faerie blade to be returned to its true nature. A changeling."

Raegan took a deep breath and nodded. "I know," she said simply, glancing at the King. "You're right. I'll try. We'll both try again to revert it with whatever time we have left." For a moment, she sank into her own mind. When she'd first started on this path back to herself, Andronica's words would've infuriated her. But only because of her insecurities, the constant voices that told her there would never be anywhere she belonged, that her true place in the world had slipped past her like a comet.

Not any longer. Because she'd found where she belonged. And she'd found who she belonged *to*—the dark-eyed faerie king who wore ferocity like armor, the owl-winged woman whose smile felt like a summer evening. And the Unseelie Court. She hadn't seen it before, but the Fair Folk accepted her for all her rage and sorrow and yearning. And that meant they'd challenge her, bare their teeth, because they knew their anger was safe with her, too. It was a terrible thing, a lovely thing, to call her own.

And she refused to let it all die on the edge of a sainted iron spear.

CHAPTER FIFTY-THREE

Sweat poured down Raegan's brow, and her entire body felt faint, but she kept going. She pulled on the long, red thread of her fury that rushed through her body like a river. And for the first time she could ever remember, she felt it threaten to snap.

She let go with a gasp, shoulders sagging as she staggered back.

Maelona caught her by the forearm, surprisingly strong despite her wiry frame. "Raegan," her aunt warned, alarm seeping into her tone.

"I'm fine," Raegan sputtered, her chest heaving. She gritted her jaw, staring down at Excalibur. The blade was submerged in one of the remaining divinatory fonts in the Temple. Maybe the shallow, marble-lipped pool in the small chamber wasn't enough water. Maybe she needed to put the sword in an actual river to gather enough energy to break the hellish working.

"I don't think I can do this, Maelona," she admitted miserably, looking up at her aunt, who had arrived with Rainer a few hours before they'd returned from Avalon. Apparently, she'd demanded the kelpie take her to her niece

483

and wouldn't take no for an answer. Since her arrival, Maelona adjusted absurdly well to being surrounded by the Unseelie Court. Raegan was pretty sure her aunt had even flirted with Andronica.

"You may not need to," Maelona replied, letting go of Raegan to cross her own arms. "I mean, the plan is good. Lure the Protectorate sieging the Temple into its walls and then collapse the pocket realm on their heads once everyone's evacuated. Meanwhile, you'll be drawing the Timekeeper's attention by battering down his front door with Excalibur, which at the very least he'll be deeply unhappy to see in your possession. Any of his remaining soldiers will be sent to deal with you and the King, leaving the Manor vulnerable for Alanna and her people to secure it."

Raegan wiped her damp hands on the front of her jeans. "Yeah," she said hoarsely. "But what if everything works perfectly until we're face-to-face with the Timekeeper and then we can't actually kill him, even with Excalibur? Or what if it's worse? What if I hand-deliver the only thing that can kill Oberon right to our greatest enemy?"

"One step at a time," Maelona said, her dark eyes glittering in the Temple's golden light. "It's very possible the King can handle the Timekeeper on his own, Excalibur or not. I mean, there's got to be a reason Kronos has tried so hard to keep the King out of the In-Between. And don't forget that you can apparently work time magic now, too."

Raegan scoffed, putting her hands on her hips. "I have no idea if I'll be able to do that again," she said, letting out a sigh. "It's just . . . *So* much is hanging in the balance, Maelona."

Raegan's gaze slid to Excalibur. The ever-present tide in all of the Temple's waters dappled the dull metal blade with gold. For the first time since she'd taken it from Avalon's low places, it actually looked magical. World-changing. God-destroying. Fate-altering.

Suddenly and fiercely, Raegan wished she could talk to the Oracle. But Octavia had long since been evacuated. As much as Raegan wanted to speak with the powerful diviner who had encouraged her to craft her own destiny, she knew safeguarding the Fey community's matriarch was more important. Cordelia—the seer who had spoken the Prophecy to life—was safe as well, probably having tea with Baba Yaga by now. It was too dangerous to contact either of them by magical means and risk exposing their location, no matter how much she craved their guidance.

"Hey," came Maelona's voice, cutting through her thoughts. "I don't think spiraling inside your own head is gonna do shit for anybody, you included."

Raegan looked up at her aunt, a wry smile pulling at the corners of her mouth. "You're right," she replied, crouching down beside the font again.

The marble was cold against her knees even through her jeans. She took a deep inhale, steeling herself, and then plunged her hands beneath the surface. Summoning the tides within her, Raegan wrapped her fingers around Excalibur's pommel. The spell woven around the sword barreled at her hungrily. She felt it reach for her, looking for a weak spot. But Raegan was half-mad, barely mortal, and nothing if not ferocious. Her magic sank its teeth into the working, and then she was yet again tumbling through the currents, locked in a battle of wills with whatever Myrddin had done to the faerie blade all those years ago.

The deeper she dove, the more Raegan could feel an impression of the famed sorcerer. The sensation crawled across her skin like an unwelcome touch. She grounded herself in the cold marble, the t-shirt sticking to her damp skin. She'd always fucking hated Myrddin. Hated his constant scheming, never-ending back-stabbing, the way everyone fawned over him when it was so clear to her that he'd been using them all for some grand plan only he knew about. Even Arthur himself had only ever been a pawn.

"Guess I ruined whatever you were planning," Raegan spat, tightening her grip on the pommel, her eyes screwed shut, "by locking you in a goddamn tree, asshole." She poured more of herself against the fabric of the spell, her blackened waters and ancient silt seeping through gaps in chainmail. A few threads of the working snapped like old, fraying rope.

Raegan rocked back on her heels, exhausted, nearly toppling over. "Shit," she said, shaking the water droplets from her hands. "This would take me *months* under the right conditions."

"And we only have a few days, if we're very lucky," Maelona sighed, extending a hand to Raegan.

She took it, grappling her aunt's forearm and pulling herself to her feet. With a sigh, she looked back at the sword. Sweat gathered uncomfortably on the base of her spine, and her legs felt unsteady. Even if they had all the time in the world, she didn't know how long she could keep this up.

"Raegan."

The sound of her name slipped around her neck like a silk scarf. She followed the feel of it, a moth to flame, to find the King leaning against the doorframe. Though he still looked exhausted, he was dressed in a clean suit. One of her favorites, actually—the deep, shimmering green he'd worn to Gossamer. She drank in the sight of him, all towering height and raven-dark waves.

"Hey," she returned, some of the tension leaving her shoulders, though another kind sparked low in her belly.

Woodsmoke and black pepper slipped into her senses, as intoxicating as ever.

"Maelona," the King said, his gaze falling away from Raegan and taking all that blessed heat with it, "may I have a word with Raegan?"

Maelona looked between her niece and the Unseelie lord she'd dedicated most of her life to hunting down. Surprisingly, that deep furrow between her brows softened. She reached out and brushed Raegan's shoulder with one hand, nodded, and then slipped out into the velveted hallway.

"Is everything okay?" Raegan asked, hoping to delay revealing that she'd gotten barely anywhere with Excalibur —that she'd failed everyone again, just as she always had.

"There are no new developments in the horrors," Oberon told her, his long strides carrying him across the creamy marble to stand before her. The moving surface of the water dappled his cool, pale skin with gold. "I do have a question for you, though."

Raegan bit the inside of her cheek, anxiety somersaulting in her stomach. "Oberon, I'm sorry. The spell on this sword . . . it's fucked. Even if I could get to a real river, it would take me a long time to make it safe for you to wield."

Oberon tilted his head in that way she liked, his eyes sliding to her mouth before returning to meet her gaze. "You have nothing to apologize for," he told her, his voice wrapping around her like a cloak that could keep her safe, keep the doubt and self-loathing at bay. "I am here for another reason entirely."

Raegan stared at him in confusion, her mind too tired to unravel whatever was going on. She opened her mouth to tell him that, but the King was already sinking down onto one knee before her. Startled and still feeling adrift, she took a step back, though her heart began to beat faster, something like anticipation careening through her veins.

"This is how mortals perform such a ritual, I am told," he said, looking up at her. His expression was all molten desire, an inferno of never-ending devotion that made the blood between her legs drum furiously. "Raegan Maeve Overhill, Nyneve Or'Afron, High Queen Titania, Witch of the Wood, and all the others—I am hopelessly in love with you."

Raegan's throat closed off, the soft light and tumbling waters of the Temple disappearing around her. Instead, she was surrounded by his dark tides, his autumnal meadow, his heathered hills at dusk. She wanted to live here forever, wanted to be buried in the rich soil of him even if it meant she'd never see the light of day again.

"I am yours," the King murmured, intense and ferocious even in this act of love. "In every life, Raegan. *Yours*. No matter the form you return to me in, I belong to you. You are the only person who has ever been mad enough and brave enough to love me."

Raegan drew a shaking inhale, choking back a wave of tears that crashed upon her shores. A soft, downy flower bloomed somewhere in her chest, the petals caressing all of her hidden, aching places until her entire body trembled.

"Though I question whether I am good enough to deserve the fierceness of your love," Oberon continued, the melody of his deep voice broken by emotion, though his eyes never left hers, "my heart cannot rest until I ask. Will you marry me?"

She bit down on her lip, but the hot tears escaped anyway, some clinging to her lashes, others falling to the marble below. Every part of her yearned to say yes without a second thought. "Oberon," she murmured, reaching out for him with unsteady hands. "You know I would. But a

Feyrish marriage? That bond is . . . eternal. And when you lose me, because you *will*, it'll be your destruction."

The King smiled, as soft and sad as anything Raegan had ever seen. He took her outstretched hand in his, leaning forward to brush his lips over her knuckles. It was only the gentlest of touches, but her body keened madly for him all the same. "And yet," the faerie king told her, the ocean of his eyes fathomless, "here I am on my knees, begging you to destroy me."

Raegan choked back a sob, sinking down to the floor. She shook her head, pulling a curl loose from her braid. "Oberon," she repeated, her voice barely more than a hoarse whisper, "think of the pain you'll feel every moment. More pain, more than what you already suffer. It'll be like someone ripped out your insides. The bond mark will turn black on your finger and poison you."

"If I cannot have you," the King replied, pulling her into his world of damp stone and autumnal rain and sweeping shadow, "I shall have the pain. Never again will I grow numb to this wild, eternal thing that grows between us."

"Your court," Raegan stammered, the words tumbling out high-pitched. She was running out of the strength to protest; she wanted him just as badly as she ever had. With his arms around her, all she wanted to do was surrender. "They'll be so angry. They'll hate me even more. They'll question your judgment."

One of Oberon's ink-dark eyebrows arched. "My court," he drawled in response, "awaits us in a chamber they have spent half a day decorating for our ceremony. If, of course, you still wish to have me in that way."

Her heart leapt. "Yes," she whispered, the word bittersweet on her tongue. "I'll have you any and every way I can."

He grinned at her—a rare, shimmering jewel—and then

dove forward to kiss her, powerful hands sliding around her waist. She pressed herself tightly against his muscular mass as his thigh slid between hers, fervently memorizing every place his hard angles met her soft curves. With all her might, Raegan tried to drown herself in his kiss. If it were up to her, she'd never surface.

When they broke apart, Oberon swept her into his arms, sending her into the kind of girlish laughter she didn't think had left her mouth in ages. She tucked herself into his chest as he carried her from the divinatory chamber, striding into the hallway. In so many other relationships, she'd always felt so heavy in her partner's arms, like she was asking them to carry too much weight.

But in the Unseelie king's embrace, Raegan felt light as a feather. She lifted her head from his chest to tell him so, but the words died on her tongue as she momentarily lost herself in his feral, unearthly beauty. She raised a hand, tracing the sharp slash of his collarbone and then the knife-like jaw.

The King leaned into her touch. "My bride," he murmured, his tone gowned in something husky and only half-restrained. Damp heat unspooled low in her belly, and she dug her fingernails into his shoulder, the other hand sliding beneath his open collar, desperate to feel more of him.

But then he ducked out of the hallway, bringing her to a room filled with flowers, beeswax candles, and people. Still in the King's arms, Raegan looked around with awe, joy filling up the places in her chest that normally burned with emptiness. Somehow, an expanse of tiny violets covered the marble floor, just as rich and thick as if it were early spring. At the far end of the room, curls of otherworldly vines crept along a wooden archway—the shape of it like a portico, like a door. At the arch's base were clusters of large pillar candles of varying heights, their flames dancing. Intricately carved ornaments hung from the walls, tiny tea lights glittering from their depths.

It was beneath the glow of the beeswax flames that Raegan caught the shine of white-blonde hair. "Blodeuwedd," she cried, any lingering homesickness for a place that didn't exist leaving her body at the sight of her dearest friend.

The owl-woman turned away from the Keeper, her entire face lighting up as she sighted Raegan. With a low rumble of pleased laughter, Oberon set Raegan down just in time for Blodeuwedd to barrel into her, wrapping the shorter woman up in a tight embrace.

"You're here," she exclaimed, the words muffled by Blodeuwedd's shoulder.

"Couldn't miss two of my favorite souls getting married," the owl-woman replied, pulling back to wink at Raegan. Then her expression fell serious, eyes darting to the King. "If anything happens, know that I will watch over him."

"Thank you," Raegan choked out, squeezing Blodeuwedd's hand. "Am I cruel for doing this?"

The owl-woman smiled, considering. Raegan drew in a deep, shaking breath, the scent of the King mingling with the dark leaf and purple petal underfoot.

"It would be crueller, I think, to deny him," Blodeuwedd replied, her expression sharp. "To deny yourself. The truest of loves often blooms in the darkest of places."

Raegan looked back at Oberon, who was talking to Andronica, and reached across the space between them for his hand. The moment their fingers interlaced—like the final weave of a tapestry—the room fell silent, a tender kind of hush that made Raegan think of angel's wings, of all things. And then, like it was Fated, like there had never been any other path, the deathless witch and the nameless king walked together toward that all-too-familiar arch.

Raegan had always thought that if she ever married, she might panic at the last moment. She might stand at the altar in a pretty dress or well-tailored suit and realize she was not worthy of this love. That she was dooming the person she claimed to love most of all to misery.

And yet, despite the fact she was dooming the King more than she ever could've with a mortal lover, Raegan felt nothing but peace. A peace she probably didn't deserve, she knew, not amidst the chaos and death and suffering that she'd had no small hand in creating.

But Oberon looked at her with that monstrous, sharp-fanged kind of love, and all she could do was offer up the few soft, tender places she had left. She wanted to be devoured. She wanted to belong to him, for him to belong to her, for there to be no question a thousand years from now that the witch and the king had loved each other with a fierceness that toppled a god.

She might've said all of that if not for the Keeper moving into her vision, asking if they were both ready for the Feyrish ritual. And then all Raegan could do was nod and cling to this moment, the last ripe berry on the vine.

The small besuited man wound a length of silver cord around their hands, speaking in the Old Tongue. Though she only understood a little, Raegan could feel the oath taking hold. She let it in without reservation, inviting it to make a nest between her bones, to lodge itself deep and true so no matter what, she would never forget him.

All the while, Oberon looked at her as if she were his beginning and not his end. She clutched his hands tighter, savoring the feel of his touch, the joy of his presence. And then, because both of them stood beneath the arch of their own free will, and because the old rite recognized the truth of their love, a silver line appeared around Raegan's ring finger. She marveled at it, how it was inked into her skin instead of sitting on the surface, how looking at it made her heart swell.

"Oberon," she told him, half-choked by the enormity of everything she felt for him. "In this life, I'd given up on love. I thought it was nothing more than a fairy tale, meant for children and adults desperate enough to keep hoping."

Raegan paused, glancing out toward the small group of people who she'd do anything for, who'd taken precious time and energy during a terrifying time to make something beautiful for her and Oberon. Then she turned back to the King, tears pouring down her face.

"I was sort of right, though," she replied, smiling through her tears. "Love *is* a fairytale, and after so much searching, after so many nights of half-remembered dreams, of aching for something I didn't think I could ever have, I finally found you. My faerie king."

CHAPTER FIFTY-FOUR

With the oath completed, Raegan reached for the King, gripping him by the lapels of his suit jacket as his large hands slipped around her waist. And then she lost herself in the ocean of his kiss, the sensation she'd wandered the fields of time and space to return to again and again.

She'd barely resurfaced from the thrall of the Unseelie king when she realized the walls of the Temple were shaking. Some of the tiny hand-cut ornaments tumbled from their places, crumpling against the floor. Raegan gripped Oberon's hands as their gazes met. Her throat closed off, and she squeezed her eyes shut. One more moment, she begged a universe that had never answered her pleas. Just one more.

"They've breached," came a shout from the hallway.

Forcing her eyes back open, Raegan watched as Kamau ran to meet the knight in the doorway, the two conferring in hushed tones she couldn't catch from across the room.

The King disentangled his hands from hers to cup her jaw in his palms. "I am yours," he breathed, those three words somehow so intense that Raegan felt like she was staring down all of the primordial darkness, the vastness of the shadowed universe before the light began. And then the King wrapped his larger hand around hers, turned, and led them to the center of the room where the rest of his court was gathering.

"I thought we had bought a few more hours at least," Andronica said miserably, her gaze flitting between Raegan and her liege. And then, louder, she called to Kamau, "What happened?"

"There's a large force too close to Hiraeth," Kamau replied, making their way over from the doorway. "Many of the kelpies were forced to retreat from our defenses to ensure the last free Fey city does not fall."

Raegan's stomach sank, nausea boiling as the lovely room crowned in beeswax light and soft petals blurred. If the Protectorate suddenly knew the location of Hiraeth right after Alanna and Reilly—whom she'd vouched for—arrived there . . .

"Don't despair," Kamau said, meeting Raegan's gaze as if reading her mind. "If—and by all the names of the gods, I hope it is not—Hiraeth is exposed, the kelpies do not think it was your people's doing. Likely the tracking spells the Protectorate's been scattering around the countryside, or just dumb luck. Regardless, we cannot be concerned about that now. They've broken through the Temple's defenses. It's time."

Andronica spat something in Old Feyrish, drawing the sword at her waist and rushing past Kamau. Blodeuwedd went still, her gaze finding Raegan's. Out of time, Raegan thought. Always out of goddamn time.

"If the Protectorate's here, I have to go," Raegan said, reaching over to grasp Blodeuwedd's hand in her own. "Go to Baba Yaga's realm. Please."

The owl woman smiled at her, slow and creeping, a

menacing thing wrapped in the prettiest of flowers. "It has been too long since we graced a battlefield together, sister," Blodeuwedd said, the angles of her face sharp and feral, "too long since I cut down the sort of men who were foolish enough to form me from the meadowsweet and the oak flowers. I wanted only to bloom toward the sun, and they made me into something that unfurls talons at dusk. Of course I must hunt."

Raegan's entire body tensed, her refusals already gathering on the back of her tongue. She couldn't lose anyone else, but certainly not Blodeuwedd.

"Besides," the owl-woman continued, seeming to sense Raegan's hesitancy, "haven't you learned to stop trying to do everything on your own yet?"

Raegan swallowed, opening her mouth and then closing it again. If she had to walk back into the Timekeeper's realm, gods, doing it with the familiar weight of owl talons on her shoulder would make all the difference. She reached up, placing both hands on either side of Blodeuwedd's face, trying to formulate the right words.

But then shouts of warning came racing down the hallway, followed by that ear-splitting battle magic she wished she'd never heard.

"If you die," Raegan said, staring into Blodeuwedd's eyes, "I'm gonna be really mad at you."

With a dangerous grin, Blodeuwedd shook off Raegan's touch and took a few steps backward. One moment, a woman, tall and sharp-featured, and then an owl, preternaturally large, its yellow eyes too vast. It opened its wings and lifted from the ground with a few strong beats, coming to land on Raegan's shoulder. The familiarity of the sensation pulled a long, slender thread of longing from somewhere deep inside her body. She grasped it, needing all of herself, even the most painful parts.

Andronica sprinted back into the room, her ballerina-like grace intact despite all the chaos, carrying something wrapped in a woolen blanket. The Fey warrior approached Raegan, holding the object out like an offering. She furrowed her brow, not understanding.

Not, at least, until she did. "Oh," Raegan murmured, parting the woolens to find Excalibur's worn leather pommel, though the sword had been tucked into a new leather scabbard with an attached belt. With a start, her memory turned over—the design was an old Unseelie make, crafted to conceal the power of magical weapons from keen eyes. Steeling herself, Raegan reached forward and wrapped her fingers around the pommel. For a moment, she wrestled with the power of the sword before it bent to her will. If she chose to drink from Excalibur's poisoned well of stolen power, it would only be at the last possible second— right before she drove the sword into the Timekeeper's chest.

"Thank you," Raegan said, meeting Andronica's gaze as she buckled the length of leather around her waist.

"Remember what I taught you," the Fey knight replied, almost looking at Raegan as if she thought the half-mortal woman might be capable of this impossible thing.

"I will," Raegan promised, tears pricking the back of her eyes. "Don't die. I was just starting to like you."

Andronica folded the woolens with a dagger-sharp grin. "Right back at you." Then the faerie knight turned and marched out of the room and back down the hallway, her spine straight as an arrow.

Raegan tested the weight of the blade, wanting to know how it felt with Blodeuwedd on her shoulders. It felt like destiny, she found. Like all her rage had been building to this moment, like all the ache had been worthwhile.

Setting her jaw, she turned, looking for the King—

always searching for him on the horizon, for the fairytale ending she never managed to get right. "Ready?" she asked as he turned toward her.

"No," he murmured, his eyes drinking her in. "But it matters not, I fear." In the space of a heartbeat, the shadows around the room pooled at his feet, slinking across his body to form hard planes of otherworldly armor. For a moment, the breath left Raegan's lungs. He was so beautiful in his violence, in his darkness, in the fury that burned low and fierce inside him.

"You are sure about this?" Kamau asked from the door, hesitating on the threshold, their words stilted.

"All the doors that I've opened," Raegan said, moving for the corridor, clutching the words like a life raft in a hurricane, "remain open to a thing like me. This will work, Kamau."

The Unseelie knight looked at her and then the King for a long moment before nodding and turning on their heel, rushing toward the front of the Temple, where the Protectorate had breached the pocket realm.

"Come," Oberon said, holding out a hand for her.

She took it, something in her soothed by the trifecta of his touch, owl talons on her shoulder, and the pommel of a heavy sword between her fingers. "The Protectorate still thinks you're injured, yes?" Raegan asked as they stepped into the hallway, moving deeper into the depths of the Temple, away from the fighting—at least, for now.

"We can hope," the King replied, his eyes roving the corridor as more Fey warriors rushed down it, headed in the opposite direction. "But the moment they see Excalibur, that will be called into question."

"Right," she said, sheathing the blade.

Blodeuwedd pushed off her shoulder with taloned claws, spreading her wings to soar down the corridor.

Seeing the owl fly ahead brought memories rushing to Raegan's mind. She clamped down on them, for now. If they won, if they freed this world, she would have time to sort through it all. To feel it all, maybe.

Oberon took a hard turn, leading them down a side hallway toward the ritual room. It was the same they'd used to follow Cormac's spellcraft, which felt as though it had happened hundreds of years ago, not a month. Uneasiness squirmed low in Raegan's belly, but she squashed it, keeping her eyes on the steady stroke of the owl's wings, focusing on the feeling of the Unseelie king at her side. Time dilated—a cruel joke—and the walk to that room felt longer than all of the moments Raegan had spent tumbling beneath sheets with Oberon or feeling the sun on her face or waking up knowing who she really was.

But then the door yawned wide and open, the marble expanse of the room cold and waiting beyond it. Beneath the filtered, golden light of the Temple, a regiment of Unseelie knights were gathered—maybe fifty at most. Raegan glanced at their faces, trying to memorize their features, in case they followed her into the Timekeeper's realm just for the god to unwind their Threads, spin them back into nothingness.

The gathered attention of the knights fell onto Raegan's shoulders, heavy and demanding, with more bite than even Blodeuwedd's claws.

"Just as we discussed," the King said, addressing the knights as Raegan walked to the center of the ritual circle. "Only come through the door if you see our signal. If not, wait until the door closes. Another will immediately open in its place, leading to Baba Yaga's realm. Get as many through as you can and then leave. Live. That is what we are fighting for. Not conquest, not riches. Only to live."

Despite knowing every step of the plan, Raegan found

herself somewhat disbelieving that after everything, she was back here in this room, standing at the center of a chalk and blood circle. She cast her eyes about the space and swallowed hard. Blodeuwedd completed a lap around the room, returning to land on Raegan's shoulders. She leaned her cheek against her friend's downy feathers.

Then the King was beside her, so she began the rite. It flowed to her like water. It shouldn't have; the Timekeeper had destroyed the pathway they'd walked last time. But she felt her magic take root, felt her rivers close in around that parched desert realm and its hungry god. She opened her eyes.

All at once, where there should have only been a smooth expanse of marble, there was instead a door—which meant there was only one choice. Had only ever been one choice.

Raegan took a deep breath and walked through it.

CHAPTER FIFTY-FIVE

The door bucked. It knew she was here now—*he* knew she was—and it wrenched itself from her grasp. But Raegan just smiled, tightening her snare. She'd spent her life learning how to hold running water in her open hands. Did this thing of dust and metal think it could twist away from her jaws now that she had closed them tight?

Nothing existed to Raegan but the door. Blodeuwedd, the King, the fabled sword on her waist, even her own body —all gone. There was only a god to be wrestled with, bested in the halls of his own home. Raegan grit her teeth hard enough to make her jaw crack in protest. Every fiber of her being protested, her magic stretched to its breaking point. She held on with all of her might.

It was not enough. Had she ever once been enough? With a cry that burrowed up from the depths of her being, Raegan lost control of the door. There was no longer a single stride over the threshold; instead, the long expanse of time snaked around her. The door slithered out of Raegan's grasp, and she was cast into a freefall. Dust filled her mouth, her head throbbing with shrill and sudden metallic clangs.

An ancient dread swelled in her chest. When the tumbling and plummeting finally stopped, she found the stillness no less terrible.

Terror turned her palms slick. With a shudder, Raegan opened her eyes to watery light. Her breath hitched. "No," she whispered, her throat constricting around the word. "No."

In front of Raegan stretched the interior of a train car. Brown leather seats lined up like soldiers, empty luggage racks looking more like prison bars. She fought for her breath, shoving away the panic. Her entire body felt limp and wrung dry from attempting to control the passage. Just standing up, she knew, would take a monumental amount of strength.

She tried anyway, biting down on her tongue, hoping a different pain might restart her body. Fear settled onto her skin like white-hot pinpricks when she realized it was not exhaustion keeping her down. It was much worse than that.

She was trapped in one of the brown leather train seats she knew far too well. Her heart hammering, nausea rising, Raegan glanced down. Her thighs were sutured to the leather. Panic exploded in her chest as she glanced to her left, eyes hunting for Excalibur.

It was still there, hanging from her belt, tucked safely into its scabbard. She hoped the spelled scabbard was enough to hide the blade's nature from the Timekeeper, though she wasn't sure it would matter—her arms were stuck fast to the seat as well. When Raegan pulled experimentally, a searing pain swept through her, so brutal and fierce that she cried out in surprise. Straining, she looked toward Excalibur again, trying to gauge the distance between her hand and its pommel.

And that was when she saw that she was not alone in the leather seat. By the window was a weathered corpse, little more than bleached bone and piles of ash. The skull splintered down the middle, slumped onto a collapsed chest. Only a few fingerbones remained, the majority turned to flakes of dull gray. Worst of all, Raegan saw, was the all-too-familiar outfit, left untouched by whatever had scavenged the corpse: brown blazer, hunter green pocket square, cream crewneck sweater marred with dirt.

"Dad," Raegan choked out through dry, cracked lips. Her father's corpse sat beside her on the Timekeeper's train. Had she even left this realm at all? Had she actually watched her father be reduced to ash? She recalled the bone-deep gnawing anxiety she'd felt after surfacing from the Rivers into the Temple—a horrible sense that none of it was real. Had she been right all along?

Despair swept through Raegan, powerful as an angry tide, drowning her defiance and rage in one massive rush. She hardly realized she was crying until she tasted the salt on her lips. So this was how it was to end—all her lives, every ounce of her spite, transmuted into power the Time-keeper could use to subjugate mortals and the Fair Folk alike.

Oberon was a fool to have believed in her. From that very first day in Camelot, he'd been a fool to think a half-mad, not-quite-mortal witch would ever be anything but his undoing. Not to mention her father and Maelona—all they'd endured so things might be better for her, for the future. She'd squandered every last bit, thinking she was fighting some incredible battle the bards would sing about one day. But she was just a rabbit in a snare. Always had been.

Eyes blurred with tears, Raegan looked over at the crumpled remains of her father. A sob wracked her chest, pulling on her body hard enough that her skin cried out in protest. As if a girl could ever topple a god. As if liberation wasn't little more than a daydream. As if the people of both realms were not destined to devour each other whole in a constant bid for more, more, *more*.

"At least I'm with you," Raegan whispered to her father, wishing she could hold his pocket square between her fingers, a small comfort in the face of a long and agonizing death. Maybe this was what she deserved. Her actions had caused so much suffering—for Oberon, for the Fair Folk, for Blodeuwedd, for Maelona. Her chest felt like it might be caving in, and she welcomed the pain.

Time tucked its tail into its own mouth and devoured the yielding flesh. Raegan waited for death to come, yearned feverishly for that old friend to pull her into the senseless void once more. At least there she might not feel like guilt and shame were boiling her alive. At least there, maybe one day, she might see her faerie king again. But no such relief appeared in the long, narrow aisle of the train car. Just harsh, unnatural light and the rattling of her own breath in her chest.

The Timekeeper did not show himself, not even to gloat. He'd wait, Raegan realized, until she was closer to death. He'd twist the knife. He always did. Maybe he'd parade in Oberon or Blodeuwedd, or simply toss the remaining funeral ash at her feet so she could spend her years wasting away thinking about everyone she'd failed.

Raegan turned her head as best she could, the train car's seat already biting deeply into the back of her neck. She looked at her father's familiar jacket again, her gaze skipping out the window. Flat plains of dust stretched endlessly in all directions, the land as dry and parched as her own tongue. The train didn't appear to be moving, though Raegan couldn't see the station from her vantage point.

Not that it mattered. The only reason she'd been looking, she knew, was because she thought the King might come save her. One last time. But no one was coming. She had only herself, and Raegan was smart enough to know when it was over. She glanced past her father's corpse and out the window again, selfishly wishing she might get to look at the sea or a rainstorm or a damp, dark autumnal forest once again.

A flash of shadow caught her eye. Hope soared defiantly in her chest, cutting through the thickly-rooted despair. Raegan squashed it; she couldn't see salvation in every shadow just because the shadows were his. Her throat closed off. When the low places of Avalon had tested her with that dream-spun realm, she should've stayed. Regret surged through her body, and more useless, stupid tears blurred her eyes. It wouldn't have been real, no, but it would've been better than this. Her body would've rotted in the caves of an ancient, magical place, her mind wrapped in the comfort of all the things she knew deep down she could never have.

A shadow of movement again. Raegan strained her eyes, realizing that if anything, it was the Timekeeper coming for her. That at least she could face—an enemy to spit venom at, a reason to summon her bravado. Let him come. She'd sink her teeth into him one last time.

But it was not the Timekeeper casting shadows on the long, wide plain. Raegan's heart pounded. No—either her grasp on reality had well and truly failed, or there on the horizon, there was an army.

An army of tattered black flags and wickedly sharp swords, an endless wellspring of defiance and power. An Unseelie army mounted on kelpies, the shadows of their King slinking into the dead world, claws experimentally flexed. The door had held just long enough for them to make it through. Suddenly, Raegan didn't care if it was all delusion or madness or if maybe she was already dead, devoured by the Timekeeper's oblivion eyes.

She was going to see him one last time. No matter the cost.

With a snarl, Raegan fought to tear her right arm from the leather. The sound morphed into a raw scream halfway through; the pain was too much. It wasn't a matter of risking large sections of torn skin, she realized. This place—this horrible, wretched place—would tear her limb from limb before it let her go.

"Fine," she snapped, a bead of sweat running down her temple. "There are other ways." She cast her gaze toward the army—it had to be real, the way it blotted out the Timekeeper's false sun, so rich and dark and lovely. Which meant her door had held. She was not powerless, not even here.

Raegan set her jaw. She'd called to the water on this very train before, just steps from where she was currently trapped, and it had not answered—not, at least, within the Timekeeper's metal confines.

"My rivers," she murmured, squeezing her eyes shut, "please. Come to me, my waters, my currents, my tides. I bid you to rise like the blood of a warrior, like the drums of war. Rise and free us from this hell of twisted magic and endless oppression. It is finally time. *Rise.*"

In all her lives, Raegan wasn't sure she'd ever said anything with so much meaning behind it, with every word so drenched in intention and blind rage. Her command bloomed crystalline and wild in the train car. She hoped and hoped and *hoped*. Her heart thudded against her chest. And then, somewhere in the distance, a roar rumbled through the Timekeeper's realm. At the exact same moment, she felt her magic churn inside of her, electrified by the words she'd uttered—the call and response of powers beyond even her understanding.

The door at the end of the train car flew open. An unremarkable man in a tweed suit and hat sitting low on his brow prowled down the aisle. Only his mouth was visible beneath the shadowed brim, curled into a cruel sneer.

"What have you done?" the Timekeeper demanded, haughty and mocking. "And why are you still stupid enough to think it will make any difference, you little bitch?"

Raegan grinned at him, all teeth. She felt the ebb of the tide rush through her, euphoric and vicious. The rumbling grew louder as the dam of this gray and lifeless realm shattered beneath the weight of her rage.

"I told you," she replied, surprised by the tone of her own voice—low and soft, just as eternal as the god before her, "that I would flood your world."

The Timekeeper shot toward her, those devouring eyes suddenly visible from beneath the brim of his hat, gloved hands reaching for her. But then the train lurched and kicked up, almost as if the hulking piece of god-made metal had been lifted from its tracks by the sweep of a river.

"Not so stupid, am I, Kronos?" Raegan shouted as the door at the end of the train car burst open, silver currents shoving through, open-mouthed and starving for violence. She threw her head back and laughed, the sound unraveled and mad to her own ears. "And I'm so much worse than a bitch. I'm a motherfucking cunt, and you are going to *drown.*"

CHAPTER FIFTY-SIX

The water took Raegan into its arms, gentle as a lover, the bonds that held her fast dissolving beneath the immutable weight of the current. She gave herself up to the tumble of the tides, trusting the river as she always had—completely. Since that first life spent on its banks, finding solace and peace in a cruel world, she had belonged to the way of the water. It would not fail her now.

The crest of the wave broke somewhere above her head, and then Raegan found herself pulling air into her lungs. Like the ocean depositing driftwood onto the shore, the rivers set her gently upon the train platform. She scrambled to her feet, completely dry despite the dampness of her surroundings, glimmering wefts of kelp draped over rod iron benches. The clocktower's hands spun around madly, furiously.

And then, looking beyond the platform, Raegan beheld a beautiful thing. Maybe two hundred paces away, the King was mounted on Rainer, formidable and deathless in his black shadow armor. His sword was raised high as the Unseelie Court rushed a force of Protectorate and clock guardians on the empty plains. For a moment, all she could do was stare at him: impossibly regal, undeniably glorious, a beautiful apocalypse.

Digging her nails into her palms, Raegan tore her gaze away from her beloved, gathering herself as she searched the platform for the Timekeeper. He was nowhere to be seen. His train lay in a crumpled heap, long sections of the tracks torn up in the river's rage.

"But what about the Gates?" Raegan murmured to herself. She glanced over her shoulder.

The Timekeeper's line of soldiers held fast, even against the force of the Unseelie Court. She chewed on her lip, her heart pounding as she sent her magic out into the space around her. Breaking the front of the Protectorate army would mean nothing if she and the King couldn't go straight for the Gates. They knew this; they'd talked this through a hundred times. If they could not find the Gates, the Timekeeper could reorganize and flank them, or do much, much worse. This was, after all, his realm.

A strange gleam caught her eye. The place where the waters had torn up the tracks shimmered slightly. Raegan stalked to the end of the empty train platform, her entire body pounding with fear and anxiety. Time was precious. She knew that better than most. She gazed down at the flickering section of tracks, eyes sharp, the rivers ready at her fingertips.

And there, beneath that metal spine, beneath the dead soil and the gray dust, was something far grander. Raegan's blood thrummed. The tracks *were* the Gates, disguised by a complex and extremely powerful glamour. With a shuddering breath, she understood that the poor souls trapped on these train cars no doubt fed the vast, endless maw of the Gates as much as they did the Timekeeper's own power.

Raegan leaned over the edge for a closer look, but then a section of damp brick crumbled beneath her weight. With a curse, she righted herself, turning on her heel to scan the platform. Nothing. Nothing but the Unseelie army in the distance, fighting hard, actually gaining ground. Her heart fluttered, beating shallow somewhere near her throat. Raegan turned back to the tracks.

She released a long exhale, preparing herself, and then bit down on her tongue until her eyes watered with the pain. Good. She needed to be present, to be sharp. And then, despite the unfathomable exhaustion and all-consuming despair she'd almost given into, Raegan called to the waters again. She raised her hands high, like some forgotten saint on a wind-buffeted hill, and commanded the tides to wash away the Timekeeper's glamour. To do as all rivers did—wear away at the surface and reveal what slept beneath.

Power coursed through her, the seams of her mortal body almost bursting, every inch of flesh screaming with pain and spite and fury. The ground trembled beneath her feet, and then the river came rushing, its mouth open, its tide unstoppable. The rivers ripped metal from the earth like sutures from a wound, tearing at the fabricated face of the Timekeeper's realm to find the darker truth that lurked beneath.

Raegan swayed, stumbling away from the edge and catching herself on the back of a bench. Dark spots swarmed her vision, but it didn't matter. Neither did the agonizing pain gnawing at her sides. Just beyond the train platform, reaching high into the blank sky, washed clean by the rivers, stood the Gates.

They were just as beautiful as her father's spellcraft papers had indicated. The metalwork looped in intricate patterns, ancient sigils and symbols of power worked into the design. Looking directly at them made Raegan feel ill. Without the glamour, she could see where the power of the

Gates leached into the In-Between, the soil a burnt black, reaching out through the gray plains with greedy fingers.

Dizziness dragged Raegan to one side. She swayed hard, trying to regain control of her own body. A clammy sweat coated her skin, and her breathing was ragged, like her lungs had been torn in two. She gasped desperately for air, feeling so alone.

But then in the distance, a clamor went up from the battlefield. No—a *cheer*, she realized. Triumph climbed up her throat like a glorious, golden vine bursting with budding blooms. They saw the Gates. Blodeuwedd appeared in the sky, rising out of the army on snow-white wings, a furious victory cry spiraling from her beak.

Raegan had finally made good on a promise. Maybe—just maybe—she and Oberon could find a little stone cottage once the world was mended. Maybe one day, people might forget their names. Maybe one day, there would be no need to call on the rivers with fury or raise a sword with the intent to destroy.

With that thought clutched to her chest, fragile as glass, Raegan stumbled away from the Gates, her legs fighting to carry her back to him. Always back to him.

She'd reached the far side of the train platform when she caught a dull glint of chainmail in her peripheral vision. Raegan turned, reaching for Excalibur's pommel, but it was too late. Always too late.

Bedwyr slammed into Raegan, taking her to the ground. The air tumbled out of her body, her chin hitting the train platform hard. She tasted blood and fought to right herself. Black flies swarmed her vision, pain piercing her abdomen.

"Your little kelpie tried to kill me," Bedwyr snarled.

Raegan ignored him, struggling to orient herself, her mind a thick, blank haze. With a pang of dread, she realized she was flat on her back. Arthur's knight straddled her waist, delivering blows to her stomach with a speed and precision that seemed unfair for someone so large and strong to possess.

"Should've tried harder," Bedwyr said, panting as he paused the barrage of his heavy fists. Just long enough for her to realize how much it hurt and how little energy she had left. Raegan curled one fist, calling for the rivers. They answered her in a rushing tide, but she couldn't contain them, couldn't direct them.

For a long moment, all Raegan saw was the wide expanse of gray sky. If she was going to die, she thought, it should at least be in her king's arms. Not in the grasp of this man turned beast, the Timekeeper's most loyal monster. She stoked the fires of her fury, shoving the pain aside. But Bedwyr just laughed—the laugh of every man who has underestimated a woman—and gripped her throat between his large hands.

Raegan sputtered, driving a knee into his groin. But the knight was faster, shifting his weight away, pressing down harder on her windpipe.

"Fuck you," she spat, finally summoning the energy to lift one hand. With a raw cry, Raegan slashed at Bedwyr's face. Her nails grazed skin, and the knight spat a curse at her. She fought to press the advantage, to drive her knee into his stomach, but Bedwyr recovered too quickly. In a heartbeat, his hands were back around her throat, pressing down harder than before. Her vision blinked in and out as she realized with a bolt of terror that she'd lost sensation in her limbs.

Not like this. Not again. She was meant to tear away the glamour concealing the Gates and then be swept into the shadow of the Unseelie army. She'd ride double on Rainer with the King, and they'd hunt down Kronos. Then she'd drive Excalibur into the god's heart and it would all be over. Couldn't Fate see how perfect it would've been that way—the kind of story that fit neatly in the mouth of a bard, that swelled and hummed in all the right places on the page?

Her fury turned bittersweet, more wound than blade. The despair found her again, hooking barbs into her skin, just as sharp and sure as the leather seats of the train car. Her heart felt strange, like it might either barrel right out of her chest or cease beating altogether. Dust coated her tongue, and the platform beneath her was rough and unyielding. At least, Raegan told herself, it might be over soon.

And then somehow, beyond all reason, the crushing weight was gone. She gasped, pulling fresh air into her lungs, her throat burning. Forcing her body to move, Raegan rolled to the side and grappled desperately for Excalibur with trembling, ice-cold fingers. Desperation clawed at her throat the way Bedwyr had, sending adrenaline skittering through her veins. Death had come for her twice a century. She knew what an ending felt like. Hers would *not* be here, not on this train platform.

With another feral shriek that tore at her bruised throat, Raegan drew Excalibur and used the blade to pull herself to her knees. She swayed, her body already feeling like a bloated corpse. For a long moment, there was nothing but the wide gray plains and the furious tick of the clock as she looked with disbelief at the scene before her. Her mind, she thought, might not be understanding. It might be offering prettier images, a softer door into death, a passage she had long since perfected.

If her mind was to be believed, then just a few feet away from her, the King was slamming Bedwyr into the ground. The viciously sharp points of his arm bracers glimmered in the strange light. Just as the knight had done to Raegan,

Oberon loomed over Bedwyr. She swallowed, her thoughts keening, her vision split by tears.

The King was a creature of control, she knew. Two goddesses had torn a wound in the night sky and crafted an impossible weapon from the obsidian jewel it bled. The sheer amount of power gathered in one body was incomprehensible. The King could not pull the pin. He could not detonate.

And yet, as Raegan watched, Oberon was more beast than Fair Folk, his shadows devouring Bedwyr from all angles. The magnitude of his rage shook the platform as if the darkness boiling deep in his marrow might be capable of tearing this entire place apart.

"I told you," her faerie king snarled, his voice ringing out like he was the realm's true god, "to *stay away* from my wife."

Despite all the pain and terror and the sinking feeling in the pit of her stomach that told Raegan her body was broken beyond repair, she threw her head back and laughed. Even if they lost this battle, if the Timekeeper consumed them all in his rampage for more power, at least she'd gotten to hear Oberon say those two words: *my wife*.

The King's head snapped toward her. The rest of his body went still as a panther on the hunt, only his eyes sliding to meet hers. "Raegan," he rasped.

"My husband," she said, the sight of him suffusing her with a strength she wouldn't have thought possible even a few moments ago. Biting down on her cheek, Raegan used Excalibur to pull herself to her feet. Without looking away from her, the King violently shook Bedwyr by his neck— something she might've seen a big jungle cat do in a documentary—and then straightened, like he was going to move toward her.

"No," Raegan said, barely biting out the word. Leaning

on Excalibur as if it were a cane and not a mythic blade, she gathered her strength and limped the three paces to where the King pinned Bedwyr to the platform. The knight was the one choking now, blood dribbling from his lips. "Hold him down for me."

"It doesn't matter," Bedwyr heaved. "I'll just come back."

With his free hand, Oberon reached up and steadied Raegan, bracketing her at the waist. His gaze landed heavy on her, the weight of his full attention heady and silken. She almost opened her mouth to explain, but of course her faerie king knew what she was going to do. Raegan watched as his fingers tightened around Bedwyr's throat, the shadows under his command holding the knight to the ground.

With the last reserves of her strength, Raegan hefted Excalibur from the ground. Bedwyr forced out another laugh, but it was hedged in desperation, the same sound she'd heard leave his lips along the River Wye.

"I will," the knight choked out against the strength of the King's long, powerful fingers, "come back."

With an unsteady lurch, Raegan slotted Excalibur against Bedwyr's chainmail, right where his heart should be. She watched with satisfaction as the knight's eyes went wide, fear flooding his expression as he recognized the sword. A wolfish laugh tore its way up from her chest, and then the deathless witch drove the mythic blade into his chest.

"Not this time."

CHAPTER FIFTY-SEVEN

Raegan expected blood, maybe. For some kind of twisted, demonic thing to fling itself from the chest of the knight, screeching and wailing. But Bedwyr's death was quiet, unremarkable. The once-mortal man who had watched a millennium pass him by simply collapsed into dust. Raegan watched, her tongue feeling too thick for her mouth, as ash drifted across the train platform.

"Raegan," the King said, pulling her into his arms.

With a sigh, she let go of Excalibur, barely registering the clatter as the blade hit the ground. All that mattered in this moment was tumbling into his expanse of autumnal meadow and dark rain and black pepper. She breathed in the scent of him, letting the King shift her in his arms so the harsh, hungry points of his armor did not pierce her.

"The Gates," she said. "Get me to the Gates." When Oberon said nothing, she forced her eyes open, tilting her head back to look at him. The expression on his otherworldly features was feral, dark eyes glinting with something mad and unrestrained.

"No," he replied, his words a low growl that thrummed

low in his chest. "I refuse to save a world that you will not live to see."

Emotions warred in Raegan's chest. She reached up for the King, brushing his jawline with her knuckles. "Oberon," she managed, her voice sounding so small, so worn-out. "You can't."

"I am the High King of the Unseelie Court," he told her, teeth bared, his face a mask of inhuman cruelty. "I will do as I please." He stood, gathering her in his arms as he turned away from the Gates. Raegan heaved a cough that left her lips bloody. She realized all at once, her mind addled and her body broken, that the King hadn't even tried to pick up Excalibur. That he was going to let the entire world burn if it meant he could have her.

She should resist. She should yell at him. She should summon whatever strength she had left and tell him he could *not* do this. But Raegan was so tired. She was so tired of fighting for so long and so hard against the same things. She was tired of funerals, of the feast table growing shorter every year. Perhaps it was kinder to let things end. Perhaps mortals needed to find their own way out.

"Oberon," she managed, one hand curling tight as a rosebud against his chest. "I—" Something hit the King hard from the side, sending Raegan sprawling onto the platform. He curled his larger body around hers protectively, but she was torn viciously from his grasp.

She lolled to the side, trying to make her body do anything at all that might mean survival. Rising up onto her hands and knees, she dragged herself across the platform, trying to get Excalibur's pommel back into her hand. The rough surface of the platform bit into her palms, the dust stinging her eyes. With a desperate lurch, Raegan grabbed the sword and looked up, only to find something that sent a chill skittering through her blood.

Her faerie king was locked in combat with the Time-keeper. She coughed hard, splattering her fingers with blood, and pulled herself up on one knee. No wonder Kronos had fortified his realm so carefully against Oberon. With one hand, those viciously-edged arm bracers glimmering like an oil spill, the King threw the Timekeeper bodily against the wall of the train station.

Gritting her teeth, Raegan tried to get to her feet. Excalibur was the only thing that might kill Kronos, might tear down the Gates. She had to get to the King, *had* to walk those ten paces. Begging her body to obey, she watched as the King stalked toward the crumpled pile of tweed, his shadow-blade drawn.

Raegan swallowed, her throat like broken glass. She managed to stand, leaning on Excalibur. The world spun and her vision played funny tricks—two Kings reaching for the mess of tweed, one Timekeeper suddenly in front of her, his eyes like the harvest, the end of all things.

Kronos drove one gloved hand straight through Raegan's chest, his hungry fingers clutching for her heart. She gasped, the pain unbelievable, unable to move until the god shoved her back onto her knees. In the distance, she heard a guttural, shattered shout from Oberon as the Time-keeper feasted on whatever time was still hers to claim. Around her, the world reduced to little more than blinding, endless pain and the gnashing of teeth.

Raegan felt her limbs grow cold and heavy even as she fought to lift them; only Excalibur's point driven into the platform kept her aloft. The Timekeeper made a meal of whatever lurked in her chest cavity, and the power there was not like the rivers. She could not bid it to flow backward or to devour that which hemmed it in.

Right as Raegan thought she might succumb to the gray-ness creeping in from all angles, something protruded from the Timekeeper's chest. A sharpened point of pure black, she saw, glinting madly in the raw-red light. Feral elation howled low in Raegan's belly. *The King.*

Death might take her in Their arms once again, sing her a sweet song she only half-remembered and usher her into that wide, vast dark. But the Timekeeper would rot, too, and all his structures would fall, buried by the silt. Raegan's mind exploded with memories, surely some final burst of her consciousness, but she fought to stay in the moment, to at least see the god she hated more than anything in the entire world dissolve into the same kind of ash he'd reduced her father to.

Instead, Kronos threw his head back and laughed. "It hurts, your power, your blade, Nameless One," the god choked out, ichor dripping from the side of his mouth, "but it will not vanquish me."

Fury flared in Raegan like a bonfire. He would not take her from her faerie king again. Damn the world and the Gates. Damn it all. None of it mattered; Oberon would *not* watch her die. Not again. Never again.

Determination swept her body—which she distantly realized was growing colder and colder—and she grappled for the Timekeeper. He ignored her, having taken what he wanted, gleeful to leave another husk in his wake, and moved to face the King. Before he could, Raegan saw something gold glimmer in the pocket of his waistcoat.

She shouldn't even still be alive, she knew, but spite was a strange thing, and she lurched forward, pulling on the short length of chain tucked away in the god's tweed vest. An ornate pocket watch with lush filigree pulled free into Raegan's bloodied fist. A howl burst out of her chest as she threw it onto the ground in front of her. Glass shattered and the Timekeeper screamed, all of his attention returned to the witch who refused to die.

With what she realized was the last ounce of strength this body would ever exert, Raegan grabbed Excalibur somewhere near its deadly point, not caring that the blade sliced into her palm with little mercy. Strangely, it was suddenly light as air, as if the sword's balance had always been crafted for this one particular Fated moment.

Despite the way life was seeping from her body, sticky as molasses, Raegan slammed the blade's tip into the pocket watch. It burst into a hundred pieces, scattering like scarab beetles across the platform.

Before her, the Timekeeper fell to his knees, clutching at his throat with those hands that had taken so much from her, from the world. She watched, death's arrival rattling in her lungs, as the god's gloved fingers began to crumble. Then his hands, wrists, arms, legs—all collapsing into nothing more than lifeless gray ash. With everything she had left in her, Raegan held his eyes, tracing the path of the wound that would finally unmake this foul thing.

As the soot-stained marks of Excalibur's bite traveled up the god's chest, the King came into view behind the Timekeeper. Blood seeped from his hairline, and the armor covering one shoulder had been torn away, revealing a deep, heavily bleeding puncture wound. His eyes were wild as he raised his sword and swung in a downward arc. The Timekeeper's head toppled from his body. Only a heartbeat, only an entire eternity, and then there was nothing left but ash, dancing in unseen currents.

Oberon took Raegan into his arms, one hand cupping her chin. "No," he whispered, his voice raw, laden with the kind of grief that destroyed most people. "*No.* I refuse to lose you again."

Raegan let herself sink into his arms, breathing in the scent of woodsmoke, black pepper, damp stone, and the torrential kind of rain that only ever came in autumn. She wished she could feel him around her once more, experience the burning heat of him against her skin, but all sensation had vanished from her body.

"Nyneve," Oberon wept, bowing his form around her, as if he might pull her back from the brink of death with nothing but the fearsome inferno of his monstrous love. "Outlive me. *Please.* I love you too much."

How she wanted to say yes, to agree, to promise him she'd do exactly as he asked. But it was beyond even her power now. The currents inside her had gone still and dark, and there was nothing to do now but sink beneath the tides.

"I love you," she managed weakly. It was a gift to die in his arms. Hadn't she always wished to drown in the fathomless depths of his impossibly beautiful gray eyes? "But I think it's time to go."

Mordred choked back a sob, his powerful shoulders wracked with grief. But he held her gaze without question, his fingertips on her jaw. "If you must go," he murmured, tears gathering on those long, dark lashes, "go now, so you may return to me all the quicker."

Nyneve smiled at him, savoring the last few moments in the arms of her faerie king. "Bury me shallow," she told him as the darkness closed in all around her. "I'll be back."

CHAPTER FIFTY-EIGHT

Sunlight poured in, dappled and soft, dancing across the waters like faerie lights. She blinked three or four times, failing to understand her surroundings: a tiled room of some kind, though there was no roof. Trees and vines climbed over the tops of the shimmering white walls, their limbs trailing down. Clear water filled the room, its tiny little waves lapping at her knees.

"Child," came a voice like stars falling.

Raegan snapped her head up from the water to find a magnificent thing standing before her—a woman with quicksilver eyes, the wings of a dove rising from behind her slim, narrow shoulders.

"You may still be a bit disorientated," the being said, her voice gentle despite the feral planes of her face.

Raegan stared at the creature, familiarity rising in her like a soft ache—a yearning she knew better than her name. The heavy tides of memory swept in behind the ache.

"Fuck you," Raegan snapped at Fate, charging forward through the knee-high water, ignoring the way she was suddenly aware of her wet, heavy boots dragging her down.

Fate held up a hand, and Raegan's body halted, as if it no longer answered to her.

"I want to speak with you," the primordial goddess said, clasping Her long-fingered hands together.

"We all want shit, you motherfucker," Raegan spat, curling her hands into fists that she ached to sink into Fate's perfect, inhuman face. "I'm very used to wanting things I can't have. Maybe *you* should try it some time."

Fate's expression tightened but didn't darken, more like a parent disappointed with their child's choice of language than an enraged power beyond Raegan's understanding. "I want," the goddess said, letting Her hands fall to Her sides, "to apologize."

Raegan's body stilled, her mind going utterly blank. "What?" she demanded weakly.

"Though I cannot say I am truly sorry for punishing you and the Nameless One as I did all those years ago," Fate said, Her tone strangely soft, the warm, dappled light dancing across the downy, creamy feathers of Her wings, "I was young then, too, and I think you know how deeply you broke the fragile rules of our universe."

Raegan crossed her arms and inhaled, the scent of tarnished silver filling her nose. How fervently she wished instead for black pepper and a curl of woodsmoke. "This is a shit apology so far."

Fate's features did darken then, that flash of primordial rage seeping into Her star-fall eyes. But the goddess's chest only rose with a long, deep inhale, and then She continued. "I am sorry for how I used you to trick the Timekeeper, for the way I moved you about the chessboard. There was no other choice. I have obscured this Thread from him for so long, hoping it might be enough. I have schemed for a millennium, child."

Raegan just stared at the goddess, the water gently

lapping at her legs, a bright red leaf floating down from one of the trees overhead. It landed on the surface of the water, sailing on the currents like a tiny boat. So her Protectorate birthright, the false Prophecy, the deal with the Timekeeper —all of it orchestrated by Fate, and not at all for the reasons she thought.

"I am sorry," Fate said, "for the way the world's destiny has depended upon your suffering. Since Camelot fell, I have been on your side. Always. I know it has rarely felt so."

Raegan narrowed her eyes at the goddess in disbelief. "Wait," she said, digging her fingers into her hair. "Does . . . does all of this mean we actually won?" Hope surged wild in her chest, an untamed thing, and she dared not breathe until Fate answered the question.

"Yes," the goddess said, Her voice impossibly gentle. "Yes, child. After you killed the Timekeeper, the King dismantled the Gates. But first, he held you as you died, Excalibur still clutched in your hand. Something about your death changed the blade, turned it back to its true nature."

Raegan stared at the goddess, opening her mouth to speak but finding no words that sufficed.

Fate glided closer, Her large eyes strangely soft. "Something, I imagine," She continued, words heavy with meaning, "about unconditional love. After all, there is a reason the power of true love has been said to break spells."

Raegan's throat closed off, and tears streamed down her face, falling like rain to the clear water below. "Love," she managed, "is as good an oath as any." She said nothing else, unable to do so without bursting into sobs. She thought about the way her tears had once torn a door into the Timekeeper's realm. How that had allowed the Morrigan to slip through with her visions. How being lured to Kronos like a lamb to slaughter had made all of it possible.

Raegan looked up at Fate, considering. "Normally," she

started, her voice hitching with tears, "an apology doesn't mean much without an effort to make amends."

One of the goddess's silvery eyebrows arched. "What do you seek, child? Do you want me to send you back to the world you just left? To the King's arms?"

Yearning unspooled in Raegan's chest, pulling at her heart, straining against her ribcage. Time stretched endless. More leaves traipsed down onto the water, coloring the room like stained glass.

"No," she replied, the single word taking all her might, all her willpower. "No. I don't want him to look at me and only see death. He needs time." Her voice broke again, fresh tears pouring down her face, nearly drowning her words. "I think the world needs him more than I do right now. And if I'm honest, I'm tired. I'm so fucking tired."

Fate watched Raegan soundlessly. Her elegant, thin lips parted, but She said nothing, only watched. Unreasonably, Raegan felt as though every divine thing in this entire universe turned its attention toward her at once.

"But I want to see my dad," she continued, pushing tears from her cheeks. "And I want to know my mom is okay. And then, at the right time, yes, please send me back."

"You wish to flit between the realms of the living and the dead as if they have no bearing on you?" Fate demanded, a hard, glinting edge in Her voice.

In response, Raegan arched her brow, a sly smile creeping onto her face despite the tears. "I am neither mortal nor magic, neither living nor dead," she replied, meeting Fate's gaze. "Such things *never* had any bearing on me, goddess."

Fate's eyes bored into hers, threaded with silver, the pupils barely more than a shining coin. Raegan held her ground. A single second or a thousand years could have passed before Fate's shoulders drooped and the primordial being nodded in acquiescence. Then She turned, the waters barely rippling around Her movements. On the far wall, there was—quite suddenly—a door. It was plain and simple, a rectangle of white wood, but it called to Raegan with all the power and might of doors encased in ironwork or inlaid with precious gems. She walked toward it, the waters parting for her.

"Wait," Raegan said, coming to a halt. A few paces ahead, Fate turned, Her impossible silver eyes sharpening. "When I go back . . . I want to be Fey. So I can actually stay with him. So he won't just be waiting for the day to come that he watches me die again. I deserve it. *We* deserve it, after you've used us like pawns for a thousand years."

The atmosphere pressed down on her all at once, like a thunderstorm appearing out of nowhere on a muggy summer day.

"Have you gone quite mad?" Fate demanded, Her voice sending a tremor through the room.

Raegan grinned. "Oh, absolutely."

EPILOGUE
FIFTEEN YEARS LATER

T he new pub atop the hill was charming. Too charming, frankly, with its stone terrace overlooking Hiraeth in the valley below. The mature oak trees hemming the south-facing side were lovely, as were the dried husks of fiddlehead ferns clustered around their roots.

From the cobblestone path leading up from the valley, the King glared at all of it with some measure of contempt. So much cheering, singing, mingling and drinking under the glorious sweep of golden hour, all in honor of Liberation Day. For the first time in fifteen years, he was supposed to be attempting to celebrate this godsdamn day like everyone else in Hiraeth.

The King leaned on his cane. He considered turning around and going home. He ground his jaw, drawing in a deep breath, the air heavy with autumn sunshine, woodsmoke and damp leaves. Like a black storm cloud hunched over the pathway, Oberon deliberated. He could admit that something about the busy pub pulled at his aching places—the throb of mortals and Fair Folk alike, the shared mirth, the deep sense of being *alive*. That is what he had fought for, was it not? For his people to *live*.

"Perhaps," he grumbled to himself, eyeing the building and its lush grounds, "the interior will hold less appeal." There was, of course, only one way to find out. So with a harsh exhale, Oberon pulled his wool overcoat closer to fend off the chill and then continued down the winding stone path.

Autumn winds rattled leaves loose from the trees surrounding the stone building, showering his broad shoulders with a gold and burgundy garland fit for a king. He slowed his pace, brushing the leaves from his overcoat with one elegant, long-fingered hand. And then, swatting aside a group of drunk young people with his cane, Oberon slipped through the tall arched door and into the pub.

He groaned as he took in the dark rafters bisecting tall ceilings and lime-washed walls studded with sconces blackened in patina. Fat beeswax pillars crowded every available windowsill and corner, throwing warm golden light into the space. Faded velvet couches lounged in the corners, where the shadows were deeper, thicker. A few long, farmhouse-style tables were tucked against the walls to accommodate larger parties. The space brimmed with mirth, the air scented with fermented apples, beeswax, and damp wool.

The King dug his fingertips into the handle of his cane and tried desperately not to think about how much she would have liked this place. How she would have held her drink in one hand, his heart in the other, and led him to one of those dark corners. His ring finger throbbed, throat tightening. If he closed his eyes right now, he would see her—those full thighs draped across his lap, that wide, feral grin on her lovely mouth.

Instead, the King kept his eyes open and walked straight to the bar. Over the years, he had learned to stop indulging his phantom ache for her. It only ever made the chasm of his loss grow wider, large enough to swallow him whole. He was glad he had decided to come to the pub early—time to gather himself before the others arrived. It hurt them all, he knew, to see him shattered like this, so he would down a few drinks and cover up the ache.

He slid onto a tall stool, his knee catching painfully, though his face remained impassive. *She* might have read the slight notch in his brow, the tension around the corners of his eyes. But Raegan was gone, he reminded himself, and it seemed unlikely she was coming back. He sighed, digging into his coat pocket for coins.

Someone at Oberon's left jostled his elbow. With a low grunt, he switched his cane to his right side, collecting the coins in his other hand as the bartender finally approached. "Cider, please," he said, handing over payment.

And then his breath caught in his chest. Distracted by his grief, Oberon had not only used his left hand to pay, but also neglected to put his gloves on before walking inside the pub. Oberon glanced down, tightening his jaw, as both he and the barkeep looked at the corrupted bond mark on his finger in unison.

The thin silver circle that had once inked his finger had long since turned soot-black. Midnight-colored despair leaked up his forearm, coloring his veins an unpleasant shade of blue-black.

Oberon sighed. *This* was precisely why he did not socialize in public. He should have turned around, should have disappeared back down the hill and into Hiraeth's mist-damp, winding streets when he had the chance. Better yet, he should have insisted on the usual private gathering in the first place—not this nonsense at the Black Hare Pub.

The barkeep glanced up at him, eyes dragging across the King's broad, muscular shoulders, then the scar that nicked the outside of his left eye. They shook their head. "Would never dream of charging you in my establishment, particularly today of all days," the barkeep replied, pushing the coins back across the polished wood.

Oberon paused, his eyes narrowing. "Appreciated," he said eventually, taking a long pull of the cider. "Though I am planning to drown my sorrows this evening, so I suggest you consider taking my coin at some point."

The barkeep offered a ghost of a smile, like they knew the taste of such sorrows, and moved to mop up a spill farther down the counter. "Alright, only one little tithe. One drink. It's a small show of gratitude for everything you've done, my liege."

Oberon inclined his head in thanks. To his relief, the bartender turned away, striding to the other side of the bar, leaving him alone again. He exhaled, some of the tension in his shoulders releasing. The barkeep's gesture had been kind, and the cider was fine—earthy and musky, only a little sweet. But there was no need for these little tithes. He had fought for all those years, sacrificed everything he had, precisely so this barkeep could open a pub on a Feyrish city's lovely outskirts. So mortals and Fair Folk could live amongst each other. So magic could thrive. So Hiraeth no longer needed to hide—though after all those years, much of the mist and rain still clung to the city. So people could spend a fine autumn day like today dancing instead of weeping.

Across the bar, a couple laughed, leaning their foreheads together before sharing a tender kiss. Oberon tore his gaze away, staring down at the polished wood counter. Fifteen years later, and yet he could barely handle the sight of someone else with their lover. His longing was too thickly wrapped around his lungs, squeezing the air out of his chest whenever he thought of her.

The cider stung his throat, or perhaps that was just the tears he was holding back. Oberon had never stopped wanting her, never stopped craving her at every hour of every day. It was the Feyrish union, yes, but it was more than that, and he knew it. She was the furious flame to his steady shadow. She was the only person who had made him believe there was nothing wrong with being a monster.

Damn the barkeep for recognizing him. Damn this pub for being something she might have loved, a place they might have gone together when the cottage they should have shared grew too quiet, too lonely. Damn the memories awakening in his depths, twisting and turning in the cages where he had locked them away. Damn the eternal heaviness of his grief, an iron chain wrapped around his ankles.

He scowled into the golden cider. It should not hurt so much; after all, he had gotten almost everything he wanted. They had saved the world. Magic had been restored. The Fair Folk and mortals lived in relative peace. No one had too much. No one had too little. Except for him, of course. He had too little because he did not have her, and it turned out she was all he had ever really wanted.

The room was growing warmer, filled with even more people now. He glanced across the room at the dial for the time. People were, understandably, not very fond of clocks any longer, and it continued to bring him a little delight to see everyone trying to reinvent the physical appearance of the devices. Still a few minutes to go before the others were due to arrive.

But sitting alone out on the terrace, he decided quite suddenly, might actually be worse. So he stayed put, even when someone recognized him and started up a humiliating chant in his honor. Like the final battle of the Great War had been a sports match and he had scored the winning goal, not lost the love of his life in a godforsaken realm of dust and death.

Despite the small, false smile on his face, Oberon's hand curled into a fist and stayed like that, even as the chant faded away and the barkeep shooed the young people off. He desperately wanted to take amusement in their joy, to share it with them—he had fought for this, had he not?

But his grief had grown so heavy. He took another long drink of his cider, the bartop in front of him now littered with offerings of alcohol from the Black Hare's patrons. The King exhaled. At least he rarely had time to wallow in the depths of his sorrow. His hands were full with an actual, restored court and the construction of an entirely new society where humans and Fey could live side-by-side. Nearly everything he had dreamed of for so many years. Some days, it was enough to keep him going.

But what truly drove the King—if he was honest—was the half-mad, foolish idea that he might get to see her again. Setting his jaw, Oberon stared down at his hands, his eyes tracing the corrupted bond mark. For all the might of the Unseelie Throne, all the unfathomable power restored to him with the opening of the Gates, he was reduced to waiting. To sleeping in an empty bed, awakening with her name on his lips. Fate refused to speak to him, and any of the Morrigan's attempts to intercede on his behalf only seemed to make matters worse. The King had begged, offered to share his seemingly endless lifeforce, or even give it up entirely. He just wanted her—as long as she still wanted him, of course. With a long, shuddering exhale, he reminded himself he had chosen the pain. Chased it, even. Because the pain was still better than forgetting her. Because the pain, at the very least, made him feel closer to her than anything else could.

The King's cider was empty and the pub was thick with

people. He sighed. Someone at his side brushed his shirt sleeve, offering some kind of flirtation. Oberon felt exhausted and immeasurably old. When he turned to decline, he wondered if the young mortal even knew who he was. If they saw eternity stretch in his ocean eyes, the way she always had. Probably not.

Oberon slid from the stool and unfolded to his full height with the help of his cane. He narrowed his eyes, searching the throngs of people, telling himself all the while it was only to thank the barkeep again. But that would of course be a lie, and apparently the Fair Folk could not lie. He put his hands into his pockets, preparing to turn for the door, when he saw a flash of red on the other side of the room.

His heart stopped in his chest, that long thread of yearning uncurling, open-mouthed and treacherous in its unrelenting desire. He fervently told himself that it was not her. It had not been her the first thousand times, so it would certainly not be her now. But all good reason seemed to flee the King when it came to his witch. He ground his jaw and told himself to leave, but his body refused, the weight and breadth of his ache rooting him to the spot. His eyes followed the tumble of dark auburn curls like nothing else had ever mattered. That thorny tangle of emotions in his chest keened with a desperation that made him feel weak and foolish.

Oberon squeezed his eyes shut, trying to stem the tears that were gathering like a thunderstorm. When he opened them, there were no deep red waves to be found in the crowd. He heaved an exhale. Not in relief—something else. He did not possess the words for whatever it was—and did not need them, because he *knew* she was not coming back. The Timekeeper had unmade Raegan, and no one—not even someone like her—came back from such a thing.

Oberon turned on his heel toward the door, pausing when he found someone blocking his path. He glanced down, his vision blurred by the tears still clinging to his eyelashes, to find a freckled face looking up at him, framed by curls the color of the leaves at the end of autumn.

"Hey," came a voice above the din—low, slightly hoarse around the edges, sweet as sin. "I've been looking for you."

His lungs pressed too tight against his ribs, his heart breaking under the heavy burden of hope. Oberon blinked the tears away. And there she was. Soft golden skin, freckles scattered across her nose and cheekbones like constellations, eyes the color of a late summer meadow. Her dress dipped low, exposing collarbones and the swell of her full bust, flaring out slightly around her ample hips, the long sleeves sensible for the chill. Good. He would not want her to be cold, not with the first frost well on its way.

Words gathered somewhere in the back of his throat, but his tongue tangled around them, half-choked by a tide of yearning that nearly swept him off his feet.

"Oberon," Raegan said, arching one brow. She wrapped a few curls around the end of her finger, and his heart followed the motion, twisting into knots. "Do you want to get out of here?"

"With you?" Oberon replied, his voice so heavy with ache he thought she might mock him, that pretty little mouth landing barbs despite his thick skin. "Yes. How far do you want to go?" His body moved of its own accord as if all these long and lonely years had not passed. In an elegant swoop, the King held his arm out for her.

"With you?" Raegan echoed, her voice husky with enough desire to unmake him. "To the ends of it all, I think." The deathless witch took his arm in that way she always did, sidling so close that he—quite suddenly— remembered what it was to be alive.

Together, they slipped through the door. He wanted to say a thousand things to her. He wanted to announce to every person in the pub that his beloved had at long last returned to him, like the tide to the shore, the heather to the hills, the dusk to the lake.

But they had barely made it a few steps down the stone walkway when Raegan unwound her arm from his. The King faltered, needing the blistering heat of her, knowing that he had always loved the pain, but then she wrapped her hand around his wrist and pulled him into the shadow of the oak trees.

"My husband," she murmured, her hands sliding up his chest to grip either side of his overcoat.

"My wife," he replied, so much ache in a few scant syllables. He set his cane against one of the tree's wide trunks and slid his hands around her waist. His large palms fit in the divot of her generous curves, just so—like they had been made for each other from the primordial dark of the universe. "Is it really you?" the King asked, one hand moving to cup the side of her face.

She gazed up at him, her meadow eyes glimmering in the sunset. In response, she stood on her tiptoes and pulled him toward her by his lapels. Oberon met her with too much eagerness, too much hunger, and the second he tasted her, he knew without a doubt that his deathless witch had returned to him. Tears tumbled down his angular face, but she did not seem to mind—if anything, she pulled him closer, deepening the kiss.

Someone lingering outside the pub spotted them and yelled a good-natured joke. They pulled apart, laughing, and Oberon found Raegan's face was damp with tears, too. He traced the line of her cheekbones, the soft curve of her hairline. He wanted to stare at her until the sun tumbled from the sky. He wanted to bury his face between her thighs until time collapsed and he did not remember what it was to be without her.

The King opened his mouth to tell her so, fingertips diving into her curls to hold her face in his hands. With a start, he found her ears were no longer softly rounded—instead, they came to a sharp, deadly curve. She must have seen the look on his face because she grinned at him, so feral and unbroken and beautiful that he had no idea how he had ever managed to deserve her.

"Would you do it again, if you knew?" Raegan murmured, drawing closer, her thighs opening for him just as they always had. His body keened with desire, hard and aching. "If you knew how much it would hurt?"

"Yes," Oberon replied in a whisper, the word spoken like a vow. "I would do it all again."

She smiled up at him, tears streaming down her face. "I love you, my faerie king," she said, just as fierce.

"I would have waited another thousand years," Oberon replied, his voice raw and breaking. "I love you, my villainous thing."

She pulled his left hand into the golden sweep of the sun, turning it over in her smaller palms. The seeping poison of heartbreak that had been slinking farther and farther up his forearm all these years was gone, replaced with a slender, shining silver band.

Oberon tangled his fingers into hers and pulled her out of the oak grove, around the side of the pub toward the stone terrace. For good measure, he kissed her again, the kind of kiss that she always said made the rest of the world stop existing. All around them, autumn shimmered in its unbroken bronze glory.

"Follow me," the King murmured as he pulled away. "I think this will make you happy." Raegan looked up at him, arching her brow in a way that made his stomach flutter.

Pressing his lips together, he just smiled, leading the way around the flagstone path.

At its end was a lovely stone terrace, currently occupied by one long, lone table. Its surface was dressed in beeswax candles, all matter of twinkling lights and snaking vines and aubergine petals. In the far corner of the terrace, a bonfire crackled merrily. The hill dropped off on one side, the mist-veiled vista of Hiraeth sitting at the bottom of the valley like a shining gray jewel.

Oberon led Raegan to the edge of the terrace, taking in the sight before him—desperately trying to memorize the feeling, to tuck it deep inside his marrow and never let it go. On the left of the table sat Reilly and Alanna, giggling infectiously about something. Andronica and Maelona were standing by the table's head, the Unseelie knight brushing the ex-Protectorate woman's knuckles with a delicate kiss. Baba Yaga, looking all the more feral when plucked from her pocket realm, crouched by the fire with a stick, Blodeuwedd laughing on the other side of its dancing flames. And at the far edge of the terrace, his black toad eyes locked on Raegan in utter disbelief, was Rainer. Apparently unable to summon actual words, the kelpie instead began to violently scrape his front hoof against the stone to get every-one's attention.

His heart fuller than he dared to believe he deserved, the King turned back toward Raegan and cupped her face in his hands. For a moment, he said nothing, marveling at the way the sunlight made emeralds out of her eyes. And then, finally, he managed to ask, "Would you like to join us?"

Raegan's lips pressed together as tears spilled down her face. "More than anything," she whispered, her voice choked with emotion as she fought to maintain a casual tone. As if she had only been gone on a short trip somewhere quiet.

His vision blurred, Oberon turned to look at their loved ones. Maelona, with both hands clamped against her mouth, tears running down her face. Blodeuwedd, her sobs taking her halfway to her knees. Reilly, a tangle of long limbs as they tried to help the owl woman stay on her feet. Alanna, standing now, her hands pressed to her heart, eyes shining. Andronica, her arms around Maelona, her lower lip quivering. Baba Yaga, barely more than a shadow at the edge of the terrace, the bonfire catching on her sharp, feral smile.

"What did you have planned for the evening?" Raegan asked, her voice rising in the breeze, the sound of it sweeter than anything else the King had ever known. That bone-deep ache he thought he would never be rid of, that kept him awake at all hours, that pulled at his Threads with unrelenting fingers, slipped out of existence, as if it had never really been there at all.

"We were planning," Oberon replied, his voice breaking, fresh tears running down his face, "to linger in the sun."

And then the witch and the King stepped out of the pub's shadow and into the glimmering light of golden hour. Whatever happened next was theirs alone. There are no more ballads, no more tales, and though a Fatesong swooped low and lovely through the late afternoon, aching and swollen, for the first time in a millennium, it did not loop.

ACKNOWLEDGMENTS

Firstly, I want to thank you, dear reader. Thank you for trusting me to ferry you to the end of this story; for trusting that the suffering would only make the ending that much sweeter. Thank you for seeing Raegan and Oberon as the complicated, messy, fierce and utterly relentless people that they are. Thank you for looking for the doors.

Thank you to my incredible publishing team: my editor Erin, my copyeditor Erin, my cover artist Robert and my interior illustrator Rachael. I write decent stories; you four turn them into actual books.

Thank you to Jordon, with whom I share a romance as great and vast as Raegan and Oberon's. Thank you for making all of this possible. Thank you for being my favorite person in the world and for believing in me. I love you in every life.

To Allison, for being gay and doing crimes with me, always. I can't for a moment imagine having taken the plunge into publishing if you weren't for you—but beyond that, I simply can't imagine my life without you. (Well, I guess I could, but I simply don't want to.) You are my dearest, fiercest friend, and you're stuck with me forever.

To my mom for loving the angry, sensitive, depressive and creative child I once was. (I'm still all those things, just an adult now.) I am not an easy creature to mother, and yet you are extraordinary in your care and guidance.

To my brother for always making me believe a better

world is possible, which is a strange conviction for someone who reads as much Russian literature as you do.

To my dearest friends who have to deal with me IRL: Lian, Alyssa, Paige, Megan, Ronan, Tiffany, Addison, Brandi and Chelsea. I love you. Thank you for your friendship and care, and thank you for letting me into your worlds.

To Katrina, Anastasia and Charlie—thank you for being such an important part of *Beneath the Buried Sea*'s writing process. Your feedback is worth its weight in gold; your friendship is priceless.

Thank you to all of the readers who have shouted about my books to the rooftops, particularly Meg, Haley, Courtney, Em, Alex, Sam, Ash, Ali, Camilla, Jess, Ebony, Ashley, Chrissy, Bianca, Cece and Grey.

And thank you to the wonderful indie booksellers and bookstores who have carried my book and graciously hosted me, in particular Multiverse Comics, Capricorn Books, Inkwood Books and A Novel Idea.

It is one thing to write and publish a book. It is another entirely to have readers—people who savor your words and identify with your characters and understand this trembling, sensitive, personal creation you have thrust into the world. Thank you for making me an author.

About the Author

Victoria Mier is a queer, disabled writer and suspected changeling. She lives and writes in Philadelphia, PA. When she's not clacking away at the keyboard, you can usually find her wandering the aisles of a thrift store, on the couch with her partner Jordon and their cat Calliope, or somewhere in a field with a horse named Castle.

Website: victoriamier.com
Instagram: @by_victoriamier
Newsletter: thechangeling.substack.com

Or scan the code below for more!

ABOUT THE ARTISTS

ROBERT KRAIZA is the cover artist and the illustrator of the case laminate design. Robert is a tattoo artist and illustrator from Philadelphia, PA. Drawing nonstop since early childhood, he's always dreamed of being a professional artist.

Robert worked as a fine artist and freelance illustrator for ten years, primarily in the mediums of watercolor, pen, ink and sculpture. Shifting to tattooing in 2016, he currently works at True Hand Society, a tattoo and graphic design studio located in a renovated 150-year-old church.

Drawing inspiration from the Art Nouveau movement, the Victoria era and the history of his hometown of Philadelphia, Robert creates large scale whimsical tattoos and illustrations of the human figure, flora, and fauna with intricate framing. Robert was chosen as a designer for the US Mint Artist Infusion program in 2023 to create designs for coins and medals. Learn more at **truehandsociety.com.**

RACHAEL WARD created the title page and chapter header art. She is an illustrator and fantasy cartographer. Her work is inspired by early 20th century book illustrations, vintage botanical art, and the beauty and whimsy of classical fantasy worlds. She currently resides in Montreal, Canada with her partner Ben and their little tabby cat Diadem. Discover more at **cartographybird.com**.